A traveler fro[...]illing oracle for a St[...] p[...] and the pawn in a primitive power struggle.

A disaffected sociologist discovers that each of his dreams for the perfect society contains the seed of a nightmare.

The War of Judgment has thrown mankind back into the Dark Ages, where the blue-eyed marauding Sky People and their victims face off in a struggle made desperate by the survival of twentieth-century technology.

Time travel provides one society with the perfect way to punish its criminals.

**THE BEST OF POUL ANDERSON**
is an original POCKET BOOK edition.

# THE BEST
# OF
# POUL ANDERSON

by

**POUL ANDERSON**

PUBLISHED BY POCKET BOOKS NEW YORK

THE BEST OF POUL ANDERSON

POCKET BOOK edition published August, 1976

This original POCKET BOOK edition is printed from brand-new
plates made from newly set, clear, easy-to-read type.
POCKET BOOK editions are published by
POCKET BOOKS,
a division of Simon & Schuster, Inc.,
A GULF+WESTERN COMPANY
630 Fifth Avenue,
New York, N.Y. 10020.
Trademarks registered in the United States
and other countries.

Printed in the U.S.A.

ACKNOWLEDGMENTS

"The Longest Voyage" copyright © 1960 by Street &
Smith Publications, Inc. First published in *Analog–Science
Fact and Fiction*.
"The Barbarian" copyright © 1956 by Fantasy House, Inc.
First published in *The Magazine of Fantasy and Science
Fiction*.

To
John and Sandra Miesel

# RECOLLECTING ANDERSON

I can still remember the joy with which I read "Sam Hall," happily evident in this volume, in the summer of 1953 when I was but fourteen years old and was not sure that anyone with my shaky grasp of ninth-grade science would be permitted to be a science-fiction reader, much less writer. (Lest it appear that I am making favorable comparisons of my age with Poul Anderson's here, let me hasten to point out that at that point in time Poul was all of twenty-seven years old, a prodigy who had been a full-time writer of science fiction for six years and is now a forty-nine-year-old prodigy who has been at it for almost thirty; next to this record of accomplishment I feel downright old.) Here was something that obviously made extrapolative and scientific sense: a rigorously imagined future society whose technology was obviously grasped, and yet the story—although it incorporated rather arcanely mythic elements—was *accessible*, structurally, characterologically, at the level of narrative pace that is perhaps almost all that a fourteen-year-old can grasp. In short, I found it a complete success. It was the first scientifically rigorous story that I had ever read with pleasure, and it marked Anderson, at that early point in our mutual careers, as a man to be attended to closely.

I am still attending, and with a good deal of that initial awe, a career that is perhaps the most remarkable in the history of the science-fiction genre. In terms of sheer output—over forty novels and over four hundred short stories, to say nothing of nonfiction—Anderson is enough even to make an old prolificist like myself mutter defensively. More remarkable is that his work has never deviated, from his first publication in 1947, from unyielding standards of scientific rigor and stylistic dignity. At his very infrequent worst, Anderson has never been less than readable; at his very best, in works like "Sam Hall" or "Kyrie" or "The Longest Voyage" (all here), or his magnificent novel, *Tau Zero,* he has been a revelation.

*Tau Zero* has long struck me as the only work published after 1955 or so that can elicit from me some of the same responses I had toward science fiction in my adolescence—a sense of timelessness, human eternity, and the order of the cosmos as reflected in the individual fate of every person who would try to measure himself against these qualities. It deals with one of Anderson's most characteristic themes: fully characterized but eventually heroic human beings abandoned to cosmic disaster, forced to reconstruct their lives in an entirely different time and place out of their qualities of human dignity, self-respect, and resourcefulness (which Anderson sees as constantly recurring within the spirit of the race). The novel builds to an overpowering climax, yet has a decent sense of humility.

*Tau Zero* suggested to me that it was not my own sense of wonder but that of the science-fiction field itself that had flagged within the last twenty years. The field exists only in terms, however, of its individual authors—among whom, on his own terms, I think Poul Anderson may be the best.

He may be the best because he brings to his kind of science fiction a reasonable narrative talent, a rigorous scientific background, a respect for the manner in which science and the human spirit may interact and, most importantly perhaps, a respect for the western literary tradition and for the reader. Along with all of these laudable qualities, he has brought energy—he is probably the most prolific of all science-fiction writers—and a dogged willingness to stay the course. After twenty-eight years as a professional writer at the top of his field, Anderson's commitment has shown no signs of flagging. At most, he strikes me as being in mid-career, and if he continues to build—as he always has—from what he has done, he will probably leave a body of work that will define American science fiction as conceived by honest and talented people from its earliest maturity to that point at which it became the dominant literature of its age.

A pleasant man, a talented writer, a good companion, an excellent (he would not, I think, object to this) drinker, a medievalist and anecdotist and popular scientist extraordinaire, Poul Anderson has brought more credit to this field than it could possibly bring to him, and I recommend him to you as giving, in his honest way, the best that he and his field have to offer.

—BARRY N. MALZBERG

*Teaneck, N.J.*
*February 20, 1976*

# CONTENTS

# INTRODUCTION

To be asked to make a selection of one's best stories is an honor both pleasing and perilous. The compliment is deeply appreciated. But what are the best? Judgments are bound to vary from person to person. The author has been closest to the work, yet this gives him the least perspective on it.

Besides, he faces practical considerations. Some things, such as novels, are too long to include. Some shorter things are so widely available elsewhere that still another reprinting seems unfair to the reader. Some have been made obsolete by events and discoveries in the real world. And some are not remotely science fiction, which this book is supposed to be.

Given these restrictions, I nevertheless found a good deal of material that appeared worthy of consideration. I let myself be guided by both my own opinions and those of people whose taste I respect. (No more than two or three of these are critics. As has been said, a writer's idea of sound criticism is five thousand words of closely reasoned adulation.) And I tried to make the ensemble representative, not merely of myself but of science fiction in general.

The second of these attempts was, of course, foredoomed. This kind of literature has far more variety than any single maker can possibly cover—a very healthy condition. However, I have tried to give you a fairly wide range of theme and treatment.

Don't ask me what science fiction is. It has as many definitions as it has definers. We can simply point to what it does. For that purpose, I've thrown in a few remarks, sometimes analytical and sometimes anecdotal, about each story. You can skip those if you wish, but I hope you will enjoy the tales themselves.

—POUL ANDERSON

WHY DO MEN EXPLORE? NO DOUBT every individual who ever did has had his own reasons, and in some cases they were strictly practical or even sordid, and probably in no case were they absolutely pure. All the great explorers have been intensely human—including today's astronauts and cosmonauts, regardless of what cocktail party intellectuals maintain. Human motives are inevitably mixed. It does seem as if the explorers have averaged more nobility of spirit than any other class of men. However that may be, in this story I tried to examine their drive to seek beyond every horizon. It got a Hugo award, which is one reason for putting it here—the judgment of readers.

Another reason is the wish to offer a suggestion of how marvelous and manifold this universe is which we have the joyous privilege of inhabiting. The scene is not a planet, but an Earth-sized moon of a monster-sized world. I had fun designing it, calculating its orbit and so on. Later Hal Clement, the master of this kind of science fiction, did me the honor of playing what he calls "The Game" with it, trying to deduce exactly what the author had in mind and where he may have gone wrong.

1

Very recent information, from the Pioneer 10 flyby past Jupiter, indicates that my satellite might well be bathed in lethally intense radiation. On the other hand, its magnetic field might protect the surface. Questions such as these are not dry technicalities; they are the stuff of wonder.

# THE LONGEST VOYAGE

<<<<<<<<<<<<<<<<<<<<<<<<<<<<<<<<<<<<<<<<<<

WHEN FIRST WE HEARD OF THE SKY SHIP, WE
were on an island whose name, as nearly as Montalirian
tongues can wrap themselves about so barbarous a noise,
was Yarzik. That was almost a year after the *Golden
Leaper* sailed from Lavre Town, and we judged we had
come halfway round the world. So befouled was our poor
caravel with weeds and shells that all sail could scarce
drag her across the sea. What drinking water remained
in the butts was turned green and evil, the biscuit was
full of worms, and the first signs of scurvy had appeared
on certain crewmen.

"Hazard or no," decreed Captain Rovic, "we must
land somewhere." A gleam I remembered appeared in
his eyes. He stroked his red beard and murmured, "Besides, it's long since we asked for the Aureate Cities. Perhaps this time they'll have intelligence of the place."

Steering by that ogre planet which climbed daily
higher as we bore westward, we crossed such an emptiness that mutinous talk broke out afresh. In my heart I
could not blame the crew. Imagine, my lords. Day upon
day upon day when we saw naught but blue waters,
white foam, high clouds in a tropic sky; heard only the
wind, *whoosh* of waves, creak of timbers, sometimes at
night the huge sucking and rushing as a sea monster
breached. These were terrible enough to common sail-

3

ors, unlettered men who still thought the world must be flat. But then to have Tambur hang forever above the bowsprit, and climb, so we could see we must eventually pass directly beneath the brooding thing . . . and what upbore it? the crew mumbled in the forecastle. Would an angered God not let it fall down on us?

At last a deputation waited on Captain Rovic. Very timid and respectful they were, those rough burly men, as they asked him to turn about. But their comrades massed below, muscled sun-blackened bodies taut in the ragged kilts, daggers and belaying pins ready to hand. We officers on the quarterdeck had swords and pistols, true. But we numbered a mere six, including that frightened boy who was myself, and aged Froad the astrologue, whose robe and white beard were reverend to see but of small use in a fight.

Rovic stood mute for a long while after the spokesman had voiced this demand. The stillness grew, until the empty shriek of wind in our shrouds, the empty glitter of ocean out to the world's rim, became all there was. Most splendid our master looked, for he had donned scarlet hose and bell-tipped shoon when he knew the deputation was coming, as well as helmet and corselet polished to mirror brightness. The plumes blew around that blinding steel head and the diamonds on his fingers flashed against the rubies in his sword hilt. Yet when he spoke, it was not as a knight of the Queen's court, but in the broad Anday of his fisher boyhood.

"So 'tis back ye'd wend, lads? Wi' a fair wind an' a warm sun, liefer ye'd come about an' beat half round the globe? How ye're changed from yere fathers! Ken ye nay the legend, that once everything did as man commanded, an' 'twas an Andayman's lazy fault that now we must work? For see ye, 'twas nay too much that he told his ax to cut down a tree for him, an' told the faggots to walk home, but when he told 'em to carry him, then God was wroth an' took the power away. Though to be sure, as recompense God gave Andaymen sea-luck, dice-luck, an' love-luck. What more d'ye ask for, lads?"

Bewildered at this response, the spokesman wrung his

hands, flushed, looked at the deck, and stammered that we'd perish miserably . . . starve, or thirst, or drown, or be crushed under that horrible moon, or sail off the world's edge . . . the *Golden Leaper* had come farther than ship had sailed since the Fall of Man, and if we returned at once, our fame would live forever—

"But can ye eat fame, Etien?" asked Rovic, still mild and smiling. "We've had fights an' storms, aye, an' merry carouses too; but devil an Aureate City we've seen, though well ye ken they lie out here someplace, stuffed wi' treasure for the first bold gang who'll come plunder 'em. What ails yere gutworks, lad? Is't nay an easy cruise? What would the foreigners say? How will yon arrogant cavaliers o' Sathayn, yon grubby chapmen o' Wondland, laugh—nay alone at us, but at all Montalir —did we turn back!"

Thus he jollied them. Only once did he touch his sword, half drawing it, as if absentmindedly, when he recalled how we had weathered the hurricane off Xingu. But they remembered the mutiny that followed then, and how that same sword had pierced three armed sailors who attacked him together. His dialect told them he would let bygones lie forgotten, if they would. His bawdy promises of sport among lascivious heathen tribes yet to be discovered, his recital of treasure legends, his appeal to their pride as seamen and Montalirians, soothed fear. And then in the end, when he saw them malleable, he dropped the provincial speech. He stood forth on the quarterdeck in burning casque and tossing plumes, and the flag of Montalir blew its sea-faded colors above him, and he said as the knights of the Queen say:

"Now you know I do not propose to turn back until the great globe has been rounded and we bring to Her Majesty that gift which is most peculiarly ours to give. The which is not gold or slaves, nor even that lore of far places that she and her most excellent Company of Merchant Adventures desire. No, what we shall lift in our hands to give her, on that day when again we lie by the long docks of Lavre, shall be our achievement: that we did this thing which no men have dared in all the world ere now, and did it to her glory."

A while longer he stood, through a silence full of the sea's noise. Then he said quietly, "Dismissed," turned on his heel and went back into his cabin.

So we continued for some days more, the men subdued but not uncheerful, the officers taking care to hide their doubts. I found myself busied, less with the clerical duties for which I was paid or the study of captaincy for which I was apprenticed—both these amounting to little by now—than with assisting Froad the astrologue. In these balmy airs he could carry on his work even on shipboard. To him it scarce mattered whether we sank or swam; he had lived more than a common span of years already. But the knowledge of the heavens to be gained here, that was something else. At night, standing on the foredeck amidst quadrant, astrolabe, and telescope, drenched in the radiance from above, he resembled some frosty-bearded saint in the windows of Provien Minster.

"See there, Zhean." His thin hand pointed above waves that glowed and rippled with light, past the purple sky and the few stars still daring to show themselves, toward Tambur. Huge it was in full phase at midnight, sprawling over seven degrees of sky, a shield or barry of soft vert and azure, splotched with angry sable that could be seen to move across its face. The firefly moon we had named Siett twinkled near the hazy edge of the giant. Balant, espied rarely and low on the horizon in our part of the world, here stood high: a crescent, but the dark part of its disk tinged by luminous Tambur.

"Observe," declared Froad, "there's no doubt left; one can *see* how the globe rotates on an axis, and how storms boil up in its air. Tambur is no longer the dimmest of frightened legends, nor a dreadful apparition seen to rise as we entered unknown waters; Tambur is real. A world like our own. Immensely bigger, certes, but still a spheroid in space, around which our own world moves, always turning the same hemisphere to her monarch. The conjectures of the ancients are triumphantly confirmed.

Not merely that our world is round—*pouf,* that's obvious to anyone—but that we move about a greater center, which in turn has an annual path about the sun. But, then, how big is the sun?"

"Siett and Balant are inner satellites of Tambur," I rehearsed, struggling for comprehension. "Vieng, Darou, and the other moons commonly seen at home have paths outside our own world's. Aye. But what holds it all up?"

"That I don't know. Mayhap the crystal sphere containing the stars exerts an inward pressure. The same pressure, maybe, that hurled mankind down onto the earth, at the time of the Fall From Heaven."

The night was warm, but I shivered, as if those had been winter stars. "Then," I breathed, "there may also be men on . . . Siett, Balant, Vieng . . . even on Tambur?"

"Who knows? We'll need many lifetimes to find out. And what lifetimes they'll be! Thank the good God, Zhean, that you were born in this dawn of the coming age."

Froad returned to making measurements. A dull business, the other officers thought; but by now I had learned enough of the mathematic arts to understand that from these endless tabulations might come the true size of the earth, of Tambur, of sun and moons and stars, the paths they took through space and the direction of Paradise. So the common sailors, who muttered and made signs against evil as they passed our instruments, were closer to fact than Rovic's gentlemen, for indeed Froad practiced a most potent gramarye.

At length we saw weeds floating on the sea, birds, towering cloud masses, the signs of land. Three days later we raised an island. It was an intense green under those calm skies. Surf, still more violent than in our hemisphere, flung against high cliffs, burst in a smother of foam and roared back down again. We coasted carefully, the palomers aloft to seek an approach, the gunners standing by our cannon with lighted matches. For not only were there unknown currents and shoals—familiar

hazards—but we had had brushes with canoe-sailing
cannibals in the past. Especially did we fear the eclipses.
My lords can visualize how in that hemisphere the sun
each day must go behind Tambur. In our longitude the
occurrence was about midafternoon and lasted nearly
ten minutes. An awesome sight: the primary planet—for
so Froad now called it, a planet akin to Diell or Coint,
with our own world humbled to a mere satellite thereof!
—became a black disk bordured red, up in a sky suddenly full of stars. A cold wind blew across the sea, and
even the breakers seemed hushed. Yet so impudent is the
soul of man that we continued about our duties, stopping
only for the briefest prayer as the sun disappeared, thinking more about the chance of shipwreck in the gloom
than of God's Majesty.

So bright is Tambur that we continued to work our
way around the island at night. From sunup to sunup,
twelve mortal hours, we kept the *Golden Leaper* slowly
moving. Toward the second noon, Captain Rovic's per-
sistence was rewarded. An opening in the cliffs revealed
a long fjord. Swampy shores overgrown with saltwater
trees told us that while the tides rose high in that bay, it
was not one of those bores dreaded by mariners. The
wind being against us, we furled sail and lowered the
boats, towing in our caravel by the power of oars. This
was a vulnerable moment, especially since we had per-
ceived a village within the fjord. "Should we not stand
out, master, and let them come first to us?" I ventured.

Rovic spat over the rail. "I've found it best never to
show doubt," said he. "If a canoe fleet should assail us,
we'll give 'em a whiff of grapeshot and trust to break
their nerve. But I think, thus showing ourselves fearless
of them from the very first, we're less likely to meet
treacherous ambuscade later."

He proved right.

In the course of time, we learned we had come upon
the eastern end of a large archipelago. The inhabitants
were mighty seafarers, considering that they had only
outrigger dugouts to travel in. These, though, were often
a hundred feet long. With forty paddles, or with three

bast-sailed masts, such a vessel could almost match our best speed, and was more maneuverable. However, the small cargo space limited their range of travel.

Albeit they lived in houses of wood and thatch, possessing only stone tools, the natives were cultivated folk. They farmed as well as fished; their priests had an alphabet. Tall and vigorous, somewhat darker and less hairy than we, they were impressive to behold, whether nude, as was common, or in full panoply of cloth and feathers and shell ornaments. They had formed a loose empire throughout the archipelago, raided islands lying farther north, and carried on a brisk trade within their own borders. Their whole nation they called the Hisagazi, and the island on which we had chanced was Yarzik.

This we learned slowly, as we mastered somewhat their tongue. For we were several weeks at that town. The duke of the island, Guzan, made us welcome, supplying us food, shelter, and helpers as we required. For our part, we pleased them with glassware, bolts of Wondish cloth, and suchlike trade goods. Nonetheless we encountered many difficulties. The shore above highwater mark being too swampy for beaching a vessel as heavy as ours, we must build a drydock before we could careen. Numerous of us took a flux from some disease, though all recovered in time, and this slowed us further.

"Yet I think our troubles will prove a blessing," Rovic told me one night. As had become his habit, once he learned I was a discreet amanuensis, he confided certain thoughts in me. The captain is ever a lonely man; and Rovic, fisher lad, freebooter, self-taught navigator, victor over the Grand Fleet of Sathayn and ennobled by the Queen herself, must have found the keeping of that necessary aloofness harder than would a gentleman born.

I waited silent, there in the grass hut they had given him. A soapstone lamp threw wavering light and enormous shadows over us; something rustled the thatch. Outside, the damp ground sloped past houses on stilts and murmurous fronded trees, to the fjord where it shimmered under Tambur. Faintly I heard drums throb, a chant and stamping of feet around a sacrificial fire. Indeed, the cool hills of Montalir seemed far.

Rovic leaned back his muscular form, y-clad a mere seaman's kilt in this heat. He had had them fetch him a civilized chair from the ship. "For see you, young fellow," he continued, "at other times we'd have established just enough communication to ask about gold. Well, we might also try to get a few sailing directions. But all in all, we'd hear little except the old story—'aye, foreign lord, indeed there's a kingdom where the very streets are paved with gold . . . a hundred miles west'—anything to get rid of us, eh? But in this prolonged stay, I've asked out the duke and the idolater priests more subtly. I've been so coy about whence we came and what we already know, that they've let slip a gobbet of knowledge they'd not otherwise have disgorged on the rack itself."

"The Aureate Cities?" I cried.

"Hush! I'd not have the crew get excited and out of hand. Not yet."

His leathery, hook-nosed face turned strange with thought. "I've always believed those cities an old wives' tale," he said. My shock must have been mirrored to his gaze, for he grinned and went on, "A useful one. Like a lodestone on a stick, it's dragging us around the world." His mirth faded. Again he got that look, which was not unlike the look of Froad considering the heavens. "Aye, of course I want gold, too. But if we find none on this voyage, I'll not care. I'll capture a few ships of Eralia or Sathayn when we're back in home waters, and pay for the voyage thus. I spoke God's truth that day on the quarterdeck, Zhean, that this journey was its own goal, until I can give it to Queen Odela, who once gave me the kiss of ennoblement."

He shook himself out of his reverie and said in a brisk tone: "Having led him to believe I already knew the most of it, I teased from Duke Guzan the admission that on the main island of this Hisagazi empire is something I scarce dare think about. A ship of the gods, he says, and an actual live god who came from the stars therein. Any of the natives will tell you that much. The secret reserved to the noble folk is that this is no legend or mummery, but sober fact. Or so Guzan claims. I know not what to think. But . . . he took me to a holy cave and showed me an object from that ship. It was some kind of clock-work mechanism, I believe. What, I know not. But of a shining silvery metal such as I've never seen before. The priest challenged me to break it. The metal was not heavy, must have been thin. But it blunted my sword, splintered a rock I pounded with, and my diamond ring would not scratch it."

I made signs against evil. A chill went along me, spine and skin and scalp, until I prickled all over. For the drums were muttering in a jungle dark, and the waters lay like quicksilver beneath gibbous Tambur, and each afternoon that planet ate the sun. Oh, the bells of Provien, heard across windswept Anday downs!

When the *Golden Leaper* was seaworthy again, Rovic had no trouble gaining permission to visit the Hisagazian emperor on the main island. He would, indeed, have found difficulty in not doing so. By now the canoes had borne word of us from one end of the realm to another, and the great lords were agog to see these blue-eyed strangers. Sleek and content once more, we disentangled ourselves from the arms of tawny wenches and em-barked. Up anchor, up sail, chanties whose echoes sent sea birds whirling above the steeps, and we stood out to sea. This time we were escorted. Guzan himself was our pilot, a big middle-aged man whose handsomeness was not much injured by the livid green tattoos his folk af-fected on face and body. Several of his sons spread their pallets on our decks, while a swarm of warriors paddled alongside.

Rovic summoned Etien the boatswain to him in his cabin. "You're a man of some wit," he said. "I give you charge of keeping our crew alert, weapons ready, how-ever peaceful this may look."

"Why, master!" The scarred brown face sagged with near dismay. "Think you the natives plot a treachery?"

"Who can tell?" answered Rovic. "Now, say naught to

the crew. They've no skill in dissembling. Did greed or fear rise among 'em, the natives would sense as much, and grow uneasy—which would worsen the attitude of our own men, until none but God's Daughter could tell what'd happen. Only see to it, as casually as you're able, that our arms are ever close by and that our folk stay together."

Etien collected himself, bowed, and left the cabin. I made bold to ask what Rovic had in mind.

"Nothing, yet," said he. "However, I did hold in these fists a piece of clockwork such as the Grand Ban of Giair never imagined; and yarns were spun me of a Ship which flew down from heaven, bearing a god or a prophet. Guzan thinks I know more than I do, and hopes we'll be a new, disturbing element in the balance of things, by which he may further his private ambitions. He did not take those many fighting men along by accident. As for me . . . I intend to learn more about this."

He sat awhile at his table, staring at a sunbeam which sickled up and down the wainscot as the ship rocked. Finally: "Scripture tells us man dwelt beyond the stars before the Fall. The astrologues of the past generation or two have told us the planets are corporeal bodies like this earth. A traveler from Paradise—"

I left with my head in a roar.

We made an easy passage among scores of islands. After several days we raised the main one, Ulas-Erkila. It is about a hundred miles long, forty miles across at the widest, rising steep and green toward central mountains dominated by a volcanic cone. The Hisagazi worship two sorts of gods, watery and fiery, and believe this Mount Ulas houses the latter. When I saw that snowpeak afloat in the sky above emerald ridges, staining the blue with smoke, I could feel what the pagans did. The holiest act a man can perform among them is to cast himself into the burning crater of Ulas, and often an aged warrior is carried up the mountain that he may do so. Women are not allowed on the slopes.

Nikum, the royal seat, is situated at the head of a fjord, like the village where we had been staying. But Nikum is rich and extensive, being about the size of Roann. Many houses are made from timber rather than thatch; there is also a massive basalt temple atop a cliff, overlooking the city, with orchards, jungle, and mountains at its back. So great are the tree trunks available to them for pilings, the Hisagazi have built here a regular set of docks like those at Lavre—instead of moorings and floats that can rise or fall with the tides, such as most harbors use throughout the world. We were offered a berth of honor at the central wharf, but Rovic made the excuse that our ship was awkward to handle and got us tied at the far end.

"In the middle, we'd have the watchtower straight above us," he muttered to me. "And they may not have discovered the bow here, but their javelin throwers are good. Furthermore, they'd have an easy approach to our ship, plus a clutter of moored canoes between us and the bay mouth. Here, though, a few of us could hold the pier whilst the others ready for quick departure."

"But have we anything to fear, master?" I asked.

He gnawed his mustache. "I know not. Much depends on what they really believe about this god-ship of theirs . . . as well as what the truth is. But come all death and hell against us, we'll not return without that truth for Queen Odela."

Drums rolled and feathered spearmen leaped as our officers disembarked. A royal catwalk stretched above highwater level. (Common townsfolk in this realm swim from house to house when the tide laps their thresholds, or take a coracle if they have burdens to carry.) Across the graceful span of vines and canes lay the palace, which was a long building made from logs, the roof pillars carved into fantastic god-shapes.

Iskilip, Priest-Emperor of the Hisagazi, was an old and corpulent man. A soaring headdress of plumes, a feather robe, a wooden scepter topped with a human skull, his facial tattoos, his motionlessness, all made him seem unhuman. He sat on a dais, under sweet-smelling torches. His sons sat crosslegged at his feet, his courtiers on either side. Down the long walls were ranged his guardsmen.

They had not our custom of standing to attention; but they were big, supple young men, bearing shields and corselets of scaly sea-monster leather, flint axes and obsidian spears that could kill as easily as iron. Their heads were shaven, which made them look the fiercer.

Iskilip greeted us well, called for refreshment, bade us be seated on a bench little lower than his dais. He asked many perceptive questions. Wide ranging, the Hisagazi knew of islands far beyond their own chain. They could even point the direction and tell us roughly the distance of a many-castled country they named Yurakadak, though none of them had traveled that far himself. Judging by their third-hand description, what could this be but Giair, which the Wondish adventurer Hanas Tolasson had reached overland? It blazed in me that we were indeed rounding the world. Only after that glory had faded a little did I again heed the talk.

"As I told Guzan," Rovic was saying, "another thing which drew us hither was the tale that you were blessed with a Ship from Heaven. And he showed me this was true."

A hissing went down the hall. The princes grew stiff, the courtiers blanked their countenances, the guardsmen stirred and muttered. Remotely through the walls I heard the rumbling, nearing tide. When Iskilip spoke, through the mask of himself, his voice had gone whetted: "Have you forgotten that these things are not for the uninitiate to see, Guzan?"

"No, Holy One," said the duke. Sweat sprang forth among the devils on his face, though not the sweat of fear. "However, this captain knew. His people also . . . as nearly as I could learn . . . he still has trouble speaking so I can understand . . . his people are initiate too. The claim seems reasonable, Holy One. Look at the marvels they brought. The hard, shining stone-which-is-not-stone, as in this long knife I was given—is that not like the stuff of which the Ship is built? The tubes which make distant things look close at hand, such as he has given you, Holy One—is this not akin to the far-seer the Messenger possesses?"

Iskilip leaned forward, toward Rovic. His scepter hand trembled till the pegged jaws of the skull clattered together. "Did the Star People themselves teach you to make all this?" he cried. "I never imagined. . . . The Messenger never spoke of any others—"

Rovic held up both palms. "Not so fast, Holy One, I pray you," said he. "We are poorly versed in your tongue. I couldn't recognize a word just now."

This was his deceit. His officers had been ordered to feign a knowledge of Hisagazi less than they really possessed. (We had improved our command of it by secret practicing with each other.) Thus he had an unimpeachable device for equivocation.

"Best we talk in private, Holy One," suggested Guzan, with a glance at the courtiers. They returned him a jealous glare.

Iskilip slouched in his gorgeous regalia. His words fell blunt, but in the weak tone of an old, uncertain man. "I know not. If these strangers are already initiate, certes we can show them what we have. But otherwise—if profane ears heard the Messenger's own tale—"

Guzan raised a dominator's hand. Bold and ambitious, long thwarted in his petty province, he had taken fire today. "Holy One," he said, "why has the full story been withheld these many years? In part to keep the commoners obedient, aye. But also, did you and your councillors not fear the whole world might swarm hither, greedy for knowledge, if it knew, and we then be overwhelmed? Well, if we let the blue-eyed men go home with curiosity unsatisfied, I think they are sure to return in strength. Thus we have naught to lose by revealing the truth to them. If they have never had a Messenger of their own, if they can be of no real use to us, time enough to kill them. But if they have indeed been visited like us, what might we and they not do together!"

This was spoken fast and softly, lest we Montalirians understand. And, indeed, our gentlemen failed to. I, having young ears, got the gist; and Rovic preserved such a fatuous smile of incomprehension that I knew he was seizing every word.

In the end they decided to take our leader—and my insignificant self, for no Hisagazian magnate goes anywhere quite unattended—to the temple. Iskilip led the way in person, Guzan and two brawny princes behind. A dozen spearmen brought up the rear. I thought Rovic's blade would be scant use if trouble came, but set my lips firmly together and made myself walk beside him. He looked as eager as a child on Thanksday Morning, teeth agleam in the pointed beard, a plumed bonnet slanted rakish over his brow. None would have thought him aware of any peril.

We left about sundown; in Tambur's hemisphere, folk make less distinction between day and night than our people must. Having observed Siett and Balant in high tide position, I was not surprised that Nikum lay nearly drowned. And yet, as we climbed the cliff trail toward the temple, methought I had never seen a view more alien.

Below us lay a sheet of water, on which the long grass roofs of the city appeared to float; the crowded docks, where our own ship's masts and spars raked above heathen figureheads; the fjord, winding between precipices toward its mouth, where the surf broke white and terrible on the skerries. The heights above us seemed altogether black, against a fire-colored sunset that filled nigh half the sky and bloodied the waters. Wan through those clouds I glimpsed the thick crescent of Tambur, banded in a heraldry no man could read. A basalt column chipped into the shape of a head loomed in outline athwart the planet. Right and left of the path grew sawtoothed turf, summer dry. The sky was pale at the zenith, dark purple in the east, where the first few stars had appeared. Tonight I found no comfort in the stars. We walked silent. The bare native feet made no noise. My shoes went pad-pad and the bells on Rovic's toes raised a tiny jingle.

The temple was a bold piece of work. Within a quadrangle of basalt walls guarded by tall stone heads lay several buildings of the same material. Only the fresh-cut fronds that roofed them were alive. Iskilip leading us, we brushed past acolytes and priests to a wooden cabin behind the sanctum. Two guardsmen stood watch at its door. They knelt for him. The emperor rapped with his curious scepter.

My mouth was dry and my heart thunderous. I expected almost any being hideous or radiant to stand in the doorway as it was opened. Astonishing, then, to see just a man, and of no great stature. By lamplight within I discerned his room, clean, austere, but not uncomfortable; this could have been an ordinary Hisagazian dwelling. He himself wore a simple bast skirt. The legs beneath were bent and thin, old man's shanks. His body was likewise thin, but still erect, the white head proudly carried. In complexion he was darker than a Montalirian, lighter than a Hisagazian, with brown eyes and sparse beard. His visage differed subtly, in nose and lips and slope of jaw, from any other race I had ever encountered. But he was human.

Naught else.

We entered the cabin, shutting out the spearmen. Iskilip doddered through a half-religious ceremony of introduction. I saw Guzan and the princes shift their stance, restless and unawed. Their class had long been party to this. Rovic's face was unreadable. He bowed in courtly wise to Val Nira, Messenger of Heaven, and explained our presence in a few words. But as he spoke, their eyes met and I saw him take the star man's measure.

"Aye, this is my home," said Val Nira. Habit spoke for him; he had given the same account to so many young nobles that the edges were worn off it. As yet he had not observed our metallic instruments, or else had not grasped their significance to him. "For . . . forty-three years, is that right, Iskilip? I have been treated as well as might be. If at times I was near screaming from loneliness, that is what an oracle must expect."

The emperor stirred, uneasy in his robe. "His demon left him," he explained. "Now he is simple human flesh. That's the real secret we keep. It was not ever thus. I remember when he first came. He prophesied immense things, and the people wailed and went on their faces. But sithence his demon has gone back to the stars, and the once-potent weapon he bore has equally been emptied of its force. The people would not believe this, however, so we still pretend otherwise, or there would be unrest among them."

"Affecting your own privileges," said Val Nira. His tone was tired and sardonic. "Iskilip was young then," he added to Rovic, "and the imperial succession was in doubt. I gave him my influence. He promised in return to do certain things for me."

"I tried, Messenger," said the monarch. "Ask all the sunken canoes and drowned men if I did not try. But the will of the gods was otherwise."

"Evidently." Val Nira shrugged. "These islands have few ores, Captain Rovic, and no person capable of recognizing those I required. It's too far to the mainland for Hisagazian canoes. But I don't deny you tried, Iskilip . . . then." He cocked an eyebrow back at us. "This is the first time foreigners have been taken deeply into the imperial confidence, my friends. Are you certain you can get back out again, alive?"

"Why, why, why, they're our guests!" blustered Iskilip and Guzan, almost in each other's mouths.

"Besides," smiled Rovic, "I had most of the secret already. My country has secrets of its own, to set against this. Yes, I think we might well do business, Holy One."

The emperor trembled. His voice cracked across. "Have you indeed a Messenger too?"

"What?" For a numbed moment Val Nira stared at us. Red and white pursued each other across his countenance. Then he sat down on the bench and began to weep.

"Well, not precisely." Rovic laid a hand on the shaking shoulder. "I confess no heavenly vessel has docked at Montalir. But we've certain other secrets, belike equally valuable." Only I, who knew his moods somewhat, could sense the tautness in him. He locked eyes with Guzan and stared the duke down as a wild animal tamer does. And meanwhile, motherly gentle, he spoke with Val Nira.

"I take it, friend, your Ship was wrecked on these shores, but could be repaired if you had certain materials?"

"Yes . . . yes . . . listen—" Stammering and gulping at the thought he might see his home again ere he died, Val Nira tried to explain.

The doctrinal implications of what he said are so astounding, even dangerous, that I feel sure my lords would not wish me to repeat much. However, I do not believe they are false. If the stars are indeed suns like our own, each attended by planets like our own, this demolishes the crystal-sphere theory. But Froad, when he was told later, did not think that matters to the true religion. Scriptures have never said that Paradise lies directly above the birthplace of God's Daughter; this was merely assumed, during those centuries when the earth was believed to be flat. Why should Paradise not be those planets of distant suns, where men dwell in magnificence, who possess the ancient arts and flit from star to star as casually as we might go from Lavre to West Alayn?

Val Nira believed our ancestors had been cast away on this world, several thousand years ago. They must have been fleeing the consequences of some crime or heresy, to come so far from any human domain. Somehow their ship was wrecked, the survivors went back to savagery, and only by degrees have their descendants regained a little knowledge. I cannot see where this explanation contradicts the dogma of the Fall. Rather, it amplifies it. The Fall was not the portion of all mankind but only a few—our own tainted blood—while the others continued to dwell prosperous and content in the heavens.

Our world still lies far off the trade lanes of the Paradise folk. Very few of them nowadays have any interest in seeking new realms. Val Nira, though, was such a one. He traveled at hazard for months until he chanced upon our earth. Then the curse seized him, too. Something went wrong. He descended upon Ulas-Erkila, and the Ship would fly no more.

"I know what the damage is," he said ardently. "I've not forgotten. How could I? No day has passed throughout these years that I didn't recite to myself what must be done. A certain subtle engine in the Ship requires quicksilver." (He and Rovic must spend some time talking ere they deduced this must be what he meant by the word he used.) "When the engine failed, I landed so hard that its tanks burst. All the quicksilver, what I had in reserve as well as what I was employing, poured forth. That much, in a hot enclosed space, would have poisoned me. I fled outside, forgetting to close the doorway. The deck being canted, the quicksilver ran after me. By the time I had recovered from blind panic, a tropical rainstorm had carried off the fluid metal. A series of unlikely accidents, yes, that's what's condemned me to a life's exile. It really would have made more sense to perish outright!"

He clutched Rovic's hand, staring up from his seat at the captain who stood over him. "Can you actually get quicksilver?" he begged. "I need no more than the volume of a man's head. Only that, and a few repairs easily made with tools in the Ship. When this cult grew up around me, I must needs release certain things I possessed, that each provincial temple might have a relic. But I took care never to give away anything important. Whatever I need is waiting there. A gallon of quicksilver, and—oh, God, my wife may even be alive, on Terra!"

Guzan, at least, had begun to understand the situation. He gestured to the princes, who hefted their axes and stepped a little closer. The door was shut on the cabin. Rovic looked from Val Nira to Guzan, whose face was grown ugly with tension. My captain laid hand on hilt. In no other way did he seem to feel any nearness of trouble.

"I take it, milord," he said lightly, "you're willing that the Heaven Ship be made to fly again."

Guzan was jarred. He had never expected this. "Why, of course," he exclaimed. "Why not?"

"Your tame god would depart you. What then becomes of your power in Hisagazia?"

"I—I'd not thought of that," Iskilip stuttered.

Val Nira's eyes shuttled among us, as if watching a

game of paddleball. His thin body shook. "No," he whispered. "You can't. You can't keep me!"

Guzan nodded. "In a few more years," he said, not unkindly, "you would depart in death's canoe anyhow. If meanwhile we held you against your will, you might not speak the right oracles for us. Nay, be at ease; we'll get your flowing stone." With a slitted glance at Rovic: "Who shall fetch it?"

"My folk," said the knight. "Our ship can readily reach Giair, where there are civilized nations who surely have the quicksilver. We could return within a year, I think."

"Accompanied by a fleet of adventurers, to help you seize the sacred vessel?" asked Guzan bluntly. "Or, once out of our islands, you might not proceed to Yurak-adak at all. You might continue the whole way home, and tell your Queen, and return with the power she commands."

Rovic lounged against a roof post, like a big pounce-cat at its ease in ruffles and hose and scarlet cape. His right hand continued to rest on his sword pommel. "None save Val Nira could make that Ship go, I suppose," he drawled. "Does it matter who aids him in making repairs? Surely you don't think either of our nations could conquer Paradise!"

"The ship is very easy to operate," chattered Val Nira. "Anyone can fly it in air. I showed many nobles what levers to use. It's navigating among the stars which is more difficult. No nation on this world could even reach my people unaided—let alone fight them—but why should you think of fighting? I've told you a thousand times, Iskilip, the dwellers in the Milky Way are dangerous to nobody. They have so much wealth they're hard put to find a use for most of it. Gladly would they spend large amounts to help the peoples of this world become civilized again." With an anxious, half-hysterical look at Rovic: "Fully civilized, I mean. We'll teach you our arts. We'll give you engines, automata, homunculi, that do all the toilsome work; and boats that fly through the air; and regular passenger service on those ships that ply between the stars—"

"These things you have promised for forty years," said Iskilip. "We've naught but your word."

"And, finally, a chance to confirm his word," I blurted.

Guzan said with calculated grimness: "Matters are not that simple, Holy One. I've watched these men from across the ocean for weeks, while they lived on Yarzik. Even on their best behavior, they're a fierce and greedy lot. I trust them no further than my eyes reach. This very night I see how they've befooled us. They know our language better than they ever admitted. And they misled us to believe they might have some inkling of a Messenger. If the Ship were indeed made to fly again, them in possession, who knows what they might choose to do?"

Rovic's tone softened still further. "What do you propose, Guzan?"

"We can discuss that another time."

I saw knuckles tighten around stone axes. For a moment, only Val Nira's unsteady breathing was heard. Guzan stood heavy in the lamplight, rubbing his chin, the small black eyes turned downward in thoughtfulness. At last he shook himself. "Perhaps," he said crisply, "a crew mainly Hisagazian could sail your ship, Rovic, and fetch the flowing stone. A few of your men could go along to instruct ours. The rest could remain here as hostages."

My captain made no reply. Val Nira groaned, "You don't understand! You're squabbling over nothing! When my people come here, there'll be no more war, no more oppression. They'll cure you of every disease. They'll show friendship to all and favor to none. I beg you—"

"Enough," said Iskilip. His own words fell ragged. "We shall sleep on this. If anyone can sleep after so much strangeness."

Rovic looked past the emperor's plumes, into the face of Guzan. "Before we decide anything . . ." His fingers tightened on the sword hilt till the nails turned white. Some thought had sprung up within him. But he kept his tone even. "First I want to see that Ship. Can we go there . tomorrow?"

Iskilip was the Holy One, but he stood huddled in his feather robe. Guzan nodded agreement.

We bade our good-nights and went forth under Tambur. The planet was waxing toward full, flooding the courtyard with cold luminance, but the hut was shadowed by the temple. It remained a black outline, a narrow lamplight rectangle of doorway in the middle. There was etched the frail body of Val Nira, who had come from the stars. He watched us till we had gone out of sight.

On the way down the path, Guzan and Rovic bargained in curt words. The Ship lay two days' march inland, on the slopes of Mount Ulas. We would go in a joint party to inspect it, but a mere dozen Montalirians were allowed. Afterward we would debate our course of action.

Lanthorns glowed yellow at our caravel's poop. Refusing Iskilip's hospitality, Rovic and I returned thither for the night. A pikeman on guard at the gangway inquired what I had learned. "Ask me tomorrow," I said feebly. "My head's in too much of a whirl."

"Come into my cabin, lad, for a stoup ere we retire," the captain invited me.

God knows I needed wine. We entered the low room, crowded with nautical instruments, books, and printed charts that looked quaint to me now I had seen a little of those spaces where the cartographer drew mermaids and windsprites. Rovic sat down behind his table, gestured me to a chair opposite, and poured from a carafe into two goblets of Quaynish crystal. Then I knew he had momentous thoughts in his head—far more than the problem of saving our lives.

We sipped a while, unspeaking. I heard the lap-lap of wavelets on our hull, the tramp of men on watch, the rustle of distant surf—otherwise nothing. At last Rovic leaned back, staring at the ruby wine on the table. I could not read his expression.

"Well, lad," said he, "what do you think?"

"I know not what to think, master."

"You and Froad are a trifle prepared for this idea

that the stars are other suns. You're educated. As for me, I've seen sufficient eldritch in my day that this seems quite believable. The rest of our people, though . . ."

"An irony that barbarians like Guzan should long have been familiar with the concept, having had the old man from the sky to preach it privily to their class for more than forty years. Is he indeed a prophet, master?"

"He denies it. He plays prophet because he must, but it's evident that the dukes and earls of this realm know it's a trick. Iskilip is senile, more than half converted to his own artificial creed. He was mumbling about prophecies Val Nira made long ago, true prophecies. Bah! Tricks of memory and wishfulness. Val Nira is as human and fallible as I am. We Montalirians are the same flesh as these Hisagazi, even if we have learned the use of metal before they did. Val Nira's people know more in turn than us; they're still mortals, by Heaven. I must remember that they are."

"Guzan remembers."

"Bravo, lad!" Rovic's mouth bent upward, one-sidedly. "He's a clever one, and bold. When he came, he saw his chance to stop stagnating as the petty lord on an outlying island. He'll not let that chance slip without a fight. Like many a double-dealer before him, he accuses us of plotting the very things he hopes to do."

"But what does he hope for?"

"My guess would be, he wants the Ship for himself. Val Nira said it was easy to fly. Navigation between the stars would be too difficult for anyone save him; nor could any man in his right mind hope to play pirate along the Milky Way. However . . . if the Ship stayed right here, on this earth, rising no higher than a mile above ground . . . the warlord who used it might conquer more widely than Lame Darveth himself."

I was aghast. "Do you mean Guzan would not even try to seek out Paradise?"

Rovic scowled so blackly at his wine that I saw he wanted solitude. I stole off to my bunk in the poop.

The captain was awake before dawn, readying our

folk. Plainly he had reached some decision, and it was
not pleasant. But once he set a course, he seldom veered.
He was long in conference with Etien, who came out of
the cabin looking frightened As if to reassure himself,
the boatswain ordered the men about harshly.

Our allowed dozen were to be Rovic, Froad, myself,
Etien, and eight crewmen. We were issued helmets and
corselets, muskets and edged weapons. Since Guzan had
told us there was a beaten path to the Ship, we assembled
a supply cart on the dock. Etien supervised its landing.
I was astonished to see that nearly all it carried, till the
axles groaned, was barrels of gunpowder. "But we're not
taking cannon!" I protested.

"Skipper's orders," rapped Etien. He turned his back
on me. After a glance at Rovic's face, nobody ventured to
ask him the reason. I remembered we would be going up
a mountainside. A wagonful of powder, with lit fuse,
set rolling down toward a hostile army, might win a battle. But did Rovic anticipate open conflict?

Certes his orders to the men and officers remaining
behind suggested as much. They were to stay aboard the
*Golden Leaper,* holding her ready for instant fight or
flight.

As the sun rose, we said our morning prayers to God's
Daughter and marched down the docks. The wood
banged hollow under our boots. A few thin mists drifted
on the bay; Tambur's crescent hung wan above. Nikum
town lay hushed as we passed through.

Guzan met us at the temple. A son of Iskilip was sup-
posedly in charge, but the duke ignored that youth as
much as we did. They had a hundred guardsmen along,
scaly-coated, shaven-headed, tattooed with storms and
dragons. The early sunlight gleamed off obsidian spear-
heads. Our approach was watched in silence. But when
we halted before those disorderly ranks, Guzan trod
forth. He was also y-clad leather, and carried the sword
Rovic had given him on Yarzik. The dew shimmered on
his feather cloak. "What have you in that wagon?" he
demanded.

"Supplies," Rovic answered.

"For four days?"

"Send home all but ten of your men," said Rovic coolly, "and I'll send back this cart."

Their eyes clashed, until Guzan turned and gave his orders. We started off, a few Montalirians surrounded by pagan warriors. The jungle lay ahead of us, a deep and burning green, rising halfway up the slope of Ulas. Then the mountain became naked black, to the snow that edged its smoking crater.

Val Nira walked between Rovic and Guzan. Strange, I thought, that the instrument of God's will for us was so shriveled. He ought to have walked tall and haughty, a star on his brow.

During the day, at night when we made camp, and again the next day, Rovic and Froad questioned him eagerly about his home. Of course, their talk was in fragments. Nor did I hear everything, since I must take my turn at pulling our wagon along that narrow, steep, damnable trail. The Hisagazi have no draft animals, therefore they make slight use of the wheel and have no proper roads. But what I did hear kept me long awake.

Ah, greater marvels than the poets have imagined for Elf Land! Entire cities built in a single tower half a mile high. The sky made to glow so that there is no true darkness after sunset. Food not grown in the earth, but manufactured in alchemical elaboratories. The lowest peasant owning a score of machines which serve him more subtly and humbly than might a thousand slaves; owning an aerial carriage which can fly him around his world in less than a day; owning a crystal window on which theatrical images appear, to beguile his abundant leisure. Argosies between suns, stuffed with the wealth of a thousand planets; yet every ship unarmed and unescorted, for there are no pirates and this realm is on such good terms with the other starfaring nations that war has also ceased. (These foreign countries, it seems, are more akin to the supernatural than Val Nira's, in that the races composing them are not human, though able to speak and reason.) In this happy land is little crime. When it does occur, the criminal is soon captured by the arts of the provost corps; yet he is not hanged, nor even transported overseas. Instead, his mind is cured of the wish to violate any law. He returns home to live as an especially honored citizen, since folk know he is now completely trustworthy. As for the government— but here I lost the thread of discourse. I believe it is in form a republic, but in practice a devoted fellowship of men, chosen by examination, who see to the welfare of everyone else.

Surely, I thought, this was Paradise!

Our sailors listened agape. Rovic's mien was reserved, but he gnawed his mustaches incessantly. Guzan, to whom this was an old tale, grew rough of manner. Plain to see, he disliked our intimacy with Val Nira, and the ease wherewith we grasped ideas that were spoken.

But, then, we came of a nation which has long encouraged natural philosophy and improvement of the mechanic arts. I myself, in my short lifetime, had witnessed the replacement of the waterwheel in regions where there are few streams by the modern form of windmill. The pendulum clock was invented the year before I was born. I had read many romances about the flying machines which no few men have tried to devise. Living at such a dizzy pace of progress, we Montalirians were all prepared to entertain still vaster concepts.

At night, sitting with Froad and Etien around a campfire, I spoke somewhat of this to the savant. "Ah," he crooned, "today Truth stood unveiled before me. Did you hear what the starman said? The three laws of planetary motion about a sun, and the one great law of attraction which explains them? Dear saints, that law can be put in a single short sentence, and yet the development will keep mathematicians busy for three hundred years!"

He stared past the flames, and the other fires around which the heathen slept, and jungle gloom, and angry volcanic glow in heaven. I started to query him. "Leave be, lad," grunted Etien. "Can ye nay tell when a man's in love?"

I shifted a little closer to the boatswain's stolid, comforting bulk. "What do you think of this?" I asked, softly, for the jungle whispered and croaked on every side.

"Me, I stopped thinking a while back," he said. "After yon day on the quarterdeck, when the skipper jested us into sailing wi' him though we went off the world's edge an' tumbled down in foam amongst the nether stars . . . well, I'm but a poor sailor man, an' my one chance o' regaining home is to follow the skipper."

"Even beyond the sky?"

"Less hazard to that, maybe, than sailing on around the world. The little man swore his vessel was safe, an' no storms blow between the suns."

"Can you trust his word?"

"Oh, aye. Even a knocked-about old palomer like me has seen enough o' men to ken when a one's too timid an' eagersome to stand by a lie. I fear not the folk in Paradise, nor does the skipper. Except in some way . . ." Etien rubbed his bearded jaw, scowling. "In some way I can nay wholly grasp, they affright Rovic. He fears nay they'll come hither wi' torch an' sword; but there's somewhat else about 'em that frets him."

I felt the ground shudder the least bit. Ulas had cleared his throat. "It does seem we'd be daring God's anger—"

"That's nay what gnaws on the skipper's mind. He was never an over-pious man." Etien scratched himself, yawned, and climbed to his feet. "Glad I am to be nay the skipper. Let him think over what's best to do. Time ye an' me was asleep."

But I slept little that night.

Rovic, I think, rested well. Yet as the next day wore on, I could see haggardness on him. I wondered why. Did he think the Hisagazi would turn on us? If so, why had he come? As the slope steepened, the wagon grew so toilsome to push and drag that my fears died for lack of breath.

Yet when we came upon the Ship, toward evening, I forgot my weariness. And after an amazed volley of

oaths, our mariners rested silent on their pikes. The
Hisagazi, never talkative, crouched low in token of awe.
Only Guzan remained erect among them. I glimpsed his
expression as he stared at the marvel. It was a look of
lust.

Wild was that place. We had gone above timberline.
The land was a green sea below us, edged with silvery
ocean. Here we stood among tumbled black boulders,
cinders and spongy tufa underfoot. The mountain rose
in steeps and scarps and ravines, on to snows and smoke,
which rose another mile into a pale chilly sky. And here
stood the Ship.

And the Ship was beauty.

I remember. In length—height, rather, since it stood
on its tail—it was about equal to our caravel, in form
not unlike a lance head, in color a shining white, un-
tarnished after forty years. That was all. But words are
paltry, my lords. What can they show of clean soaring
curves, of iridescence on burnished metal, of a thing
which was proud and lovely and in its very shape aquiver
to be off? How can I conjure back the glamour which
hazed that Ship whose keel had cloven starlight?

We stood there a long time. My vision blurred. I wiped
my eyes, angry to be seen thus affected, until I noticed a
tear glisten in Rovic's red beard. But the captain's visage was quite blank. When he spoke, he said merely, in
a flat voice, "Come, let's make camp."

The Hisagazian guardsmen dared approach no closer
than these several hundred yards to as potent an idol as
the Ship had become. Our mariners were glad to maintain the same distance. But after dark, when everything
else was in order, Val Nira led Rovic, Froad, Guzan,
and myself to the vessel.

As we approached, a double door in the side swung
noiselessly open and a metal gangplank descended there-
from. Glowing in Tambur's light, and in the dull clotted
red reflected off the smoke clouds, the Ship was already as
strange as I could endure. When it thus beckoned me,
as if a ghost stood guard, I whimpered and fled. The

cinders crunched beneath my boots; I caught a whiff of
sulfurous air.

But at the edge of camp I rallied myself enough to
look again. The dark ground blotted up light, so that the
Ship appeared alone with its grandeur. Presently I went
back.

The interior was lit by luminous panels, cool to the
touch. Val Nira explained that the great engine which
drove it—as if the troll of folklore were put on a tread-
mill—was intact, and would furnish power at the flick
of a lever. As nearly as I could understand what he said,
this was done by changing the metallic part of salt into
light . . . thus I do not understand after all. The quicksilver was required for a part of the controls, which chan-
neled power from the engine into another mechanism
that hurtled the Ship skyward. We inspected the broken
container. Enormous indeed had been the impact of landing, to twist and bend that thick alloy. And yet Val Nira
had been shielded by invisible forces, and the rest of the
Ship had not suffered important damage. He fetched
some tools, which flamed and hummed and whirled, and
demonstrated a few repair operations on the broken part.
Obviously he would have no trouble completing the work
—and then he need only pour in a gallon of quicksilver,
to bring his vessel alive again.

Much else did he show us that night. I shall say naught
of it, for I cannot even remember such strangeness very
clearly, let alone find words. Suffice that Rovic, Froad,
and Zhean spent a few hours in Elf Hill.

So, too, did Guzan. Though he had been taken here
before, as part of his initiation, he had never been shown
this much ere now. Watching him, however, I saw less
marveling in him than greed.

No doubt Rovic observed the same. There was little
which Rovic did not observe. When we departed the
Ship, his silence was not stunned like Froad's or mine. At
the time, I thought in a vague fashion that he fretted over
the trouble Guzan was certain to make. Now, looking
back, I believe his mood was sadness.

Sure it is that long after we others were in our bedrolls, he stood by himself, looking at the planet-lit Ship.

Early in a cold dawn, Etien shook me awake. "Up, lad, we've work to do. Load yere pistols an' belt on yere dirk."

"What? What's to happen?" I fumbled with a hoar-frosted blanket. Last night seemed a dream.

"The skipper's nay said, but plainly he awaits a fight. Report to the wagon an' help us move into yon flying tower." Etien's thick form heelsquatted a moment longer beside me. Then, slowly: "Methinks Guzan has some idea o' murdering us here on the mountain. One officer an' a few crewmen can be made to sail the *Golden Leaper* for him, to Giair an' back. The rest o' us would be less trouble to him wi' our weasands slit."

I crawled forth, teeth clattering in my head. After arming myself, I snatched some food from the common store. The Hisagazi on the march carry dried fish and a sort of bread made from a powdered weed. The saints alone knew when I'd next get a chance to eat. I was the last to join Rovic at the cart. The natives were drifting sullenly toward us, unsure what we intended.

"Let's go, lads," said Rovic. He gave his orders. Four men started manhandling the wagon across the rocky trail toward the Ship, where this gleamed among mists. We others stood by, weapons ready. Guzan hastened toward us, Val Nira toiled in his wake.

Anger darkened his countenance. "What are you doing?" he barked.

Rovic gave him a calm stare. "Why, milord, as we may be here for some time, inspecting the wonders aboard the Ship—"

"What?" exclaimed Guzan. "What do you mean? Have you not seen ample for a first visit? We must get home again, and prepare to sail after the flowing stone."

"Go if you wish," said Rovic. "I choose to linger. And since you don't trust me, I reciprocate the feeling. My folk will stay in the Ship, which can be defended if necessary."

Guzan stormed and raged, but Rovic ignored him. Our men continued hauling the cart over the uneven ground. Guzan signaled his spearmen, who approached in a disordered but alert mass. Etien spoke a command. We fell into line. Pikes slanted forward, muskets took aim.

Guzan stepped back. We had demonstrated firearms for him at his home island. Doubtless he could overwhelm us with sheer numbers, were he determined, but the cost would be heavy. "No reason to fight, is there?" purred Rovic. "I am only taking a sensible precaution. The Ship is a most valuable prize. It could bring Paradise for all . . . or dominion over this earth for a few. There are those who'd prefer the latter. I've not accused you of being among them. However, in prudence I'd liefer keep the Ship for my hostage and my fortress, as long as it pleases me to remain here."

I think then I was convinced of Guzan's real intentions, not as a surmise of ours but as plain fact. Had he truly wished to attain the stars, his single concern would have been to keep the Ship safe. He would not have reached out, snatched little Val Nira in his powerful hands, and dragged the starman backward like a shield against our fire. Not that his intent matters, save to my own conscience. Wrath distorted his patterned visage. He screamed at us, "Then I'll keep a hostage too! And much good may your shelter do you!"

The Hisagazi milled about, muttering, hefting their spears and axes, but not prepared to follow us. We grunted our way across the black mountainside. The sun strengthened. Froad twisted his beard. "Dear me, master captain," he said, "think you they'll lay siege to us?"

"I'd not advise anyone to venture forth alone," said Rovic dryly.

"But without Val Nira to explain things, what use for us to stay at the Ship? Best we go back. I've mathematic texts to consult. My head's aspin with the law that binds the turning planets. I must ask the man from Paradise what he knows of—"

Rovic interrupted with a gruff order to three men, that

they help lift a wheel wedged between two stones. He
was in a savage temper. I confess his action seemed mad
to me. If Guzan intended treachery, we had gained little
by immobilizing ourselves in the Ship, where he could
starve us. Better to let him attack in the open, where we
would have a chance of fighting our way through. And
if Guzan did not plan to fall on us in the jungle—or
any other time—then this was senseless provocation on
our part. But I dared not question.

When we had brought our wagon to the Ship, its gangplank again descended for us. The sailors started and
cursed. Rovic forced himself out of his bitterness, to
speak soothing words. "Easy, lads. I've been aboard already, ye ken. Naught harmful within. Now we must
tote our powder thither, an' stow it as I've planned."

Being slight of frame, I was not set to carrying the
heavy casks, but put at the foot of the gangplank to watch
the Hisagazi. Although we were too far away to distinguish words, I saw how Guzan stood on a boulder and
harangued them. They shook their weapons at us and
whooped. They did not venture to attack. I wondered
wretchedly what this was all about. If Rovic had fore-
seen us besieged, that would explain why he brought
the powder along. . . . No, it would not, for there was
more than a dozen men could shoot off in weeks of mus-
ketry, even if we had enough bullets . . . and we had almost no food! I looked past the poisonous volcano clouds,
to Tambur where storms raged that could engulf our
whole earth, and wondered what demons lurked here to
possess men.

I sprang to alertness at an indignant shout from within. Froad! Almost, I ran up the gangway, then remembered my duty. I heard Rovic roar him down and order
the crewfolk to carry on. Froad and Rovic must have
gone by themselves into the pilot's compartment and
talked for an hour or more. When the old man emerged,
he protested no longer. But as he walked down the gangway, he wept.

Rovic followed, grimmer of countenance than I had

ever seen ere now. The sailors filed after, some looking appalled, some relieved, but chiefly watching the Hisagazian camp. They were simply mariners; the Ship was little to them save a weird and disquieting object. Last came Etien, walking backward down the metal plank as he uncoiled a long string.

"Form square!" barked Rovic. The men snapped into position. "Get at the middle, Zhean and Froad," said the captain. "You can better carry extra ammunition than fight." He placed himself in the van.

I tugged Froad's sleeve. "Please, I beg you, master, what's happening?" He sobbed too much to answer.

Etien crouched, flint and steel in his hands. He heard me—for otherwise we were deathly silent—and said in a hard voice: "We placed casks o' powder throughout this hull, lad, wi' powder trains to join 'em. Here's the fuse to the whole."

I could not speak, could not even think, so monstrous was this. As if from immensely far away, I heard the click of stone on metal in Etien's fingers, heard him blow on the spark and add: "A good idea, methinks. I said t'other eventide, I'd follow the skipper wi'out fear o' God's curse—but let's not tempt Him overmuch."

"Forward march!" Rovic's sword blazed clear of the scabbard.

Our feet scrunched loud and horrible on the mountain as we quick-stepped away. I did not look back. I could not. I was still fumbling in a nightmare. Since Guzan would have moved to intercept us anyhow, we proceeded straight toward his band. He stepped forth as we halted at the camp's edge. Val Nira slunk shivering after him. I heard the words dimly.

"Well, Rovic, what now? Are you ready to go home?"

"Yes," said the captain. His voice was dull. "All the way home."

Guzan squinted in rising suspiciousness. "Why did you abandon your wagon? What did you leave behind?"

"Supplies. Come, let's march."

Val Nira stared at the cruel shapes of our pikes. He must wet his lips a few times ere he could quaver, "What are you talking about? There's no reason to leave food there. It would spoil in the time until . . . until—" He faltered as he looked into Rovic's eyes. The blood drained from him.

"What have you done?" he whispered.

Suddenly Rovic's free hand arose, to cover his face. "What I must," he said thickly. "Daughter of God, forgive me."

The starman regarded us an instant more. Then he turned and ran. Past the astonished warriors he burst, out onto the cindery slope, toward his Ship.

"Come back!" bellowed Rovic. "You fool, you'll never—"

He swallowed hard. As he looked after that small, stumbling, lonely shape, hurrying across a fire mountain toward the Beautiful One, the sword sank in his grasp. "Perhaps it's best," he said, like a benediction.

Guzan raised his own sword. In scaly coat and blowing feathers, he was a figure as impressive as steel-clad Rovic. "Tell me what you've done," he snarled, "or I'll kill you this moment!"

He paid our muskets no heed. He, too, had had dreams.

He, too, saw them end, when the Ship exploded.

Even that adamantine hull could not withstand a wagonload of carefully placed gunpowder, set off at the same time. A crash knocked me to my knees, and the hull cracked open. White-hot chunks of metal screamed across the slopes. I saw one of them strike a boulder and split it in twain. Val Nira vanished, destroyed too quickly to have seen what happened; thus, in the ultimate, God was merciful to him. Through the flames and smokes and doomsday noise which followed, I saw the Ship fall. It rolled down the slope, strewing its mangled guts behind. Then the mountainside grumbled and slid in pursuit, and buried it, and dust hid the sky.

More than this, I have no heart to remember.

The Hisagazi shrieked and fled. They must have thought hell was come to earth. Guzan stood his ground. As the dust enveloped us, hiding the grave of the Ship and the white volcano crater, turning the sun red, he sprang at Rovic. A musketeer raised his weapon. Etien slapped it down. We stood and watched those two men fight, up and over the shaken cinder land, and knew in our private darkness that this was their right. Sparks flew where the blades clamored together. At last Rovic's skill prevailed. He took his foe in the throat.

We gave Guzan decent burial and went down through the jungle.

That night the guardsmen rallied their courage to attack us. We were aided by our muskets, but must chiefly use sword and pike. We hewed our way through them because we had no place else to go than the sea.

They retreated, but carried word ahead of us. When we reached Nikum, all the forces Iskilip could raise were besieging the *Golden Leaper* and waiting to oppose Rovic's entry. We formed a square again, and no matter how many thousands they had, only a score or so could reach us at any time. Nonetheless, we left six good men in the crimsoned mud of those streets. When our people on the caravel realized Rovic was coming back, they bombarded the town. This ignited the thatch roofs and distracted the enemy enough that a sortie from the ship was able to effect a juncture with us. We chopped our way to the pier, got aboard, and manned the capstan.

Outraged and very brave, the Hisagazi paddled their canoes up to our hull, where our cannon could not be brought to bear. They stood on each other's shoulders to reach our rail. One band forced itself aboard, and the fight was fierce which cleared them from the decks. That was when I got the shattered collarbone which plagues me to this day.

But in the end, we came out of the fjord. A fresh east wind was blowing. Sail aloft, we outran the foe. We counted our dead, bound our wounds, and slept.

Next dawning, awakened by the pain of my wound and the worse pain within, I mounted the quarterdeck. The sky was overcast. The wind had stiffened; the sea ran cold and green, whitecaps out to a cloudy-gray horizon. Timbers groaned and rigging thrummed. I stood an hour facing aft, into the chill wind that numbs pain.

When I heard boots behind me, I did not turn around. I knew they were Rovic's. He stood beside me a long while, bareheaded. I noticed that he was starting to turn gray.

Finally, not yet regarding me, still squinting into the air that lashed tears from our eyes, he said: "I had a chance to talk Froad over, that day. He was grieved, but owned I was right. Has he spoken to you about it?"

"No," I said.

"None of us are ever likely to speak of it much," said Rovic.

After another time: "I was not afraid Guzan or anyone else would seize the Ship and try to turn conqueror. We men of Montalir should well be able to deal with any such rogues. Nor was I afraid of the Paradise dwellers. That poor little man could only have been telling truth. They would never have harmed us . . . willingly. They would have brought precious gifts, and taught us their esoteric arts, and let us visit their stars."

"Then why?" I got out.

"Someday Froad's successors will solve the riddles of the universe," he said. "Someday our descendants will build their own Ship, and go forth to whatever destiny they wish."

Spume blew around us until our hair was wet. I tasted the salt on my lips.

"Meanwhile," said Rovic, "we'll sail the seas of this earth, and walk its mountains, and chart and subdue and come to understand it. Do you see, Zhean? That is what the Ship would have taken from us."

Then I was also made able to weep. He laid his hand on my uninjured shoulder and stood with me while the *Golden Leaper*, all sail set, proceeded westward.

OCCASIONALLY I WRITE A HEROIC fantasy, the protagonist of which bears not a gun but a sword and faces not scientific technology and extraterrestrial intelligences but magic and elves—or gods. Some readers like this the best of anything I do. By now the class includes three novels, *The Broken Sword, Three Hearts and Three Lions,* and *Hrolf Kraki's Saga,* plus two on the borderline, *Operation Chaos* and *A Midsummer Tempest.* There are also a few shorter tales, but none that would quite fit in here, except this little spoof of the entire genre.

Since it was first published, a gentleman by the name of Walter Cronkite has gained a certain prominence. I therefore considered changing the name of my chief character, but finally decided against it. After all, the reference is to that archetypal figure Conan the Cimmerian. Know, Mr. Cronkite, that I don't agree with every opinion you hold, but for your wonderful coverage of the Apollo missions, I love you!

2

# THE BARBARIAN

<<<<<<<<<<<<<<<<<<<<<<<<<<<<<<<<<<<<<<<<<

SINCE THE HOWARD-DE CAMP SYSTEM FOR *deciphering preglacial inscriptions first appeared, much progress has been made in tracing the history, ethnology, and even daily life of the great cultures which flourished till the Pleistocene ice age wiped them out and forced man to start over. We know, for instance, that magic was practiced; that there were some highly civilized countries in what is now central Asia, the Near East, North Africa, southern Europe, and various oceans; and that elsewhere the world was occupied by barbarians, of whom the northern Europeans were the biggest, strongest, and most warlike. At least, so the scholars inform us, and being of northern European ancestry, they ought to know.*

*The following is a translation of a letter recently discovered in the ruins of Cyrenne. This was a provincial town of the Sarmian Empire, a great though decadent realm in the eastern Mediterranean area, whose capital, Sarmia, was at once the most beautiful and the most lustful, depraved city of its time. The Sarmians' northern neighbors were primitive horse nomads and/or Centaurs; but to the east lay the Kingdom of Chathakh, and to the south was the Herpetarchy of Serpens, ruled by a priestly cast of snake worshipers—or possibly snakes.*

*The letter was obviously written in Sarmia and posted
to Cyrenne. Its date is approximately 175,000* B.C.

Maxilion Quaestos, sub-sub-sub-prefect of the Impe-
rial Waterworks of Sarmia, to his nephew Thyaston,
Chancellor of the Bureau of Thaumaturgy, Province of
Cyrenne:

Greetings!

I trust this finds you in good health, and that the gods
will continue to favor you. As for me, I am well, though
somewhat plagued by the gout, for which I have tried
[*here follows the description of a home remedy, both
tedious and unprintable*]. This has not availed, however,
save to exhaust my purse and myself.

You must indeed have been out of touch during your
Atlantean journey, if you must write to inquire about
the Barbarian affair. Now that events have settled down
again, I can, I hope, give you an adequate and dis-
passionate account of the whole ill-starred business. By
the favor of the Triplet Goddesses, holy Sarmia has
survived the episode; and though we are still rather
shaken, things are improving. If at times I seem to
depart from the philosophic calm I have always tried
to cultivate, blame it on the Barbarian. I am not the man
I used to be. None of us are.

To begin, then, about three years ago the war with
Chathakh had settled down to border skirmishes. An
occasional raid by one side or the other would penetrate
deeply into the countries themselves, but with no decisive effect. Indeed, since these operations yielded a more
or less equal amount of booty for both lands, and the
slave trade grew brisk, it was good for business.

Our chief concern was the ambiguous attitude of
Serpens. As you well know, the Herpetarchs have no
love for us, and a major object of our diplomacy was
to keep them from entering the war on the side of
Chathakh. We had, of course, no hope of making them
our allies. But as long as we maintained a posture of
strength, it was likely that they would at least stay neu-
tral.

Thus matters stood when the Barbarian came to Sarmia.

We had heard rumors of him for a long time. He was a wandering soldier of fortune, from some kingdom of swordsmen and seafarers up in the northern forests, who had drifted south, alone, in search of adventure or perhaps only a better climate. Seven feet tall, and broad in proportion, he was one mass of muscle, with a mane of tawny hair and sullen blue eyes. He was adept with any weapon, but preferred a four-foot double-edged sword with which he could cleave helmet, skull, neck, and so on down at one blow. He was additionally said to be a drinker and lover of awesome capacity.

Having overcome the Centaurs singlehanded, he tramped down through our northern provinces and one day stood at the gates of Sarmia herself. It was a curious vision—the turreted walls rearing over the stone-paved road, the guards bearing helmet and shield and corselet, and the towering, near-naked giant who rattled his blade before them. As their pikes slanted down to bar his way, he cried in a voice of thunder:

"I yam Cronkheit duh Barbarian, an' I wanna audience widjer queen!"

His accent was so ludicrously uneducated that the watch burst into laughter. This angered him; flushing darkly, he drew his sword and advanced stiff-legged. The guardsmen reeled back before him, and the Barbarian swaggered through.

As the captain of the watch explained it to me afterward: "There he came, and there we stood. A spear length away, we caught the smell. Ye gods, *when* did he last bathe?"

So with people running from the streets and bazaars as he neared, Cronkheit made his way down the Avenue of Sphinxes, past the baths and the Temple of Loccar, till he reached the Imperial Palace. Its gates stood open as usual, and he looked in at the gardens and the alabaster walls beyond, and grunted. When the Golden Guardsmen approached him upwind and asked his business, he grunted again. They lifted their bows and would

have made short work of him, but a slave came hastily
to bid them desist.

You see, by the will of some malignant god, the Empress was standing on a balcony and saw him.

As is well known, our beloved Empress, Her Seductive
Majesty the Illustrious Lady Larra the Voluptuous, is
built like a mountain highway and is commonly believed
to be an incarnation of her tutelary deity, Aphrosex, the
Mink Goddess. She stood on the balcony, the wind blowing her thin transparent garments and thick black hair,
and a sudden eagerness lit her proud lovely face. This
was understandable, for Cronkheit wore simply a bearskin kilt.

Hence the slave was dispatched, to bow low before the
stranger and say: "Most noble lord, the divine Empress
would have private speech with you."

Cronkheit smacked his lips and strutted into the palace. The chamberlain wrung his hands when he saw
those large muddy feet treading on priceless rugs, but
there was no help for it, and the Barbarian was led upstairs to the Imperial bedchamber.

What befell there is known to all, for of course in such
interviews the Lady Larra posts mute slaves at convenient peepholes, to summon the guards if danger seems to
threaten; and the courtiers have quietly taught these
mutes to write. Our Empress had a cold, and had furthermore been eating a garlic salad, so her aristocratically
curved nose was not offended. After a few formalities,
she began to pant. Slowly, then, she held out her arms
and let the purple robe slide down from her creamy
shoulders and across the silken thighs.

"Come," she whispered. "Come, magnificent male."

Cronkheit snorted, pawed the ground, rushed forth,
and clasped her to him.

"Yowww!" cried the Empress as a rib cracked.
"Leggo! Help!"

The mutes ran for the Golden Guardsmen, who entered at once. They got ropes around the Barbarian and
dragged him from their poor lady. Though in considerable pain, and much shaken, she did not order his exe-

cution; she is known to be very patient with some types.

Indeed, after gulping a cup of wine to steady her, she invited Cronkheit to be her guest. After he had been conducted off to his rooms, she summoned the Duchess of Thyle, a supple, agile little minx.

"I have a task for you, my dear," she murmured. "You will fulfill it as a loyal lady-in-waiting."

"Yes, Your Seductive Majesty," said the Duchess, who could well guess what the task was and thought she had been waiting long enough. For a whole week, in fact. Her assignment was to take the edge off the Barbarian's impetuosity.

She greased herself so she could slip free if in peril of being crushed, and hurried to Cronkheit's suite. Her musky perfume drowned out his odor, and she slipped off her dress and crooned with half-shut eyes: "Take me, my lord!"

"Yahoo!" howled the warrior. "I yam Cronkheit duh Strong, Cronkheit duh Bold, Cronkheit what slew a mammot' single-handed an' made hisself chief o' duh Centaurs, an' dis's muh night! C'mere!"

The Duchess did, and he folded her in his mighty arms. A moment later came another shriek. The palace attendants were treated to the sight of a naked and furious duchess speeding down the jade corridor.

"Fleas he's got!" she cried, scratching as she ran.

So all in all, Cronkheit the Barbarian was no great success as a lover. Even the women in the Street of Joy used to hide when they saw him coming. They said they'd been exposed to clumsy technique before, but this was just too much.

However, his fame was so great that the Lady Larra put him in command of a brigade, infantry and cavalry, and sent him to join General Grythion on the Chathakh border. He made the march in record time and came shouting into the city of tents which had grown up at our main base.

Now, admittedly our good General Grythion is somewhat of a dandy, who curls his beard and is henpecked by his wives. But he has always been a competent sol-

dier, winning honors at the Academy and leading troops
in battle many times before rising to the strategic-
planning post. One could understand Cronkheit's incivil-
ity at their meeting. But when the general courteously
declined to go forth in the van of the army and pointed
out how much more valuable he was as a coordinator
behind the lines—that was no excuse for Cronkheit to
knock his superior officer to the ground and call him a
coward, damned of the gods. Grythion was thoroughly
justified in having him put in irons, despite the casualties
involved. Even as it was, the spectacle had so demoral-
ized our troops that they lost three important engage-
ments in the following month.

Alas! Word of this reached the Empress, and she did
not order Cronkheit's head struck off. Indeed, she sent
back a command that he be released and reinstated. Perhaps she still cherished a hope of civilizing him enough
to be an acceptable bed partner.

Grythion swallowed his pride and apologized to the
Barbarian, who accepted with an ill grace. His restored
rank made it necessary to invite him to a dinner and conference in the headquarters tent.

That was a flat failure. Cronkheit stamped in and at
once made sneering remarks about the elegant togas of
his brother officers. He belched when he ate and couldn't
distinguish the product of any vineyard from another.
His conversation consisted of hour-long monologues
about his own prowess. General Grythion saw morale
zooming downward, and hastily called for maps and
planning.

"Now, most noble sirs," he began, "we have to lay out
the summer campaign. As you know, we have the Eastern Desert between us and the nearest important enemy
positions. This raises difficult questions of logistics and
catapult emplacement." He turned politely to the Barbarian. "Have you any suggestion, my lord?"

"Duh," said Cronkheit.

"I think," ventured Colonel Pharaon, "that if we advanced to the Chunling Oasis and dug in there, building
a supply road—"

"Dat reminds me," said Cronkheit. "One time up in duh Norriki marshes, I run acrost some swamp men an' dey uses poisoned arrers—"

"I fail to see what that has to do with this problem," said General Grythion.

"Nuttin'," admitted Cronkheit cheerfully. "But don't innerup' me. Like I was sayin' . . ." And he was off for a whole dreary hour.

At the end of a conference which had gotten nowhere, the general stroked his beard and said shrewdly: "Lord Cronkheit, it appears your abilities are more in the tactical than the strategic field."

The Barbarian snatched for his sword.

"I mean," said Grythion quickly, "I have a task which only the boldest and strongest leader can accomplish."

Cronkheit beamed and listened closely for a change. He was to lead an expedition to capture Chantsay. This was a fort in the mountain passes across the Eastern Desert, and a major obstacle to our advance. However, in spite of Grythion's judicious flattery, a full brigade should have been able to take it with little difficulty, for it was known to be undermanned.

Cronkheit rode off at the head of his men, tossing his sword in the air and bellowing some uncouth battle chant. Then he was not heard of for six weeks.

At the close of that time, the ragged, starving, fever-stricken remnant of his troops staggered back to the base and reported utter failure. Cronkheit, who was in excellent health himself, made sullen excuses. But he had never imagined that men who march twenty hours a day aren't fit for battle at the end of the trip—the more so if they outrun their supply train.

Because of the Empress' wish, General Grythion could not do the sensible thing and cashier the Barbarian. He could not even reduce him to the ranks. Instead, he used his well-known guile and invited the giant to a private dinner.

"Obviously, most valiant lord," he purred, "the fault is mine. I should have realized that a man of your type is too much for us decadent southerners. You are a lone wolf who fights best by himself."

"Duh," agreed Cronkheit, ripping a fowl apart with his fingers and wiping them on the damask tablecloth.

Grythion winced, but easily talked him into going out on a one-man guerrilla operation. When he left the next morning, the officers' corps congratulated themselves on having gotten rid of the lout forever.

In the face of subsequent criticism and demands for an investigation, I still maintain that Grythion did the only rational thing under the circumstances. Who could have known that Cronkheit the Barbarian was so primitive that rationality simply slid off his hairy skin?

The full story will never be known. But apparently, in the course of the following year, while the border war continued as usual, Cronkheit struck off into the northern uplands. There he raised a band of horse nomads as ignorant and brutal as himself. He also rounded up a herd of mammoths and drove them into Chathakh, stampeding them at the foe. By such means, he reached their very capital, and the King offered terms of surrender.

But Cronkheit would have none of this. Not he! His idea of warfare was to kill or enslave every last man, woman, and child of the enemy nation. Also, his irregulars were supposed to be paid in loot. Also, being too unsanitary even for the nomad girls, he felt a certain urgency.

So he stormed the capital of Chathakh and burned it to the ground. This cost him most of his own men. It also destroyed several priceless books and works of art, and any possibility of tribute to Sarmia.

Then he had the nerve to organize a triumphal procession and ride back to our own city!

This was too much even for the Empress. When he stood before her—for he was too crude for the simple courtesy of a knee bend—she exceeded herself in describing the many kinds of fool, idiot, and all-around blockhead he was.

"Duh," said Cronkheit. "But I won duh war. Look, I won duh war, I did. I won duh war."

"Yes," hissed the Lady Larra. "You smashed an ancient and noble culture to irretrievable ruin. And did you know that half our peacetime trade was with Chathakh? There'll be a business depression now such as history has never seen before."

General Grythion, who had returned, added his own reproaches. "Why do you think wars are fought?" he asked bitterly. "War is an extension of diplomacy. It's the final means of making somebody else do what you want. The object is *not* to kill them all off. How can corpses obey you?"

Cronkheit growled in his throat.

"We would have negotiated a peace in which Chathakh became our ally against Serpens," went on the general. "Then we'd have been safe against all comers. But you —you've left a howling wilderness which we must garrison with our own troops lest the nomads take it over. Your atrocities have alienated every civilized state. You've left us alone and friendless. You've won this war by losing the next one!"

"And on top of the depression which is coming," said the Empress, "we'll have the cost of maintaining those garrisons. Taxes down and expenditures up—it may break the treasury, and then where are we?"

Cronkheit spat on the floor. "Yuh're decadent, dat's what yuh are," he snarled. "Be good for yuh if yer empire breaks up. Yuh oughtta get dat city rabble o' yers out in duh woods an' make hunters of 'em, like me. Let 'em eat steak."

The Lady Larra stamped an exquisite gold-shod foot. "Do you think we've nothing better to do with our time than spend the whole day hunting, and sit around in mud hovels at night licking the grease off our fingers?" she cried. "What the hell do you think civilization is for, anyway?"

Cronkheit drew his great sword. It flashed before their eyes. "I hadda nuff!" he bellowed. "I'm t'rough widjuh! It's time yuh was wiped off duh face o' duh eart, an I'm jus' duh guy t' do it!"

And now General Grythion showed the qualities

which had raised him to his high post. Artfully, he quailed. "Oh, no!" he whimpered. "You're not going to —to—to fight on the side of Serpens?"

"I yam," said Cronkheit. "So long." The last we saw of him was a broad, indignant, flea-bitten back, headed south, and the reflection of the sun on a sword.

Since then, of course, our affairs have prospered and Serpens is now frantically suing for peace. But we intend to prosecute the war till they meet our terms. We are most assuredly not going to be ensnared by their treacherous pleas and take the Barbarian back!

SCIENCE-FICTION WRITERS ARE NOT prophets. They have no more of a pipeline to the future than anyone else who has given the subject some thought. For that matter, nobody is a prophet. As Herman Kahn has remarked, the greatest surprise the future could hold is that it will hold no surprises.

But the inevitability of surprise is the very theme of this story. And, oddly enough, though it was written quite a long time ago, some of the possibilities it suggests have since begun to develop into realities here and there in our country. I do *not* believe these trends will continue to completion; the odds against that are overwhelming. Indeed, other parts of the story now look a bit old-fashioned. I had to revise a few paragraphs in order not to be hopelessly outdated. The changes are, deliberately, very minor, to allow you, if you wish, to compare this projection from the past with the world around you. Then you might ask yourself what the chances are that, among the many maps now being offered us of the time into which we are headed, any of them has any accuracy. And if so, how shall we know which one it is?

3

# THE LAST OF THE DELIVERERS

<<<<<<<<<<<<<<<<<<<<<<<<<<<<<<<<<<<<<<<<<<<

TILL I WAS NINE YEARS OLD, WE HAD A CRAZY man living in our town. He was almost a hundred himself, I suppose, and none of his kin were left. But in those days every town still had a few people who did not belong to any family.

Uncle Jim was harmless, even useful. He wanted to work, and did a bit of cobbling. His shop was in his house, always neat, and when you stood there among the good smells of leather and oil, you could see his living room beyond. He did not have many books, but shelf after shelf was loaded with tall bright sheaves cased in plastic—cracked and yellowed by age like their owner. He called them his magazines, and if we children behaved nicely he sometimes let us look at the pictures in them. After he was dead I had a chance to read the texts. They didn't make sense. Nobody would worry about the things the people in those stories and articles made such a fuss over. He also had a big antique television set, though why he kept it when there was nothing to receive but announcements and the town had a perfectly good set, I don't know. Well, he was crazy.

Every morning he took a walk down Main Street. The trees along it were mostly elms, tall, overshadowing in summer except where gold sunflecks got through. Uncle Jim always dressed his long stiff body in ancient clothes,

52

no matter how hot the day, and Ohio can get plenty hot; so no doubt the shadiness was the reason for his route. He wore frayed white shirts with scratchy, choky collars and a strip of cloth knotted around his neck, long trousers, a clumsy kind of jacket, and narrow shoes that pinched his feet. The outfit was ugly, though painfully clean. We children, being young and therefore cruel, thought at first that because we never saw him unclothed he must be hiding some awful deformity, and teased him about it. My aunt's brother John made us stop, and Uncle Jim never held our bad ways against us. In fact, he used to give us candy he had made himself, till the dentist complained. Then we had solemn talks with our parents and learned that sugar rots the teeth.

Finally we decided that Uncle Jim—we called him that, without saying on which side he was anyone's uncle, because he wasn't really—wore those things as a sort of background for his button that said "WIN WITH WILLARD." He told me once, when I asked, that Willard had been the last Republican President of the United States and a very great man who tried to avert disaster but was too late because the people were already far gone in sloth and decadence. That was a big lading for a nine-year-old head and I still don't really understand it, except that the towns did not govern themselves then and the country was divided between the two big groups who were not even clans but who more or less took turns furnishing a President; and the President was not an umpire between towns and states, but ran everything.

Uncle Jim used to creak down Main Street past Townhall and the sunpower plant, then turn at the fountain and go by my father's great-uncle Conrad's house to the edge of town where the fields and Trees rolled to the rim of the world. At the airport he would turn and come back by Joseph Arakelian's, where he always looked in at the hand looms and sneered and talked about automatic machinery; though what he had against the looms I don't know, because Joseph's weavery was famous. He also made harsh remarks about our ratty little airport and the town's half-dozen flitters. That wasn't fair; we

had a good airport, surfaced with concrete ripped out of
the old highway, and plenty of flitters for our longer trips.
You'd never get more than six groups going anywhere
at any one time in a town this size.

But I wanted to tell about the Communist.

This was in spring. The snow had melted and the
ground begun to dry and our farmers were out planting.
The rest of our town bustled with preparations for the
Fete, cooking and baking, oh, such a smell as filled the
air, women trading recipes from porch to porch, artisans
hammering and sawing and welding, the washlines afire
with Sunday-best clothes taken out of winter chests,
lovers hand in hand whispering of the festivals to come.
Red and Bob and Stinky and I were playing marbles by
the airport. It used to be mumbletypeg, but some of the
kids flipped their knives into Trees and the Elders made
a rule that no kid could carry a knife unless a grown-up
was along.

So it was a fair sweet morning, the sky a dizzy-high
arch of blue, sunlight bouncing off puffy white clouds and
down to the earth, and the first pale whisper of green had
been breathed across the hills. Dust leaped where our
marbles hit, a small wind blew up from the south and slid
across my skin and rumpled my hair, the world and the
season and we were young.

We were about to quit, fetch our guns and take into
the woods after rabbit, when a shadow fell across us and
we saw Uncle Jim and my mother's cousin Andy. Uncle
Jim wore a long coat above his other clothes, and still
shivered as he leaned on his cane, and the shrunken
hands were blue from cold. Andy wore a kilt, for the
pockets, and sandals. He was our town engineer, a stocky
man of forty. In the prehistoric past before I was born he
had been on an expedition to Mars, and this made him a
hero for us kids. We never understood why he was not a
swaggering corsair. He owned three thousand books at
least, more than twice the average in our town. He spent a
lot of time with Uncle Jim, too, and I didn't know why.
Now I see that he was trying to learn about the past from

him, not the dead past mummified in the history books but the people who had once been alive.

The old man looked down at us and said: "You boys aren't wearing a stitch. You'll catch your death of cold." He had a high, thin voice, but steady. In the many years alone, he must have learned how to be firm with himself.

"Oh, nonsense," said Andy. "I'll bet it's sixty in the sun."

"We was going after rabbits," I said importantly. "I'll bring mine to your place and your wife can make us a stew." Like all children, I spent as much time with kinfolk as I did with my ortho-parents, but I favored Andy's home. His wife was a wonderful cook, his oldest son was better than most on the guitar, and his daughter's chess was just about my speed, neither too good nor too bad.

I'd won most of the marbles this game, so now I gave them back. "When I was a boy," said Uncle Jim, "we played for keeps."

"What happened after the best shooter had won all the marbles in town?" said Stinky. "It's hard work making a good marble, Uncle Jim. I can't hardly replace what I lose anyway."

"You could have bought more," he told him. "There were stores where you could buy anything."

"But who made those marbles?"

"There were factories—"

Imagine that! Big grown men spending their time making colored glass balls!

We were almost ready to leave when the Communist showed up. We saw him as he rounded the clump of Trees at the north quarter-section, which was pasture that year. He was on the Middleton road, and dust scuffed up from his bare feet.

A stranger in town is always big news. We kids started running to meet him till Andy recalled us with a sharp word and reminded us that he was entitled to proper courtesy. Then we waited, our eyes bugging out, till he reached us.

But this was a woebegone stranger. He was tall, like Uncle Jim, but his cape hung in rags about a narrow chest where you could count the ribs, and under a bald dome of a head was a dirty white beard down to his waist. He walked heavily, leaning on a staff, heavy as Time, and even then I sensed the loneliness like a weight on his thin shoulders.

Andy stepped forward and bowed. "Greetings and welcome, Freeborn," he said. "I am Andrew Jackson Welles, town engineer, and on behalf of the Folks I bid you stay and rest and refresh yourself." He didn't just rattle the words off as he would for someone he knew, but declaimed them with great care.

Uncle Jim smiled then, a smile like thawing after a nine year's winter, for this man was as old as himself and born in the same forgotten world. He trod forth and held out his hand."Hello, sir," he said. "My name is Robbins. Pleased to meet you." They didn't have very good manners in his day.

"Thank you, Comrade Welles, Comrade Robbins," said the stranger. His smile was lost somewhere in that tangled mold of whiskers. "I'm Harry Miller."

*"Comrade?"* Uncle Jim spoke it slowly, like a word out of a nightmare. His hand crept back again. "What do you mean?"

The wanderer straightened and looked at us in a way that frightened me. "I meant what I said," he answered. "I don't make any bones about it. Harry Miller, of the Communist Party of the United States of America!"

Uncle Jim sucked in a long breath. "But—" he stammered, "but I thought . . . at the very least, I thought all you rats were dead."

"Now hold on," said Andy. "Your pardon, Freeborn Miller. Our friend isn't, uh, isn't quite himself. Don't take it personally, I beg you."

There was a grimness in Miller's chuckle. "Oh, I don't mind. I've been called worse than that."

"And deserved it!" I had never seen Uncle Jim angry before. His face got red and he stamped his cane in the dust. "Andy, this, this man is a traitor. D'you hear? He's a foreign agent!"

"You mean you come clear from Russia?" murmured

Andy, and we boys clustered near, our ears stiff in the breeze, because a foreigner was a seldom sight.

"No," said Miller. "No, I'm from Pittsburgh. Never been to Russia. Wouldn't want to go. Too awful—they *had* socialism once."

"Didn't know anybody was left in Pittsburgh," said Andy. "I was there last year with a salvage crew, after steel and copper, and we never saw anything but birds."

"A few. A few. My wife and I. But she died, and I couldn't stay in that rotten empty shell of a city, so I went out on the road."

"And you can go back on the road," snarled Uncle Jim.

"Now, please be quiet," said Andy. "Come on into town, Freeborn Miller—Comrade Miller, if you prefer. May I invite you to stay with me?"

Uncle Jim grabbed Andy's arm. He shook like a dead leaf in fall, under the heartless fall winds. "You can't!" he shrieked. "Don't you see, he'll poison your minds, he'll subvert you, we'll end up slaves to him and his gang of bandits!"

"It seems you've been doing a little mind-poisoning of your own, Mister Robbins," said Miller.

Uncle Jim stood for a moment, head bent to the ground, and the quick tears of an old man glimmered in his eyes. Then he lifted his face and pride rang in the words: "I am a Republican."

"I thought so." The Communist glanced around and nodded to himself. "Typical bourgeois pseudo-culture. Look at those men, each out on his own little tractor in his own field, hugging his own little selfishness to him."

Andy scratched his head. "What are you talking about, Freeborn?" he asked. "Those are town machines. Who wants to be bothered keeping his own tractor and plow and harvester?"

"Oh . . . you mean—" I glimpsed a light of wonder in the Communist's eyes. He half-stretched out his hands. They were aged hands; I could see bones just under the dried-out skin. "You mean you do work the land collectively?"

"Why, no. What on earth would be the point of that?"
replied Andy. "A man's entitled to what he raises himself, isn't he?"

"So the land, which should be the property of all the
people, is parcelled among those kulaks!" flared Miller.

"How in hell's name can land be anybody's property?
It's . . . it's land. You can't put forty acres in your pocket
and walk off with them." Andy took a long breath. "You
must have been pretty well cut off from things in Pittsburgh. Ate the ancient canned stuff, didn't you? I thought
so. It's easy enough to explain. Look, that section yonder is being planted in corn by my mother's cousin Glenn.
It's his corn, that he swaps for whatever else he needs.
But next year, to conserve the soil, it'll be put in alfalfa,
and my sister's son Willy takes care of it. As for garden
truck and fruit, most of us raise our own, just to get
outdoors each day."

The light faded in our visitor. "That doesn't make
sense," said Miller, and I could hear how tired he was.
It must have been a long hike from Pittsburgh, living off
handouts from gypsies and the Lone Farmers.

"I quite agree," said Uncle Jim with a stiff kind of
smile. "In my father's day—" He closed his mouth. I
knew his father had died in Korea, in some war when he
himself was a baby, and Uncle Jim had been left to keep
the memory and the sad barren pride of it. I remembered
my history, which Freeborn Levinsohn taught in our
town because he knew it best, and a shiver crept in my
skin. A *Communist!* Why, they had killed and tortured
Americans . . . only this was a faded rag of a man, who
couldn't kill a puppy. It was very odd.

We started towards Townhall. People saw us and began to crowd around, staring and whispering as much as
decorum allowed. I strutted with Red and Bob and Stinky,
right next to the stranger, the real live Communist, under
the eyes of the other kids.

We passed Joseph's weavery. His family and apprentices came out to join the gogglers. Miller spat in the
street. "I imagine those people are hired," he said.

"You don't expect them to work for nothing, do you?" asked Andy.

"They should work for the common good."

"But they do. Every time somebody needs a garment or a blanket, Joseph gets his boys together and they make one. You can buy better stuff from him than most women can make at home."

"I knew it. The bourgeois exploiter—"

"I only wish that were the case," said Uncle Jim, tight-lipped.

"You would," snapped Miller.

"But it isn't. People don't have any drive these days. No spirit of competition. No desire to improve their living standard. No . . . they buy what they need, and wear it while it lasts—and it's made to last damn near forever." Uncle Jim waved his cane in the air. "I tell you, Andy, the country's gone to hell. The economy is stagnant. Business has become a bunch of miserable little shops and people making for themselves what they used to buy!"

"I think we're pretty well fed and clothed and housed," said Andy.

"But where's your . . . your drive? Where's the get-up-and-go, the hustling, that made America great? Look—your wife wears the same model of gown her mother wore. You use a flitter that was built in your father's time. Don't you want anything better?"

"Our machinery works well enough." Andy spoke in a bored voice. This was an old argument to him, while the Communist was new. I saw Miller's tattered cape swirl into Si Johansen's carpenter shop and followed.

Si was making a chest of drawers for George Hulme, who was getting married this spring. He put down his tools and answered politely.

"Yes . . . yes, Freeborn . . . sure, I work here . . . Organize? What for? Social-like, you mean? But my apprentices got too damn much social life as is. Every third day a holiday, damn near. . . . No, they *aren't* oppressed. Hell, they're my own kin! . . . But there aren't any people who haven't got good furniture. Not unless they're lousy carpenters and too uppity to get help—"

"But the people all over the world!" cried Miller. "Don't you have any heart, man? What about the Mexican peons?"

Si Johansen shrugged. "What about them? If they want to run things different down there, it's their own business." He put away his electric sander and hollered to his apprentices that they could have the rest of the day off. They'd have taken it anyway, of course, but Si was a wee bit bossy.

Andy got Miller out in the street again. At Townhall the Mayor came in from the fields and received him. Since good weather was predicted for the whole week, we decided there was no hurry about the planting and we'd spend the afternoon welcoming our guest.

"Bunch of bums!" snorted Uncle Jim. "Your ancestors stuck by a job till it was finished."

"This'll get finished in time," said the Mayor, as if he were talking to a baby. "What's the rush, Jim?"

"Rush? To get on with it—finish it and go on to something else. Better things for better living!"

"For the benefit of your exploiters," cackled Miller. He stood on the Townhall steps like a starved and angry rooster.

"What exploiters?" The Mayor was as puzzled as me.

"The . . . the big businessmen, the—"

"There aren't any more businessmen," said Uncle Jim. A little more life seemed to trickle out of him as he admitted it. "Our shopkeepers? . . . No. They only want to make a living. They've never heard of making a profit. They're too lazy to expand."

"Then why haven't you got socialism?" Miller glared around as if looking for some hidden enemy. "It's every family for itself. Where's your solidarity?"

"We get along pretty well with each other, Freeborn," said the Mayor. "We got courts to settle any arguments."

"But don't you want to go on, to advance, to—"

"We get enough," declared the Mayor, patting his belly. "I couldn't eat any more than I do."

"But you could wear more!" said Uncle Jim. He jittered on the steps, the poor crazy man, dancing before our eyes like the puppets in a traveling show. "You could have your own car, a new model every year with beautiful chrome plate all over it, and new machines to lighten your labor, and—"

"And to buy those shoddy things, meant only to wear out, you would have to slave your lives away for the capitalists," said Miller. "The people must produce for the people."

Andy traded a glance with the Mayor. "Look, Freeborn," he said gently, "you don't seem to get the point. We don't *want* such gadgets. It isn't worthwhile scheming and working to get more than we have, not while there are girls to love in springtime and deer to hunt in fall. And when we do work, we'd rather work for ourselves, not for somebody else, whether you call the somebody else a capitalist or the people. Now let's go sit down and take it easy before lunch."

Wedged between the legs of the Folks, I heard Si Johansen mutter to Joseph Arakelian: "I don't get it. What would we do with that machinery? If I had some damn machine to make furniture for me, what'd I do with my hands?"

Joseph lifted his shoulders. "Beats me, Si. Personally, I'd go nuts watching two people wear the same identical pattern."

"It might be kind of nice at that," said Red to me, "having a car like they show in Uncle Jim's ma-gazines."

"Where'd you go in it?" asked Bob.

"Gee, I dunno. To Canada, maybe. But shucks, I can go to Canada any time I can talk my dad into checking out a flitter."

"Sure," said Bob. "And if you're going less than a hundred miles, you got a horse, haven't you? Who wants an old car?"

I wriggled through the crowd toward the Plaza, where the women were setting up outdoor tables and bringing food for a banquet. The crowd was so thick around our guest where he sat that I couldn't get near, but Stinky and I skun up into the Plaza Tree, a huge gray oak, and crawled along a branch till we hung just above his head.

It was a bare and liver-spotted head, wobbling on a thread of neck, but he darted it around and spoke shrill.

Andy and the Mayor sat near him, puffing their pipes, and Uncle Jim was there too. The Folks had let him in so they could watch the fireworks. That was thoughtless, but how could we know? Uncle Jim had always been peaceful, and we'd never had two crazy men in twon.

". . . forces of reaction," Comrade Miller was saying. "I'm not sure precisely which forces engineered the dissolution of the Soviet Union. News was already getting hard to come by, not many telecasts anymore and—well, I must admit I doubt either the capitalists or the Chinese were behind the tragedy. Both those systems were pretty far gone by then."

"Whatever did happen in Russia?" wondered Ed Mulligan. He was the town psychocounsellor, who'd trained at Menninger, clear out in Kansas. "Actual events, I mean. I never would have thought the Communists would allow freedom, not from what I've read of them."

"What you call freedom," Miller said scornfully. "I suspect, myself, revisionism took hold. Once that had led to corruption, the whole poor country was ripe for a counter-revolutionary takeover."

"Now that isn't true," said Uncle Jim. "I followed the news too, remember. The Communists in Russia got corrupt and easygoing of their own accord. Tyrants always do. They didn't foresee what changes the new technology would make, and blithely introduced it. Soon their Iron Curtain rusted away. Nobody *listened* to them anymore."

"Pretty correct, Jim," said Andy. He saw my face among the twigs, and winked at me. "Some violence did occur, the breakup was more complicated than you think, but that's essentially what happened. Trouble is, you can't seem to realize it happened in the U.S.A. also."

Miller shook his withered head. "Marx proved that technological advances mean inevitable progress towards socialism," he said. "Oh, the cause has been set back, but the day is coming."

"Why, maybe you're right up to a point," said Andy.

"But you see, science and society went beyond that point. Maybe I can give you a simple explanation."

"If you wish," said Miller, grumpy-like.

"Well, I've studied the period. Technology made it possible for a few people and acres to feed the whole country, till millions of acres were lying idle; you could buy them for peanuts. Meanwhile the cities were overtaxed, underrepresented, and choked by their own traffic. Along came the cheap sunpower unit and the high-capacity accumulator. Those let a man supply most of his own wants, not work his heart out for someone else to pay the inflated prices demanded by an economy where every single business was subsidized or protected at the taxpayer's expense. Also, by living in the new way, a man cut down his money income to the point where he had to pay almost no taxes—he actually lived better on a shorter work week.

"More and more, people tended to drift out and settle in small country communities. They consumed less, which brought on a great depression, and that drove still more people out to fend for themselves. By the time big business and organized labor realized what was happening and tried to get laws passed against what they called un-American practices, it was too late; nobody was interested. Everything happened so gradually, you see. But it happened, and I think for the better."

"Ridiculous!" said Miller. "Capitalism went bankrupt, as Marx foresaw two hundred years ago, but its vicious influence was still so powerful that instead of advancing to collectivism you went back to being peasants."

"Please," said the Mayor. I could see he was annoyed, and thought that maybe peasants were somebody not Freeborn. "Uh, maybe we can pass the time with a little singing."

Though he had no voice to speak of, courtesy demanded that Miller be asked to perform first. He rose and quavered out something about a guy named Joe Hill. It had a nice tune, but even a nine-year-old like me knew it was lousy poetics. A childish a-b-c-b scheme of masculine rhymes and not a double metaphor anywhere. Be-

sides, who cares what happened to some little tramp
when we have hunting songs and epics about interplanetary explorers to make? I was glad when Andy took over
and gave us some music with muscle in it.

Lunch was called. I slipped down from the Tree and
found a seat nearby. Comrade Miller and Uncle Jim
glowered at each other across the table, but nothing
much was said till after the meal, a couple of hours later.
People had kind of lost interest in the stranger as they
learned he'd spent his time huddled in a dead city, and
wandered off for the dancing and games. Andy hung
around, not wanting to but because he was Miller's host.

The Communist sighed and got up. "You've been nice
to me," he said.

"I thought we were a bunch of capitalists," sneered
Uncle Jim.

"It's man I'm interested in, wherever he is and whatever conditions he has to live under," said Miller.

Uncle Jim lifted his voice with his cane: "Man! You
claim to care for man, you who killed and enslaved
him?"

"Oh, come off it, Jim," said Andy. "That was a long
time ago. Who cares at this late date?"

"I do!" Uncle Jim started crying, but he looked at
Miller and walked toward him, stiff-legged, fingers
crooked. "They killed my father. Men died by the tens
of thousands—for an ideal. And you don't care! The
whole damn country has lost its guts!"

I stood under the Tree, one hand on the rough comfort of its bark. I was a little afraid, because I did not
understand. Surely Andy, who had been sent by the
United Townships Research Foundation the long black
way to Mars, just to gather knowledge, was no coward.
Surely my father, a gentle man and full of laughter, did
not lack guts. What was it we were supposed to want?

"Why, you bootlicking belly-crawling lackey," yelled
Miller, "it was you who gutted them! It was you who
murdered working men, and roped their sons into your
dummy unions, and . . . and . . . what about the Mexican
peons?"

Andy tried to come between them. Miller's staff clattered on his head. Andy stepped back, wiping blood off, looking helpless, as the old crazy men howled at each other. He couldn't use force; he might hurt them.

Perhaps, in that moment, he realized. "It's all **right**, Freeborns," he said quickly. "It's all right. We'll listen to you. Look, you can have a nice debate tonight, right in Townhall, and everybody will come and—"

He was too late. Uncle Jim and Comrade Miller were already fighting, thin arms locked and dim eyes full of tears because they had no strength left to destroy what they hated. But I think, now, that the hate arose from a baffled love. They both loved us in a queer, maimed fashion, and we did not care, we did not care.

Andy got some men together and separated the two and they were led off to different houses for a nap. When Dr. Simmons looked in on Uncle Jim a few hours later, he was gone. The doctor hurried off to find the Communist, and he was gone, too.

I only learned that afterward, since I went off to play tag and pom-pom-pullaway with the other kids down where the river flowed cool and dark. It was in the same river, next morning, that Constable Thompson found the Communist and the Republican. Nobody knew what had happened. They met under the Trees, alone, at dusk, when bonfires were being lit and the Elders making merry around them and lovers stealing off into the woods. That's all we can be sure of. We gave them a decent funeral.

It was the talk of the town for a week, and in fact the whole Ohio region heard about it; but after a while the talk died and the old crazy men lay forgotten. That was the year the Brotherhood came to power in the north, and men wondered what this could mean. The next spring they learned, and there was an alliance made and war went across the hills. For the Brotherhood gang, just as it had threatened, cut Trees down wholesale and planted none. Such evil cannot go unpunished.

WHERE DOES SCIENCE FICTION LEAVE off and fantasy begin? I honestly can't tell you. A famous schoolboy definition said, "A fantasy is a story about goblins, ghosts, werewolves, virgins, and other supernatural beings." Meanwhile, science fiction was supposed to include no out-and-out, provable impossibilities; yet among its standard themes were travel faster than light and travel through time.

So I went ahead and used these without worrying much about it. I would, at all events, have wanted a time-travel yarn in this book, as representative of a motif too important to ignore.

Then—well, in the past several years, the whole question of that light-speed limitation has been reopened by a number of highly reputable physicists. And very recently, the question of time travel has been too! It seems there are good theoretical grounds for supposing that under certain conditions, a body can move into its own past.

This remains to be investigated, of course. But whatever the answer to any particular scientific problem, we can say with Eddington (rephrasing him slightly, because words also are changeable things) that the universe is not only stranger than we know, it is stranger than we can imagine.

4

# MY OBJECT ALL SUBLIME

<<<<<<<<<<<<<<<<<<<<<<<<<<<<<<<<<<<<<<<<<<<

WE MET IN LINE OF BUSINESS. MICHAELS'
firm wanted to start a subdivision on the far side of
Evanston and discovered that I held title to some of the
most promising acreage. They made me a good offer, but
I was stubborn; they raised it and I stayed stubborn;
finally the boss himself looked me up. He wasn't entirely
what I'd expected—aggressive, of course, but in so polite
a way that it didn't offend, his manners so urbane you
rarely noticed his lack of formal education. This lack
he was remedying quite rapidly, anyhow, via night
classes and extension courses as well as omnivorous
reading.

We went out for a drink while we talked the matter
over. He led me to a bar that had little of Chicago about
it: quiet, shabby, no jukebox, no television, a bookshelf
and several chess sets, but none of the freaks and
phonies who usually infest such places. Besides ourselves, there were only half a dozen customers—a
professor-emeritus type among the books, people arguing
politics with a degree of factual relevance, a young man
debating with the bartender whether Bartók was more
original than Schönberg or vice versa. Michaels and I
found a corner table and some Danish beer.

I explained that I didn't care about money, either way,
but objected to bulldozing some rather good-looking
countryside in order to erect still another chrome-plated

68

slum. Michaels stuffed his pipe before answering. He was a lean, erect man, long-chinned and Roman-nosed, his hair grizzled, his eyes dark and luminous. "Didn't my representative explain?" he said. "We aren't planning a row of identical split-level sties. We have six basic designs in mind, with variations, to be located in a pattern . . . so."

He took out pencil and paper and began to sketch. As he talked, his accent thickened, but the fluency remained. And he made his own case better than anyone had done for him. Like it or not, he said, this was the middle twentieth century and mass production was here to stay. A community need not be less attractive for being ready-made, could in fact gain an artistic unity. He proceeded to show me how.

He didn't press me too hard, and conversation wandered.

"Delightful spot, this," I remarked. "How'd you find it?"

He shrugged. "I often prowl about, especially at night. Exploring."

"Isn't that rather dangerous?"

"Not in comparison," he said—a touch of grimness.

"Uh . . . I gather you weren't born over here?"

"No. I didn't arrive in the United States until 1946. What they called a DP, a displaced person. I became Thad Michaels because I got tired of spelling out Tadeusz Michalowski. Nor did I want any part of old-country sentimentalism; I'm a zealous assimilationist."

Otherwise he seldom talked much about himself. Later I got a few details of his early rise in business, from admiring and envious competitors. Several of them didn't yet believe it was possible to sell a house with radiant heating for less than twenty thousand dollars and show a profit. Michaels had found ways, though. Not bad for a penniless immigrant.

I checked up and found he'd been admitted on a special visa, in consideration of services rendered the U.S. Army in the last stages of the European war. Those services had taken nerve as well as quick-wittedness.

Meanwhile our acquaintance developed. I sold him the land he wanted, but we continued to see each other, sometimes at my bachelor apartment, most often in his lakeshore penthouse. He had a stunning blonde wife and a couple of bright, well-mannered boys. Nonetheless he was a lonely man, and I fulfilled a need for friendship.

A year after we first met, he told me the story. I'd been invited over for Thanksgiving dinner. Afterward we sat around and talked. And talked. And talked. When we had ranged from the chances of an upset in the next city election to the chances of other planets following the same general course of history as ours, Amalie excused herself and went to bed. This was long past midnight. Michaels and I kept on talking. I had not seen him so excited before. It was as if that last subject had opened a door for him. Finally he got up, refilled our whisky glasses with a motion not altogether steady, and walked across the living room (noiseless on that deep green carpet) to the picture window.

The night was clear and sharp. We overlooked the city, streaks and webs and coils of glittering color, ruby, amethyst, emerald, topaz, and the dark sheet of Lake Michigan; almost it seemed we could glimpse endless white plains beyond. But overhead arched the sky, crystal black, where the Great Bear stood on his tail and Orion went striding along the Milky Way. I had not often seen so big and frosty a view.

"After all," he said, "I know what I'm talking about."

I stirred, deep in my armchair. The fire on the hearth spat tiny blue flames. Besides this, only one shaded lamp lit the room; the star swarms had also been visible to me when I passed by the window earlier. I gibed a little: "Personally?"

He glanced back toward me. His face was stiff. "What would you say if I answered yes?"

I sipped my drink. King's Ransom is a noble and comforting brew, most especially when the Earth itself seems to tone with a deepening chill. "I'd suppose you had your reasons and wait to see what they were."

He grinned one-sidedly. "Oh, well, I'm from this planet too," he said. "And yet—yet the sky is wide and strange. Don't you think the strangeness would affect men who went there? Wouldn't it seep into them, till they carried it home in their bones, and Earth was never quite the same afterward?"

"Go on. You know I like fantasies."

He stared outward, and then back again, and suddenly he tossed off his drink. The violent gesture was unlike him. But so had his hesitation been.

He said in a harsh tone, with all the former accent: "Okay, then, I shall tell you a fantasy. It is a story for winter, though, a cold story, that you are best advised not to take serious."

I drew on the excellent cigar he had given me and waited in the silence he needed.

He paced a few times back and forth before the window, eyes on the floor, until he filled his glass anew and sat down near me. He didn't look at me but at a picture on the wall, a somber, unintelligible thing which no one else liked. He seemed to get strength from it, for he began talking, fast and softly.

"Once upon a time, a very, very long time in the future was a civilization. I shall not describe it to you, for that would not be possible. Could you go back to the time of the Egyptian pyramid builders and tell them about this city below us? I don't mean they wouldn't believe you; of course they wouldn't, but that hardly matters. I mean they would not understand. Nothing you said could make sense to them. And the way people work and think and believe would be less comprehensible than those lights and towers and machines. Right? If I spoke to you of people in the future living among great psychocosmic energies, and of genetic changelings, and imaginary wars, and talking stones, and a certain blind hunter, you might feel anything at all, but you would not understand.

"So I ask you only to imagine how many thousands of times this planet has circled the sun, how deeply buried and forgotten we are; and then also to imagine

that this other civilization thinks in patterns so foreign
that it has ignored every limitation of logic and natural
law, to discover means of traveling in time. While the
ordinary dweller in that age (I can't exactly call him a
citizen, or anything else for which we have a word,
because it would be too misleading), the average educated dweller knows in a vague, uninterested way that
millennia ago some semi-savages were the first to split
the atom, only one or two men have actually been here,
walked among us, studied and mapped us and returned
with a file of information for the central brain, if I may
call it by such a name. No one else is concerned about
us, any more than you are concerned about early
Mesopotamian archeology. You see?"

He dropped his gaze to the tumbler in his hand and
held it there, as if the whisky were an oracular pool. The
silence grew. At last I said, "Very well. For the sake of
the story, I'll accept the premise. I imagine time trav-
elers would be unnoticeable. They'd have techniques
of disguise and whatnot. Wouldn't want to change their
own past."

"Oh, no danger of that," he said. "It's mainly that
they couldn't learn much if they went around insisting
they were from the future. Just imagine."

I chuckled.

Michaels gave me a shadowed look. "Apart from the
scientific," he said, "can you guess what use there
might be for time travel?"

"Well," I suggested, "trade in objects of art or natural
resources. Go back to the dinosaur age and dig up iron
before man appeared to strip the richest mines."

He shook his head. "Think again. They'd only want a
limited number of Minoan statuettes, Ming vases, or
Third World Hegemony dwarfs, chiefly for their mu-
seums. If 'museum' isn't too inaccurate a word. I tell
you, they are *not* like us. As for natural resources,
they're beyond the point of needing any; they make their
own."

He paused, as if before a final plunge. Then: "What
was that penal colony the French abandoned?"

"Devil's Island?"

"Yes, that was it. Can you imagine a better revenge on a condemned criminal than to maroon him in the past?"

"Why, I should think they'd be above any concept of revenge, or deterrence by horrible examples. Even in this century, we're aware that that doesn't work."

"Are you sure?" he asked quietly. "Side by side with the growth of today's enlightened penology, haven't we a corresponding growth of crime itself? You were wondering, some time ago, how I dared walk the night streets alone. Furthermore, punishment is a catharsis of society as a whole. Up in the future they'd tell you that public hangings did reduce the crime rate, which would otherwise have been still higher. And more important, these spectacles made possible the eighteenth-century birth of real humanitarianism." He raised a sardonic brow. "Or so they claim in the future. It doesn't matter whether they are right, or simply rationalizing a degraded element in their own civilization. All you need assume is that they do send their worst criminals back into the past."

"Rather rough on the past," I said.

"No, not really. For a number of reasons, including the fact that everything they cause to happen has already happened. . . . Damn! English isn't built for talking about these paradoxes. Mainly, though, you must remember that they don't waste all this effort on ordinary miscreants. One has to be a very rare evildoer to deserve exile in time. And the worst crime in the world depends on the particular year of the world's history. Murder, brigandage, treason, heresy, narcotics peddling, slaving, patriotism, the whole catalogue, all have rated capital punishment in some epochs, and been lightly regarded in others, and positively commended in still others. Think back and see if I'm not right."

I regarded him for a while, observing how deep the lines were in his face and recalling that at his age he shouldn't be gray. "Very well," I said. "Agreed. But would not a man from the future, possessing its knowledge—"

He set his glass down, audibly hard. "What knowledge?" he rapped. "Use your brains! Imagine yourself left naked and alone in Babylon. How much Babylonian language or history do you know? Who's the present king, how much longer will he reign, who'll succeed him? What are the laws and customs you must obey? You remember that eventually the Assyrians or the Persians or someone will conquer Babylon and there'll be hell to pay. But when? How? Is the current war a mere border skirmish or an all-out struggle? If the latter, is Babylon going to win? If not, what peace terms will be imposed? Why, there wouldn't be twenty men today who could answer those questions without looking in a book. And you're not one of them; nor have you been given a book."

"I think," I said slowly, "I'd head for the nearest temple, after I'd picked up enough of the language. I'd tell the priest I could make . . . oh . . . fireworks—"

He laughed. "How? You're in Babylon, remember. Where do you find sulfur and saltpeter? If you can get across to the priest what you want, and somehow persuade him to obtain the stuff for you, how do you compound a powder that'll actually go off instead of just fizzing? For your information, that's quite an art. Hell, you couldn't even get a berth as a deckhand. You'd be lucky if you ended up scrubbing floors. A slave in the fields is a likelier career. Isn't it?"

The fire sank low.

"All right," I conceded. "True."

"They pick the era with care, you know." He looked back toward the window. Seen from our chairs, reflection on the glass blotted out the stars, leaving us only aware of the night itself.

"When a man is sentenced to banishment," he said, "the experts confer, pointing out what the periods of their specialties would be like for this particular individual. You can see how a squeamish, intellectual type, dropped into Homeric Greece, would find it a living nightmare, whereas a rowdy type might get along fairly well—might even become a respected warrior. If the rowdy was not the blackest of criminals, they might actually leave him near the hall of Agamemnon, condemning him to no more than danger, discomfort, and homesickness.

"Oh God," he whispered. "The homesickness!"

Such a darkness rose in him as he spoke that I sought to steady him by a dry remark. "They must immunize the convict to every ancient disease. Otherwise this'd just be an elaborate death sentence."

His eyes focused on me again. "Yes," he said. "And of course the longevity serum is still active in his veins. That's it, however. He's dropped in an unfrequented spot after dark, the machine vanishes, he's cut off for the rest of his life. All he knows is that they've chosen an era for him with . . . characteristics . . . that they expect will make the punishment fit his crime."

Stillness fell once more upon us, until the clock on the mantel became the loudest thing in the world, as if every other sound had frozen to death outside. I glanced at its dial. The night was old; soon the east would be turning pale.

When I looked back, he was still watching me, disconcertingly intent. "What was your crime?" I asked.

He didn't seem taken aback, and said wearily, "What does it matter? I told you the crimes of one age are the heroisms of another. If my attempt had succeeded, the centuries to come would have adored my name. But I failed."

"A lot of people must have got hurt," I said. "A whole world must have hated you."

"True," he said. And after a minute: "This is a fantasy I'm telling you, of course. To pass the time."

"I'm playing along," I smiled.

His tension eased a trifle. He leaned back, his legs stretched across that glorious carpet. "Well. Given as much of the fantasy as I've related, how did you deduce the extent of my alleged guilt?"

"Your past life. When and where were you left?"

He said, in as bleak a voice as I've ever heard, "Near Warsaw, in August, 1939."

"I don't imagine you care to talk about the war years."

"No, I don't."

However, he went on when enough defiance had accumulated. "My enemies blundered. The confusion following the German attack gave me a chance to escape from police custody before I could be stuck in a concentration camp. Gradually I learned what the situation was. Of course, I couldn't predict anything. I still can't; only specialists know, or care, what happened in the twentieth century. But by the time I'd become a Polish conscript in the German forces, I realized this was the losing side. Therefore I slipped across to the Americans, told them what I'd observed, became a scout for them. Risky—but if I'd stopped a bullet, what the hell? I didn't; and I acquired plenty of sponsors to get me over here; and the rest of the story is conventional."

My cigar had gone out. I relit it, for Michaels' cigars were not to be taken casually. He had them especially flown in from Amsterdam.

"The alien corn," I said.

"What?"

"You know. Ruth in exile. She wasn't badly treated, but she stood weeping for her homeland."

"No, I don't know that story."

"It's in the Bible."

"Ah, yes. I really must read the Bible sometime." His mood was changing by the moment, toward the assurance I had first encountered. He swallowed his whisky with a gesture almost debonair. His expression was alert and confident.

"Yes," he said, "that aspect was pretty bad. Not so much the physical conditions of life. You've doubtless gone camping and noticed how soon you stop missing hot running water, electric lights, all the gadgets that their manufacturers assure us are absolute necessities. I'd be glad of a gravity reducer or a cell stimulator if I had one, but I get along fine without. The homesickness, though, that's what eats you. Little things you never noticed, a particular food, the way people walk, the games played, the small-talk topics. Even the constellations. They're different in the future. The sun has traveled that far in its galactic orbit.

"But, voluntary or forced, people have always been emigrating. We're descended from those who could stand the shock. I adapted."

A scowl crossed his brows. "I wouldn't go back now even if I were given a free pardon," he said, "the way those traitors are running things."

I finished my own drink, tasting it across my whole tongue and palate, for it was a marvelous whisky, and listened to him with only half an ear. "You like it here?"

"Yes," he said. "By now I do. I'm over the emotional hump. Being busy the first few years just staying alive, and then busy establishing myself after I came to this country, that helped. I never had much time for self-pity. Now my business interests me more and more, a fascinating game, and pleasantly free of extreme penalties for wrong moves. I've discovered qualities here that the future has lost. . . . I'll bet you have no idea how exotic this city is. Think. At this moment, within five miles of us, there's a soldier on guard at an atomic laboratory, a bum freezing in a doorway, an orgy in a millionaire's apartment, a priest making ready for sunrise rites, a merchant from Araby, a spy from Muscovy, a ship from the Indies . . ."

His excitement softened. He looked from the window and the night, inward, toward the bedrooms. "And my wife and kids," he finished, most gently. "No, I wouldn't go back, no matter what happened."

I took a final breath of my cigar. "You *have* done rather well."

Liberated from his gray mood, he grinned at me. "You know, I think you believe that yarn."

"Oh, I do." I stubbed out the cigar, rose, and stretched. "The hour is late. We'd better be going."

He didn't notice at once. When he did, he came out of his chair like a big cat. "We?"

"Of course." I drew a nerve gun from my pocket. He

stopped in his tracks. "This sort of thing isn't left to chance. We check up. Come along, now."

The blood drained from his face. "No," he mouthed, "no, no, no, you can't, it isn't fair, not to Amalie, the children—"

"That," I told him, "is part of the punishment."

I left him in Damascus the year before Tamerlane sacked it.

A WRITER MUST LEARN TO LIVE WITH the fact that half the people he meets will ask him, "Where do you get your ideas?" If he writes science fiction, the question is apt to take the form, "Where do you get those crazy ideas?"

The answer, of course, is: "Everywhere. If you have that sort of mind, anything—an incident, a remark, a glimpse, something read, something watched—can suggest a story. The problem is not to get the idea, it's what to do with it."

The genesis of this particular tale is a good example. Too many years ago, young and unattached, I spent several months batting around Europe on a bicycle. It was grand fun, but there were a few annoyances. One was the requirement of filling out a silly little card wherever I spent the night—name, nationality, etc.—a card that obviously would only molder in local police archives. We've since been getting the same kind of nonsense in America, but those were less cramped days. Being seldom asked to show my passport, at last I took to signing fictitious names whenever I was in a grumpy mood, and one of the names was Sam Hall, the hero of the ballad herein quoted. Today's youth did not invent useless protest against the System.

5

79

Returning, I found the heyday of Senator Joseph McCarthy. Now this wasn't quite the horror that academic folklore maintains. While no doubt a few innocent people did get harmed, the fact is that others *had* been the dangerous agents of an implacable enemy; and in any event, as a shrewd observer remarked, the period consisted mainly of intellectuals screaming from the rooftops that they were afraid to speak above a whisper. Actual suppression, when it occurred, was almost always the result of private unofficial hysteria. Still, it didn't take great imagination to see the trend continuing until we really got a dictatorship.

Nor did it take great imagination to see the potentialities in computer systems. At that time they were few, crude, sharply limited in their capabilities; but they were bound to develop, and thinkers such as Norbert Wiener were already considering what this might bring about. I saw the possibility of government keeping a day-by-day eye on everybody; I remembered Europe and Sam Hall; and there was my story.

It was published by John Campbell, editor of *Astounding* (as the magazine was then called), himself a political conservative. It was republished elsewhere, earning me a nice total sum. So much for the repression of the McCarthy era.

We outlived that, as we had outlived similar things before. And yet I don't think this fable is obsolete. Some changes may be slower than a shift in emotional climate, but far less reversible. Today we have in fact almost completed the building of the system I described; its initials are IRS. And now they talk about a national data bank. . . .

But, *nota bene*: We, in the real-world United States of the 1970s, are still very, very far from the situation here depicted. Indeed, that was supposed to have arisen because of defeat in a major war. Despite every crime and encroachment, our government has not yet lost its legitimacy. Revolution now would only deliver us to totalitarianism, whether that be of foreigners or of Berkeley's bearded *fascisti*. The duty of those who love freedom is to ward off tyrants both outside and inside their countries. Then perhaps revolution will never be necessary.

# SAM HALL

<<<<<<<<<<<<<<<<<<<<<<<<<<<<<<<<<<<<<<<<<<<

CLICK. BZZZ. WHRRR.

Citizen Blank Blank, Anytown, Somewhere, U.S.A., approaches the hotel desk. "Single with bath."

"Sorry, sir, our fuel ration doesn't permit individual baths. We can draw one for you; that will be twenty-five dollars extra."

"Oh, is that all? Okay."

Citizen Blank takes out his wallet, extracts his card, gives it to the registry machine, an automatic set of gestures. Aluminum jaws close on it, copper teeth feel for the magnetic encodings, electronic tongue tastes the life of Citizen Blank.

Place and date of birth. Parents. Race. Religion. Educational, military, and civilian service records. Marital status. Children. Occupations, from the beginning to the present. Affiliations. Physical measurements, fingerprints, retinals, blood type. Basic psychotype. Loyalty rating. Loyalty index as a function of time to moment of last test given. Click, click. Bzzz.

"Why are you here, sir?"

"Salesman. I expect to be in Cincinnati tomorrow night."

The clerk (32 yrs., married, two children; NB, confidential: Jewish. To be kept out of key occupations) punches buttons.

81

Click, click. The machine returns the card. Citizen Blank puts it back in his wallet.

"Front!"

The bellboy (19 yrs., unmarried; NB confidential: Catholic. To be kept out of key occupations) takes the guest's suitcase. The elevator creaks upstairs. The clerk resumes his reading. The article is entitled "Has Britain Betrayed Us?" Companion articles in the magazine include "New Indoctrination Program for the Armed Forces," "Labor Hunting on Mars," "I Was a Union Man for the Security Police," "More Plans for YOUR Future."

The machine talks to itself. Click, click. A bulb winks at its neighbor as if they shared a private joke. The total signal goes out over the wires.

Accompanied by a thousand others, it shoots down the last cable and into the sorter unit of Central Records. Click, click. Bzzz. Whrrr. Wink and glow. The distorted molecules in a particular spool show the pattern of Citizen Blank, and this is sent back. It enters the comparison unit, to which the incoming signal corresponding to him has also been shunted. The two are perfectly in phase; nothing wrong. Citizen Blank is staying in the town where, last night, he said he would, so he has not had to file a correction.

The new information is added to the record of Citizen Blank. The whole of his life returns to the memory bank. It is wiped from the scanner and comparison units, that these may be free for the next arrival.

The machine has swallowed and digested another day. It is content.

Thornberg entered his office at the usual time. His secretary glanced up to say "Good morning," and looked closer. She had been with him for enough years to read the nuances in his carefully controlled face. "Anything wrong, chief?"

"No." He spoke harshly, which was also peculiar. "No, nothing wrong. I feel a bit under the weather, maybe."

"Oh." The secretary nodded. You learned discretion

in the government. "Well, I hope you get better soon."

"Thanks. It's nothing." Thornberg limped over to his desk, sat down, and took out a pack of cigarettes. He held one for a moment in nicotine-yellowed fingers before lighting it, and there was an emptiness in his eyes. Then he puffed ferociously and turned to his mail. As chief technician of Central Records, he received a generous tobacco ration and used it all.

The office was a windowless cubicle, furnished in gaunt orderliness, its only decorations pictures of his son and his late wife. Thornberg seemed too big for the space. He was tall and lean, with thin straight features and neatly brushed graying hair. He wore a plain version of the Security uniform, insignia of Technical Division and major's rank but none of the ribbons to which he was entitled. The priesthood of Matilda the Machine were a pretty informal lot.

He chain-smoked his way through the mail. Most was related to the changeover. "Come on, June," he said. Recording and later transcription sufficed for routine stuff, but best that his secretary take notes as well while he dictated anything unusual. "Let's get this out of the way fast. I've got work to do."

He held a letter before him. "To Senator E. W. Harmison, S.O.B., New Washington. Dear Sir: In re your communication of the 14th inst., requesting my personal opinion of the new ID system, may I say that it is not a technician's business to express opinions. The directive that every citizen shall have a single number for his records—birth certificate, education, rations, taxes, wages, transactions, public service, family, travel, etc.—has obvious long-range advantages, but naturally entails a good deal of work both in reconversion and interim data control. The President having decided that the gain justifies our present difficulties, the duty of citizens is to conform, not complain. Yours, and so forth." He let a cold smile flicker. "There, that'll fix him! I don't know what use Congress is anyway, except to plague honest bureaucrats."

Privately, June decided to modify the letter. Maybe a

senator was only a rubber stamp, but you couldn't brush him off that curtly. Part of a secretary's job is to keep the boss out of trouble.

"Okay, let's get to the next," said Thornberg. "To Colonel M. R. Hubert, Director of Liaison Division, Central Records Agency, Security Police, etc. Dear Sir: In re your memorandum of the 14th inst., requiring a definite date for completion of the ID conversion, may I respectfully state that it is impossible for me honestly to set one. You realize we must develop a memory-modification unit which will make the changeover in our records without our having to take out and alter each of three hundred million spools. You realize too that we cannot predict the exact time needed to complete such a project. However, research is progressing satisfactorily (refer him to my last report, will you?), and I can confidently say that conversion will be finished and all citizens notified of their numbers within three months at the latest. Respectfully, and so on. Put that in a nice form, June."

She nodded. Thornberg continued through his mail, throwing most into a basket for her to answer alone. When he was done he yawned and lit a fresh cigarette. "Praise Allah that's over. Now I can get down to the lab."

"You have afternoon appointments," she reminded him.

"I'll be back after lunch. See you." He got up and went out of the office.

Down the escalator to a still lower sublevel, walking along a corridor, he returned the salutes of passing subordinates automatically. His expression did not bespeak anything; perhaps the stiff swinging of his arms did.

*Jimmy,* he thought. *Jimmy, boy.*

At the guard chamber, he presented hand and eye to the scanners. Finger and retinal patterns were his pass. No alarm sounded. The door opened for him and he walked into the temple of Matilda.

She squatted huge, tier upon tier of control panels, meters, indicator lights to the lofty ceiling. The spectacle always suggested to Thornberg an Aztec pyramid, whose gods winked red eyes at the acolytes and suppliants creeping about base and flanks. But they got their sacrifices elsewhere.

For a moment Thornberg stood and watched. He smiled again, a tired smile that creased his face on the left side only. A recollection touched him, booklegged stuff from the forties and fifties of the last century which he had read: French, German, British, Italian. The intellectuals had been fretful about the Americanization of Europe, the crumbling of old culture before the mechanized barbarism of soft drinks, hard sells, enormous chrome-plated automobiles (dollar grins, the Danes had called them), chewing gum, plastics. . . . None of them had protested the simultaneous Europeanization of America: bloated government, unlimited armament, official nosiness, censors, secret police, chauvinism. . . . Well, for a while there had been objectors, but first their own excesses and sillinesses discredited them, then later. . . .

Oh, well.

*But Jimmy, lad, where are you now, what are they doing to you?*

Thornberg sought a bench where his top engineer, Rodney, was testing a unit. "How're you coming along?" he asked.

"Pretty good, chief." Rodney didn't bother to salute. Thornberg had, in fact, forbidden it in the labs as a waste of time. "A few bugs yet, but we're chasing them out."

The project was, essentially, to develop a gimmick that would change numbers without altering anything else—not too easy a task, since the memory banks depended on individual magnetic domains. "Okay," said Thornberg. "Look, I want to run a few checks myself, out of the main coordinator. The program they've written for Section Thirteen during the conversion doesn't quite satisfy me."

"Want an assistant?"

"No, thanks. I just want not to be bothered."

Thornberg resumed his way across the floor. Hardness resounded dully under his shoes. The main coordinator was in a special armored booth nestled against the great

pyramid. He must go through a second scan before the
door admitted him. Not many were allowed in here. The
complete archives of the nation were too valuable to risk.

Thornberg's loyalty rating was AAB-2—not absolutely perfect, but the best available among men and
women of his professional caliber. His last drugged checkup had revealed certain doubts and reservations about
government policy, but there was no question of disobe-
dience. *Prima facie,* he was certainly bound to be loyal.
He had served with distinction in the war against Brazil,
losing a leg in action; his wife had been killed in the
abortive Chinese rocket raids ten years ago; his son was
a rising young Space Guard officer on Venus. He had
read and listened to illegal stuff, blacklisted books, underground and foreign propaganda—but then, every intellectual dabbled with that; it was not a serious offense if
your record was otherwise good and if you laughed off
what the things said.

He sat for a moment regarding the board inside the
booth. Its complexity would have baffled most engineers,
but he had been with Matilda so long that he didn't even
need the reference tables.

*Well* . . .

It took nerve, this. A hypnoquiz was sure to reveal
what he was about to do. But such raids were, necessarily, in a random pattern. He wouldn't likely be called
up again for years, especially given his rating. By the
time he was found out, Jack should have risen far enough
in the Guard ranks to be safe.

In the privacy of the booth Thornberg permitted himself a harsh grin. "This," he murmured to the machine,
"will hurt me worse than it does you."

He began punching buttons.

Here were circuits which could alter the records, take
out an entire spool and write whatever was desired in the
molecules. Thornberg had done the job a few times for
high officials. Now he was doing it for himself.

Jimmy Obrenowicz, son of his second cousin, had been
hustled off at night by Security Police on suspicion of
treason. The file showed what no private citizen was sup-

posed to know: the prisoner was in Camp Fieldstone. Those who returned from there, not a big percentage, were very quiet, and said absolutely nothing about their experiences. Sometimes they were incapable of speech.

The chief of the Technical Division, Central Records, had damn well better not have a relative in Fieldstone. Thornberg toiled at the screens and buttons for an hour, erasing, changing. The job was tough; he had to go back several generations, altering lines of descent. But when he was through, James Obrenowicz had no kinship whatsoever to the Thornbergs.

*And I thought the world of that boy. Well, I'm not doing this for me, Jimmy. It's for Jack. When the cops pull your file, later today no doubt, I can't let them find you're related to Captain Thornberg on Venus and a friend of his father.*

He slapped the switch that returned the spool to the memory banks. *With this act do I disown thee.*

After that he sat for a while, relishing the quiet of the booth and the clean impersonality of the instruments. He didn't even want to smoke. Presently, though, he began to think.

So now they were going to give every citizen a number, one number for everything. Already they discussed tattooing it on. Thornberg foresaw popular slang referring to the numbers as "brands" and Security cracking down on those who used the term. Disloyal language.

Well, the underground was dangerous. It was supported by foreign countries who didn't like an American-dominated world—at least, not one dominated by today's kind of America, though once "U.S.A." had meant "hope." The rebels were said to have their own base out in space somewhere and to have honeycombed the country with their agents. That could well be. Their propaganda was subtle: we don't want to overthrow the nation; we simply want to restore the Bill of Rights. It could attract a lot of unstable souls. But Security's spy hunt was bound to drag in any number of citizens who had never meditated treason. Like Jimmy—or had Jimmy been an undergrounder after all? You never knew. Nobody ever told you.

There was a sour taste in Thornberg's mouth. He grimaced. A line of a song came back to him. *"I hate you one and all."* How had it gone? They used to sing it in his college days. Something about a very bitter character who'd committed a murder.

Oh, yes. "Sam Hall." How did it go, now? You needed a gravely bass to sing it properly.

> Oh, my name it is Sam Hall, it is Sam Hall.
> Yes, my name is Sam Hall, it is Sam Hall.
>   Oh, my name it is Sam Hall,
>   And I hate you one and all,
> Yes, I hate you one and all, God damn your eyes.

That was it. And Sam Hall was about to swing for murder. Thornberg remembered now. He felt like Sam Hall himself. He looked at the machine and wondered how many Sam Halls were in it.

Idly, postponing his return to work, he punched for the data-name, Samuel Hall, no further specifications. The machine mumbled. Presently it spewed out a stack of papers, microprinted on the spot from the memory banks. Complete dossier on every Sam Hall, living and dead, from the time the records began to be kept. To hell with it. Thornberg chucked the sheets down the incinerator slot.

*"Oh, I killed a man, they say, so they say—"*

The impulse was blinding in its savagery. They were dealing with Jimmy at this moment, probably pounding him over the kidneys, and he, Thornberg, sat here waiting for the cops to requisition Jimmy's file, and there was nothing he could do. His hands were empty.

*By God,* he thought, *I'll give them Sam Hall!*

His fingers began to race; he lost his nausea in the intricate technical problem. Slipping a fake spool into Matilda wasn't easy. You couldn't duplicate numbers, and every citizen had a lot of them. You had to account for each day of his life.

Well, some of that could be simplified. The machine had only existed for twenty-five years; before then, records had been kept in a dozen different offices. Let's make Sam Hall a resident of New York, his dossier there lost in the bombing thirty years ago. Such of his papers as were in New Washington had also been lost, in the Chinese attack. That meant he simply reported as much detail as he could remember, which needn't be a lot.

Let's see. "Sam Hall" was an English song, so Sam Hall should be British himself. Came over with his parents, oh, thirty-eight years ago, when he was three, and got naturalized with them; that was before the total ban on immigration. Grew up on New York's Lower East Side, a tough kid, a slum kid. School records lost in the bombing, but he claimed to have gone through the tenth grade. No living relatives. No family. No definite occupation, just a series of unskilled jobs. Loyalty rating BBA-O, which meant that purely routine questions showed him to have no political opinions that mattered.

Too colorless. Give him some violence in his background. Thornberg punched for information on New York police stations and civilian-police officers destroyed in the last raids. He used them as the source of records that Sam Hall had been continually in trouble—drunkenness, disorderly conduct, brawls, a suspicion of holdups and burglary, but not strong enough to warrant calling in Security's hypnotechnicians for quizzing him.

Hmm. Better make him 4-F, no military service. Reason? Well, a slight drug addiction; men weren't so badly needed nowadays that hopheads had to be cured. Neocoke didn't impair the faculties too much. Indeed, the addict was abnormally fast and strong under the influence, though he suffered a tough reaction afterwards.

Then he would have had to put in an additional term of civilian service. Let's see. He spent his four years as a common laborer on the Colorado Dam project. In such a mess of men, who would remember him? At any rate, it would be hard finding somebody who did.

Now to fill in. Thornberg called on a number of automatic devices to help him. He must account for every day in twenty-five years; but of course the majority would show no change of circumstances. Thornberg punched for cheap hotels, the kind which didn't bother keeping records of their own after the data went to Matilda. Who could remember a shabby individual patron? For Sam Hall's current address he chose the Triton, a glorified flophouse on the East Side not far from the craters. At present his man was unemployed, putatively living off savings, likelier off odd jobs and petty crime. Oh, blast! Income tax returns. Thornberg could be sketchy in creating those, however. The poor weren't expected to be meticulous, nor were they audited annually like the middle class and the rich.

Hmm . . . physical ID. Make him of average height, stocky, black-haired and black-eyed, a bent nose, a scar on his forehead—tough-looking, though not enough to be unusually memorable. Thornberg entered the precise measurements. Fingerprints and retinals being encoded, they were easy to fake; he wrote a censor into his ongoing program, lest he duplicate somebody else's by chance.

Finally he leaned back and sighed. The record was still shot full of holes, but he could plug those at his leisure. The main job was done—a couple of hours' hard work, utterly pointless, except that he had blown off steam. He felt a lot better.

He glanced at his watch. *Time to get back on the job, son.* For a rebellious moment he wished no one had ever invented clocks. They had made possible the science he loved, but they had then proceeded to mechanize man. Oh, well, too late now. He left the booth. The door closed itself behind him.

About a month later, Sam Hall committed his first murder.

The night before, Thornberg had been at home. His rank entitled him to good housing in spite of his living alone: two rooms and bath on the ninety-eighth floor of a unit in town, not far from the camouflaged entrance to Matilda's underground domain. The fact that he was in Security, even if he didn't belong to the man-hunting branch, got him so much deference that he often felt lonely. The superintendent had offered him his daughter once—"Only twenty-three, sir, just released by a gentleman of marshal's rank, and looking for a nice patron, sir." Thornberg had refused, trying not to be prissy about it. *Autres temps, autres moeurs*—but still, she wouldn't have had any choice about getting client status, the first time anyway. And Thornberg's marriage had been a long and happy one.

He had been looking through his bookshelves for something to read. The Literary Bureau was trumpeting Whitman as an early example of Americanism, but though Thornberg had always liked the poet, his hands strayed perversely to a dog-eared volume of Marlowe. Was that escapism? The L.B. was very down on escapism. These were tough times. It wasn't easy to belong to the nation which was enforcing peace on a sullen world. You must be realistic and energetic and all the rest, no doubt.

The phone buzzed. He clicked on the receiver. Martha Obrenowicz's plain plump face showed in the screen; her gray hair was wild and her voice a harsh croak.

"Uh—hello," he said uneasily. He hadn't called her since the news of her son's arrest. "How are you?"

"Jimmy is dead," she told him.

He stood for a long while. His skull felt hollow.

"I got word today that he died in camp," said Martha. "I thought you'd want to know."

Thornberg shook his head, back and forth, quite slowly. "That isn't news I ever wanted, Martha," he said.

"It isn't *right!*" she shrieked. "Jimmy wasn't a traitor. I knew my son. Who ought to know him better? He had some friends I was kind of doubtful of, but Jimmy, he wouldn't ever—"

Something cold formed in Thornberg's breast. You never knew when calls were being tapped.

"I'm sorry, Martha," he said without tone. "But the police are careful about these things. They wouldn't act till they were sure. Justice is in our traditions."

She regarded him for a long time. Her eyes held a hard glitter. "You too," she said at last.

"Be careful, Martha," he warned her. "I know this is a blow to you, but don't say anything you might regret later. After all, Jimmy may have died accidentally. Those things happen."

"I—forgot," she said jerkily. "You . . . are in Security . . . yourself."

"Be calm," he said. "Think of it as a sacrifice for the national interest."

She switched off on him. He knew she wouldn't call him again. And he couldn't safely see her.

"Good-bye, Martha," he said aloud. It was like a stranger speaking.

He turned back to the bookshelf. *Not for me,* he told himself. *For Jack.* He touched the binding of *Leaves of Grass. Oh, Whitman, old rebel,* he thought, a curious dry laughter in him, *are they calling you Whirling Walt now?*

That night he took an extra sleeping pill. His head still felt fuzzy when he reported for work, and after a while he gave up trying to answer the mail and went down to the lab.

While he was engaged with Rodney, and making a poor job of understanding the technical problem under discussion, his eyes strayed to Matilda. Suddenly he realized what he needed for a cathartic. He broke off as soon as possible and went into the coordinator booth.

For a moment he paused at the keyboard. The day-by-day creation of Sam Hall had been an odd experience. He, quiet and introverted, had shaped a rowdy life and painted a rugged personality. Sam Hall was more real to him than many of his associates. *Well, I'm a schizoid type myself. Maybe I should have been a writer.* No, that would have meant too many restrictions, too much fear of offending the censor. He had done exactly as he pleased with Sam Hall.

He drew a breath and punched for unsolved murders of Security officers, New York City area, during the past month. They were surprisingly common. Could dissatisfaction be more general than the government admitted? But when the bulk of a nation harbors thoughts labeled treasonous, does the label still apply?

He found what he wanted. Sergeant Brady had incautiously entered the Crater district after dark on the twenty-seventh on a routine checkup mission; he had worn the black uniform, presumably to give himself the full weight of authority. The next morning he had been found in an alley, his skull shattered.

Oh, I killed a man, they say, so they say.
Yes, I killed a man, they say, so they say.
   I beat him on the head,
And I left him there for dead,
Yes, I left him there for dead, God damn his eyes.

Newspapers had no doubt deplored this brutality perpetrated by the treacherous agent of enemy powers. (*"Oh, the parson, he did come, he did come."*) A number of suspects had been rounded up and given a stiff quizzing. (*"And the sheriff, he came too, he came too.*") Nothing was proven as yet, though a Joe Nikolsky (fifth generation American, mechanic, married, four children, underground pamphlets found in his room) had been arrested yesterday on suspicion.

Thornberg sighed. He knew enough of Security methods to be sure they would get somebody for such a killing. They couldn't allow their reputation for infallibility to be smirched by a lack of conclusive evidence. Maybe Nikolsky had done the crime—he couldn't *prove* he had simply been out for a walk that evening—and maybe he hadn't. But, hell's fire, why not give him a break? He had four kids. With such a black mark, their mother would find work only in a recreation house.

Thornberg scratched his head. This had to be done carefully. Let's see. Brady's body would have been cremated by now, but of course there had been a thorough study first. Thornberg withdrew the dead man's file from the machine and microprinted a replica of the evidence —zero. Erasing that, he entered the statement that a blurred thumbprint had been found on the victim's collar and referred to ID labs for reconstruction. In the ID file he inserted the report of such a job, finished only yesterday due to a great press of work. (Plausible. They were busy lately on material sent from Mars, seized in a raid on a rebel meeting place.) The probable pattern of the whorls was—and here he inserted Sam Hall's right thumb.

He returned the spools and leaned back in his chair. It was risky; if anyone thought to query the ID lab, he was in trouble. But that was unlikely. The chances were that New York would accept the findings with a routine acknowledgement which some clerk at the lab would file without studying. The more obvious dangers were not too great either: a busy police force would not stop to ask if any of their fingerprint men had actually developed that smudge; and as for hypnoquizzing showing Nikolsky really was the murderer, well, then the print would be assumed that of a passerby who had found the body and not reported it.

So now Sam Hall had killed a Security officer—grabbed him by the neck and smashed his brainpan with a weighted club. Thornberg felt considerably happier.

New York Security shot a request to Central Records for any new material on the Brady case. An automaton compared the codes and saw that fresh information had been added. The message flashed back, plus the dossier on Sam Hall and two others—for the reconstruction could not be absolutely accurate.

The two were safe, as it turned out. Both had alibis. The squad that stormed into the Triton Hotel and demanded Sam Hall met blank stares. No such person was registered. No one of that description was known there. A thorough quizzing corroborated this. Then Sam Hall had managed to fake an address. He could have done that easily by punching the buttons on the hotel register when nobody was looking. Sam Hall could be anywhere!

Joe Nikolsky, having been hypnoed and found harmless, was released. The fine for possessing subversive lit-

erature would put him in debt for the next few years—
he had no influential friends to get it suspended—but
he'd be all right if he watched his step. Security sent out
an alarm for Sam Hall.

Thornberg derived a sardonic amusement from watching the progress of the hunt as it came to Matilda. No
man with that ID card had bought tickets on any public
transportation. That proved nothing. Of the hundreds
who vanished every year, some at least must have been
murdered for their cards, and their bodies disposed of.
Matilda was set to give the alarm when the ID of a disappeared person showed up somewhere. Thornberg faked
a few such reports, just to give the police something to do.

He slept more poorly each night, and his work suffered. Once he met Martha Obrenowicz on the street—
passed by hastily without greeting her—and couldn't
sleep at all, even after maximum permissible drugging.

The new ID system was completed. Machines sent no-
tices to every citizen, with orders to have their numbers
tatooed on the right shoulder blade within six weeks. As
each center reported that such-and-such a person had
had the job done, Matilda changed the record appropri-
ately. Sam Hall, AX-428-399-075, did not report for his
tattoo. Thornberg chuckled at the AX symbol.

Then the telecasts flashed a story that made the nation
exclaim. Bandits had held up the First National Bank in
Americatown, Idaho (formerly Moscow), collecting a
good five million dollars in assorted bills. From their discipline and equipment it was assumed that they were
rebel agents, possibly having come in a spaceship from
their unknown interplanetary base, and that the raid was
intended to help finance their nefarious activities. Security was cooperating with the armed forces to track down
the evildoers, and arrests were expected hourly, etc., etc.

Thornberg went to Matilda for a complete account. It
had been a bold job. The robbers had apparently worn
plastic face masks and light body armor under ordinary
clothes. In the scuffle of the getaway one man's mask had
slipped aside—only for a moment, but a clerk who saw
had, under hypnosis, given a fairly good description. A

brown-haired, heavyset fellow, Roman nose, thin lips,
toothbrush mustache.

Thornberg hesitated. A joke was a joke; and helping
poor Nikolsky was perhaps morally defensible; but aid-
ing and abetting a felony which was in all likelihood an
act of treason—

He grinned to himself, with scant humor. It was too
much fun playing God. Swiftly he changed the record.
The crook had been of medium height, dark, scar-faced,
broken-nosed. . . . He sat for a while wondering how
sane he was. How sane anybody was.

Security Central requisitioned complete data on the incident and any correlations the logic units could make.
The description they got could have fitted many men, but
geography left just a single possibility. *Sam Hall*.

The hounds bayed forth. That night Thornberg slept
well.


Dear Dad,

Sorry I haven't written before. We've been too
busy here. I myself was on patrol duty in the Austin
Highlands. The idea was, if we can take advantage
of reduced atmospheric pressure at that altitude to
construct a military spaceport, a foreign country
might sneak in and do the same, probably for the
benefit of our domestic insurrectionists. I'm glad to
say we found nothing. But it was grim going for us.
Frankly, everything here is. Sometimes I wonder if
I'll ever see the sun again. And lakes and forests—
life; who wrote that line about the green hills of
Earth? My mind feels rusty as well. We don't get
much to read, and I don't care for the taped shows.
Not that I'm complaining, of course. This is a necessary job.

We'd hardly gotten back when we were bundled
into bathyplanes and ferried to the lowlands. I'd
never been there before—thought Venus was awful,
but you have to get down in that red-black ocean of
hell-hot air, way down, before you know what "awful" means. Then we transferred straight to mobile

sealtanks and went into action. The convicts in the new thorium mine were refusing to work on account of conditions and casualties. We needed guns to bring them to reason. Dad, I hated that. I actually felt sorry for the poor devils, I don't mind admitting it. Rocks and hammers and sluice hoses against machine guns! And conditions *are* rugged. They DE- .. LETED BY CENSOR someone has to do that job too, and if no one will volunteer, for any kind of pay, they have to assign convicts. It's for the state.

Otherwise nothing new. Life is pretty monotonous. Don't believe the adventure stories. Adventure is weeks of boredom punctuated by moments of being scared gutless. Sorry to be so brief, but I want to get this on the outbound rocket. Won't be another for a couple of months. Everything well, really. I hope the same for you and live for the day we'll meet again. Thanks a million for the cookies—you know you can't afford to pay the freight, you old spendthrift! Martha baked them, didn't she? I recognized the Obrenowicz touch. Say hello to her and Jim for me. And most of all, my kindest thoughts go to you.

As ever,
Jack

The telecasts carried "Wanted" messages for Sam Hall. No photographs of him were available, but an artist could draw an accurate likeness from Matilda's description, and his truculent face began to adorn public places. Not long thereafter, the Security offices in Denver were wrecked by a grenade tossed from a speeding car that vanished into traffic. A witness said he had glimpsed the thrower, and the fragmentary picture given under hypnosis was not unlike Sam Hall's. Thornberg doctored the record a bit to make it still more similar. The tampering was risky; if Security ever became suspicious, they could easily check back with their witnesses. But the chance was not too big to take, for a scientifically quizzed man told everything germane to the subject which his memory, conscious, subconscious, and cellular, held. There was never any reason to repeat such an interrogation.

Thornberg often tried to analyze his motives. Plainly, he disliked the government. He must have contained that hate all his life, carefully suppressed from awareness, and recently it had been forced into his conscious mind. Not even his subconscious could have formulated it earlier, or he would have been caught by the loyalty probes. The hate derived from a lifetime of doubts (Had there been any real reason to fight Brazil, other than to obtain those bases and mineral concessions? Had the Chinese attack perhaps been provoked—or even faked, for their government denied it?) and the million petty frustrations of the garrison state. Still—the strength of his feelings! The violence!

By creating Sam Hall he had struck back. But that was an ineffectual blow, a timid gesture. Most likely his basic motive was simply to find a halfway safe release. In Sam Hall he lived vicariously the things that the beast within him wanted to do. Several times he had intended to discontinue his sabotage, but it was like a drug: Sam Hall was becoming necessary to his own stability.

The thought was alarming. He ought to see a psychiatrist—but no, the doctor would be bound to report his tale, he would go to camp, and Jack, if not exactly ruined, would be under a cloud for the rest of his life. Thornberg had no desire to go to camp, anyway. His existence had compensations, interesting work, a few good friends, art and music and literature, decent wine, sunsets and mountains, memories. He had started this game on impulse, and now he was simply too late to stop it.

For Sam Hall had been promoted to Public Enemy Number One.

Winter came, and the slopes of the Rockies under which Matilda lay were white beneath a cold greenish sky. Air traffic around the nearby town was lost in that hugeness: brief hurtling meteors against infinity, ground traffic that could not be seen from the Records entrance. Thornberg took the special tubeway to work every morn-

ing, but he often walked the ten kilometers back, and his
Sundays were usually spent in long hikes over slippery
trails. That was a foolish thing to do alone in winter, except that he felt reckless.

He was in his office shortly before Christmas when the
intercom said: "Major Sorensen to see you, sir. From Investigation."

Thornberg felt his stomach tie itself into a cold knot.
"All right," he answered in a voice whose levelness sur-
prised him. "Cancel any other appointments." Security
Investigation took AAA priority.

Sorensen walked in with a clack of bootheels. He was
a big blond man, heavy-shouldered, face expressionless,
eyes pale and remote as the winter sky. His black uniform fitted him like a skin; against it, the lightning badge
of his service glittered frosty. He halted before the desk.
Thornberg rose to give him an awkward salute.

"Please sit down, Major Sorensen. What can I do for
you?"

"Thanks." The agent's tone crackled. He lowered
his bulk into a chair and let his gaze drill Thornberg.
"I've come about the Sam Hall case."

"Oh, the rebel?" Thornberg's flesh prickled. He could
barely meet those eyes.

"How do you know he's a rebel?" Sorensen demanded.
"That's never been stated officially."

"Why—I assumed—bank raid—attacks on personnel
in your service—"

Sorensen slightly inclined his cropped head. When he
spoke again, he sounded relaxed, almost casual. "Tell
me, Major Thornberg, have you followed the Hall devel-
opments in detail?"

Thornberg hesitated. He was not supposed to do so
unless ordered; he only kept the machine running. He remembered a principle from reading and, yes, furtively
cynical conversation. "When suspected of a major sin,
admit minor ones frankly. That may satisfy them."

"As a matter of fact, I have," he said. "I know it's
against regs, but I was interested and—well, I couldn't

see any harm in it. I've not discussed it with anybody, of course."

"No matter." Sorensen waved a muscular hand. "If you hadn't, I'd have ordered you to. I want your opinion on this."

"Why—I'm not a detective—"

"You know more about Records, though, than any other person. I'll be frank with you—under the rose, naturally." Sorensen seemed almost friendly now. *Was it a trick to put his prey off guard?* "You see, there are some puzzling features about this case."

Thornberg kept silent. He wondered if Sorensen could hear the thudding of his heart.

"Sam Hall is a shadow," said the agent. "The most careful checkups eliminate any chance of his being identical with anyone else of that name. In fact, we've learned that the name occurs in a violent old drinking song. Is this coincidence, or did the song suggest crime to Sam Hall, or did he by some incredible process get that alias into his record instead of his real name? Whatever the answer there, we know that he's ostensibly without military training, yet he's pulled off some beautiful pieces of precision attack. His IQ is only 110, but he evades our traps. He has no politics, yet he turns on Security without warning. We have not been able to find a single individual who remembers him—not one, and believe me, we have been thorough. Oh, there are a few subconscious memories which might be of him, but probably aren't; and so aggressive a personality should be remembered consciously. No undergrounder or foreign operative we've caught had any knowledge of him, which defies probability. The whole business seems impossible."

Thornberg licked his lips. Sorensen, the hunter of men, must know he was frightened; but would he assume that to be the normal nervousness of a man in the presence of a Security officer?

Sorensen's face broke into a hard smile. "As Sherlock Holmes remarked," he said, "when you have eliminated every other hypothesis, then the one which remains, however improbable, must be right."

Despite himself, Thornberg was jolted. Sorensen hadn't struck him as a reader.

"Well," he asked slowly, "what is your remaining hypothesis?"

His visitor watched him for a long time, it seemed forever, before replying. "The underground is more powerful and widespread than people realize. They've had seventy years to prepare, and many good brains in their ranks. They carry on scientific research of their own. It's top secret, but we know they have perfected a type of weapon we cannot duplicate yet. It seems to be a hand gun throwing bolts of energy—a blaster, you might call it —of immense power. Sooner or later they're going to wage open war against the government.

"Now, could they have done something comparable in psychology? Could they have found a way to erase or cover up memories selectively, even on the cellular level? Could they know how to fool a personality tester, how to disguise the mind itself? If so, we may have any number of Sam Halls in our midst, undetectable until the moment comes for them to strike."

Thornberg felt almost boneless. He couldn't help gasping his relief, and hoped Sorensen would take it for a sign of alarm.

"The possibility is frightening, no?" The blond man laughed metallically. "You can imagine what is being felt in high official circles. We've put all the psychological researchers we could get to work on the problem—bah! Fools! They go by the book; they're afraid to be original even when the state tells them to.

"This may just be a wild fancy, of course. I hope it is. But we have to *know*. That's why I approached you personally, instead of sending the usual requisition. I want you to make a search of the records—everything pertaining to the subject, every man, every discovery, every hypothesis. You have a broad technical background and, from your psychorecord, an unusual amount of creative imagination. I want you to do what you can to correlate your data. Co-opt whoever you need. Submit to my office a report on the possibility—or should I say probability—

of this notion; and if you find any likelihood of its being true, sketch out a research program which will enable us to duplicate the results and counteract them."

Thornberg fumbled for words. "I'll try," he said lamely. "I'll do my best."

"Good. It's for the state."

Sorensen had finished his official business, but he didn't go at once. "Rebel propaganda is subtle stuff," he said quietly, after a pause. "It's dangerous because it uses our own slogans, with a twisted meaning. Liberty, equality, justice, peace. Too many people can't appreciate that times have changed and the meanings of words have necessarily changed likewise."

"I suppose not," said Thornberg. He added the lie: "I never thought much about that kind of question."

"You should," said Sorensen. "Study your history. When we lost World War III we had to militarize to win World War IV, and after that mount guard on the whole human race. The people demanded it at the time."

*The people,* thought Thornberg, *never appreciated freedom till they'd lost it. They were always willing to sell their birthright. Or was it merely that, being untrained in thinking, they couldn't see through demagoguery, couldn't visualize the ultimate consequences of their wishes?* He was vaguely shocked at the thought; wasn't he able to control his mind any longer?

"The rebels," said Sorensen, "claim that conditions have changed, that militarization is no longer necessary —if it ever was—and that America would be safe in a union of free countries. Devilishly clever propaganda, Major Thornberg. Watch out for it."

He got up and took his leave. Thornberg sat for a long time staring at the door. Sorensen's last words had been odd, to say the least. Were they a hint—or a bait?

The next day Matilda received a news item which was carefully edited for the public channels. An insurrectionist force had landed aircraft in the stockade of Camp Forbes, in Utah, gunned down the guards, and taken away the prisoners. The institution's doctor had been spared, and related that the leader of the raid, a stocky man in a mask, had said to him: "Tell your friends I'll call again. My name is Sam Hall."

Space Guard ship blown up on Mesa Verde Field. On a fragment of metal someone has scrawled: "Compliments of Sam Hall."

Squad of Security Police, raiding a suspected underground hideout in Philadelphia, cut down by tommy-gun fire. Voice from a hidden bull horn cries: "My name, it is Sam Hall!"

Matthew Williamson, chemist in Seattle, suspected of subversive connections, is gone when the arresting officers break into his home. A note left on his desk says: "Off to visit Sam Hall. Back for liberation. M.W."

Defense plant producing important robomb components near Miami is sabotaged by a planted bomb, after a phone warning gives the workers time to evacuate. The caller, who leaves the visio circuit off, styles himself Sam Hall. Various similar places get similar warnings. These are fakes, but each costs a day's valuable work in the alarm and the search.

Scribbled on walls from New York to San Diego, from Duluth to El Paso, Sam Hall, Sam Hall, Sam Hall.

Obviously, thought Thornberg, the underground had seized on the invisible and invincible man of legend and turned him to their own purposes. Reports of him poured in from all over the country, hundreds every day—Sam Hall seen here, Sam Hall seen there. Ninety-nine percent could be dismissed as hoaxes, hallucinations, mistakes; it was another national craze, fruit of a jittery time, like the sixteenth- and seventeenth-century witch hunts or the twentieth-century flying saucers. But Security and civilian police had to check on every one.

Thornberg planted a number of them himself.

Mostly, though, he was busy on his assignment. He could understand what it meant to the government. Life in the garrison state was inevitably founded on fear and mistrust, every man's eye on his neighbor; but at least

psychotyping and hypnoquizzing had given a degree of
surety. Now, that staff knocked out from under them—

His preliminary studies indicated that an invention
such as Sorensen had hypothesized, while not impossible,
was too far beyond the scope of contemporary science for
the rebels to have perfected. Such research carried on
nowadays would, from the standpoint of practicality if
not of knowledge, be a waste of time and trained men.

He spent a good many sleepless hours and a month's
cigarette ration before he could decide what to do. All
right, he'd aided insurrection in a small way, and he
shouldn't boggle at the next step. Still—nevertheless—
did he want to?

Jack—his son had a career lined out for himself. He
loved the big deeps beyond the sky as he would love a
woman. If things changed, what then of Jack's career?

Well, what was it now? Stuck on a dreary planet as
guardsman and executioner of homesick starvelings poisoned by radioactivity; never even seeing the sun. Come
the day, Jack could surely wangle a berth on a real
spacer. They'd need bold men to explore beyond Saturn.
Jack was too honest to make a good rebel, but Thornberg
felt that after the initial shock he would welcome a new
government.

But treason! Oaths!

*When in the course of human events . . .*

It was a small thing that decided Thornberg. He
passed a shop downtown and noticed a group of the
Youth Guard smashing the windows and spattering yellow paint over the goods, O Moses, Jesus, Mendelssohn,
Hertz, and Einstein! Once he had chosen his path, a curious serenity possessed him. He stole a vial of prussic acid
from a chemist friend and carried it in his pocket; and as
for Jack, the boy would have to take his chances too.

The work was demanding and dangerous. He had to
alter recorded facts which were available elsewhere, in
books and journals and the minds of men. Nothing could
be done about basic theory. But quantitative results could
be juggled a little to set the overall picture subtly askew.
He would co-opt carefully chosen experts, men whose

psychotypes indicated they would take the easy course of
relying on Matilda instead of checking original sources.
And the correlation and integration of innumerable data,
the empirical equations and extrapolations thereof, could
be tampered with.

He turned his regular job over to Rodney and devoted
himself entirely to the new one. He grew thin and testy;
when Sorensen called, trying to hurry him, he snapped
back: "Do you want speed or quality?" and wasn't too
surprised at himself afterward. He got little sleep, but his
mind seemed unnaturally clear.

Winter faded into spring while Thornberg and his experts labored and while the nation shook, psychically and
physically, under the growing violence of Sam Hall. The
report Thornberg submitted in May was so voluminous
and detailed that he didn't think the government researchers would bother referring to any other source. Its
conclusion: Yes, given a brilliant man applying Belloni
matrices to cybernetic formulas and using some unknown
kind of colloidal probe, a psychological masking technique was plausible.

The government yanked every man it could find into
research. Thornberg knew it was only a matter of time
before they realized they had been had. How much time,
he couldn't say. But when they were sure . . .

Now up the rope I go, up I go.
Now up the rope I go, up I go.
  And the bastards down below,
  They say, "Sam, we told you so."
They say, "Sam, we told you so," God damn
    their eyes.

REBELS ATTACK
SPACESHIPS LAND UNDER COVER OF
RAINSTORM, SEIZE POINTS NEAR
N. DETROIT
FLAME WEAPONS USED AGAINST ARMY
BY REBELS

"The infamous legions of the traitors have taken ground throughout the nation, but already our gallant forces have hurled them back. They have come out in early summer like toadstools, and will wither as fast— WHEEEEEE-OOOOOO!" Silence.

"All citizens will keep calm, remain loyal to their country, and stay at their usual tasks, until otherwise ordered. Civilians will report to their local defense officers. Military reservists will report immediately for active duty."

"Hello, Hawaii! Are you there? Come in, Hawaii! Calling Hawaii!"

"CQ, Mars GHQ calling . . . bzzz, wheeee . . . seized Syrtis Major Colony and . . . whoooo . . . help needed . . ."

The lunar rocket bases are assaulted and carried. The commander blows them up rather than surrender. A pinpoint flash on the moon's face, a new crater; what will they name it?

"So they've got Seattle, have they? Send a robomb flight. Scrub the place off the map. . . . Citizens?. To hell with citizens! This is war!"

". . . in New York. Secretly drilled rebels emerged from the notorious Crater district and stormed . . ."

". . . assassins were shot down. The new President has already been sworn in and . . ."

### BRITAIN, CANADA, AUSTRALIA REFUSE ASSISTANCE TO GOV'T

". . . no, sir. The bombs reached Seattle all right. But they were stopped before they hit—some kind of energy gun. . . ."

"COMECO to army commanders in Florida and Georgia: Enemy action has made Florida and the keys temporarily untenable. Your units will withdraw as follows . . ."

"Today a rebel force engaging a military convoy in Donner Pass was annihilated by a well-placed tactical atomic bomb. Though our own men suffered losses on this account . . ."

"COMWECO to army commanders in California: the mutiny of units stationed around San Francisco poses a grave problem. . . ."

### SP RAID REBEL HIDEOUT, BAG FIVE OFFICERS

"Okay, so the enemy is about to capture Boston. We *can't* issue weapons to the citizens. They might turn them on us!"

### SPACE GUARD UNITS EXPECTED FROM VENUS

*Jack, Jack, Jack!*

It was strange, living in the midst of a war. Thornberg had never thought it would be like this. Drawn faces, furtive looks, chaos in the telecast news and the irregularly arriving papers, blackouts, civil defense drills, shortages, occasional panic when a rebel jet whistled overhead—but nothing else. No gunfire, no bombs, no more than the unreal combats you heard about. The only local casualty list were due to Security; people kept disappearing, and nobody spoke about them.

But then, why should the enemy bother with this unimportant mountain town? The self-styled Libertarian Army was grabbing key points of manufacture, transportation, communication, was engaging in pitched battles, sabotaging buildings and machines, assassinating officials. By its very purpose, it couldn't wage total war, couldn't annihilate the folk it wanted to free—an attitude historically rare among revolutionaries, Thornberg knew. Rumor said the defenders were less finicky.

Most citizens were passive. They always are. Probably no more than one-fourth of the population was ever in earshot of an engagement. City dwellers might see fire in the sky, hear crump and whistle and crash of artillery, scramble aside from soldiers and armored vehicles, cower in shelters when rockets arced overhead; but the action was outside of town. If matters came to street fighting, the rebels never pushed far in. They would either lay siege or they would rely on agents inside the town. Then a citizen might hear the crack of rifles and grenades, rattle of machine guns, sizzle of lasers, and see corpses. But the end was either a return of military government or the rebels marching in and setting up their own provisional councils. (They rarely met cheers and flowers. Nobody knew how the war would end. But they heard words whispered, and usually got good service.) As nearly as possible, the average American continued his average life.

Thornberg stayed on his personal rails. Matilda, the information nexus, was in such demand that users queued for their shared time. If the rebels ever learned where she was—

*Or did they know?*

He got few opportunities to conduct his private sabotages, but on that account planned each of them extra carefully. The Sam Hall reports were almost standardized in his mind—Sam Hall here, Sam Hall there, pulling off this or that incredible stunt. But what did one superman count for in these gigantic days? He needed something more.

Television and newspapers jubilantly announced that Venus had finally been contacted. Luna and Mars had fallen, but the Guard units on Venus had quickly smashed a few feeble uprisings. Mere survival there demanded quantities of powerful, sophisticated equipment, readily adaptable to military purposes. The troops would be returning at once, fully armed. Given present planetary configurations, the highest boost could not deliver them on Earth for a good six weeks. But then they might prove a decisive reinforcement.

"Looks like you may see your boy soon, chief," Rodney remarked.

"Yes," said Thornberg, "I may."

"Tough fighting." Rodney shook his head. "I'd sure as hell hate to be in it."

*If Jack is killed by a rebel gun, when I have aided the rebels' cause . . .*

Sam Hall, reflected Thornberg, had lived a hard life, all violence and enmity and suspicion. Even his wife hadn't trusted him.

> . . . And my Nellie dressed in blue,
> Says, "Your trifling days are through.
> Now I know that you'll be true, God damn
>      your eyes."

Poor Sam Hall. No wonder he had killed a man.

*Suspicion!*

Thornberg stood for a moment while a tingle went through him. The police state was founded on suspicion. Nobody could trust anybody else. And with the new fear of psychomasking, and research on that project suspended during the crisis—

*Steady, boy, steady. Can't rush into action. Have to plan very carefully.*

Thornberg punched for the dossiers of key men in the administration, in the military, in Security. He did this in the presence of two assistants, for he thought that his own frequent sessions alone in the coordination booth were beginning to look funny.

"Top secret," he warned them, pleased with his cool manner. He was becoming a regular Machiavelli. "You'll be skinned alive if you mention it to anyone."

Rodney gave him a shrewd glance. "So they're not even sure of their top men now, are they?" he murmured.

"I've been told to make some checks," snapped Thornberg. "That's all you need to know."

He studied the files for many hours before coming to a decision. Secret observations were, of course, made of everyone from time to time. A cross check with Matilda showed that the cop who filed the last report on Lindahl had been killed the next day in a spontaneous and abor-

tive uprising. The report was innocuous: Lindahl had
stayed at home, studying various papers; he had been
alone in the house except for a bodyguard in another
room who had not seen him. And Lindahl was Under-
secretary of Defense.

Thornberg changed the record. A masked man—
stocky, black-haired—had come in and talked for three
hours with Lindahl. They had spoken low, so that the
cop's ears, outside the window, couldn't catch what was
said. After the visitor left, Lindahl had retired. The cop
went back in great excitement, made out his report, and
gave it to the signalman, who had sent it on to Matilda.

*Tough on the signalman,* thought Thornberg. *They'll
want to know why he didn't tell this to his chief in New
Washington, if the observer was killed before doing so.
He'll deny every such report, and they'll hypnoquiz him
—but they don't trust that method anymore!*

His sympathy quickly faded. What counted was
having the war over before Jack got home. He refilled
the altered spool and did a little backtracking, shifting
the last report of Sam Hall from Salt Lake City to
Atlanta. More plausible. Then, as opportunity permitted,
he worked on real men's records.

He must wait two haggard days before the next
order came from Security for a check on Sam Hall. The
scanners trod out their intricate measure, transistors
awoke, in due course a cog turned. LINDAHL unrolled
before the microprinter. Cross references ramified in all
directions. Thornberg attached a query to the preliminary report: this looked interesting; did his superiors
want more information?

They did!

Next day the telecast announced a shake-up in the
Department of Defense. Nobody heard more about
Lindahl.

*And I,* Thornberg reflected, *have grabbed a very large
tiger by the tail. Now they'll have to check everybody.
How does a solitary man keep ahead of the Security Police?*

Lindahl is a traitor. How did his chief ever let him get such a sensitive position? Secretary Hoheimer was a personal friend of Lindahl, too. Have Records check Hoheimer.

What's this? Hoheimer himself! Five years ago, yes, but even so—the dossier shows he lived in an apartment unit where *Sam Hall* was janitor! Grab Hoheimer! Who'll take his place? General Halliburton? That stupid old bastard? Well, at least his nose is clean. Can't trust those slick characters.

Hoheimer has a brother in Security, general's rank, good detection record. A blind? Who knows? Slap the brother in jail, at least for the duration. Better check his staff. . . . Central Records shows that his chief field agent, Jones, has five days unaccounted for a year ago; he claimed Security secrecy at the time, but a double cross check shows it wasn't true. Shoot Jones! He has a nephew in the army, a captain. Pull that unit out of the firing line till we can study it man by man! We've had too many mutinies already.

Lindahl was also a close friend of Benson, in charge of the Tennessee Atomic Ordnance Works. Haul Benson in! Check every man connected with him! No trusting those scientists; they're always blabbing secrets.

The first Hoheimer's son is an industralist, owns a petroleum-synthesis plant in Texas. Nab him! His wife is a sister of Leslie, head of the War Production Coordination Board. Get Leslie too. Sure, he's doing a good job, but he may be sending information to the enemy. Or he may just be waiting for the signal to sabotage the whole works. We can't trust *anybody,* I tell you!

What's this? Records relays an Intelligence report that the mayor of Tampa was in cahoots with the rebels. It's marked "Unreliable, Rumor"—but Tampa did surrender without a fight. The mayor's business partner is Gale, who has a cousin in the army, commanding a robomb base in New Mexico. Check both the Gales, Records. . . . So the cousin was absent four days without filing his whereabouts, was he? Military privilege or not, arrest him and find out where he was!

• Attention, Records, attention, Records, urgent. Brigadier John Harmsworth Gale, etc., etc., refused to divulge information required by Security Officers, claiming to have been at his base all the time. Can this be an error on your part?

• Records to Security Central, ref: etc., etc. No possibility of error exists except in information received.

• to Records, ref: etc., etc. Gale's story corroborated by three of his officers.

Put that whole damned base under arrest! Recheck those reports! Who sent them in, anyway?

• to Records, ref: etc., etc. On attempt to arrest entire personnel, Robomb Base 37-J fired on Security detachment and repulsed it. At last reports Gale was calling for rebel forces fifty miles off to assist him. Details will follow for the files as soon as possible.

So Gale was a traitor. Or was he driven by fear? Have Records find out who filed that information about him in the first place.

*We can't trust anybody!*

Thornberg was not much surprised when his door was kicked open and the Security squad entered. He had been expecting it for days, maybe weeks. A solitary man can't keep ahead of the game forever. No doubt accumulated inconsistencies had finally drawn suspicion his way; or, ironically, the chains of accusation he forged had by chance led to him; perhaps somebody here, like Rodney, had decided something was amiss and lodged a tip.

Were that last the case, he laid no blame. The tragedy of civil war was that it turned brother against brother. Millions of decent people were with the government because they had pledged themselves to be, or simply because they didn't believe in the alternative. Mostly, Thornberg felt tired.

He looked down the barrel of a revolver and up to the eyes of the blackcoat behind. They were equally empty of feeling. "I assume I'm under arrest?" he said tonelessly.

"On your feet," the leader snapped.

June could not hold back a whimper of pain. The man who held her was twisting her arm behind her back, obviously enjoying himself. "Don't do that," Thornberg said. "She's innocent. Had no idea what I was carrying out."

"On your feet, I told you." The leader thrust his gun closer.

"I suggest you leave me alone, too." Thornberg lifted his right hand, to show a ball he had taken from his desk when the squad arrived. "Do you see this? A thing I made against contingencies. Not a bomb *per se*—but a radio trigger. If my fingers relax, the rubber will expand and close a circuit. I believe such a device is called a dead-man switch."

The squad stiffened. Thornberg heard an oath. "Release the lady," he said.

"You surrender first!" said June's captor. He wrenched. She screamed.

"No," Thornberg said. "June, dear, I'm sorry. But have no fears. You see, I expected this visit, and made my preparations. The radio signaller won't touch off anything as melodramatic as a bomb. No, instead it will close a relay which will activate a certain program in Matilda—the Records computer, you know, the data machine. Every spool will be wiped. The government will have not a record left. Myself, I am prepared to die. But if you men let me complete that circuit, I imagine you'll wish there had been a bomb. Now do let go of the lady."

The blackcoat did, as if she had suddenly turned incandescent. She slumped sobbing to the floor.

"A bluff!" the leader shouted. Sweat made his face shiny.

"Do you wish to call it?" Thornberg made a smile. "By all means."

"You traitor—"

"I prefer 'patriot,' if you please. But be the semantics as they may, you must admit I was effective. The government has been turned end for end and upside down.

The army is breaking apart, officers deserting right and left for fear they'll be arrested next, or defecting, or leading mutinies. Security is chasing its own tail around half a continent. Far more administrators are being murdered by their colleagues than the underground could possibly assassinate. The Libertarians take city after city without resistance. My guess is that they will occupy New Washington inside another week."

"Your doing!" Finger quivered on trigger.

"Oh, no. Spare my blushes. But I did make a contribution of some significance, yes. Unless you say Sam Hall did, which is fine by me."

"What . . . will . . . you do now?"

"That depends on you, my friend. Whether I am killed or only rendered unconscious, Matilda dies. You could have the technicians check out whether I'm telling the truth, and if I am, you could have them yank that program. However, at the first sign of any such move on your part, I will naturally let the ball go. Look in my mouth." He opened it briefly. "Yes, the conventional glass vial of prussic acid. I apologize for the cliché, but you will understand that I have no wish to share the fate that you people bring on yourselves."

Bafflement wrestled rage in the countenances before Thornberg. They weren't used to thinking, those men.

"Of course," he went on, "you have an alternative. At last reports, a Liberation unit was established less than two hundred kilometers from here. We could call and ask them to send a force, explaining the importance of this place. That would be to your advantage too. There is going to be a day of reckoning with you blackcoats. My influence could help you personally, however little you deserve to get off the hook."

The stared at each other. After a very long while, wherein the only sounds were June's diminishing sobs, unevenly drawn breaths among the police, and Thornberg's pulse rapid in his ears, the leader spat, "No! You lie!" He aimed his gun.

The man behind him drew and shot him in the head. The result was ugly to see. As soon as he knew he was fully in charge, Thornberg did his best to comfort June.

"As a matter of fact," he told Sorensen, "I *was* bluffing. That was just a ball; the poison alone was real. Not that it made much difference at that stage, except to me."

"We'll need Matilda for a while yet," said Sorensen. "Want to stay on?"

"Sure, provided I can take a vacation when my son comes home."

"That shouldn't be long now. You'll be glad to hear we've finally contacted the Venus units of the Space Guard, on their way back. The commander agreed to stay out of fighting, on the grounds that his service's obligation is to the legitimate government and we'll need an election to determine what that is. Your boy will be safe."

Thornberg could find no words of response. Instead he remarked with hard-held casualness, "You know, I'm surprised to learn you were an undergrounder."

"We got a few into Security, who wangled things so they gave each other clearances and loyalty checks." Sorensen grimaced. "That was the only part of it I enjoyed, though, till quite lately."

He leaned back in his chair which creaked under his weight. In civilian clothes which nothing but an armband made into the uniform of a Libertarian officer, he did seem an altogether different man. Where his bulk had formerly crowded Thornberg's office, today his vitality irradiated it.

"Then Sam Hall came along," he said. "They had their suspicions at first in Security. My bosses were evil but not stupid. Well, I got myself assigned to the job of checking you out. Right away I guessed you harbored disruptive thoughts; so I gave you a clean bill of health. Afterward I cooked up that fantasy of the psychological mask and got several high-ranking men worried. When you followed my lead, I was sure you were on our side. Consequently, though the Libertarian command knew all along where Matilda was, of course they left her alone!"

"You must have joined them in person very recently."

"Yeah, the witch hunt you started inside of Security was getting too close to me. Well worth a risk, though, to see those cockroaches busily stepping on each other."

Thornberg sat quiet awhile, then leaned over his desk. "I haven't enlisted under your banner yet," he said gravely. "I had to assume the Libertarian words about freedom were not mere rhetoric. But . . . you mentioned Matilda. You want me to continue in my work here. What are your plans for her?"

Sorensen turned equally serious. "I was waiting for you to ask that, Thorny. Look. Besides needing her to help us find some people we want rather badly, we are resonsible for the sheer physical survival of the country. I'd feel easier too if we could take her apart this minute. But—"

"Yes?"

"But we've got to transcribe a lot of information first, strictly practical facts. *Then* we wipe everything else and ceremoniously dynamite this building. You're invited, no, urgently asked to sit on the board that decides the details —in other words, we want you to help work yourself out of a job."

"Thank you," Thornberg whispered.

After a moment, in a sudden tide of happiness, he chuckled. "And that will be the end of Sam Hall," he said. "He'll go to whatever Valhalla there is for the great characters of fiction. I can see him squabbling with Sherlock Holmes and shocking the hell out of King Arthur and striking up a beautiful friendship with Long John Silver. Do you know how the ballad ends?" He sang softly: "Now up in heaven I dwell, in heaven I dwell. . . ."

Unfortunately, the conclusion is rugged. Sam Hall never was satisfied.

REALITY KEEPS OVERTAKING SCIENCE fiction. You will note a quotation from the Latin mass in this story; it was written just before Vatican Two decreed the vernacular be used. However, I leave the passage as is— first, because I prefer it thus; second, because the Latin mass is not quite extinct and may possibly someday make a comeback in some services.

Scientific obsolescence is harder to explain away. The picture of a collapsing star given here is the one most generally accepted by astrophysicists at the time I was writing this. They've learned a great deal more since then. But I don't believe their discoveries have— yet—made "Kyrie" as unacceptable as, for instance, practically every story ever published about Jupiter became at the end of 1973.

The assumptions about the nature of telepathy, including the assumption that it occurs at all, are a different matter, of course; they are beyond the area of known science. True, many physicists will balk at the idea that a message can be transmitted instantaneously (or nearly so) and without loss across interstellar distances—not to mention the idea that ships may evade the light-speed limit

6

117

through bypassing the space between starting point and goal. But these speculations are no longer as disreputable as they were only a short while ago. Let me merely repeat to the physicists a few such phrases as "tachyon," "Kerr metric space warp," and "scalar field radiation." How little we know for sure!

The intelligent nonhuman character in the form of a plasma is just as speculative. However, the existence of *some* kinds of thinking nonhumans looks more than plausible. What reasonable person can seriously believe that in this entire enormous, mysterious cosmos, ours is the single awareness?

# KYRIE

≪≪≪≪≪≪≪≪≪≪≪≪≪≪≪≪≪≪≪≪≪≪≪≪≪≪≪≪≪≪≪≪≪≪≪≪

ON A HIGH PEAK IN THE LUNAR CARPATHIANS stands a convent of St. Martha of Bethany. The walls are native rock; they lift, dark and cragged as the mountainside itself, into a sky that is always black. As you approach from Northpole along Route Plato, you see the cross which surmounts the tower, stark athwart Earth's blue disc. No bells resound from there—not in airlessness.

You may hear them inside at the canonical hours, and throughout the crypts below where machines toil to maintain a semblance of terrestrial environment. If you linger awhile you will also hear them calling to requiem mass. For it has become a tradition that prayers be offered at St. Martha's for those who have perished in space; and they are more with every passing year.

This is not the work of the sisters. They minister to the sick, the needy, the crippled, the insane, all whom space has broken and cast back. Luna is full of such, exiles because they can no longer endure Earth's pull or because it is feared they may be incubating a plague from some unknown planet or because men are so busy with their frontiers that they have no time to spare for the failures. The sisters wear spacesuits as often as habits, are as likely to hold a medikit as a rosary.

But they are granted some time for contemplation. At

119

night, when for half a month the sun's glare has departed, the chapel is unshuttered and stars look down through the glazedome to the candles. They do not wink and their light is winter cold. One of the nuns in particular is there as often as may be, praying for her own dead. And the abbess sees to it that she can be present when the yearly mass, that she endowed before she took her vows, is sung.

> *Requiem aeternam dona eis, Domine, et lux*
> *perpetua luceat eis.*
> *Kyrie eleison, Christe eleison, Kyrie eleison.*

The Supernova Sagittarii expedition comprised fifty human beings and a flame. It went the long way around from Earth orbit, stopping at Epsilon Lyrae to pick up its last member. Thence it approached its destination by stages.

This is the paradox: time and space are aspects of each other. The explosion was more than a hundred years past when noted by men on Lasthope. They were part of a generations-long effort to fathom the civilization of creatures altogether unlike us; but one night they looked up and saw a light so brilliant it cast shadows.

That wave front would reach Earth several centuries hence. By then it would be so tenuous that nothing but another bright point would appear in the sky. Meanwhile, though, a ship overleaping the space through which light must creep could track the great star's death across time.

Suitably far off, instruments recorded what had been before the outburst, incandescence collapsing upon itself after the last nuclear fuel was burned out. A jump, and they saw what happened a century ago: convulsion, storm of quanta and neutrinos, radiation equal to the massed hundred billion suns of this galaxy.

It faded, leaving an emptiness in heaven, and the *Raven* moved closer. Fifty light-years—fifty years—inward, she studied a shrinking fieriness in the midst of a fog which shone like lightning.

Twenty-five years later the central globe had dwindled more, the nebula had expanded and dimmed. But because the distance was now so much less, everything seemed larger and brighter. The naked eye saw a dazzle too fierce to look straight at, making the constellations pale by contrast. Telescopes showed a blue-white spark in the heart of an opalescent cloud delicately filamented at the edges.

The *Raven* made ready for her final jump, to the immediate neighborhood of the supernova.

Captain Teodor Szili went on a last-minute inspection tour. The ship murmured around him, running at one gravity of acceleration to reach the desired intrinsic velocity. Power droned, regulators whickered, ventilation systems rustled. He felt the energies quiver in his bones. But metal surrounded him, blank and comfortless. Viewpoints gave on a dragon's hoard of stars, the ghostly arch of the Milky Way: on vacuum, cosmic rays, cold not far above absolute zero, distance beyond imagination to the nearest human hearthfire. He was about to take his people where none had ever been before, into conditions none was sure about, and that was a heavy burden on him.

He found Eloise Waggoner at her post, a cubbyhole with intercom connections directly to the command bridge. Music drew him, a triumphant serenity he did not recognize. Stopping in the doorway, he saw her seated with a small tape machine on the desk.

"What's this?" he demanded.

"Oh!" The woman (he could not think of her as a girl, though she was barely out of her teens) started. "I . . . I was waiting for the jump."

"You were to wait at the alert."

"What have I to do?" she answered less timidly than was her wont. "I mean, I'm not a crewman or a scientist."

"You are in the crew. Special communications technician."

"With Lucifer. And he likes the music. He says we come closer to oneness with it than in anything else he knows about us."

Szili arched his brows. "Oneness?"

A blush went up Eloise's thin cheeks. She stared at

the deck and her hands twisted together. "Maybe that isn't the right word. Peace, harmony, unity . . . God? . . . I sense what he means, but we haven't any word that fits."

"Hm. Well, you are supposed to keep him happy." The skipper regarded her with a return of the distaste he had tried to suppress. She was a decent enough sort, he supposed, in her gauche and inhibited way; but her looks! Scrawny, big-footed, big-nosed, pop eyes and stringy dust-colored hair—and, to be sure, telepaths always made him uncomfortable. She said she could only read Lucifer's mind, but was that true?

No. Don't think such things. Loneliness and otherness can come near breaking you out here, without adding suspicion of your fellows.

If Eloise Waggoner was really human. She must be some kind of mutant at the very least. Whoever could communicate thought to thought with a living vortex had to be.

"What are you playing, anyhow?" Szili asked.

"Bach. The Third Brandenburg Concerto. He, Lucifer, he doesn't care for the modern stuff. I don't either."

You wouldn't, Szili decided. Aloud: "Listen, we jump in half an hour. No telling what we'll emerge in. This is the first time anyone's been close to a recent supernova. We can only be certain of enough hard radiation that we'll be dead if the screenfields give way. Otherwise we've nothing to go on except theory. And a collapsing stellar core is so unlike anything anywhere else in the universe that I'm skeptical about how good the theory is. We can't sit daydreaming. We have to prepare."

"Yes, sir." Whispering, her voice lost its usual harshness.

He stared past her, past the ophidian eyes of meters and controls, as if he could penetrate the steel beyond and look straight into space. There, he knew, floated Lucifer.

The image grew in him: a fireball twenty meters across, shimmering white, red, gold, royal blue, flames dancing like Medusa locks, cometary tail burning for a hundred meters behind, a shiningness, a glory, a piece of hell. Not the least of what troubled him was the thought of that which paced his ship.

He hugged scientific explanations to his breast, though they were little better than guesses. In the multiple star system of Epsilon Aurigae, in the gas and energy pervading the space around, things took place which no laboratory could imitate. Ball lightning on a planet was perhaps analogous, as the formation of simple organic compounds in a primordial ocean is analogous to the life which finally evolves. In Epsilon Aurigae, magnetohydrodynamics had done what chemistry did on Earth. Stable plasma vortices had appeared, had grown, had added complexity, until after millions of years they became something you must needs call an organism. It was a form of ions, nuclei, and force-fields. It metabolized electrons, nucleons, X rays; it maintained its configuration for a long lifetime; it reproduced; it thought.

But what did it think? The few telepaths who could communicate with the Aurigeans, who had first made humankind aware that the Aurigeans existed, never explained clearly. They were a queer lot themselves.

Wherefore Captain Szili said, "I want you to pass this on to him."

"Yes, sir." Eloise turned down the volume on her taper. Her eyes unfocused. Through her ears went words, and her brain (how efficient a transducer was it?) passed the meanings on out to him who loped alongside *Raven* on his own reaction drive.

"Listen, Lucifer. You have heard this often before, I know, but I want to be positive you understand in full. Your psychology must be very foreign to ours. Why did you agree to come with us? I don't know. Technician Waggoner said you were curious and adventurous. Is that the whole truth?

"No matter. In half an hour we jump. We'll come within five hundred million kilometers of the supernova. That's where your work begins. You can go where we dare not, observe what we can't, tell us more than our instruments would ever hint at. But first we have to verify we can stay in orbit around the star. This concerns you too. Dead men can't transport you home again.

"So. In order to enclose you within the jumpfield, without disrupting your body, we have to switch off the shield screens. We'll emerge in a lethal radiation zone. You must promptly retreat from the ship, because we'll start the screen generator up sixty seconds after transit. Then you must investigate the vicinity. The hazards to look for—" Szili listed them. "Those are only what we can foresee. Perhaps we'll hit other garbage we haven't predicted. If anything seems like a menace, return at once, warn us, and prepare for a jump back to here. Do you have that? Repeat."

Words jerked from Eloise. They were a correct recital; but how much was she leaving out?

"Very good." Szili hesitated. "Proceed with your concert if you like. But break it off at zero minus ten minutes and stand by."

"Yes, sir." She didn't look at him. She didn't appear to be looking anywhere in particular.

His footsteps clacked down the corridor and were lost.

—Why did he say the same things over? asked Lucifer.

"He is afraid," Eloise said.

—?—.

"I guess you don't know about fear," she said.

—Can you show me? . . . No, do not. I sense it is hurtful. You must not be hurt.

"I can't be afraid anyway, when your mind is holding mine."

(Warmth filled her. Merriment was there, playing like little flames over the surface of Father-leading-her-by-the-hand-when-she-was-just-a-child-and-they-went-out-one-summer's-day-to-pick-wild-flowers; over strength and gentleness and Bach and God.) Lucifer swept around the hull in an exuberant curve. Sparks danced in his wake.

—Think flowers again. Please.

She tried.

—They are like (image, as nearly as a human brain

could grasp, of fountains blossoming with gamma-ray colors in the middle of light, everywhere light). But so tiny.
So brief a sweetness.

"I don't understand how you can understand," she
whispered.

—You understand for me. I did not have that kind of
thing to love, before you came.

"But you have so much else. I try to share it, but I'm
not made to realize what a star is."

—Nor I for planets. Yet ourselves may touch.

Her cheeks burned anew. The thought rolled on, inter-
weaving its counterpoint to the marching music. —That
is why I came, do you know? For you. I am fire and air.
I had not tasted the coolness of water, the patience of
earth, until you showed me. You are moonlight on an
ocean.

"No, don't," she said. "Please."

Puzzlement: —Why not? Does joy hurt? Are you not
used to it?

"I, I guess that's right." She flung her head back. "No!
Be damned if I'll feel sorry for myself!"

—Why should you? Have we not all reality to be in,
and is it not full of suns and songs?

"Yes. To you. Teach me."

—If you in turn will teach me— The thought broke
off. A contact remained, unspeaking, such as she imagined must often prevail among lovers.

She glowered at Motilal Mazundar's chocolate face,
where the physicist stood in the doorway. "What do you
want?"

He was surprised. "Only to see if everything is well
with you, Miss Waggoner."

She bit her lip. He had tried harder than most aboard
to be kind to her. "I'm sorry," she said. "I didn't mean to
bark at you. Nerves."

"We are everyone on edge." He smiled. "Exciting
though this venture is, it will be good to come home, correct?"

Home, she thought: four walls of an apartment above
a banging city street. Books and television. She might

present a paper at the next scientific meeting, but no one would invite her to the parties afterward.

Am I that horrible? she wondered. I know I'm not anything to look at, but I try to be nice and interesting. Maybe I try too hard.

—You do not with me, Lucifer said.

"You're different," she told him.

Mazundar blinked. "Beg pardon?"

"Nothing," she said in haste.

"I have wondered about an item," Mazundar said in an effort at conversation. "Presumably Lucifer will go quite near the supernova. Can you still maintain contact with him? The time dilation effect, will that not change the frequency of his thoughts too much?"

"What time dilation?" She forced a chuckle. "I'm no physicist. Only a little librarian who turned out to have a wild talent."

"You were not told? Why, I assumed everybody was. An intense gravitational field affects time just as a high velocity does. Roughly speaking, processes take place more slowly than they do in clear space. That is why light from a massive star is somewhat reddened. And our supernova core retains almost three solar masses. Furthermore, it has acquired such a density that its attraction at the surface is, ah, incredibly high. Thus by our clocks it will take infinite time to shrink to the Schwarzschild radius; but an observer on the star itself would experience this whole shrinkage in a fairly short period."

"Schwarzschild radius? Please explain." Eloise realized that Lucifer had spoken through her.

"If I can without mathematics. You see, this mass we are to study is so great and so concentrated that no force exceeds the gravitational. Nothing can counterbalance. Therefore the process will continue until no energy can escape. The star will have vanished out of the universe. In fact, theoretically the contraction will proceed to zero volume. Of course, as I said, that will take forever as far as we are concerned. And the theory neglects quantum-mechanical considerations which come into play toward the end. Those are still not very well understood. I hope,

from this expedition, to acquire more knowledge."
Mazundar shrugged. "At any rate, Miss Waggoner, I was
wondering if the frequency shift involved would not prevent our friend from communicating with us when he is
near the star."

"I doubt that." Still Lucifer spoke; she was his instrument, and never had she known how good it was to be
used by one who cared. "Telepathy is not a wave phenomenon. Since it transmits instantaneously, it cannot be.
Nor does it appear limited by distance. Rather, it is a
resonance. Being attuned, we two may well be able to
continue thus across the entire breadth of the cosmos;
and I am not aware of any material phenomenon which
could interfere."

"I see." Mazundar gave her a long look. "Thank you,"
he said uncomfortably. "Ah . . . I must get to my own
station. Good luck." He bustled off without stopping for
an answer.

Eloise didn't notice. Her mind was become a torch
and a song. "Lucifer!" she cried aloud. "Is that true?"

—I believe so. My entire people are telepaths, hence
we have more knowledge of such matters than yours do.
Our experience leads us to think there is no limit.

"You can always be with me? You always will?"

—If you so wish, I am gladdened.

The comet body curvetted and danced, the brain of
fire laughed low. —Yes, Eloise, I would like very much
to remain with you. No one else has ever—Joy. Joy. Joy.

They named you better than they knew, Lucifer, she
wanted to say, and perhaps she did. They thought it was
a joke; they thought by calling you after the devil they
could make you safely small like themselves. But Lucifer
isn't the devil's real name. It means only "light bearer."
One Latin prayer even addresses Christ as Lucifer. Forgive me, God, I can't help remembering that. Do You
mind? He isn't Christian, but I think he doesn't need to
be; I think he must never have felt sin, Lucifer, Lucifer.

She sent the music soaring for as long as she was permitted.

The ship jumped. In one shift of world line parameters she crossed twenty-five light-years to destruction.

Each knew it in his own way, save for Eloise who also lived it with Lucifer.

She felt the shock and heard the outraged metal scream, she smelled the ozone and scorch and tumbled through the infinite falling that is weightlessness. Dazed, she fumbled at the intercom. Words crackled through: ". . . unit blown . . . back EMF surge . . . how should I know how long to fix the blasted thing? . . . Stand by, stand by. . . ." Over all hooted the emergency siren.

Terror rose in her, until she gripped the crucifix around her neck and the mind of Lucifer. Then she laughed in the pride of his might.

He had whipped clear of the ship immediately on arrival. Now he floated in the same orbit. Everywhere around, the nebula filled space with unrestful rainbows. To him, *Raven* was not the metal cylinder which human eyes would have seen, but a lambency, the shield screen reflecting a whole spectrum. Ahead lay the supernova core, tiny at this remove but alight, alight.

—Have no fears (he caressed her). I comprehend. Turbulence is extensive, this soon after the detonation. We emerged in a region where the plasma is especially dense. Unprotected for the moment before the guardian field was reestablished, your main generator outside the hull was short-circuited. But you are safe. You can make repairs. And I, I am in an ocean of energy. Never was I more alive. Come, swim these tides with me.

Captain Szili's voice yanked her back. "Waggoner! Tell that Aurigean to get busy. We've spotted a radiation source on an intercept orbit, and it may be too much for our screen." He specified coordinates. "What is it?"

For the first time, Eloise felt alarm in Lucifer. He curved about and streaked from the ship.

Presently his thought came to her, no less vivid. She lacked words for the terrible splendor she viewed with him: a million-kilometer ball of ionized gas where luminance blazed and electric discharges leaped, booming through the haze around the star's exposed heart. The thing could not have made any sound, for space here was still almost a vacuum by Earth's parochial standards; but she heard it thunder, and felt the fury that spat from it.

She said for him: "A mass of expelled material. It must have lost radial velocity to friction and static gradients, been drawn into a cometary orbit, held together for a while by internal potentials. As if this sun were trying yet to bring planets to birth—"

"It'll strike us before we're in shape to accelerate," Szili said, "and overload our shield. If you know any prayers, use them."

"Lucifer!" she called; for she did not want to die, when he must remain.

—I think I can deflect it enough, he told her with a grimness she had not hitherto met in him. —My own fields, to mesh with its; and free energy to drink; and an unstable configuration; yes, perhaps I can help you. But help me, Eloise. Fight by my side.

His brightness moved toward the juggernaut shape.

She felt how its chaotic electromagnetism clawed at his. She felt him tossed and torn. The pain was hers. He battled to keep his own cohesion, and the combat was hers. They locked together, Aurigean and gas cloud. The forces that shaped him grappled as arms might; he poured power from his core, hauling that vast tenuous mass with him down the magnetic torrent which streamed from the sun; he gulped atoms and thrust them backward until the jet splashed across heaven.

She sat in her cubicle, lending him what will to live and prevail she could, and beat her fists bloody on the desk.

The hours brawled past.

In the end, she could scarcely catch the message that flickered out of his exhaustion: —Victory.

"Yours," she wept.

—Ours.

Through instruments, men saw the luminous death pass them by. A cheer lifted.

"Come back," Eloise begged.

—I cannot. I am too spent. We are merged, the cloud and I, and are tumbling in toward the star. (Like a hurt hand reaching forth to comfort her:) Do not be afraid for me. As we get closer, I will draw fresh strength from its glow, fresh substance from the nebula. I will need a while to spiral out against that pull. But how can I fail to come back to you, Eloise? Wait for me. Rest. Sleep.

Her shipmates led her to sickbay. Lucifer sent her dreams of fire flowers and mirth and the suns that were his home.

But she woke at last, screaming. The medic had to put her under heavy sedation.

He had not really understood what it would mean to confront something so violent that space and time themselves were twisted thereby.

His speed increased appallingly. That was in his own measure; from *Raven* they saw him fall through several days. The properties of matter were changed. He could not push hard enough or fast enough to escape.

Radiation, stripped nuclei, particles born and destroyed and born again, sleeted and shouted through him. His substance was peeled away, layer by layer. The supernova core was a white delirium before him. It shrank as he approached, ever smaller, denser, so brilliant that brilliance ceased to have meaning. Finally the gravitational forces laid their full grip upon him.

—Eloise! he shrieked in the agony of his disintegration —Oh, Eloise, help me!

The star swallowed him up. He was stretched infinitely long, compressed infinitely thin, and vanished with it from existence.

The ship prowled the farther reaches. Much might yet be learned.

Captain Szili visited Eloise in sickbay. Physically she was recovering.

"I'd call him a man," he declared through the machine mumble, "except that's not praise enough. We weren't even his kin, and he died to save us."

She regarded him from eyes more dry than seemed natural. He could just make out her answer. "He is a man. Doesn't he have an immortal soul too?"

"Well, uh, yes, if you believe in souls, yes, I'd agree."

She shook her head. "But why can't he go to his rest?"

He glanced about for the medic and found they were alone in the narrow metal room. "What do you mean?" He made himself pat her hand. "I know, he was a good friend of yours. Still, his must have been a merciful death. Quick, clean; I wouldn't mind going out like that."

"For him . . . yes, I suppose so. It has to be. But—" She could not continue. Suddenly she covered her ears. "Stop! Please!"

Szili made soothing noises and left. In the corridor he encountered Mazundar. "How is she?" the physicist asked.

The captain scowled. "Not good. I hope she doesn't crack entirely before we can get her to a psychiatrist."

"Why, what is wrong?"

"She thinks she can hear him."

Mazundar smote fist into palm. "I hoped otherwise," he breathed.

Szili braced himself and waited.

"She does," Mazundar said. "Obviously she does."

"But that's impossible! He's dead!"

"Remember the time dilation," Mazundar replied. "He fell from the sky and perished swiftly, yes. But in supernova time. Not the same as ours. To us, the final stellar collapse takes an infinite number of years. And telepathy has no distance limits." The physicist started walking fast, away from that cabin. "He will always be with her."

ONE UNIQUENESS OF SCIENCE FICtion is its freemasonry. In no other kind of literature do authors, editors, artists, publishers, and readers have such widespread and often intimate personal acquaintance. To be sure, the fans who seek contact are a very small percentage of the total audience; still, attendance at the annual world convention these days runs to a couple of thousand. And as for the professionals, only a few hold themselves entirely aloof. Many of my dearest friends I met through science fiction, as well as a girl who soon became what my life is all about.

Because of this, a lot of what is done in the field has wildly informal origins. People will start kicking an idea around, and somebody will exclaim, "Hey, suppose—" and somebody else will happen to know that such-and-such an editor should like the proposal, and away we go. I believe the project of which this story was a part began thus; and I know that my own contribution is due to the chance that I was present when Keith Laumer and Gordon Dickson were discussing the notion.

The notion was that Keith would provide five different writers, including himself, with

7

133

a short narrative passage; each would take off from there in any direction he saw fit; and the results would be published between the same covers. The others co-opted were Frank Herbert and Harlan Ellison; the book was *Five Fates;* and Keith's gift to us was the section, ending with a deliberate misquotation of certain famous lines, with which this story opens.

# THE FATAL FULFILLMENT

<<<<<<<<<<<<<<<<<<<<<<<<<<<<<<<<<<<<<<<<<<<<<<<<<<<<<

## Prologue

"LEFT HAND," THE THIN MAN SAID TONE-
lessly. "Wrist up."

Douglas Bailey peeled back his cuff; the thin man put
something cold against it, nodded toward the nearest
door.

"Through there, first slab on the right," he said.

"Just a minute," Bailey started. "I wanted—"

"Let's get going, buddy," the thin man said. "That stuff
is fast."

Bailey felt something stab up under his heart. "You
mean—you've already . . . that's all there is to it?"

"That's what you came for, right? Slab one, friend.
Let's go."

"But—I haven't been here two minutes—"

"Whaddayou expect—organ music? Look, pal." The
thin man shot a glance at the wall clock. "I'm on my
break, know what I mean?"

"I thought I'd at least have time for . . . for . . . "

"Have a heart, chum. You make it under your own
power, I don't have to haul you, see?" The thin man was
pushing open the door, urging Bailey through into an odor
of chemicals and unalive flesh. In a narrow, curtained al-
cove, he indicated a padded cot.

"On your back, arms and legs straight out."

Bailey assumed the position, tensed as the thin man began fitting straps over his ankles.

"Relax. It's just if we get a little behind and I don't get back to a client for maybe a couple hours and they stiffen up . . . well, them issue boxes is just the one size, you know what I mean?"

A wave of softness, warmness swept over Bailey as he lay back.

"Hey, you didn't eat nothing the last twelve hours?" The thin man's face was a hazy pink blur.

"I awrrr mmmm," Bailey heard himself say.

"Okay, sleep tight, paisan. . . ." The thin man's voice boomed and faded. Bailey's last thought as the endless blackness closed in was of the words cut in the granite over the portal to the Euthanasia Center:

". . . Send me your tired, your poor, your hopeless, yearning to be free. To them I raise the lamp beside the brazen door. . . ."

Then the poison immobilized his hemoglobin and he was dead.

Death was a stormwind. It was as if he were blown, whirled, cast up and down and up again, in a howl and a whistle and a noise of monstrous gallopings. He did not know whether the wind was searing him with cold or heat. Nor did he wonder about it, for the lightnings blinded his eyes and the thunders rattled his teeth.

Eyes? flashed a moment's startlement. Teeth? But I'm dead. That application I had to fill out in triplicate will be stamped "COMPLETED," and a bored attendant will wheel me and my box to the crematorium chute and yo-heave-ho. And I will be transfigured; I will no more be Douglas Bailey but a statistic.

He clawed after reality, any reality, but grabbed only chaos. Dizziness sucked him through an infinite spiral. Somewhere and everywhere God was counting, "Zero, one, ten, eleven, one hundred, one hundred one, one hundred ten, one hundred eleven, one thousand, one thousand one, one thousand ten," in a small dry voice. Bailey believed that his nonexistent stomach had turned into an octopus with guts for tentacles. It would eat him and thus itself, but that was all right, because the universe inside Douglas Bailey was topologically identical with Douglas Bailey inside the universe, and so maybe when the universe swallowed itself he would be free of his madness.

Must be sensory deprivation, he thought in the maelstrom. Being dead, I have no body, therefore no senses, therefore no sensory input, therefore I hallucinate, therefore I must already have been reduced to ash; as I have no way to gauge time, if time has any meaning after death, centuries may have gone since I became a statistic. Poor little statistic, blown forever in the storm and the counting. I shouldn't have been in such a hurry to die.

Why was I?

I can't remember. I can't remember. There were the buildings, yes, and tastefully landscaped grounds. I entered—did I?—yes, I think I came in looking for, oh, counsel. Maybe someone to tell me I wasn't that badly off yet, that I ought to go home and think it over. But already my transformation had begun. The moment I crossed that threshold, I was not a man but a category, to be shunted from desk to desk, courteously, smoothly, but so fast I had no chance to think, inexorably to that room at the corridor's end.

What went before my last hour? I don't know.

"One hundred thousand one hundred ten," counted God, "one hundred thousand one hundred eleven, one hundred thousand one thousand."

I don't know! the statistic screamed. I can't remember!

"One hundred thousand one thousand one, one hundred thousand one thousand ten."

Why did they do it to me? cried the fragments. Why did they let me? They knew I was too sick to think.

"One hundred thousand one thousand eleven."

More than that. Too many more of us. But giving us our freedom to choose death was no freedom. They murdered us.

"One hundred thousand one thousand one hundred."

Shut up, damn You! Where were You when they murdered me? Why did You let them? They were no saner

than the pathetic swarms, psychotic, neurotic, psychoneurotic, they invited to come to die. That was no way to
behave. They could have cured us—could have tried,
anyhow—they should not have—

*Click,* said God. And there was silence, and darkness
was upon the face of the deep.

—not have given us that saving-their-own-smugness
"choice." They should have shouldered their responsibility to us, committed us, compelled us to get well.

Let there be Douglas Bailey. And there was Douglas
Bailey.

### Fate the Second

They caught him practicing solitary vice in his affluent
bachelor's apartment. The door flew open. Two large men
entered. "Stop where you're at," one of them said in a
gravel-truck basso. "Hands up. Stand back. This is a
raid."

The fact was like a boot to the stomach. Bailey
lurched, almost fell, and strangled for breath. Sunlight
and traffic murmurs through an open window, familiar
shapes of chairs, tables, drapes, clean smell of turpentine,
were suddenly unreal in his awareness. Instead he knew
his pulsebeat, sweat on his skin, strength gone from his
knees.

"Okay," said the other detective to the building superintendent. That little man cowered in the hall. "Beat it."

"Y—yes, sir. Right away!"

"But don't leave your own place. Somebody will want
to talk with you later."

"Of course," chattered the superintendent. "Anything
I can do to help." He scuttled from sight.

He must have furnished a passkey, Bailey thought in
the sickness that held him by the throat. So every precaution had been for nothing.

"Well, well, well." The first detective planted himself
before the easel. "Whaddayou think of this, Joe?"

"Looks like a case for sure." They were hard to tell apart, those two, when one's mind was splitting with terror. They were dressed alike in correctly drab civilian clothes; they were both crew-cut, slab-faced, and over-poweringly big; they regarded his work with equal, slightly sickened distaste, as if it were the leftovers from an ax murder.

"But that's just a hobby of mine!" Bailey heard himself croak. "I never—I never—never any secret—everybody knows I paint pictures—why, the President recommends hobbies—"

"This kind of picture?" Joe snorted.

"You don't show stuff like this around, do you, now?" Joe's companion added.

*No,* Bailey thought. *I was careful.*

Item: The conventional works he turned out, landscapes, portraits, tinkering with them like Penelope with her web. They bored him, but should have forestalled any curiosity about the art supplies in his home.

Item: His door locked whenever he painted in earnest. A false-backed cabinet open, ready to receive and conceal the canvas, a standard picture half-finished and ready to substitute, in a total fifteen seconds of well-rehearsed motions . . . should there be a knock. Since the apartment was on a third floor, with a warehouse across the street, he had not needed to arouse suspicion by drawing any blinds.

Item: The location, not very convenient to his work, but right in the Haight-Ashbury district. Before the Mental Health Act, this had been a traditional hangout for eccentrics. Therefore it had been so thoroughly treated and cleansed—the very buildings torn down, reconstructed in hygienic styles, redevoted to sound purposes—that it became the most respectable part of San Francisco. Surveillance was close around the waterfront or Nob Hill. But the bourgeoisie of Haight-Ashbury? Why, they had the highest average stability index in the city.

Item: The whole concealment that was his life.

Was that what betrayed him in the end: himself? Too much laughter, or too little; insufficient ambition; negligence within social organizations; too little chastity or too much—had something like that made someone think Douglas Bailey had better be reported as a possible psycho? Maybe, maybe, maybe. But how was a sane man supposed to behave?

"Awright," Joe said, "let's see your cards."

"But it—it's only a painting . . . manner of Van Gogh—"

"Which ear do you figure to cut off?" Joe asked surprisingly. Or perhaps not surprisingly. They said the mental health squad of this town maintained a collection of pathological, pornographic, and other prohibited work that compared favorably with the FBI's.

The second man continued staring at the violent blues and yellows of the buttercup field Bailey had been doing. "Flowers don't grow that big," he said. "And you got no perspeckative." He shook his head, clicked his tongue. "Man, you're sick."

"That's for the Clinic to decide," Joe said. "But let's see those cards, Mac."

Bailey got out his wallet in a mechanical fashion. Joe flipped through the driver's license, work permit, draft card, immunization record, permit to consume alcoholic beverages, social security, library card—"Hey, whatcha doing with a Class B?"

"I'm a sociologist," Bailey mumbled. "Research. I need to consult specialized books sometimes . . . journals—"

"Yeah? Next thing you'll put in for a Class A, huh, and maybe check out a copy of Krafft-Ebing?" Joe laughed, but kept on until he found the psychocheck record.

"See," Bailey got past the dryness in his gullet. "Properly punched. Every year for the—the . . . past six years? . . . Just as the law requires. Last time was . . . four months ago?"

"Look, friend," Joe said with elaborate weariness, "let's not play games. You know how much one lousy annual EEG shows, when you got three hundred million people in the country to give it to. If that could spot all the whackos, I'd be out of a job, wouldn't I, now?" He

tucked the wallet inside his coat. "You might as well
sit down, Bailey. In that corner, out of the way. Come on,
Sam, let's give this place the once over quick."

The other man nodded and went to the bookshelf.
From his pocket he extracted a list of titles which he compared with those on the volumes. It was a slow process,
especially since everything in a dust wrapper must be
opened, and others at random to be certain nothing had
been re-bound. His lips moved. Joe was more organized,
ransacking drawers like a terrier chasing rats.

Bailey sat in an armchair as directed. A numbness
crept up into him. Why care? What did it matter? If only
he could sleep. *Perchance to dream, to sleep, to die. . . .
No, wait, there you go. Withdrawal. Retreat. The wish
for isolation. The basic schizoid pattern, that you've
fought, adapted to (?), hidden ever since the treatment
of mental illness was made compulsory—because I am
not insane, not, not, not.*

*But I am so tired. If only the world would go away and
leave me alone.*

After an hour, Joe and Sam compared notes. They
hadn't found the secret compartment, but there appeared
to be significance in various items. Bailey didn't know
what or which. He was sure that he'd left nothing forbidden out in the open. But no doubt the law allowed a good
many things, simply because their possession was indic-
ative to the trained eye. Bailey had no idea what the
things might be—psychiatric information above the most
elementary level wasn't available to anyone without an A
card—and the detectives muttered too low for him to
overhear much.

It didn't matter. His apathy had reached black full
tide.

"Okay, we'll take him in and arrange for a detail to
come and pull this joint apart," Joe said.

"You mean you and me didn't?" Sam must be new to
this business, probably transferred from another division.

"Sheest, no! Why'd you think orders is to put everything back the way you found it? A real expert can tell
you from, uh, the way his underwear is folded whether

down underneath the whacko wants to murder his father or hump his mother."

"Or both?" Sam grinned.

"In this case, could be, I guess. You remember we got an urgency warrant on him. 'Nother reason why we better get him up there pronto." Joe strode to the chair—the floor trembled ever so faintly beneath his weight—and grabbed Bailey's arm. "On your feet, tubehead. Got a nice doctor waiting to see you."

Bailey dragged along with them. They stopped to lock the door and placard it. Word must have run through the building, for the corridors and stairs were empty. Footfalls echoed.

The sunlight outside was heartlessly brilliant, pouring from a summer sky where a few gulls wheeled on rakish wings. Such a day even managed to brighten the stiff utilitarian façades that lined the street, the stiff utilitarian garments of pedestrians going soberly about their business. Cars purred past with electric quiet; they still had a certain gaudiness, Bailey thought. The police vehicle was unmarked, a 1989 Chevrolet, and therefore it had a bubble canopy.

In a flicker of rebellion, Bailey exclaimed, "Why?"

Joe gave him a hard look. "Why what?"

"Civilian cars. Required to have fully visible interiors. Isn't that carrying our anti-privacy fetish to ridiculous extremes?"

Sam pulled out a notebook and started writing. "How do you spell 'ridiculous'?" he asked.

"Oh, never mind," Joe said. Bailey fell silent again. Joe unlocked the car and took the wheel. The other two sat in the rear. Because Bailey had no wish to look at either of his captors, he stared out at the view as it passed.

They went by the local service telly. For the first time since he had moved to this area and learned to ignore that screen, he paid attention. It was set into a wall near a bus stop. As usual when there was no particular announcement to make, it urged hygiene upon the public.

"Not like this!" it shouted, and for a moment flashed

the image of a squalid person who crouched and gibbered while picking imaginary fleas off himself. The moment was short, lest a latent hypochondria be triggered in some viewer. "Like this!" There followed an all-American family: stalwart father, beautiful though decorous and not too bosomy mother, four healthful children, marching into the future with toothpaste smiles. The children were, in order, one Nordic, one Negro, one Oriental, and one whose Jewish nose was exaggerated precisely enough to be unmistakable. The avoidance of tension-producing minority-group grievances was, after all, more important than strict genetics. "Yes, like this!" (Flourish of trumpets.) "To be clean, to be straight, to be happy—" (Ruffle of drums.) "THINK CLEAN! THINK STRAIGHT! THINK HAPPY!"

A little farther on was a poster which, Bailey recalled, offered a reward of ten thousand dollars ($10,000) for information leading to the arrest and treatment of any person suffering from unreported psychic disorder.

On the sidewalk nearby, a uniformed policeman handed a summons to a middle-aged woman. Maybe she'd back-talked him, maybe it was a spot check; at any rate, Bailey recognized the pink slip. "You are hereby directed to report to the center at which you are registered . . . prior to the date of . . . examination and recertification of nervous stability . . . failure to comply without proof of impossibility will result in—" The woman looked more annoyed than frightened. You wouldn't have gotten as drastic a measure as the Act passed if a majority of the public had not felt something ought to be done about the growing incidence of mental illness. And the law would not have been enforceable without the cooperation of that same majority.

The police car took a route through a corner of Golden Gate Park, past Kezar Stadium. A grade-school hygiene class sat on the lawn, in neat white uniforms. Before them stood their teacher. She was young and comely, and you didn't often see that much exposed female flesh anymore. (What a narrow tightrope to walk, between causing shame at natural functions on the one hand and exciting prurient interest on the other!) Once Bailey had enjoyed such spectacles. He would switch his attention from what she chanted: "Now, children, this is Good-thinking time. Let us first think about the beautiful sunshine. A-one, and a-two, and a-three, and a-four. . . ." But today he was enclosed in his private night. And the car whipped him by too fast.

The street climbed steeply, until at its crest the Clinic buildings appeared like sheer cliffs. Bailey remembered when this had been the University Medical Center. But that was before a single class of diseases got absolute priority.

The car stopped at the main gate for identification. Beyond a pair of burly guards could be seen the usual queue at the dispensary: outpatients, borderline cases require to report daily for their prescribed tranquilizers. In spite of all the propaganda about emotional problems being no more disgraceful than any other kind, the line shuffled in the entrance with hanging heads, and slunk out the exit, each individual alone. The attendant who kept them moving was bored and hardly polite.

*Still . . . maybe I could have escaped with that,* Bailey thought. *Had I confessed the turmoil in me at the very beginning, maybe it could have been arrested; I could have been adjusted—but no.* He slumped. *I didn't want to be adjusted. I wanted to go my own way. And now it's too late.* In his wretchedness, he hardly noticed when the car started again, or when it stopped and he was conducted into the very biggest house. The elevator that bore him upward, though, was so like a coffin built for three that he must struggle not to scream.

Afterward there was a long hall, featureless, white, faintly rustling, faintly odorous of antiseptic. At the end was an office with a counter. An orderly sat behind it. Behind him, in turn, worked a number of secretaries and machines. They paid no attention to the new arrival.

"Here he is," Joe said. "Bailey."

"So let's get positive ID," the orderly said. He picked a form off a stack and handed it, with a pen, to Bailey.

It was clipped together with several carbons. "Fill this out."

# UNITED STATES DEPARTMENT OF HYGIENE
## Northern California Facility

### APPLICATION FOR TREATMENT

Form 1066                                                    Print or type

Name_____     Date_____
      (last)    (first)    (middle)              (month)   (day)   (year)

Sex M___ F___ MH___ FH ___   Other (specify)_____

Registry number_____     Birthdate_____
                                                (month)   (day)   (year)

Address_____     Occupation_____

Employer_____      Address_____

Name of spouse_____    Registry number_____
              (If none, write "none.")

(NB: If status is widowed or divorced, attach Schedule B-1.) Children
(List name, age, and sex of each minor child now living. Put only one
child per line and use only one line per child. If none, write "none." If
more space is needed, attach Schedule C-2.)

_____

_____

_____


Other dependents . . . Religious preference (If none,
write "Ecumenical.") . . . Outstanding debts . . .

Bailey raised his eyes.

"But this is an application," he said weakly. "I don't
have to fill it out, do I?"

"I guess not," the orderly said. "Only if you don't,
that proves you're incapable and you get an automatic
commitment."

Bailey wrote. Afterward he was finger-scanned and

retino-scoped. "Yep, that's him," the orderly said. "You boys can go now." He scribbled on a slip. "Your receipt."

"Thanks," Joe said. "So long, Mac. See you in the nut bowl. Come on, Sam." The detectives left.

The orderly spoke on an intercom. "You're in luck, Bailey," he reported. "Dr. Vogelsang can see you right away. I've known 'em to wait for three days before a doctor is free. Gets kind of dull."

Bailey followed him out into the hall, as a man walks helplessly through a dream. But the office which he reached startled him back to alertness. It was like nothing he had met hitherto: fumed-oak paneling; deep rugs; a couple of tasteful Chinese scrolls; music, yes, by heaven, soft but absolutely the "Moonlight Sonata"; and the man behind the desk, small, white-haired, kindly featured, almost recklessly colorful in his garb. He rose to shake hands.

"Welcome aboard, Mr. Bailey," he smiled. "I'm so glad to meet you. That'll be all, Roger."

"You don't think he should be, uh, restrained?" the orderly asked.

"Oh, no," Dr. Vogelsang said. "Of course not." When the door had closed and they were alone: "You must excuse him, Mr. Bailey. Frankly, he's not too bright. But we have so big a job here, so much to do, we must manage with what personnel we can get. Please sit down. Cigarette? Or I have cigars here, if you prefer."

Bailey lowered himself into an extraordinarily comfortable chair. "I . . . I don't smoke," he said. "But if— a drink, maybe? . . ."

Vogelsang astounded him with a laugh. "Why, sure! Excellent idea. Don't mind if I do myself. The oldest tranquilizer, and still one of the best, eh? How about Scotch?" He used his intercom.

Bailey couldn't meet the twinkling eyes, but he did ask, "What got me brought here?"

"Oh, various information. People who have your welfare at heart. They suggested we check on you. And, frankly, there were some rather disturbing things in your record. Things that should have been studied more closely a long time ago—and would have been, eventually, but as I said, we're understaffed. We must depend to a large extent, as yet, on the patient himself, on his educated ability to recognize early symptoms, his educated willingness to come straight in for help.". Dr. Vogelsang beamed. "But please don't imagine anyone is angry that you didn't. We realize that you aren't fully your own master at present. Our one desire is to cure you. You have a fine mind, intrinsically, you know, Mr. Bailey. Your IQ puts you in the upper five percent. Society needs minds like yours—minds liberated from guilts, terrors, metabolic imbalances, whatever makes them operate at less than half efficiency and makes the person so very unhappy—ah. Here we are."

A nurse came in with a tray. On the tray stood bottle, ice bucket, glasses, soda. She smiled on Bailey as warmly as her boss.

"To your very good health," Vogelsang toasted.

"What . . . are you going to do?" Bailey dared say.

"Why, nothing much. We'll want to run a lot of diagnostic tests and so on before we decide on any course of action. Don't worry. I'm convinced we'll have you out of here before Christmas."

The Scotch was good. The talk was pleasant. Bailey wondered if rumor might not have exaggerated what went on in the Clinic.

And, indeed, the first few days consisted of little more than interviews, multiphasic questionnaires, Rorschachs, narcosynthesis, laboratory studies—exhausting, often embarrassing, but in no way unendurable.

However, then they decided he belonged in Ward Seven. That was for the seriously disturbed cases.

In Ward Seven they tried shock, both insulin and electric. This reduced the notable IQ by a noticeable percentage. When that didn't work, they considered surgery, either prefrontal lobotomy or transorbital leucotomy. Since Bailey had by now met quite a few of the two-legged vegetables that resulted from such treatment, he screamed and tried to fight. He sobbed his grat-

itude when Dr. Vogelsang overruled the suggestion and
ordered the new, somewhat experimental excitation
therapy. For this, he was strapped down while a low-
frequency current passed through his nerves. It was the
ultimate pain. Dr. Vogelsang watched every minute.

"Tsk, tsk," he said after a week or two, and shook
his white head. "No success, eh? Well, I'm afraid we
can't continue like this. But we must dissolve those bad
thought patterns somehow, must we not? Your trouble
doesn't seem to be in your glandular chemistry, you
know. Nothing that simple. We'll use a few Pavlovian
techniques and hope for the best."

Dream deprivation. Sleep deprivation. Cold. Heat.
Hunger. Thirst. Ringing bells. Rewards when the proper
thoughts were recited. Punishment when they were not.
But the effects remained disappointing. At least, according to depth analysis they were; Bailey no longer knew
what he believed. "Dear me, dear me," Dr. Vogelsang
said, "I'm afraid we must go one step further. The
Pavlovians often get decisive results with castration."

Bailey leaped to attack him, but the choke-collar leash
brought him up short. *"You can't do this to me!"* he
howled. "I've got my rights!"

"Come, now. Come, now. Be reasonable. You know
as well as I, the Supreme Court declared the Mental
Health Act constitutional under the interstate commerce
clause. Please don't worry. The operation won't hurt a
bit. I'll preform it myself. And of course, first we'll
deep-freeze some spermatozoa. You'll want children
after you're cured. Every normal man does."

But that didn't work either.

"I don't believe we should go further along these
lines," said gentle Dr. Vogelsang. "They do have their
distressing aspects, don't they? And in your case, for
some reason they only seem to increase your basic hos-
tility. I think we had better rebuild you."

"Rebuild?" Bailey's mind groped through the haze
that had lately enclosed it. "Wuh. Kill me? You gonna
kill me?"

"Oh, no! No, no, no! Gossip is *so* distorted, no matter

how hard we attempt to enlighten the public. True, rebuilding has replaced capital punishment. But that
doesn't mean you are a criminal. Rather, it means that
the criminal is a sick man also, like you. We wouldn't
dream of going back to the barbaric waste of legalized
murder." Dr. Vogelsang grew quite indignant. "Especially in your case. You have a wonderful potential. It's
merely being held down by bad attitudes that, unfortunately, have become integral to your personality.
So"—he glowed—"we start over again. Eh? A recent
technique, but perfectly safe, perfectly reliable. Electro-
chemical treatment reverses the RNA formation which
is the physical basis of memory. Every memory, every
habit, every last, bad, old engram goes. You start out
clean, fresh, sparkling new. A *tabula rasa* on which
experts will inscribe a different, sane, outgoing, friendly,
adjusted, efficient personality! Won't that be nice?"

"Uh," said Bailey. He wished they'd go away and let
him sleep.

But when at length he was boxed in the helmet,
secured to a bed while drugs dripped into his veins, and
the whine rose, rose, rose, and he felt the departure of—

—sundown purple on the East Bay hills; the first girl
he had ever kissed, and the last; a curious old tavern,
one summer when he was young and on a walking tour
through England; white rush down a ski slope in the
High Sierra; Shakespeare, Beethoven, Van Gogh; work,
friends, father, mother, mother—

—the animal instincts revived, and he screamed aloud
in his agony of terror: "If this isn't death, what is?"

Then the last trace of what he had done with his
genetic endowment, and what had been done to it, was
scrubbed from him and he was dead.

Death was a stormwind. It was as if he were blown,
whirled, cast up and down and up again, in a howl and
a whistle and a noise of monstrous gallopings. He did not
know whether the wind was searing him with cold or
heat. Nor did he wonder about it, for the lightnings
blinded his eyes and the thunders rattled his teeth.

Eyes? flashed a moment's startlement. Teeth? But I'm dead. They'll use my body to make someone else. No, wait, that's not right. They'll cremate my body. I took voluntary euthanasia when I couldn't endure my own misery any longer. No, I didn't, either. I was wiped out of my own brain after they'd made me so miserable that it didn't really matter.

"Zero," God counted, "one, ten, eleven, one hundred, one hundred ten."

Bailey grabbed for reality, any reality, in the torrents of night. Dizziness sucked him through an infinite spiral. But the only reality was himself. He clutched that to him. I am Douglas Bailey, he thought against the devouring octopus. I am . . . I am . . . a sociologist. A madman. What else? I died twice, after two different horrible lives.

Were there more? I can't remember. The wind blows too hard.

Wait. A glimpse. No, gone.

"One thousand eleven," counted God the Simulator, "one thousand one hundred, one thousand one hundred one, one thousand one hundred ten."

Why are You doing this to me? Bailey screamed. You're as bad as they are. They killed me twice. Once with indifference. They called it freedom—freedom to choose death—but they didn't care about us, except they hoped we would reduce our own numbers. They withdrew from us, established automatic social machinery to process us, did their best to forget us. And again they killed me with hate. It had to be hate, cruelty, death wish, no matter how much they talked of cure. What else? How can you take a human being and make an object(ive) of him, unless your real aim is to make him less than human—make him a thing that crawls at your feet—because you hate his humanity?

"Ten thousand, ten thousand one, ten thousand ten, ten thousand eleven."

Space twisted back on itself and time split like the delta of the Styx. The wind blew and blew.

My problem was real. I was suffering. I needed help and love.

*Click.* The wind stopped. The darkness waited.

Please, wept Douglas Bailey. Help me. Care about me. Give me your love.

It was so.

## Fate the Third

Having finished his bathroom business, he suddenly spread his legs and looked between them.

*Now why should I do that?* he wondered. *I'm all there. Of course.*

*But not well,* he reminded himself. *Severe nervous breakdown, possible incipient schizophrenia. I was doing less rational things than this before they persuaded me to come here.*

Pulling his trousers up again, he stared into the mirror above the sink. The image was tall and broad-shouldered. He didn't think Birdie Carol was lying to him when she praised his body, at least. It was deteriorating, though: too little exercise, too many drugs. He didn't like that, but never got together the energy to do anything about it. And the face was shocking, waxy cheeks, sunken smudge-circled eyes, the dark hair unkempt.

He had no way of measuring exactly his downhill progress. Few people did. The thing happened so gradually. But he knew that, after the brief euphoria that followed his admission to the hospital, he was getting worse fast. Mentally as well as physically—physically because mentally—he was in far poorer shape than when he entered.

Which shouldn't be. By every theory, it shouldn't be.

A tic in one eyelid. He turned from the spectacle. This made him confront the walls. They were pink, with painted teddy bears and hobby horses. He detested pink. "And I could do without kiddy pictures in the can, too," he had grumbled.

Birdie had patted his knee. They were side by side on the living-room couch. "I know, dear," she said, "but Dr. Breed thinks it's helpful in the long run. And frankly, I think he's right."

"How so?"

"Well, the idea is to re-create your childhood. That is, the love and trust and innocence you had then. I know that sounds silly, but a nursery motif ought to remind your poor subconscious of what it's lost, and remind it that there's a way back."

"What love and trust and innocence?" Bailey said. "I remember my childhood quite well, and it was perfectly typical. I was dragooned into school and loathed every minute. The neighborhood bully used to lie in wait for me on my way home and beat me up. But for some reason I never could tell my parents. Once or twice I read a ghost story, and lay awake every night for weeks, full of the horrors. My puppy was run over. I got caught at—"

"Hush, darling." She laid one large smooth hand across his lips and leaned close to him. The cologne she always wore smelled overpoweringly sweet. "I know. We mean an ideal childhood. You have to learn—deep, deep down inside—you have to learn how to love. And how to be loved. Then you'll be well."

"Look," he said, his exasperation growing geometrically, "suppose my trouble isn't an autistic neurosis or whatever label you've hung on. Suppose it's organic schizophrenia. What's that got to do with this love you keep mooing about?"

Birdie smiled with infinite patience. "Love is a basic requirement of the mammalian life form," she said. "We are mammalian life forms." Her build left no doubt of that. "Little babies in orphanages used to die because they weren't cuddled. If you get some love, but not enough, you mature starved for it. The deficiency warps and weakens you as rickets would. What we are doing is giving you the love you need to become straight and strong."

He jumped to his feet. "I've heard that over and over till I'm ready to vomit!" he shouted. "What about true psychosis?"

"Well, yes, I suppose that is a metabolic thing," Birdie answered. "Or so the scientists believe. Though I think every such illness must also start because there wasn't enough love. Don't you think so?"

"I—I—"

"In any event," she said, "schizophrenia amounts to a loss of communication with the outside world. We have no hope of a cure without reestablishing communication, have we? Just think, darling, and you'll see I'm right. But love is the bridge across all gaps."

Bailey longed to reply with a swear word, preferably obscene. But those he could recall were too feeble. Birdie rose, tossed back her blonde hair, and unbuttoned her dress. "I think we should make love again," she said briskly.

He hadn't much wanted to, but she urged him—and what the hell else was there to do—so they ended in the bedroom. Only this time he hadn't been able to make anything happen. She was very sympathetic, cradled him in her arms and sang him to sleep. However, first he had needed a barbiturate.

Maybe that recollection was what had now made him worry about—*Nuts! Not a thing wrong with me in that department, except I've gotten so bloody fed up with*—

He left the bathroom. His suite was not large, but comfortable and pleasantly furnished. He prowled to the living-room window and looked out. It was barred, but only against possible sleepwalking, he had been assured. He had the entire freedom of the grounds. As soon as he got better, he could draw weekend passes. Meanwhile, any loved ones he wished could come here to visit him.

The view, from this twentieth floor of the largest building in the Medical Center, was magnificent in its distances. Golden Gate Park spread green toward the ocean, which blazed with sunlight. He glimpsed the bridge that soared across the bay's mouth, water glittering away to the hills of the eastern shore, gulls, boats, ships, aircraft. A breeze wandered in, cool, smelling of the sea, and brought a remote traffic sound.

Too remote, though; too muted; and apart from the pride that was this hilltop complex, San Francisco showed decay, here a vacant store window, there a seedy tenement. Business was spiraling downward just like Douglas Bailey. As a sociologist, he had seen the data. No doubt existed, nor any reasonable doubt about the cause. If mental illness, at every level from mild eccentricity to complete insanity, was approaching epidemic proportions, and if the United States had assumed a national obligation to care for the victims as lavishly as was the case, the bill must be paid somehow. Between them, taxes and inflation were collecting it, with their usual side effects.

He'd argued against the policy. He still would, he supposed, in spite of having become one of its beneficiaries. But the warnings of that tiny minority to which he belonged were so much spent air. Either people refused to believe the facts of economic life, or they looked at you wide-eyed and asked, "Do you mean anything could be more important than the well-being of the people we love?"

Perhaps, he thought with brief and discouraged humor, the futility of his efforts had helped bring on the collapse that put him in here.

Then the sense of being caged and baited rose in him till he had no other awareness. He smashed his fist against the window sill, again and again and again. "God damn God. God damn God. God damn God." The chant gathered speed. "Goddamngod, goddamngod, goddamngod-goddamngod-goddamngodgoddamngodgoddamngodgoddamngod, WHOOOO, WHOO-OO, ch-ch-ch, ch-ch-ch, ch-ch-ch—"

"Duggie! What are you doing?"

Bailey stopped. Very slowly he turned around. Birdie Carol's plump figure filled the hall doorway. She carried a bouquet of buttercups. As always, her dress was civilian, rather flamboyant, with merely a pin to indicate that she was a psychiatric technician.

He swallowed some of his rage, though he nearly strangled on it, and retorted, "I might ask you the same."

"Why, I came to see you." She closed the door and bustled toward him. "Look, I've brought you flowers. You told me once you like buttercups. I love them, myself."

"Busting in on me like a—like a—a buster-in—"

"But darling, I couldn't leave you isolated. That's your whole problem, you know, isolation. Think for a minute and you'll see that I'm right. You should go out more." Having reached him, she stopped and patted his shoulder. "You really should. Go join the other patients in the recreation rooms. They're wonderful people when you get to know them, really they are. And the social hostesses are such dears too. They want to help you . . . help you enjoy yourself, help you get strong again. What is that beautiful old German saying? You know the one, it means—"

"*Kraft durch Freude,*" Bailey suggested.

"Does that mean 'strength through joy'? Because that's what I mean. But oh, dear, I must put these poor thirsty blossoms in water, mustn't I?" Birdie started off. Her yellow ringlets jiggled, but her hips swung like solid masses. There was, in fact, a solidity about every aspect of her, a kind of absolute physical control—even in bed with him on a hot afternoon, she hadn't sweated—that had been comforting at first: the Earth Mother image.

Only, should the Earth Mother babble?

"That was a Nazi motto," Bailey said.

"Oh, really? How interesting. You know so much, Duggie, darling. Once we get you well again, you'll be able to find so many wonderful ways to help others. Won't you?" She took an unbreakable plastic vase off a table and shook her head sadly at the dethorned roses already within. "Poor things. They have had their little day, I'm afraid. But if they helped brighten your life, that was their service, wasn't it?"

Bailey clenched his fists. "For instance," he said, "I

know the Nazis gassed people who didn't fit into their scheme. But at least they didn't preach positive thinking at them."

"No, I suppose not." Birdie sent the roses reverently down the waste chute and took the vase, the buttercups, and her enormous handbag into the bathroom. "That poor man—Hitler, was that his name?—how he must have been starved for love!"

She left the door open. He could have avoided seeing pink walls, teddy bears, and hobby horses by looking out the window. But for some morbid reason, he had to stare in that direction. Maybe, he thought, this enabled him to hate them better.

"No doubt it was most unkind of other countries to make war on the Nazis," he said around his teeth.

Birdie set her handbag down on the flush tank and rummaged in it. "Certainly," she replied. "I'm not saying that their prisoners should not have been rescued. If there really were prisoners. You know what wartime propaganda is like. With—what is it?—fifty years' perspective, do you really and truly believe any human beings could behave that way? Honestly, I can't."

"I can. I know what historical evidence is. I also know how human beings behave right now. Committing violent crimes, say."

"Yes, yes, darling, but don't you understand? Let's suppose those awful things were true. Or let's be realistic and think about those deeds today that, yes, I know, they are done . . . by poor, bewildered victims of an unfeeling society. Now, suppose that the people being attacked— or even people being herded into gas chambers and ovens, if they ever were—suppose they turned around and said, with love shining out of their eyes, 'You too are victims. You are our brothers. Come, let us embrace each other.'" Birdie leaned past the door to lay her own china-blue gaze directly upon him. "Don't you see what that would do? Can't you feel what a change would occur?"

"The method doesn't seem to have improved me any," Bailey said with a jerky gesture of shoulders.

"Well, it does take time." Birdie returned to her task. From her handbag she drew a pocketknife and began trimming the buttercup stems. "But true love is infinite," she said. "True love knows no impatience, no anger, no despair, no end."

He couldn't stop himself; he must take first one step toward her, then another, while a roaring mounted in his skull. "Do you love me?" he said in a voice that sounded remote and hollow to him. "Or am I only your assignment?"

"I love everyone," she cooed.

"In bed, too?"

"Oh, Duggie, love isn't jealous. Love is sharing. I use my body as just one way of loving you."

He was at the bathroom entrance, swaying on his feet. "But do you care for me?" he cried. "Me, alone, especially, not because I'm a—a—a featherless biped, but because I'm me!"

She didn't blush. He had never seen any such change in her creamy skin. But she did flutter her lashes downward. "Well," she murmured, "I have thought, sometimes, if it would make you happy, we could get married when you're well. Such a sweet name, don't you think? Birdie Bailey."

He screamed in his torment, snatched the knife from her, and cut and cut and cut.

"Please don't do that," she said. "That's not a loving act."

He slashed her belly open. For a moment, through the darkness that brawled around him, he saw the wires, transistors, thermogenic superconductor leads, heavy-duty accumulator. He would have stopped his assault, but his arm was already in motion.

The knife sliced the insulation around a cable. The powerplant short-circuited through him. It felt like hatred, lovely, clean, hell-blue hatred coursing inward, possessing him, making him one with its Ragnarok tide. But when his heart went into fibrillation, that hurt.

In a cloud of smoke, Douglas Bailey fell on Birdie Carol.

*Of course she's a machine,* thought his last fragment of consciousness. *No human being could've kept that up.*

Then his pulse stopped and he was dead.

Death was a stormwind. It was as if he were blown, whirled, cast up and down and up again, in a howl and a whistle and a noise of monstrous gallopings. He did not know whether the wind was searing him with cold or heat. Nor did he wonder about it, for the lightnings blinded his eyes and the thunders rattled his teeth.

Eyes? flashed a moment's startlement. Teeth? But I'm dead. . . . Wait a minute. Wait one bloody minute. How many deaths does that make?

"Zero," God counted, "one, ten, eleven, one hundred."

Why don't You give me a chance to think? he yelled.

By concentrating, he could maintain a certain equilibrium in chaos. He was Douglas Bailey. Sociologist. Psychoneurotic. Ending his life in an institution—three different lives and three different institutions, each as bad as the others.

Why was the Simulator doing this to him?

Well, the problem was real enough. Psychopathology was on the increase. Society had to cope somehow.

But none of those three attempts was successful. Not really. Murderous indifference; murderous malevolence; murderous love. Which latter wasn't actually love at all —anyhow, not a healthy kind. It was nothing but another way of trying to force people back into the very structure that had warped them.

Love was acceptance of the loved one, whether he seem right or wrong; adjusting your behavior to his, within reasonable limits, not his to yours; giving him his freedom while always standing by to help if there should come trouble.

"One hundred eleven, one thousand, one thousand one."

If social conditions were responsible for the epidemic, the cure lay in a basic reform. Change the conditions. Take off the unendurable pressures.

*Click.* Chaos rested.

No more compulsions, ordered Douglas Bailey. Let's have the world's first genuinely free civilization.

This he was granted.

## Fate the Fourth

"Sure, I'm bitter," said the man who sat at Bailey's left. He was in his thirties, medium-sized, sandy-haired, and very drunk. "Who wouldn't be?" He finished his bourbon on the rocks and set it noisily down on the bar. " 'Nother," he called. To his companion: "You care for 'nother?"

"No, thanks," Bailey said.

"Aw, c'mon. I'll buy. Leas' I can do, way I been bending your ear. Good o' you t'listen, me a stranger an' so forth. But if Jim Wyman—tha's my name, Jim Wyman —if Jim Wyman weeps on a shoulder, Jim Wyman 'spec's t' pay f' privilege."

"That's okay," Bailey said. "I'm interested in what you're telling me. I've been away for some years, you see. Just got back today. Things have changed."

"They sure have, Mr., uh, Mr.—they sure have. Place'll never be 'erself again, tha's f' sure. Bartender!" Wyman roared. "Where's 'at refill?"

Bailey clenched his jaw for an embarrassing scene. He didn't want to be thrown out. He wanted to rest in cool darkness, in the remembered elegance of mahogany and thick carpeting, nurse the single weak Scotch and water he dare allow himself, and spend an hour gathering back his courage. They had warned him that San Francisco, like every American city, had changed; they had not told him how shocking the change would be.

The bartender considered Wyman for a moment, shrugged, and poured. Another symptom, Bailey thought. The Drake's Tavern would never have served an obvious drunk aforetime. But when you looked twice, you also saw how dusty and shabby the Elizabethan decor had gone.

"You were telling me you do R and D on computers," he said in the hope of quieting Wyman.

It worked. The man's voice even became less slurred. "Yes. At the Med Center. Or rather, I did. Till yestiddy. Not now. Projec' canceled. And it would'a been the bigges' breakthrough since—since . . . No, bigger. Fun-damental!"

"What was the project?"

It turned out to be something that Bailey had seen discussed in theoretical terms before he fell sick. Direct man-machine linkages were an old idea, and of course the powered prosthetic limbs, hooked into an amputee's nervous system, that had been developed around 1980, were a familiar case. But integration of the human brain and a computer presented difficulties on another order of magnitude. The connection wasn't the problem. You didn't need wires into the skull or any such nonsense. By amplification and induction, impulses could flow both ways, neuron to transistor and back again, through purely electromagnetic channels. But how to develop a common language, that was the question. It had never been shown that any particular encephalographic pattern corresponded to any particular thought, and indeed the evidence was against it. Thought appeared to be the incredibly complex functioning of the entire cortical network.

"But we got th' basic approach," Wyman said. "We figured how to proceed. Idea is, you don't need any special codes. Jus' need a one-one match. Kind of like languages. You can say same thing in English an' German, to th' extent diff'rent words mean same thing. They proved in neurophysiology section, brain can incorporate any digital code into own processes, long's there's unique correspondence. Nex' the math boys worked out a bunch o' theorems. You see, new data made the whole problem one o' conformal mapping. Topological. You see? Once we had those theorems in our hot li'l fists, why, away we go. R and D. Develop right kind o' computer an' right kind programmin'—not easy, take effort, staff, sev'ral years' work—but we know damn well we can do it. An' do you know what success'd mean?"

Bailey nodded eagerly. He was feeling better minute by minute. Intoxicated though Wyman was, he talked the language of science. And to hear that, after the past lost years, was like homecoming. Bailey's discipline had been sociology, but it too was pretty well mathematized these days, and—

And the man-computer system had fantastic potentialities. In effect, the machine's immense store of data, memory-scanning rate, ability to perform logical operations in microseconds, would be added to—integrated with—the human's creativity and conation. During their linkage, the two would be one, a continuously self-programming calculator, a mind so powerful that IQ would have no meaning. They/he/it would, for the first time in intellectual history, consider the totality of a problem.

Certain obvious dangers must be guarded against, and no doubt less obvious ones would manifest themselves as work progressed. But the ultimate rewards seemed worth any risk.

"Well, we're not gonna do it." Wyman sagged above his glass. "No funds 'vailable. Got final word yestiddy. So now I'm busy gettin' stonkered."

"Why no funds?" Bailey asked. "I should think NSF would bury any such proposal under a truckload of gigabucks."

"Huh? Where you been, pal? Time past when NSF had money t' hand out. Nor NIH. We applied to 'em both. To ever'body in sight. Nope. Mental health too 'spensive. Otherwise government can barely keep a few existin' programs goin'. Defense—think Defense'd be in'ested, wouldn' you? Well, hell, yes, sure they're int-'rested, but you know what shape they're in. Air Force takin' payin' passengers, USS *Puerto Rico* on the high seas as a floatin' casino . . . jus' so the service can finance a nickel's worth o' defense. Tha's why we backed down on the Guyana issue last year. Oh, the President tried t' save face, yattered 'bout 'honorable settlement without military pressure' . . . but damn it, whole world knows

there was military pressure—on us—by *Venezuela,* f'
Chris' sake!'"

A tear dropped into Wyman's drink. "Damn that
man," he mumbled. "Damn him to the smoggies' pit in
Hell. Damn him till half pas' eternity. He's the one ruined
us. I bet the French government put 'im up to it. I bet
any 'mount you like, he wrote his books an' made his
speeches on purpose."

"Who are you talking about?" Bailey inquired.

"You know. The professor. The Frenchman. Can't
p'rnounce's goddamn name. One with th' ideas 'bout pre-
servin' the nuts."

"Wait a minute." Bailey stiffened in his chair. His skin
prickled. "You don't mean Michel Chanson d'Oiseau?"

"Tha's uh man. Tha's uh man. Shansong Dwahso. Bet
he was really a Chinese agent, name like that. He knew
this big, sloppy, soft-hearted, fat-headed country 'ud go
for his ideas—go overboard for'm—fall overboard, into
a sea o' manure. He's the one ruined us. Ruined my projec'. Ruined my country. Now we can't do damn thing
but support buncha worthless crackpated bums." Wyman
raised his glass. "Destruction to Shansong Dwaho!'"

"No." Bailey rose. His chair clattered to the floor.

"Huh?" Wyman blinked at him.

*I shouldn't let myself get angry,* Bailey knew. *I'm not
well yet. They told me I must be careful, not get excited,
always keep my emotions under control, till my nerves
have grown much steadier.* But the rage mounted nevertheless, chilling, nauseating, shaking him. He said
harshly, "For your information, I am one of those worthless crackpated bums."

"Uh? You?"

"Don't believe me?" Bailey drew his wallet out of his
pants. (He had said they really needn't issue him so good
a suit, but they told him that morale was important to his
recovery.) He flipped it open to the card that certified
him as mentally ill. "I was discharged this morning, after
five years in Napa State Hospital," he said. "Before I
took sick, I was a useful member of society. But then I
went through such a nightmare as you in your smugness

can't begin to imagine. They saved me at Napa. They couldn't have been more kind. As well as their knowledge permitted, they patched my mind together again. I'm on an outpatient basis now. When I'm fully cured, as I hope eventually I will be, I'll go back to work. And I'll gladly pay my share of the tax bill for helping those who aren't well."

"Bu—but—" Wyman tried to talk. Bailey trampled over him.

"What would you have the country do? In the past twenty years, the rate of mental illness has grown almost exponentially. You have to do something. What's your choice? Kill us? Brainscrub us? Exile us? Leave us to starve? Those are all possible policies. But I, along with a good many million fellow human beings, I say thank God that Chanson d'Oiseau showed us the decent way to handle the problem—and I say to hell with you!"

He dashed the contents of his glass in Wyman's face.

"Bartender!" Wyman screamed. "You see what he did? You see what this suck-the-public-tit psycho did uh me?"

"Watch your language," the bartender replied. "He's certified, isn't he? So the law says we gotta make allowances."

"It does?" Bailey exclaimed. Delighted, he emptied Wyman's glass over Wyman's head.

"Hey," the bartender said. "Have a heart, buddy. I got to clean up the mess."

Bailey turned on his heel and strode out.

Sunlight fell brilliant on the street from a cloudless sky full of wind and gulls. Bailey tried to ignore its illumination of the shabbiness of once-proud buildings, dirty sidewalks, drab display windows, scanty traffic, ill-clad pedestrians. The cost was certainly great, but the obligation must be met. As Chanson d'Oiseau had written—Bailey savored the noble, often-read passage in his mind, and turned it to English while he walked:

"Having shown in the foregoing chapters that epidemic madness arises from a situation that man has created, collectively (through overpopulation, overmechanization, regimentation, depersonalization, everything against

which the deepest instincts of the human animal revolt),
I now consider what must be done about these revolting
human animals. Their numbers are, in truth, creating
such a burden and a hazard that compassion for them
tends to die. Yet their condition, it is due not to any fault
of their own, but to a massive failure of society. Hence
one must find a social cure for this social disease.

"The solution that I shall propose and develop in detail
is of the most radical. But what does 'radical' mean? The
word comes from the Latin *radix,* meaning Racine—
meaning root, and thus radical proposals are those which
go to the root of the matter.

"Obviously, clinical services must be provided free, to
the maximum extent required in every individual case.
But psychiatry is imperfect. There are few or no absolute
cures. The patient who verges on instability, or who has
regained a measure of stability after institutionalization,
he should not be subjected ever to the same intolerable
pressures that brought on his illness. Rather, he must be
freed from them. His whole task is to recover, or at least
not to grow worse. Therefore he should receive a public
stipend, adequate for the support of him and his dependents at a decent standard of living. And, as long as his
behavior does not constitute an outright menace to others, he should be free of legal restrictions, permitted to
work off his impulses in any way that it has necessity—"

Brakes screamed. A car skidded to a halt. White-faced,
the driver leaned out and yelled, "Why'n'cha watch where
you're going, you crazy nut?"

"Oh." Bailey came to himself with a shock and realized
that he stood in the middle of Post Street, the light against
him. "I—"

Cars stopped perforce around the tableau and honked.
A crowd gathered. A large blue policeman pushed
through. "Awright, awright," he said, "what's going on?"
He assessed the circumstances. "Jaywalking, huh? You
wanna get killed, Mac?"

"I—I—" Fear, irrational but terribly real, closed fingers around Bailey's throat.

"Give him a ticket, officer," the driver demanded.

"Haul him off right now. He's a menace to radiator grilles."

*Toot! Toot! Toot!* "Judas Priest," the policeman groaned, "we'll get traffic snarled from here to Daly City account of you. Come over here! Off the street! Lessee your—" But Bailey had already offered his wallet.

The policeman's jaw dropped. "Why the hell didn't you say so right off?" he exclaimed. The car was starting again. He ran and whistled it to a halt. "You, there! Pull over! Don't you know you damn near killed an unfortunate?"

The driver blanched afresh. "Yes," said a voice in the crowd, "and abused him too. Called him a crazy nut."

"For sure?" the policeman asked.

"Yes, indeed." The speaker stepped forth. "I heard him myself, officer. Goodness knows what psychic damage that brute inflicted."

Several witnesses added corroboration. The policeman said, "I'm sorry, Mr. Bailey, but I can't book him for felony abuse less'n you come down to the station and swear out a complaint. You want to do that?"

Bailey gulped and shook his head.

"Well, anyhow, I can summons him on a 666," the policeman said grimly. "And he'll appear before Judge Jeffreys. I'll see to that personal. Nobody gets away with abuse on my beat."

Bailey felt he ought to put in a word somewhere, but he was too shaken. Wanting only escape, he faded into the crowd, which made way for him, and onto Union Square. Its grass was long overdue for mowing, and badly littered, but the flags still flew on their staffs—

Wait. Those were supposed to be American and Californian flags, weren't they? Not the Jolly Roger, and SPQR, and a Campbell tartan, and Friends United in Close Kinship, and—

The man who had been his first witness touched his arm. "May I be of service, dear boy?" he murmured. "You are evidently new to our fair city."

"Well, I . . . I've been in Napa," Bailey said.

"And now alone. How perfectly awful! You might have

been simply days about finding your real sort." The man
was small, neat, clean, educated of speech; in fact, no
matter how closely Bailey looked, the sole remarkable
thing about him was his strapless blue velvet evening
gown. He shook hands, lingeringly, and said, "Call me
Jules."

"Bailey. Douglas Bailey. I—uh—you too—an, uh, unfortunate?"

"But of course, delightful boy, but of course. You are
so lucky that I happened to be there. Few of us come
down to this area. Without a guide, you could have been
stranded among absolute *tessies*."

A man in a black uniform emerged from the throng,
mounted a bench, and trumpeted: "Friends! My dear
subhuman friends! Listen to me. This is a very vital message. You will note that I am of Caucasian stock. Well,
friends, I have a surprise for you. I am something rather
unique. I am a racist—a dedicated, fanatical racist—who
maintains, and can scientifically prove, that his own race
is inferior. The only true humans on Earth, my friends,
the main line of evolution, the masters of the future, are
the lordly Melanesians."

Bailey and Jules wandered upwind. "But there do
seem to be, well, individualistic types here," Bailey said.

"Oh, my poor innocent," replied Jules. "How can you
count them? Don't be so naïve. It's charming in you, but
it is still naïveté. Half the Union Square orators are sane.
They merely indulge themselves, knowing that an over-
worked police force will seldom ask to see their certifi-
cates. And the other half—now really, darling, don't you
agree that they are as bad as the tessies?"

"Tessies?"

Jules patted Bailey on the rear. "I see that I shall have
to take you in hand. I shall truly have to. No, no, don't
feel obligated. My pleasure. My, shall I say, soul-artistry.
I shall introduce you to the people who matter. I shall
inform you. I shall remold your personality. I shall, in a
word, make you."

"What? Uh, hey, look here, I don't—"

Jules took Bailey's elbow and urged him along. "Tes-

sies," he said, "are tesseracts. Four-dimensional squares.
The stolidly, immovably sane. But I insist that these
downtown psychoceramics, even the certified ones, are
tessies themselves. They have the same preoccupations,
society, success, display, no dimmest concept of inner
space. Why, I heard one ranting about God once, and
asked him if he had ever apprehended the infinite by simple contemplation of an antique Quaker Oaks box, and
he positively *spit!*" They crossed the street. "I shall take
you straight to Genghiz's. I'm sure a party will be starting. It's that time of day. And he has the most delightful
friends. . . . Ah, here we are." Jules stopped at a Volks-
wagen. It was overparked, but evidently the U sticker on
the windshield, or perhaps the flounces around the chas-
sis, took care of that.

"You have a driver's license?" Bailey asked in his bewilderment.

Jules nodded. "It makes me very much in demand in
my little circle. Not many of them are allowed to drive,
you realize. Some wax positively furious about it. But I
must agree, just between the two of us, dear, that society
has some rights as against the unfortunate. Not many, but
some. However, can you think of any reason why a ho-
mosexual should not drive?"

"What? But, uh, but—your case—"

Jules trilled merriment. "Oh, my love, how did they
treat you in Napa? Were you never allowed newspapers?
Newscasts? Why, it was *the* big issue of the last election.
We were even divided among ourselves. The Mattachine
Society said they had worked so hard to get us accepted
as normal, if un-average, citizens. Poor dears. They were
just unrealistic. The rewards of 'unfortunate' status are
well worth the label. And it isn't supposed to be a stigma
anyway, is it? Every candidate—I mean simply every
candidate throughout the nation—who favored changing
the law to declare us mental cases, was elected by an
overwhelming majority. I had no idea there were so many
of us. Now, do hippity-hop in, doll child, and let us be
on our merry way."

Bailey climbed in, automatically, recognizing his own

weakness but unable to do much about it. *Besides,* he thought, *I was at loose ends. This could be fun. I can always leave if it isn't. I hope.*

They drove west, over the hills, toward Haight-Ashbury. Jules pointed out the sights as they went. The Temple of Ishtar: "Well, I may have certain prejudices of my own, but I do think those satyriasis and nymphomania sufferers are a teensy bit vulgar, making a religion of it incorporated under the laws of the State of California, don't you? And so unnecessary." The marijuana maze in Hamilton Playground: "That litigation went to the Supreme Court. What may or may not certified parents do about the rearing of their children? The Court found that, under the Fourteenth Amendment, it was discriminatory to exercise official control over such families when no physical harm was being inflicted." The distant view of Oakland's blackened ruins: "So tragic. But I suppose, with the load they have, not to mention the demand for admissions far exceeding the available space, institutions must be forgiven for believing that an occasional arsonist has been cured." A gaggle of men and women, dressed in artistic paint designs and nothing else, posing for the cameras of a foreign-looking couple: "I believe those tourists are Russian. We get a great many Russians these days. They laugh and laugh. I wonder why."

When the car stopped, Bailey gulped and had half a mind to run. The street was lined with old houses whose glass was broken, doors sagging, shingles loose, frames unpainted and tottery. The sidewalks were ankle deep in rubbish. The next block was unpassable because two automobiles had locked horns there and never been removed; they were rusted hulks now, and a rat scuttled from one. Nobody else was about, except a mainliner happily injecting himself on a decayed front porch. The smell of garbage blew strong on a cold breeze, and shadows deepened between the lean walls. Someone, somewhere, was crowing, loud and with a horrible regularity.

Jules sensed Bailey's unease and patted his head.

"Don't worry," the little man said. "I know this may strike you as the least bit . . . sinister? But really, that handsome head of yours is quite safe here. It's merely that—well, the tessies have their own areas, but they can't monopolize the entire city, can they? This section has been turned over to the unfortunates, to do with exactly as they like. Because wasn't excessive conformity one reason they become ill?"

Bailey mustered his nerve and accompanied Jules to an Edwardian mansion, turreted, scaled, and three stories high, which had been subdivided into apartments. "Shouldn't we, uh, bring something?" he said. "If we're crashing a party . . . a bottle or a sixpack?"

Jules stamped his foot. "You *must* shake off those preoccupations!" he cried. "What could be duller than a 'party'?" He all but enunciated the quotation marks. "How do you organize fun? And as for beverages, if you really haven't the inner resources to get high by an act of will, why, they'll be around. You see, Genghiz Khan knows Hairless Joe."

"He does?"

Jules calmed down and explained. "We have an unfortunate who thinks he's Hairless Joe. Surely you remember your classics. Hairless Joe made liquors. Therefore anyone who thinks he is Hairless Joe must be allowed to make liquors. And licensing or taxing him would hurt his psyche. So the cost is negligible." He winked and dug a thumb in Bailey's ribs. "It wasn't easy to get that certification. Hairless Joe is the subtlest man I have ever met."

From a gloomy, cobwebby entrance hall, a flight of stairs led up to the sound of voices and what Bailey supposed was music. "Uh, who'd you say our host is?" he asked.

"Oh!" Jules smote his breast. "I am so glad you reminded me! It could have been simply dreadful if you didn't know you must humor his delusion. Be sure to call him Genghiz Khan. His name is—was—really Ole Swenson, but we don't mention that. As long as you oblige him in a few reasonable ways—you know, kowtow when introduced, tremble in fear, inquire how his conquest of China is going—he's really a love. But otherwise, well, I must admit he can get terribly, terribly vicious."

"Violent?"

"Oh, no! Gracious no!" Jules threw up his hands. "Where do you get these distorted impressions? I admit some of my friends are a little strange, but it isn't their fault, it's society's, and they are all, I am sure, such dear, good people at bottom." He dropped his voice. "However, as for Genghiz, do be careful. If you don't treat him as the Emperor of All Men, he . . . he *sues* you. For psychic damage. He often wins, too."

Bailey moistened lips gone dry and creaked after Jules.

But once he got into the swing of it, the party turned out to be harmless. Ineed, he was reminded of student days in Berkeley. The odd clothes, the rather grubby bodies, the earnest and somewhat pompous conversations, the necking in various corners of the rooms, which were painted black or hung with parachute cloth or otherwise decorated in the latest nonconformist mode, were very familiar. He remembered that this company were certified safe, able to cope with the world provided merely that the world paid their way. Like him.

The affair got larger and noisier as day slid into night. Volunteers took a collection—unlike other Bohemias, this one did not lack for cash—and brought back sandwich makings. Bailey stayed in the apartment, circulating, getting acquainted, talking, admitting that Jules had probably done him a favor. This was an interesting bash.

He did suffer occasional disillusionments. For example, a young man in a robe, hair to his waist, interrupted Bailey's discussion with a former professor of economics. "Hey, Phil, you hear about Tommy?"

"No, what?" replied the professor. He was a gentle, soft-spoken gray man who seemed more resigned to his own untidiness than rejoicing in it.

"He got busted," the young man said. "Cops caught him with his wife."

"Well, well." The professor shook his head. "I can't say I sympathize overly much. You know I never approved."

"Now, come off that tessie kick of yours," the young man said. "We can't let the fuzz pull this kind of stuff. We got to do something."

"What's the trouble?" Bailey asked. By now, a glass of wine in his hand and another inside him, he felt almost bold.

"New, chum?" the young man said. " 'S like so. Tommy got himself certified last year. Stubborn case of marital impotence."

"You mean it wasn't?"

"Hell, no. Tommy's the biggest stud on the West Coast. Like, he towers. But I guess word got to the fuzz. Imagine that! Snooping on a man's private life. What kind of police state are we getting, anyhow?"

"But a malingerer—" Bailey found he was addressing the back of the robe.

The professor smiled. "I'm afraid that that's become so common it's positively respectable in some circles," he said. "Our young friend makes no secret among his friends that his religious monomania is nothing but a way he has found to live without working."

"And you don't report him?"

"No, I regret to say I lack the courage to be a fink." The professor sighed. "My own breakdown was quite genuine. *You* try explaining modern American fiscal policies."

—An hour or two later, Bailey stood on the fringes of a group which listened to a voluble Negro explain an idea.

"Man, I tell you, we can do it. All we need's the organization. If the fairies did it, why not the colored? Way back in Brown vs. Board of Education, the Supreme Court found how discrimination effects the psyche. Right? Right. And law or no law, we still got discrimination in this country. So why shouldn't we get a bill passed saying every black person's a mental case? Don't Whitey owe us that much?"

"Well," answered Genghiz Khan, "if the same thought could be applied to Mongols and Swedes—"

"Sure," said the Negro. "Why not? I was thinking we should get together with the Jews. But too many Jews got tessie hangups. So why not you instead? Logrolling, they call it."

A red-haired girl tugged Bailey's sleeve, nodded toward the speaker, and whispered, "Now that's a marvelous irony. Ferd wants certification so bad he can taste it. You should hear him rave about how the black man ought to rise and kill every dirty white in the world. But he's never gotten past any examining board. The bastards always say he's not paranoiac, he's just expressing a political opinion. You see, down underneath, he likes white people. He can't help it; he does. So now he's hatched this scheme that ought to get him certified as an individual. Only I'll bet it doesn't. I'll bet that inside ten years it'll be the law of the land."

—Toward midnight they started dancing. By that time, probably half the population of the district was crowded into the house, every one of its apartments, and spilling downstairs into the street. But they discovered they could hop to recorded bongo drums if they did so in unison.

Bailey's head ached. He felt a trifle dizzy. Too much alcohol, smoke, warmth, stale air, excitement, in his weakened condition. But he didn't want to leave. His inner disturbances were lost in a roseate glow. His loneliness was no more. This world-within-the-world accepted him. The red-haired girl had talked about her analysis, and talked and talked and talked. But she was nice-looking, and active as they sprang belly to belly, and he thought he could get her into bed later on. He danced.

The company danced. The floor boomed. The chandeliers rocked. Plaster fell. Windowpanes shattered. *Rat-a-plan, rat-a-plan, paradiddle, flan, flan! Hey, ha!*

Until the entire dry-rotted, termite-infested building

collapsed. Bailey had an instant to know that he and the roof were falling.

Then the rubble buried him and he was dead.

Death was a stormwind. It was as if he were blown, whirled, cast up and down and here we go again. But by concentrating his will, by resolutely ignoring things like thunder and lightning and octopuses, he could stay somewhat on a level course.

"Zero," God counted, "one, ten, eleven—"

Oh, shut up, he snarled.

What was happening to him? Would this succession of sticky endings go on forever? Had he died his real death and been consigned to Hell?

No. For what was the point of Hell if you couldn't remember what you were there for?

He focused himself on that one riddle. Who was he? Why was he? Not being so confused and frightened this time around, he discovered that he could recall his entire past in each of his lives. And up to a point they were the same. Ordinary boyhood, studies, travels, books, music, friends, marriage, divorce, other women, other hobbies, promising career as a young research sociologist attached to the University Medical Center in San Francisco, because he'd written his thesis on the problem posed by the rising incidence of mental illness and was now trying to find cause and cure in terms of his own science. . . . The lives diverged several years ago, in 1984 as nearly as he could place it.

"One thousand, one thousand one, one thousand ten."

But which of the four was his real existence? Or were they all? No. Couldn't be. Nothing in their common past suggested that his psyche would ever disintegrate. And yet it had. Four times. Then weren't those episodes the illusion, the not-so-merry-go-round that he had to get off?

How?

Well, how had he gotten on in the first place?

He didn't know! The "incarnations" camouflaged that last segment of his life. Ye gods and witches, was he doomed to repeat death in one lunatic world after the next, until at last he actually did go mad?

Think, he thought with growing desperation. Think hard. What is it you do that catapults you from here into a different pseudo-existence?

"One thousand one hundred eleven."

You consider where you were last. You see what was wrong with their way of handling the situation. You believe you see a better way. Then God says *click,* and you're in business at a new stand, and you find that it doesn't pay either.

For instance, take this last world. They did have the germ of an idea. Remove the pressures that make the weaker personalities buckle. Trouble is, society won't function without some measure of intolerance and compulsion.

At least, this one won't. Technological, city-dominated, rationalism-oriented society has to put strains on people, and maybe those strains will always be too brutal for some. But how about an altogether different culture? Not Noble Savages, of course, but . . . well, post-technological man, who uses machinery only for the hard, dull, dangerous tasks, who has otherwise rid his world of ugliness and overcomplexity, who's gone back to a nature made safe and clean, so that while satisfying his animal instincts he also cultivates his intellectual, spiritual, uniquely human capabilities—

*Click.* The womb of time was impregnated.

No! cried Douglas Bailey in horror. I didn't mean that!

He was too late.

### Fate the Fifth

The area-maintenance robot had broken down beyond its capacity for self-repair. Bailey sent for an Engineer. The man couldn't come for several days. Bailey wasn't annoyed at keeping house in the meantime. In fact, he usually did his gardening himself. To cut and split wood, cook, make minor repairs on the plumbing and the sun-power unit, by hand, consititued a pleasant change of pace. It was a joy to work outdoors. These hills above the bay, on which he and the robot had raised the cabin, had never been more beautiful.

But no one man could patrol an entire region. And Bailey had no neighbors. (He wasn't a hermit by any means; he had simply withdrawn for a while from his community, in order that he might develop certain aspects of a philosophical idea.) If nothing else, fire was an omnipresent menace in the dry season. He couldn't risk that, when the forest was making such a promising come-back. Besides, he'd hate to see Sausalito ruined, whether by conflagration or neglect. The deserted town had a curious, melancholy charm for him.

Thus he activated his radiophone and called Fairfax. Avis Carmen, who directed cooperative activities this year, happened to take the message in person. "Why, certainly, Doug," she said. "You ought to have notified us earlier. I'll get you a crew in—well, a lot of the boys went boating in the Delta, so we may not be able to spare enough here. But I can ask for volunteers from elsewhere. How many do you estimate we'll need? Twenty? Okay, we'll be at your place day after tomorrow at the latest."

"Thanks a lot, Avis," he said.

"Why, what's to thank for? It's our plain duty to the land. Besides, a joint job like that is fun."

"I've kept the habit of thanking people for kindness. Guess I'm old-fashioned."

"You are that, dear." Her voice got huskier. "Tell you what. I'll delegate the organization to Jim Wyman, and come today by myself."

"Oh, that's not necessary. I'm not in any trouble yet."

"I know. But wouldn't you like a helping hand? And some companionship and sex? You've been alone for weeks."

Bailey hesitated. "To be quite honest, yes," he said. "I'm sufficiently worried that I can't maintain deep serenity. Which means I'm not accomplishing anything in the insight line anyhow. But can you leave on such short notice?"

Avis laughed. "Relax! You must try to overcome those geases. I swear, if the Change hadn't occurred, you'd eventually have fretted yourself into a nervous breakdown. It won't hurt a thing if I don't lead the folk dances and community sings and handicraft classes for a bit. My only vital obligation is the training in gentleness, and I'm sure Roger Breed will take charge of my six-year-olds while I'm gone. If you insist on being stuffy and self-righteous, I could say that my most urgent task is you. You sound as if loneliness has stimulated your aggressions."

" 'Make love, not war,' " he quoted with a chuckle.

"Isn't that the basic principle of the modern world?" she replied soberly. "Not that you'd ever hurt anyone else, dear. But that means that any undischarged tensions are turned inward."

Bailey broke the connection as soon as decently possible, which wasn't very soon, given a canon of leisureliness and sociability. Avis Carmen talked too much, and was a little too bustlingly sincere, for his entire liking.

Nevertheless, he looked forward to her arrival.

That was in late afternoon. Being in a hurry, she didn't walk, bicycle, or ride horseback the fifteen or twenty miles. After making sure no one else needed it, she took one of the village's hovercars. The vehicle set down in a soft whirr outside the cabin. Bailey ran to meet it. Avis climbed forth. She was a big woman, her blonde hair a startling, sun-bleached brightness against the tanned unclothed skin. When they embraced, she was warm and smooth and smelled of summer.

"Hey, big boy," she said, "are you in that urgent a case?"

He nuzzled the hollow between her neck and shoulder. "Now that you bring it up," he said, "yes."

"Well . . . all right. I've missed you too, Doug."

Afterward they stepped back outdoors to fetch her suitcase. But she halted, and whispered with shaken, unaffected reverence, "My God, have you got a view here!" and they opened their awareness and knew themselves one with the world.

The sun was westering behind the live oak and eucalyptus that crowned this ridge. From its great golden shield there streamed spears, which flamed where they struck. The cabin walls, the surrounding trees, the air itself were saturated with light. Ahead, the ground tumbled steeply, down into woods, until at last the bay shone blue, mile after calm mile to the tawny eastern hills. Southward lay San Francisco, towers lifting elfin out of luminous mists. Silence brimmed the sky.

Bailey was the first to return to his isolated self. He saw tears on Avis' face and said, "But what's wrong?"

She came back slowly, with some reluctance, from her communion. "Nothing," she answered him. "The loveliness. And the pity."

"Pity?"

"For everyone who lived before the Change. Who never knew this."

"Now, now, we weren't that miserable, sweetheart. And why make me feel ancient? You were born in the prior civilization too."

"I don't remember much, though," she said gravely. "I suppose the . . . the judgment time made such an impression on me that I forgot a great deal of childhood. Same thing for nearly all the survivors. You seem to recall the old days better than most. The rest of us, well, you might say the judgment scrubbed us clean."

He guessed that she wanted to expel whatever sorrow had brushed her, for she went on almost fiercely: "It had to be. We had to be shaken loose from the ways of our fathers. Then we saw what the unnaturalness, the compulsions, the dirty little inhibitions, had done to the earth and mankind. We were liberated from the past and really could start afresh."

"I'm not sure we're all that liberated," Bailey said.

"Oh, we've kept what was good." Avis glanced at San Francisco. "Take the city, for instance. It does add a magic to the scene. I'm glad it's there, glad the machines keep it up, glad children get taken on visits as part of their education. But live there?" She grimaced.

"I liked it," Bailey said.

"You didn't know any better. Did you?"

"N-n-no." His memories demanded release. "But I had friends. They died. Everyone I knew. What's the estimate? The plague killed ninety-five percent? Of the whole world's population—in months! Even you have to weep for them once in a while."

"For their poor, wasted lives," Avis said. "Not their deaths. Death was a release, I'm sure. And what other way was there out of the trap man had built around himself? Now we have room to breathe, and the wealth and resources and knowledge to do anything we like, and we're turning our planet into paradise."

"Are we?" Bailey wondered. "We know the Bay Area. We make occasional radio contact with a few other fragments, here and there around the world. But otherwise— okay, suppose you tell me what's happening as close to us as the Russian River."

"Probably nothing," Avis said. "No people. We'll expand and occupy the empty lands. But not in haste." Her fist thudded on the soil. "And we'll *never* breed, and build, and mine and log and pollute and destroy, in the old obscene fashion. Never! We've learned our lesson!"

Bailey decided the conversation had grown depressing and should be changed. He laid an arm around her waist. "You're a sweet girl," he said, as much to calm her as because he meant it. "If jealousy were permitted, I'd be jealous of your other lovers. Think you might like to be a parent with me?"

She eased her tautness, kissed his cheek and nestled close. "I'm young yet," she said. "Not ready to assume the ultimate responsibility. But someday . . . yes, Doug, if you still want, I think I'll want to. You must have very good chromosomes, and you'd play the father role well— and, aw, I'm fond of you."

Their talk wandered off into amiable nonsense until twilight and hunger drove them inside. After dinner, on a synthetic bearskin rug (although bears were coming back, so far the species was protected), before the flames that danced in a genuine stone fireplace, they made love again, to the accompaniment of Ravel's *Bolero* played on a rustic stereo hi-fi. That was such fun that they repeated with Stravinsky's *Le Sacre du Printemps,* and Bach's Toccata and Fugue in D Minor, and Beethoven's Ninth, and finally something by Delius. The modern way of life did wonders for that particular capability.

The next afternoon a dozen of their friends arrived from Fairfax with a carrier load of gear. Toward evening, a contingent from across the bay moored their yawl and hiked uphill. They were made welcome as new acquaintances always were. The total force was greater than needed or expected, because several girls had come along to help cook. But everyone carried food—venison, wild pork, smoked fish, dried fruit, nuts, raisins, honey, stone-ground bread—which went into the common stock. One man had thoughtfully added a case of Livermore wine. That night saw a great party. No one got drunk— you never got drunk in this culture—but they grew mellow, sang songs, danced, swapped partners, vied in athletic feats, extended invitations to come visit.

There followed two days of earnest effort. The men ranged widely on foot, checking potential trouble spots, clearing deadwood from firebreaks, eradicating poison oak, medicating for plant diseases, maintaining trails and roads, everything the robot had handled. At night, they were too tired to do more than eat and sleep. But the sense of comradeship and accomplishment was precious.

Finally the Engineer arrived. The sunpower unit was giving new trouble, so Bailey happened to be at the cabin with the women when the hovertruck descended from heaven. They bowed their heads respectfully as the tall, saffron-robed figure emerged, followed by his bell-ringing acolytes.

.The Engineer lifted his slide rule. "Peace be upon you, my children," he intoned. "I pray you, lead me to the sufferer."

"Will you not take refreshment first, Doctor?" Avis asked.

The feather bonnet bobbed and swayed with head shaking. "My daughter is gracious. Later we will avail ourselves of her hospitality in the spirit in which it is proffered. But first we must, if naught else, inspect the robot. To the degree that anything, aye, even a machine, is not in harmony with itself, unto that degree are the world and the starry universe awry. All malfunction is evil, all evil is malfunction."

"The Doctor has instructed me, his chela," Avis said humbly.

Bailey led Engineer and acolytes to the shed where the robot was kept. They took off their robes, broke out their tools, and went quite matter-of-factly to work. Bailey watched. He had no further call on his services. Once the robot was fixed, it would repair everything better and quicker than he could.

"You must forgive the delay, my son," the Engineer said while he unscrewed a cover plate. "I have so many calls over so wide an area. Would that more people would enter the Profession."

"Well, it's a hard one," Bailey said. "I don't think the younger generation has incentive to undergo years of intensive training."

"You're probably right. Let's hope we succeed in instilling the true cooperative spirit."

"Uh, don't you think the Profession could be made less difficult? If nothing else, coudn't the ceremonial duties be omitted? I'll bet you spent months learning the Mass of Matter, for instance."

Again the Engineer shook his grizzled head. "The spirit of the times requires it," he stated. "I suspect you remember pre-Change conditions quite well. So do I. We can both look at our present environment with some objectivity. Don't you agree, one of the best features about it is this rite, pageantry, desire to give a religious meaning to every act we perform? I think the spiritual barrenness of the old world was one reason the judgment destroyed it so thoroughly. What did most people have to live for? Lacking the will, they lacked resistance to the plague." He returned to his job. "Of course," he said, "that worked out for the best."

"What?"

"Why, sure. Without a really clean sweep, how could we have been free to develop as we have?"

The trouble with the robot was nothing serious, a burned-out circuit that was soon replaced. The Engineer did not stay longer than necessary for a cup of coffee and the briefest thanksgiving song. He was expected in too many other places.

When the men came back at dusk, they felt something more was needed. They must celebrate, not only the end of their work, but the fact that the land had escaped harm. It was decided that next day they'd hike to Muir Woods.

That was a gorgeous tramp, sometimes along the crumbling road, sometimes straight across the huge, windy, poppy-flaming hills. They sang, talked, jested, laughed, or simply took joy in the sunshine and air that enveloped them. Bailey found himself most of the time walking beside Cynara. She was one of the Eastbay crew, a small, fine-boned, red-haired girl with the most magnificent large eyes he had ever seen. And he liked her conversation, too; she had a puckish humor that Avis lacked. Toward the end, she went hand in hand with him.

Having started early and being in top condition, the party reached their goal not long after noon. They meant to enter the great redwood grove and commune with its awesomeness. Later they'd have a picnic supper, spend some mirthful hours like their first night together, spread sleeping bags, and rest beneath the stars. In the morning they'd wend their separate homeward ways.

"But the first order of business is lunch," Cynara declared. Several others nodded agreement.

Avis frowned. "I don't know, my friends," she said. "We came here for sanctification."

"Not on an empty stomach, please," Cynara answered.

Avis unbent. "Very well. I suppose holiness is a little

difficult under those circumstances." She genuflected to the trees that rose sheer beyond the Custodian's house.

The sun gave benediction. The earth breathed incense. A lark chanted.

They opened their packs and built sandwiches ad libitum. Bailey and Cynara were thigh by thigh, resting their backs against a solitary oak, when Avis happened past. "Well, well," she smiled. "A developing relationship, hm?"

"Do you mind?" Bailey asked.

She rumpled both their heads. "Of course not, sillies."

Having eaten, the group laid prayer cloaks over what clothes they did or did not happen to wear and approached the grove. The Custodian emerged from his house. They knelt, the old man blessed them, they passed in under the silent, sun-flecked shadows.

Bailey's eyes kept straying from the cathedral archways that reached before him, to Cynara at his side. *Well*, he thought, *what's wrong with that? Even in today's religion. Especially in today's religion. What higher purpose does man have than to give and receive happiness, to care for the land and be cared for by it, and know that he is one with the cosmos?*

*Oneness, yes, also with our fellow human beings. When I am with this girl, I will also somehow be with Avis; and when I am with Avis or any other I will also somehow be with Cynara, and thus we cannot ever be unkind or unfaithful.* A tune lilted through Bailey's mind, something from old times, or had it been a poem, or both? He couldn't quite remember.

> But I'm always true to you, Cynara, in my
>     fashion.
> Yes, I'm always true to you, Cynara, in my
>     way—

A woman shrieked.

The noise went like a buzz saw in this hush. Bailey leaped backward. Cynara choked on her own scream.

Their companions who had preceded them retreated, halted, stared out of eyes in which there was no belief.

All save one man. He sprawled on the path, face down, in a puddle of blood that was impossibly brilliant scarlet and that spread and spread and spread without end.

Above him grinned his killer. The creature was huge, burly, dressed in stinking skins. Through a greasy thicket of hair and beard could be seen the smallpox scars. A crude machete dripped in his hand.

Bailey reacted with an instinct he had not known remained to him. He grabbed Cynara, threw her and himself into the hollow that a fire had made in a vast bole, and stood before her with his hands crooked for battle.

Others loped into view, as filthy as the first. They howled and yelped in what might once have been English. A couple of Bay Area men bolted. One went down, his skull split by an ax blow. His comrade fell with a spear through him, lay there and ululated in agony. The killer laughed.

"Joe," Bailey whispered. "Sam. But they're my friends!"

Rage drove out terror. Never had he seen with such starkness, snuffed blood and sweat at such distances, felt each microscopic breath of air cold across his skin. His thoughts went in lightning flashes: *Those are savages. Must have come from the north. Survivors in those parts after all. People that really went back to nature.*

The pilgrims stood numb. The invaders encircled them. The two groups were about equal in numbers—no, the civilized men amounted yet to four or five more— and the girls were in good physical shape too. Why didn't they fight? An athlete could get in under one of those clumsily handled swords, pikes, clubs . . . take it away from the enemy . . . or at least make the enemy pay!

Bailey had almost jumped forth to begin combat when Avis collected her wits, lifted both hands, and cried, "What is this? My fellow souls, my brothers, what are you doing?"

A northerner barked a command. His company got to

work. One or two of the victims tried to run, but didn't get far. The slaughter of the men was over in seconds, though some would obviously take hours to die. Thereafter the gang seized the women.

"No!" Avis wailed. "Not with animals!"

She struggled until, impatiently, her attacker knocked her out with his fist. He broke her jaw. The other girls gave less trouble. While waiting their turn, a couple of northerners cut pieces off a dead man and ate them raw.

Cynara had fainted. *I've got to get her away,* Bailey thought in his nightmare. *Away from . . . this whole area? We've forgotten how to fight. We've no weapons, no training, no will even to defend ourselves. And now the savages have discovered us. They'll swarm in, killing, raping, enslaving, looting, burning. It was a mistake to believe we'd succeeded in making history stop.*

*But no. I can't desert my people.*

Maybe, just maybe he and she would be overlooked in this hollow, until the invaders and their captured women —if they didn't simply murder the girls—had gone away. Maybe he and she could flee across the land, carrying their warning, somehow rally their gentle folk before it was too late.

They might perhaps have done so. They might conceivably have become the leaders of a civilization that would apply scientific method to the perfection of war, exterminate the enemy, and proceed on momentum to conquer a good-sized empire. But Cynara woke, and moaned, precisely as a few woods-runners passed by on their way to the Custodian's house. They called the rest.

Had he been armed, Bailey might have held the entrance to his refuge for a while. But the first spear thrust in his shoulder convinced him that he needed room to operate, if he wasn't helplessly to be butchered. He charged forth and did manage to acquire an ax. With much satisfaction, he killed its owner and backed toward his tree. But the northerners were already behind him.

Then a club spattered his brains and he was dead.

Death was a stormwind. No, wait, this wasn't death,

wasn't chaos, was merely the senselessness of total sensory deprivation.

"Zero," God counted, "one, ten, eleven—"

Oh, come off it, Bailey growled. Do You think I don't recognize binary digits?

That was the worst world so far, his thoughts continued. And not because of the cannibals, either. They were only poor and ignorant. But the civilized people, who never bothered to find out what was going on beyond their little bailiwick, who blandly accepted the deaths of I don't know how many human creatures as a reasonable price for their own superior culture—ugh!

Hey, now. What do I mean, "so far"? I want out, not further in.

I should be able to find the way. I'd better be able to. Otherwise, good-bye, sanity.

"—one hundred, one hundred one, one hundred ten—"

Or in Arabic, four, five, six, et cetera. That's a computer. My nerves detect its impulses while it's on standby. This indicates that somehow I'm coupled to it. When the thing goes into action—yes, the Simulator.

The man-machine system. I the man, it the machine. Together we consider a problem in totality.

What problem?

Well, I'm a sociologist, working on the cause and cure of mental illness. Many kinds of solutions are being proposed. . . . I remember talk of voluntary euthanasia. . . . But oftentimes in the past, remedies proved worse than troubles. Consider the long-range effect of bread and circuses on the Roman proletariat; consider most revolutions and attempted utopias. We need a way to improve in a less blind, trial-and-error fashion. And it's not enough to devise a theoretically workable system. We have to know beforehand how it'll feel in action, to those it acts on. For instance, a dole might make good economic sense under some circumstances, but might demoralize the recipients. How can you test a social reform in advance, from the inside?

Why, sure. The man-machine linkage. The human

component supplies more than a general directive. He furnishes his entire conscious-unconscious-visceral-genetic understanding of what it is to be human. This goes into the data banks, along with every other piece of information the machine already has. Then, as one unit, brain and computer assume a social change and deduce the consequences. Since the objective is to explore those consequences from an immediate, emotional standpoint, the result of the logic is presented as a "dream."

Perhaps the machine is a bit too literal-minded.

Be that as it may . . . clearly, if an imaginary world turns out to be undesirable, there's no point in exploring it further. The system must allow me to order that sequence broken off. Sort of like the way a person can tell himself to awake from a bad dream.

Only in this case, for some damn depth-psychological reason, the signal for switch-off took the form of my own realistically simulated death. And that shocked me into partial amnesia. Hence I didn't issue an unequivocal order to end the whole show. Hence the machine waited on standby, till my stream of semiconsciousness tossed up something that it could interpret as a command.

The mind shuddered. Christ! I could've gone on this way till—till—

Okay, Simulator. Take me home and stop operation.
*Click?*
You heard me, said Douglas Bailey.

Creation began.

## O Ye of Little Fate

He opened his eyes. Darkness lay upon them. He yelled and flung his arms about.

"I say there, what's the matter? Wait a tick. I'm right here."

Douglas Bailey forced himself to lie quietly. His chest heaved and his pulse thuttered.

The induction helmet was pulled off his head. He

looked into the blessed, familiar, British face of Michael Birdsong, his immediate superior, and at the wonder of his own laboratory. The knowledge of deliverance went through him in a wave.

"Are you all right?" Birdsong asked. "Something go wrong?"

"I . . . I dunno." Bailey sat up on the couch, letting his legs hang down. He still trembled. "How long was I under?"

"I didn't clock you. But tell you in a minute." Birdsong punched a key. The instrument-studded board clicked and extruded a printout. He tore the slip loose and read. " 'Bout five seconds."

"Huh? Oh, well." Struck with a sudden suspicion, Bailey said, "This is the real world, isn't it?"

"What? What? Indeed. What else? Unless you want to go the Bishop Berkeley route. But do tell me—"

"No, wait." Bailey waved a hand. "This is too important. I have my complete memory back, but it could be false. Let me check with yours. That might provide a clue. What's the status of the mental epidemic?"

Birdsong considered him narrowly before saying, "Well, as you wish. It's following the usual yeast-cell growth law. Starting to level off, y' know. Thus we should in time be able to commence large-scale treatment and cure. Meanwhile we're dealing with the victims one way or another, best's we can improvise. This program of yours and mine is aimed at finding a quicker, more basic answer." Eagerness burst forth. "Did you?"

"I don't know." Bailey slid his legs down till he stood erect, walked to the window and looked out across the city and the bay. "We'll have to evaluate my data, and probably collect more, after we've installed a safety factor I've discovered we need. But later, later." He laughed, with a slight lingering hysteria. "Right now, I'm content to know there are no basic answers—that we're muddling along, in our slow, left-handed, wasteful, piecemeal, unimaginative human fashion—that, by God, I *am* back in the real world!"

ONE DANGER SCIENCE FICTION FACES in this era of its growing respectability stems from the fact that some people are taking it too bloody seriously. I don't mean that it should never, or seldom, treat serious themes. Nor do I mean that the writer should not give every story he writes the very best he has to give at the time. But where in today's critical essays, academic conferences, and the fictional dooms and frustrations with which they are concerned is there any room for old-fashioned fun?

Oh well, whether or not English professors do, the reading public continues to like adventures, exotic settings, and—in science fiction—exploration of a few of the infinite possible forms which worlds and the life upon them may take. With every respect and, indeed, admiration for my colleagues whose interests lie elsewhere, I'll continue to spend a good part of my time as a spinner of yarns.

8

# HIDING PLACE

<<<<<<<<<<<<<<<<<<<<<<<<<<<<<<<<<<<<<<<<<<<<

CAPTAIN BAHADUR TORRANCE RECEIVED THE news as befitted a Lodgemaster in the Federated Brotherhood of Spacemen. He heard it out, interrupting only with a few knowledgeable questions. At the end, he said calmly, "Well done, Freeman Yamamura. Please keep this to yourself till further notice. I'll think about what's to be done. Carry on." But when the engineer officer had left the cabin—the news had not been the sort you tell on the intercom—he poured himself a triple whisky, sat down, and stared emptily at the viewscreen.

He had traveled far, seen much, and been well rewarded. However, promotion being swift in his difficult line of work, he was still too young not to feel cold at hearing his death sentence.

The screen showed such a multitude of stars, hard and winter-brilliant, that only an astronaut could recognize individuals. Torrance sought past the Milky Way until he identified Polaris. Then Valhalla would lie so-and-so-many degrees away, in that direction. Not that he could see a type-G sun at this distance, without optical instruments more powerful than any aboard the *Hebe G.B.* But he found a certain comfort in knowing his eyes were sighted toward the nearest League base (houses, ships, humans, nestled in a green valley on Freya) in this almost uncharted section of our galactic arm. Especially when he didn't expect to land there, ever again.

The ship hummed around him, pulsing in and out of four-space with a quasi-speed that left light far behind and yet was still too slow to save him.

Well . . . it became the captain to think first of the others. Torrance sighed and stood up. He spent a moment checking his appearance; morale was important, never more so than now. Rather than the usual gray coverall of shipboard, he preferred full uniform: blue tunic, white cape and culottes, gold braid. As a citizen of Ramanujan planet, he kept a turban on his dark aquiline head, pinned with the Ship-and-Sunburst of the Polesotechnic League.

He went down a passageway to the owner's suite. The steward was just leaving, a tray in his hand. Torrance signaled the door to remain open, clicked his heels and bowed. "I pray pardon for the interruption, sir," he said. "May I speak privately with you? Urgent."

Nicholas van Rijn hoisted the two-liter tankard which had been brought him. His several chins quivered under the stiff goatee; the noise of his gulping filled the room, from the desk littered with papers to the Huy Brasealian jewel-tapestry hung on the opposite bulkhead. Something by Mozart lilted out of a taper. Blond, big-eyed, and thoroughly three-dimensional, Jeri Kofoed curled on a couch, within easy reach of him where he sprawled in his lounger. Torrance, who was married but had been away from home for some time, forced his gaze back to the merchant.

"Ahhh!" Van Rijn banged the empty mug down on a table and wiped foam from his mustaches. "Pox and pestilence, but the first beer of the day is good! Something with it is so quite cool and—um—by damn, what word do I want?" He thumped his sloping forehead with one hairy fist. "I get more absent in the mind every week. Ah, Torrance, when you are too a poor old lonely fat man with all powers failing him, you will look back and remember me and wish you was more good to me. But then is too late." He sighed like a minor tornado and scratched the pelt on his chest. In the near tropic temperature at which he insisted on maintaining his quarters, he need wrap only a sarong about his huge body. "Well, what begobbled stupiding is it I must be dragged from my all-too-much work to fix up for you, ha?"

His tone was genial. He had, in fact, been in a good mood ever since they escaped the Adderkops. (Who wouldn't be? For a mere space yacht, even an armed one with ultrapowered engines, to get away from three cruisers was more than an accomplishment; it was nearly a miracle. Van Rijn still kept four grateful candles burning before his Martian sandroot statuette of St. Dismas.) True, he sometimes threw crockery at the steward when a drink arrived later than he wished, and he fired everybody aboard ship at least once a day. But that was normal.

Jeri Kofoed arched her brows. "Your first beer, Nicky?" she murmured. "Now really! Two hours ago—"

"*Ja*, but that was before midnight time. If not Greenwich midnight, then surely on some planet somewhere, *nie?* So is a new day." Van Rijn took his churchwarden off the table and began stuffing it. "Well, sit down, Captain Torrance, make yourself to be comfortable and lend me your lighter. You look like a dynamited custard, boy. All you youngsters got no stamina. When I was a working spaceman, by Judas, we made solve our own problems. These days, death and damnation, you come ask me how to wipe your noses! Nobody has any guts but me." He slapped his barrel belly. "So what is be-jingle-bang gone wrong now?"

Torrance wet his lips. "I'd rather speak to you alone, sir."

He saw the color leave Jeri's face. She was no coward. Frontier planets, even the pleasant ones like Freya, didn't breed that sort. She had come along on what she knew would be a hazardous trip because a chance like this— to get an in with the merchant prince of the Solar Spice & Liquors Company, which was one of the major forces within the whole Polesotechnic League—was too good for an opportunistic girl to refuse. She had kept her nerve

during the fight and the subsequent escape, though death
came very close. But they were still far from her planet,
among unknown stars, with the enemy hunting them.

"So go in the bedroom," van Rijn ordered her.

"Please," she whispered. "I'd be happier hearing the
truth."

The small black eyes, set close to van Rijn's hook nose,
flared. "Foulness and fulminate!" he bellowed. "What is
this poppies with cocking? When I say frog, by billy
damn, you jump!"

She sprang to her feet, mutinous. Without rising, he
slapped her on the appropriate spot. It sounded like a
pistol going off. She gasped, choked back an indignant
screech, and stamped into the inner suite. Van Rijn rang
for the steward.

"More beer this calls for," he said to Torrance. "Well,
don't stand there making bug's eyes! I got no time for
fumblydiddles, even if you overpaid loafers do. I got to
make revises of all price schedules on pepper and nutmeg
for Freya before we get there. Satan and stenches! At
least ten percent more that idiot of a factor could charge
them, and not reduce volume of sales. I swear it! All
good saints, hear me and help a poor old man saddled
with oatmeal-brained squatpots for workers!"

Torrance curbed his temper with an effort. "Very well,
sir. I just had a report from Yamamura. You know we
took a near miss during the fight, which hulled us at the
engine room. The converter didn't seem damaged, but after patching the hole, the gang's been checking to make
sure. And it turns out that about half the circuitry for the
infrashield generator was fused. We can't replace more
than a fraction of it. If we continue to run at full quasi-
speed, we'll burn out the whole converter in another fifty
hours."

"Ah, s-s-so." Van Rijn grew serious. The snap of the
lighter, as he touched it to his pipe, came startlingly loud.
"No chance of stopping altogether to make fixings? Once
out of hyperdrive, we would be much too small a thing
for the bestinkered Adderkops to find. Hey?"

"No, sir. I said we haven't enough replacement parts. This is a yacht, not a warship."

"Hokay, we must continue in hyperdrive. How slow must we go, to make sure we come within calling distance of Freya before our engine burns out?"

"One-tenth of top speed. It'd take us six months."

"No, my captain friend, not that long. We never reach Valhalla star at all. The Adderkops find us first."

"I suppose so. We haven't got six months' stores aboard anyway." Torrance stared at the deck. "What occurs to me is, well, we could reach one of the nearby stars. There barely might be a planet with an industrial civilization, whose people could eventually be taught to make the circuits we need. A habitable planet, at least—maybe . . ."

*"Nie!"* Van Rijn shook his head till the greasy black ringlets swirled about his shoulders. "All us men and one woman, for life on some garbagey rock where they have not even wine grapes? I'll take an Adderkop shell and go out like a gentleman, by damn!" The steward appeared. "Where you been snoozing? Beer, with God's curses on you! I need to make thinks! How you expect I can think with a mouth like a desert in midsummer?"

Torrance chose his words carefully. Van Rijn would have to be reminded that the captain, in space, was the final boss. And yet the old devil must not be antagonized, for he had a record of squirming between the horns of dilemmas. "I'm open to suggestions, sir, but I can't take the responsibility of courting enemy attack."

Van Rijn rose and lumbered about the cabin, fuming obscenities and volcanic blue clouds. As he passed the shelf where St. Dismas stood, he pinched the candles out in a marked manner. That seemed to trigger something in him. He turned about and said, "Ha! Industrial civilizations, *ja,* maybe. Not only the pest-begotten Adderkops ply this region of space. Gives some chance perhaps we can come in detection range of an un-beat-up ship, *nie?* You go get Yamamura to jack up our detector sensitivities till we can feel a gnat twiddle its wings back in my Djakarta office on Earth, so lazy the cleaners are. Then

we go off this direct course and run a standard naval
search pattern at reduced speed."

"And if we find a ship? Could belong to the enemy,
you know."

"That chance we take."

"In all events, sir, we'll lose time. The pursuit will gain
on us while we follow a search-helix. Especially if we
spend days persuading some nonhuman crew who've
never heard of the human race that we have to be taken
to Valhalla immediately if not sooner."

"We burn that bridge when we come to it. You have
might be a more hopeful scheme?"

"Well . . . ." Torrance pondered awhile, blackly.

The steward came in with a fresh tankard. Van Rijn
snatched it.

"I think you're right, sir," said Torrance. "I'll go
and—"

"Virginal!" bellowed van Rijn.

Torrance jumped. "What?"

"Virginal! That's the word I was looking for. The first
beer of the day, you idiot!"

The cabin door chimed. Torrance groaned. He'd been
hoping for some sleep, at least, after more hours on deck
than he cared to number. But when the ship prowled
through darkness, seeking another ship which might or
might not be out there, and the hunters drew closer. . . .
"Come in."

Jeri Kofoed entered. Torrance gaped, sprang to his
feet, and bowed. "Freelady! What—what—what a surprise! Is there anything I can do?"

"Please." She laid a hand on his. Her gown was of
shimmerite and shameless in cut, because van Rijn hadn't
provided any different sort, but the look she gave Torrance had nothing to do with that. "I had to come, Lodgemaster. If you've any pity at all, you'll listen to me."

He waved her to a chair, offered cigarettes, and struck
one for himself. The smoke, drawn deep into his lungs,
calmed him a little. He sat down on the opposite side of
the table. "If I can be of help to you, Freelady Kofoed,

you know I'm happy to oblige. Uh . . . Freeman van Rijn . . ."

"He's asleep. Not that he has any claims on me. I haven't signed a contract or any such thing." Her irritation gave way to a wry smile. "Oh, admitted, we're all his inferiors, in fact as well as in status. I'm not contravening his wishes, not really. It's just that he won't answer my questions, and if I don't find out what's going on I'll have to start screaming."

Torrance weighed a number of factors. A private explanation, in more detail than the crew had required, might indeed be best for her. "As you wish, Freelady," he said, and related what had happened to the converter. "We can't fix it ourselves," he concluded. "If we continued traveling at high quasi-speed, we'd burn it out before we arrived; and then, without power, we'd soon die. If we proceed slowly enough to preserve it, we'd need half a year to reach Valhalla, which is more time than we have supplies for. Though the Adderkops would doubtless track us down within a week or two."

She shivered. "Why? I don't understand." She stared at her glowing cigarette end for a moment, until a degree of composure returned, and with it a touch of humor. "I may pass for a fast, sophisticated girl on Freya, Captain. But you know even better than I, Freya is a jerkwater planet on the very fringe of human civilization. We've hardly any spatial traffic, except the League merchant ships, and they never stay long in port. I really know nothing about military or political technology. No one told me this was anything more important than a scouting mission, because I never thought to inquire. Why should the Adderkops be so anxious to catch us?"

Torrance considered the total picture before framing a reply. As a spaceman of the League, he must make an effort before he could appreciate how little the enemy actually meant to colonists who seldom left their home world. The name "Adderkop" was Freyan, a term of scorn for outlaws who'd been booted off the planet a century ago. Since then, however, the Freyans had had no direct contact with them. Somewhere in the unexplored deeps beyond Valhalla, the fugitives had settled on some unknown planet. Over the generations, their numbers grew, and the numbers of their warships. But Freya was still too strong for them to raid, and had no extraplanetary enterprises of her own to be harried. Why should Freya care?

Torrance decided to explain systematically, even if he must repeat the obvious. "Well," he said, "the Adderkops aren't stupid. They keep somewhat in touch with events, and know the Polesotechnic League wants to expand its operations into this region. They don't like that. It'd mean the end of their attacks on planets which can't fight back, their squeezing of tribute and their overpriced trade. Not that the League is composed of saints; we don't tolerate that sort of thing, but merely because freebooting cuts into the profits of our member companies. So the Adderkops undertook not to fight a full-dress war against us, but to harass our outposts till we gave it up as a bad job. They have the advantage of knowing their own sector of space, which we hardly do at all. And we were, indeed, at the point of writing this whole region off and trying someplace else. Freeman van Rijn wanted to make one last attempt. The opposition to this was so great that he had to come here and lead the expedition himself.

"I suppose you know what he did: used an unholy skill at bribery and bluff, at extracting what little information the prisoners we'd taken possessed, at fitting odd facts together. He got a clue to a hitherto untried segment. We flitted there, picked up a neutrino trail, and followed it to a human-colonized planet. As you know, it's almost certainly their own home world.

"If we bring back that information, there'll be no more trouble with the Adderkops. Not after the League sends in a few Star-class battleships and threatens to bombard their planet. They realize as much. We were spotted; several warcraft jumped us; we were lucky to get away. Their ships are obsolete, and so far we've shown them a clean pair of heels. But I hardly think they've quit hunting for us. They'll send their entire fleet cruising in search. Hyperdrive vibrations transmit instantaneously, and can be detected out to about one light-year distance. So if any Adderkop observes our 'wake' and homes in on it—with us crippled—that's the end."

She drew hard on her cigarette, but remained otherwise calm. "What are your plans?"

"A countermove. Instead of trying to make Freya— uh—I mean, we're proceeding in a search-helix at medium speed, straining our own detectors. If we discover another ship, we'll use the last gasp of our engines to close in. If it's an Adderkop vessel, well, perhaps we can seize it or something; we do have a couple of light guns in our turrets. It may be a nonhuman craft, though. Our intelligence reports, interrogation of prisoners, evaluation of explorers' observations, et cetera, indicate that three or four different species in this region possess the hyperdrive. The Adderkops themselves aren't certain about all of them. Space is so damned huge."

"If it does turn out to be nonhuman?"

"Then we'll do what seems indicated."

"I see." Her bright head nodded. She sat for a while, unspeaking, before she dazzled him with a smile. "Thanks, Captain. You don't know how much you've helped me."

Torrance suppressed a foolish grin. "A pleasure, Freelady."

"I'm coming to Earth with you. Did you know that? Freeman van Rijn has promised me a very good job."

*He always does,* thought Torrance.

Jeri leaned closer. "I hope we'll have a chance on the Earthward trip to get better acquainted, Captain. Or even right now."

The alarm bell chose that moment to ring.

The *Hebe G.B.* was a yacht, not a buccaneer frigate. When Nicholas van Rijn was aboard, though, the distinction sometimes got a little blurred. Thus she had more legs than most ships, detectors of uncommon sensitivity, and a crew experienced in the tactics of overhauling.

She was able to get a bearing on the hyperemission of

the other craft long before her own vibrations were observed. Pacing the unseen one, she established the set course it was following, then poured on all available juice to intercept. If the stranger had maintained quasi-velocity, there would have been contact in three or four hours. Instead, its wake indicated a sheering off, an attempt to flee. The *Hebe G.B.* changed course too, and continued gaining on her slower quarry.

"They're afraid of us," decided Torrance. "And they're not running back toward the Adderkop sun. Which two facts indicate they're not Adderkops themselves, but do have reason to be scared of strangers." He nodded, rather grimly, for during the preliminary investigations he had inspected a few backward planets which the bandit nation had visited.

Seeing that the pursuer kept shortening her distance, the pursued turned off their hyperdrive. Reverting to intrinsic sublight velocity, converter throttled down to minimal output, their ship became an infinitesimal speck in an effectively infinite space. The maneuver often works; after casting about futilely for a while, the enemy gives up and goes home. The *Hebe G. B.*, though, was prepared. The known superlight vector, together with the instant of cutoff, gave her computers a rough idea of where the prey was. She continued to that volume of space and then hopped about in a well-designed search pattern, reverting to normal state at intervals to sample the neutrino haze which any nuclear engine emits. Those nuclear engines known as stars provided most; but by statistical analysis, the computers presently isolated one feeble nearby source. The yacht went thither . . . and wan against the glittering sky, the other ship appeared in her screens.

It was several times her size, a cylinder with bluntly rounded nose and massive drive cones, numerous housings for auxiliary boats, a single gun turret. The principles of physics dictate that the general conformation of all ships intended for a given purpose shall be roughly the same. But any spaceman could see that this one had never been built by members of Technic civilization.

Fire blazed. Even with the automatic stopping-down of his viewscreen, Torrance was momentarily blinded. Instruments told him that the stranger had fired a fusion shell which his own robogunners had intercepted with a missile. The attack had been miserably slow and feeble. This was not a warcraft in any sense; it was no more a match for the *Hebe G.B.* than the yacht was for one of the Adderkops chasing her.

"Hokay, now we got that foolishness out of the way and we can talk business," said van Rijn. "Get them on the telecom and develop a common language. Fast! Then explain we mean no harm but want just a lift to Valhalla." He hesitated before adding, with a distinct wince, "We can pay well."

"Might prove difficult, sir," said Torrance. "Our ship is identifiably human-built, but chances are that the only humans they've ever met are Adderkops."

"Well, so if it makes needful, we can board them and force them to transport us, *nie?* Hurry up, for Satan's sake! If we wait too long here, like bebobbled snoozers, we'll get caught."

Torrance was about to point out they were safe enough. The Adderkops were far behind the swifter Terrestrial ship. They could have no idea that her hyperdrive was now cut off; when they began to suspect it, they could have no measurable probability of finding her. Then he remembered that the case was not so simple. If the parleying with these strangers took unduly long—more than a week, at best—Adderkop squadrons would have penetrated this general region and gone beyond. They would probably remain on picket for months, which the humans could not do for lack of food. When a hyperdrive did start up, they'd detect it and run down this awkward merchantman with ease. The only hope was to hitch a ride to Valhalla *soon,* using the head start already gained to offset the disadvantage of reduced speed.

"We're trying all bands, sir," he said. "No response so far." He frowned worriedly. "I don't understand. They must know we've got them cold, and they must have picked up our calls and realize we want to talk. Why don't they respond? Wouldn't cost them anything."

"Maybe they abandoned ship," suggested the communications officer. "They might have hyperdriven lifeboats."

"No." Torrance shook his head. "We'd have spotted that. . . . Keep trying, Freeman Betancourt. If we haven't gotten an answer in an hour, we'll lay alongside and board."

The receiver screens remained blank. But at the end of the grace period, when Torrance was issuing space armor, Yamamura reported something new. Neutrino output had increased from a source near the stern of the alien. Some process involving moderate amounts of energy was being carried out.

Torrance clamped down his helmet. "We'll have a look at that."

He posted a skeleton crew—van Rijn himself, loudly protesting, took over the bridge—and led his boarding party to the main air lock. Smooth as a gliding shark (the old swine was a blue-ribbon spaceman after all, the captain realized in some astonishment), the *Hebe G.B.* clamped on a tractor beam and hauled herself toward the bigger vessel.

It disappeared. Recoil sent the yacht staggering.

"Beelzebub and botulism!" snarled van Rijn. "He went back into hyper, ha? We see about that!" The ulcerated converter shrieked as he called upon it, but the engines were given power. On a lung and a half, the Terrestrial ship again overtook the foreigner. Van Rijn phased in so casually that Torrance almost forgot this was a job considered difficult by master pilots. He evaded a frantic pressor beam and tied his yacht to the larger hull with unshearable bands of force. He cut off his hyperdrive again, for the converter couldn't take much more. Being within the force-field of the alien, the *Hebe G.B.* was carried along, though the "drag" of extra mass reduced quasi-speed considerably. If he had hoped the grappled vessel would quit and revert to normal state, he was disappointed. The linked hulls continued plunging faster than light toward an unnamed constellation.

Torrance bit back an oath, summoned his men, and went outside.

He had never forced entry on a hostile craft before, but assumed it wasn't much different from burning his way into a derelict. Having chosen his spot, he set up a balloon tent to conserve air; no use killing the alien crew. The torches of his men spewed flame; blue actinic sparks fountained backward and danced through zero gravity. Meanwhile the rest of the squad stood by with blasters and grenades.

Beyond, the curves of the two hulls dropped off to infinity. Without compensating electronic viewscreens, the sky was weirdly distorted by aberration and Doppler effect, as if the men were already dead and beating through the other existence toward Judgment. Torrance held his mind firmly to practical worries. Once inboard, the non-humans made prisoner, how was he to communicate? Especially if he first had to gun down several of them . . .

The outer shell was peeled back. He studied the inner structure of the plate with fascination. He'd never seen anything like it before. Surely this race had developed space travel quite independently of mankind. Though their engineering must obey the same natural laws, it was radically different in detail. What was that tough but corky substance lining the inner shell? And was the circuitry embedded in it, for he didn't see any elsewhere?

The last defense gave way. Torrance swallowed hard and shot a flashbeam into the interior. Darkness and vacuum met him. When he entered the hull, he floated, weightless; artificial gravity had been turned off. The crew was hiding someplace and . . .

And . . .

Torrance returned to the yacht in an hour. When he came on the bridge, he found van Rijn seated by Jeri. The girl started to speak, took a closer look at the captain's face, and clamped her teeth together.

"Well?" snapped the merchant peevishly.

Torrance cleared his throat. His voice sounded unfamiliar and faraway to him. "I think you'd better come have a look, sir."

"You found the crew, wherever the sputtering hell they holed up? What are they like? What kind of ship is this we've gotten us, ha?"

Torrance chose to answer the last question first. "It seems to be an interstellar animal collector's transport vessel. The main hold is full of cages—environmentally controlled compartments, I should say—with the damnedest assortment of creatures I've ever seen outside Luna City Zoo."

"So what the pox is that to me? Where is the collector himself, and his fig-plucking friends?"

"Well, sir." Torrance gulped. "We're pretty sure by now they're hiding from us. Among the other animals."

A tube was run between the yacht's main lock and the entry cut into the other ship. Through this, air was pumped and electric lines were strung, to illuminate the prize. By some fancy juggling with the gravitic generator of the *Hebe G.B.*, Yamamura supplied about one-fourth Earth-weight to the foreigner, though he couldn't get the direction uniform and its decks felt canted in wildly varying degrees.

Even under such conditions, van Rijn walked ponderously. He stood with a salami in one hand and a raw onion in the other, glaring around the captured bridge. It could only be that, though it was in the bows rather than the waist. The viewscreens were still in operation, smaller than human eyes found comfortable, but revealing the same pattern of stars, surely by the same kind of optical compensators. A control console made a semicircle at the forward bulkhead, too big for a solitary human to operate. Yet presumably the designer had only had one pilot in mind, for a single seat had been placed in the middle of the arc.

Had been. A short metal post rose from the deck. Similar structures stood at other points, and boltholes showed where chairs were once fastened to them. But the seats had been removed.

"Pilot sat there at the center, I'd guess, when they weren't simply running on automatic," Torrance hazarded. "Navigator and communications officer . . . here and here? I'm not sure. Anyhow, they probably didn't use a copilot, but that chair bollard at the after end of the room suggests that an extra officer sat in reserve, ready to take over."

Van Rijn munched his onion and tugged his goatee. "Pestish big, this panel," he said. "Must be a race of bloody-be-damned octopussies, ha? Look how complicated."

He waved the salami around the half circle. The console, which seemed to be of some fluorocarbon polymer, held very few switches or buttons, but scores of flat luminous plates, each about twenty centimeters square. Some of them were depressed. Evidently these were the controls. Cautious experiment had shown that a stiff push was needed to budge them. The experiment had ended then and there, for the ship's cargo lock had opened and a good deal of air was lost before Torrance slapped the plate he had been testing hard enough to make the hull reseal itself. One should not tinker with the atomic-powered unknown, most especially not in galactic space.

"They must be strong like horses, to steer by this system without getting exhausted," went on van Rijn. "The size of everything tells likewise, *nie?*"

"Well, not exactly, sir," said Torrance. "The viewscreens seem made for dwarfs. The meters even more so." He pointed to a bank of instruments, no larger than buttons, on each of which a single number glowed. (Or letter, or ideogram, or what? They looked vaguely Old Chinese.) Occasionally a symbol changed value. "A human couldn't use these long without severe eyestrain. Of course, having eyes better adapted to close work than ours doesn't prove they are not giants. Certainly that switch couldn't be reached from here without long arms, and it seems meant for big hands." By standing on tiptoe, he touched it himself, an outsize double-pole affair set overhead, just above the pilot's hypothetical seat.

The switch fell open.

A roar came from aft. Torrance lurched backward under a sudden force. He caught at a shelf on the after bulkhead to steady himself. Its thin metal buckled as he clutched. "Devilfish and dunderheads!" cried van Rijn. Bracing his columnar legs, he reached up and shoved the switch back into position. The noise ended. Normality returned. Torrance hastened to the bridge doorway, a tall arch, and shouted down the corridor beyond: "It's okay! Don't worry! We've got it under control!"

"What the blue blinking blazes happened?" demanded van Rijn, in somewhat more high-powered words.

Torrance mastered a slight case of the shakes. "Emergency switch, I'd say." His tone wavered. "Turns on the gravitic field full speed ahead, not wasting any force on acceleration compensators. Of course, we being in hyperdrive, it wasn't very effective. Only gave us a—uh—less than one-G push, intrinsic. In normal state we'd have accelerated several Gs, at least. It's for quick getaways and ... and ..."

"And you, with brains like fermented gravy and bananas for fingers, went ahead and yanked it open!"

Torrance felt himself redden. "How was I to know, sir? I must've applied less than half a kilo of force. Emergency switches aren't hair-triggered, after all. Considering how much it takes to move one of those control plates, who'd have thought the switch would respond to so little?"

Van Rijn took a closer look. "I see now there is a hook to secure it by," he said. "Must be they use that when the ship's on a high-gravity planet." He peered down a hole near the center of the panel, about one centimeter in diameter and fifteen deep. At the bottom a small key projected. "This must be another special control, ha? Safer than that switch. You would need thin-nosed pliers to make a turning of it." He scratched his pomaded curls. "But then, why is not the pliers hanging handy? I don't see even a hook or bracket or drawer for them."

"I don't care," said Torrance. "When the whole interior's been stripped— There's nothing but a slagheap in the engine room, I tell you—fused metal, carbonized plastic . . . bedding, furniture, anything they thought might give us a clue to their identity, all melted down in a jury-rigged cauldron. They used their own converter to supply heat. That was the cause of the neutrino flux Yamamura observed. They must have worked like demons."

"But they did not destroy all needful tools and machines, surely? Simpler then they should blow up their whole ship, and us with it. I was sweating like a hog, me, for fear they would do that. Not so good a way for a poor sinful old man to end his days, blown into radioactive stinks three hundred light-years from the vineyards of Earth."

"N-n-no. As far as we can tell from a cursory examination, they didn't sabotage anything absolutely vital. We can't be sure, of course. Yamamura's gang would need weeks just to get a general idea of how this ship is put together, let alone the practical details of operating it. But I agree, the crew isn't bent on suicide. They've got us more neatly trapped than they know, even. Bound helplessly through space—toward their home star, maybe. In any event, almost at right angles to the course we want."

Torrance led the way out. "Suppose we go have a more thorough look at the zoo, sir," he went on. "Yamamura talked about setting up some equipment . . . to help us tell the crew from the animals!"

The main hold comprised almost half the volume of the great ship. A corridor below, a catwalk above, ran through a double row of two-decker cubicles. These numbered ninety-six, and were identical. Each was about five meters on a side, with adjustable fluorescent plates in the ceiling and a springy, presumably inert plastic on the floor. Shelves and parallel bars ran along the side walls, for the benefit of creatures that liked jumping or climbing. The rear wall was connected to well-shielded machines; Yamamura didn't dare tamper with these, but said they obviously regulated atmosphere, temperature, gravity, sanitation, and other environmental factors within each "cage." The front wall, facing on corridor and catwalk, was transparent. It held a stout air lock, almost as high as the cubicle itself, motorized but controlled by simple wheels inside and out. Only a few compartments were empty.

The humans had not strung fluoros in this hold, for it wasn't necessary. Torrance and Van Rijn walked through shadows, among monsters; the simulated light of a dozen different suns streamed around them: red, orange, yellow, greenish, and harsh electric blue.

A thing like a giant shark, save that tendrils fluttered about its head, swam in a water-filled cubicle among fronded seaweeds. Next to it was a cageful of tiny flying reptiles, their scales aglitter in prismatic hues, weaving and dodging through the air. On the opposite side, four mammals crouched among yellow mists—beautiful creatures, the size of a bear, vividly tiger-striped, walking mostly on all fours but occasionally standing up; then you noticed the retractable claws between stubby fingers, and the carnivore jaws on the massive heads. Farther on, the humans passed half a dozen sleek red beasts like six-legged otters, frolicking in a tank of water provided for them. The environmental machines must have decided this was their feeding time, for a hopper spewed chunks of proteinaceous material into a trough and the animals lolloped over to rip it with their fangs.

"Automatic feeding," Torrance observed. "I think probably the food is synthesized on the spot, according to the specifications of each individual species as determined by biochemical methods. For the crew, also. At least, we haven't found anything like a galley."

Van Rijn shuddered. "Nothing but synthetics? Not even a little glass Genever before dinner?" He brightened. "Ha, maybe here we find a good new market. And until they learn the situation, we can charge them triple prices."

"First," clipped Torrance, "we've got to find them."

Yamamura stood near the middle of the hold, focusing a set of instruments on a certain cage. Jeri stood by, handing him what he asked for, plugging and unplugging at a small powerpack. Van Rijn hove into view. "What goes on, anyhows?" he asked.

The chief engineer turned a patient brown face to him. "I've got the rest of the crew examining the shop in detail, sir," he said. "I'll join them as soon as I've gotten Freelady Kofoed trained at this particular job. She can handle the routine of it while the rest of us use our special skills to . . ." His words trailed off. He grinned ruefully. "To poke and prod gizmos we can't possibly understand in less than a month of work, with our limited research tools."

"A month we have not got," said van Rijn. "You are here checking conditions inside each individual cage?"

"Yes, sir. They're metered, of course, but we can't read the meters, so we have to do the job ourselves. I've haywired this stuff together, to give an approximate value of gravity, atmospheric pressure and composition, temperature, illumination spectrum, and so forth. It's slow work, mostly because of all the arithmetic needed to turn the dial readings into such data. Luckily, we don't have to test every cubicle, or even most of them."

"No," said van Rijn. "Even to a union organizer, obvious this ship was never made by fishes or birds. In fact, some kind of hands is always necessary."

"Or tentacles." Yamamura nodded at the compartment before him. The light within was dim red. Several black creatures could be seen walking restlessly about. They had stumpy-legged quadrupedal bodies, from which torsos rose, centaur fashion, toward heads armored in some bony material. Below the faceless heads were six thick, ropy arms, set in triplets. Two of these ended in three boneless but probably strong fingers.

"I suspect these are our coy friends," said Yamamura. "If so, we'll have a deuce of a time. They breathe hydrogen under high pressure and triple gravity, at a temperature of seventy below."

"Are they the only ones who like that kind of weather?" asked Torrance.

Yamamura gave him a sharp look. "I see what you're

getting at, Skipper. No, they aren't. In the course of putting this apparatus together and testing it, I've already found three other cubicles where conditions are similar. And in those, the animals are obviously just animals, snakes and so on, which couldn't possibly have built this ship."

"But then these octopus-horses can't be the crew, can they?" asked Jeri timidly. "I mean, if the crew were collecting animals from other planets, they wouldn't take home animals along, would they?"

"They might," said van Rijn. "We have a cat and a couple parrots aboard the *Hebe G.B.*, *nie?* Or, there are many planets with very similar conditions of the hydrogen sort, just like Earth and Freya are much-alike oxygen planets. So that proves nothings." He turned toward Yamamura, rather like a rotating globe himself. "But see here, even if the crew did pump out the air before we boarded, why not check their reserve tanks? If we find air stored away just like these diddlers here are breathing . . ."

"I thought of that," said Yamamura. "In fact, it was almost the first thing I told the men to look for. They've located nothing. I don't think they'll have any success, either. Because what they did find was an adjustable catalytic manifold. At least, it looks as if it should be, though we'd need days to find out for certain. Anyhow, my guess is that it renews exhausted air and acts as a chemosynthesizer to replace losses from a charge of simple inorganic compounds. The crew probably bled the ship's atmosphere into space before we boarded. When we go away, if we do, they'll open the door of their particular cage a crack, so its air can trickle out. The environmental adjuster will automatically force the chemosynthesizer to replace this. Eventually the ship'll be full of enough of their kind of gas for them to venture forth and adjust things more precisely." He shrugged. "That's assuming they even need to. Perhaps Earth-type conditions suit them perfectly well."

"Uh, yes," said Torrance. "Suppose we look around some more, and line up the possibly intelligent species."

Van Rijn trundled along with him. "What sort intelligence they got, these bespattered aliens?" he grumbled. "Why try this stupid masquerade in the first places?"

"It's not too stupid to have worked so far," said Torrance dryly. "We're being carried along on a ship we don't know how to stop. They must hope we'll either give up and depart, or else that we'll remain baffled until the ship enters their home region. At which time, quite probably a naval vessel—or whatever they've got —will detect us, close in, and board us to check up on what's happened."

He paused before a compartment. "I wonder . . ."

The quadruped within was the size of an elephant, though with a more slender build, indicating a lower gravity than Earth's. Its skin was green and faintly scaled, a ruff of hair along the back. The eyes with which it looked out were alert and enigmatic. It had an elephantlike trunk, terminating in a ring of pseudodactyls which must be as strong and sensitive as human fingers.

"How much could a one-armed race accomplish?" mused Torrance. "About as much as we, I imagine, if not quite as easily. And sheer strength would compensate. That trunk could bend an iron bar."

Van Rijn grunted and went past a cubicle of feathered ungulates. He stopped before the next. "Now here are some beasts might do," he said. "We had one like them on Earth once. What they called it? Quintilla? No, gorilla. Or chimpanzee, better, of gorilla size."

Torrance felt his heart thud. Two adjoining sections each held four animals of a kind which looked extremely hopeful. They were bipedal, short-legged and long-armed. Standing two meters tall, with a three-meter arm span, one of them could certainly operate that control console alone. The wrists, thick as a man's thighs, ended in proportionate hands, four-digited including a true thumb. The three-toed feet were specialized for walking, like man's feet. Their bodies were covered with brown fleece. Their heads were comparatively small, rising almost to a point, with massive snouts and beady eyes under cavernous brow ridges. As they wandered aimlessly about, Torrance saw that they were divided among males and females. On the sides of each neck he noticed two lumens closed by sphincters. The light upon them was the familiar yellowish white of a Sol-type star.

He forced himself to say, "I'm not sure. Those huge jaws must demand corresponding maxillary muscles, attaching to a ridge on top of the skull. Which'd restrict the cranial capacity."

"Suppose they got brains in their bellies," said van Rijn.

"Well, some people do," murmured Torrance. As the merchant choked, he added in haste, "No, actually, sir, that's hardly believable. Neural paths would get too long and so forth. Every animal I know of, if it has a central nervous system at all, keeps the brain close to the principal sense organs, which are usually located in the head. To be sure, a relatively small brain, within limits, doesn't mean these creatures are not intelligent. Their neurons might well be more efficient than ours."

"Humph and hassenpfeffer!" said van Rijn. "Might, might, might!" As they continued among strange shapes; "We can't go too much by atmosphere or light, either. If hiding, the crew could vary conditions quite a bit from their norm without hurting themselves. Gravity, too, by twenty or thirty percent."

"I hope they breathe oxygen, though—hoy!" Torrance stopped. After a moment, he realized what was so eerie about the several forms under the orange glow. They were chitinous-armored, not much bigger than a squarish military helmet and about the same shape. Four stumpy legs projected from beneath to carry them awkwardly about on taloned feet, also a pair of short tentacles ending in a bush of cilia. There was nothing special about them, as extraterrestrial animals go, except the two eyes which gazed from beneath each helmet: as large and somehow human as—well—the eyes of an octopus.

"Turtles," snorted van Rijn. "Armadillos at most."

"There can't be any harm in letting Jer—Freelady Kofoed check their environment too," said Torrance.

"It can waste time."

"I wonder what they eat. I don't see any mouths."

"Those tentacles look like capillary suckers. I bet they are parasites, or overgrown leeches, or something else like one of my competitors. Come along."

"What do we do after we've established which species could possibly be the crew?" said Torrance. "Try to communicate with each in turn?"

"Not much use, that. They hide because they don't want to communicate. Unless we can prove to them we are not Adderkops . . . but hard to see how."

"Wait! Why'd they conceal themselves at all, if they've had contact with the Adderkops? It wouldn't work."

"I think I tell you that, by damn," said van Rijn. "To give them a name, let us call this unknown race the Eksers. So. The Eksers been traveling space for some time, but space is so big they never bumped into humans. Then the Adderkop nation arises, in this sector where humans never was before. The Eksers hear about this awful new species which has gotten into space also. They land on primitive planets where Adderkops have made raids, talk to natives, maybe plant automatic cameras where they think raids will soon come, maybe spy on Adderkop camps from afar or capture a lone Adderkop ship. So they know what humans look like, but not much else. They do not want humans to know about them, so they shun contact; they are not looking for trouble. Not before they are well prepared to fight a war, at least. Hell's sputtering griddles! Torrance, we have got to establish our bona fides with this crew, so they take us to Freya and afterward go tell their leaders all humans are not so bad as the slime-begotten Adderkops. Otherwise, maybe we wake up one day with some planets attacked by Eksers, and before the fighting ends, we have spent billions of credits." He shook his fists in the air and bellowed like a wounded bull. "It is our duty to prevent this!"

"Our first duty is to get home alive, I'd say," Torrance answered curtly. "I have a wife and kids."

"Then stop throwing sheepish eyes at Jeri Kofoed. I saw her first."

The search turned up one more possibility. Four organisms the length of a man and the build of thick-legged caterpillars dwelt under greenish light. Their bodies were dark blue, spotted with silver. A torso akin to that of the tentacled centauroids, but stockier, carried two true arms. The hands lacked thumbs, but six fingers arranged around a three-quarter circle could accomplish much the same things. Not that adequate hands prove effective intelligence; on Earth, not only simians but a number of reptiles and amphibia boast as much, even if a man has the best, and man's apish ancestors were as well equipped in this respect as we are today. However, the round flat-faced heads of these beings, the large bright eyes beneath feathery antennae of obscure function, the small jaws and delicate lips, all looked promising.

*Promising of what?* thought Torrance.

Three Earth-days later, he hurried down a central corridor toward the Ekser engine room.

The passage was a great hemicylinder lined with the same rubbery gray plastic as the cages, making footfalls silent and spoken words weirdly unresonant. But a deeper vibration went through it, the almost subliminal drone of the hyperengine, driving the ship into darkness toward an unknown star, and announcing their presence to any hunter straying within a light-year of them. The flouros strung by the humans were far apart, so that one passed through bands of humming shadow. Doorless rooms opened off the hallway. Some were still full of supplies, and however peculiar the shape of tools and containers might be, however unguessable their purpose, this was a reassurance that one still lived, was not yet a ghost aboard the Flying Dutchman. Other cabins, however had been inhabited. And their bareness made Torrance's skin crawl.

Nowhere did a personal trace remain. Books, both codex and micro, survived, but in the finely printed symbology of a foreign planet. Empty places on the shelves suggested that all illustrated volumes had been sacrificed. Certainly he could see where pictures stuck on the walls had been ripped down. In the big private cabins, in the still larger one which might have been a saloon, as well as in the engine room and workshop and bridge, only the bollards to which furniture had been bolted were left. Long low niches and small cubbyholes were built into the cabin bulkheads, but when bedding had been thrown into a white-hot cauldron, how could a man guess which were the bunks . . . if either kind were? Clothing, ornaments, cooking and eating utensils, everything was destroyed. One room must have been a lavatory, but the facilities had been ripped out. Another might have been used for scientific studies, presumably of captured animals, but was so gutted that no human was certain.

*By God, you've got to admire them,* Torrance thought. Captured by beings whom they had every reason to think of as conscienceless monsters, the aliens had not taken the easy way out, the atomic explosion that would annihilate both crews. They might have, except for the chance of this being a zoo ship. But given a hope of survival, they snatched it, with an imaginative daring few humans could have matched. Now they sat in plain view, waiting for the monsters to depart—without wrecking their ship in mere spitefulness—or for a naval vessel of their own to rescue them. They had no means of knowing their captors were not Adderkops, or that this sector would soon be filled with Adderkop squadrons; the bandits rarely ventured even this close to Valhalla. Within the limits of available information, the aliens were acting with complete logic. But the nerve it took!

*I wish we could identify them and make friends,* thought Torrance. *The Eksers would be damned good friends for Earth to have. Or Ramanujan, or Freya, or the entire Polesotechnic League.* With a lopsided grin: *I'll bet they'd be nowhere near as easy to swindle as Old Nick thinks. They might well swindle him. That I'd love to see!*

*My reason is more personal, though,* he thought with a return of bleakness. *If we don't clear up this misunder-*

*standing soon, neither they nor we will be around. I mean
soon. If we have another three or four days of grace,
we're lucky.*

The passage opened on a well, with ramps curving
down either side to a pair of automatic doors. One door
led to the engine room, Torrance knew. Behind it, a nuclear converter powered the ship's electrical system,
gravitic cones, and hyperdrive; the principles on which
this was done were familiar to him, but the actual
machines were engines cased in metal and in foreign symbols. He took the other door, which opened on a workshop. A good deal of the equipment here was identifiable,
however distorted to his eyes: lathe, drill press, oscil-
loscope, crystal tester. Much else was mystery. Yamamura
sat at an improvised workbench, fitting together a piece
of electronic apparatus. Several other devices, haywired
on breadboards, stood close by. His face was shockingly
haggard, and his hands trembled. He'd been laboring this
whole time, stimpills holding him awake.

As Torrance approached, the engineer was talking
with Betancourt, the communications man. The entire
crew of the *Hebe G.B.* were under Yamamura's direction, in a frantic attempt to outflank the Eksers by learning on their own how to operate this ship.

"I've identified the basic electrical arrangement, sir,"
Betancourt was saying. "They don't tap the converter
directly like us; evidently they haven't developed our
stepdown methods. Instead, they use a heat exchanger to
run an extremely large generator—yeah, the same thing
you guessed was an armature-type dynamo—and draw
AC for the ship off that. Where DC is needed, the AC
passes through a set of rectifier plates which, by looking
at 'em, I'm sure must be copper oxide. They're bare,
behind a safety screen, though so much current goes
through that they're too hot to look at close up. It all
seems kind of primitive to me."

"Or else merely different," sighed Yamamura. "We
use a light-element fusion converter, one of whose advantages is that it can develop electric current directly.
They may have perfected a power plant which utilizes

moderately heavy elements with small positive packing fractions. I remember that was tried on Earth a long while ago, and given up as impractical. But maybe the Eksers are better engineers than us. Such a system would have the advantage of needing less refinement of fuel—which'd be a real advantage to a ship knocking about among unexplored planets. Maybe enough to justify that clumsy heat exchanger and rectifier system. We simply don't know."

He stared head-shakingly at the wires he was soldering. "We don't know a damn thing," he said. Seeing Torrance: "Well, carry on, Freeman Betancourt. And remember, *festina lente*."

"For fear of wrecking the ship?" asked the captain.

Yamamura nodded. "The Eksers would've known a small craft like ours couldn't generate a big enough hyperforce field to tug their own ship home," he replied. "So they'll have made sure no prize crew could make off with it. Some of the stuff may be booby-trapped to wreck itself if it isn't handled just right; and how'd we ever make repairs? Hence we're proceeding with the utmost caution. So cautiously that we haven't a prayer of figuring out the controls before the Adderkops find us."

"It keeps the crew busy, though."

"Which is useful. Uh-huh. Well, sir, I've about got my basic apparatus set up. Everything seems to test okay. Now, let me know which animal you want to investigate first." As Torrance hesitated, the engineer explained: "I have to adapt the equipment for the creature in question, you see. Especially if it's a hydrogen breather."

Torrance shook his head. "Oxygen. In fact, they live under conditions so much like ours that we can walk right into their cages. The gorilloids. That's what Jeri and I have named them. Those woolly, two-meter-tall bipeds with the ape faces."

Yamamura made an ape face of his own. "Brutes that powerful? Have they shown any sign of intelligence?"

"No. But then, would you expect the Eksers to? Jeri Kofoed and I have been parading in front of the cages of the possible species, making signs, drawing pictures, everything we could think of, trying to get the message across that we are not Adderkops and the genuine article is chasing us. No luck, of course. All the animals did give us an interested regard, though, except the gorilloids . . . which may or may not prove anything."

"What animals, now? I've been so blinking busy—"

"Well, we call 'em the tiger apes, the tentacle centaurs, the elephantoid, the helmet beasts, and the caterpiggles. That's stretching things, I know; the tiger apes and the helmet beasts are highly improbable, to say the least, and the elephantoid isn't much more convincing. The gorilloids have the right size and the most effective-looking hands, and they're oxygen breathers, as I said, so we may well take them first. Next in order of likelihood, I'd guess, are the caterpiggles and the tentacle centaurs. But the caterpiggles, though oxygen breathers, are from a high-gravity planet; their air pressure would give us narcosis in no time. The tentacle centaurs breathe hydrogen. In either case, we'd have to work in space armor."

"The gorilloids will be quite bad enough, thank you kindly."

Torrance looked at the workbench. "What exactly do you plan to do?" he asked. "I've been too busy with my own end of this affair to learn any details of yours."

"I've adapted some things from the medical kit," said Yamamura. "A sort of ophthalmoscope, for example, because the ship's instruments use color codes and finely printed symbols, so that the Eksers are bound to have eyes at least as good as ours. Then this here's a nervous-impulse tracer. It detects synaptic flows and casts a three-dimensional image into yonder crystal box, shows us the whole nervous system functioning as a set of luminous traces. By correlating this with gross anatomy, we can roughly identify the sympathetic and parasympathetic systems—or their equivalents—I hope. And the brain. And, what's really to the point, the degrees of brain activity more or less independent of the other nerve paths. That is, whether the animal is thinking."

He shrugged. "It tests out fine on me. Whether it'll

work on a nonhuman, especially in a different sort of atmosphere, I do not know. I'm sure it'll develop bugs."

" 'We can but try,' " quoted Torrance wearily.

"I suppose Old Nick is sitting and thinking," said Yamamura in an edged voice. "I haven't seen him for quite some time."

"He's not been helping Jeri and me either," said Torrance. "Told us our attempt to communicate was futile until we could prove to the Eksers that we know who they are. And even after that, he said, the only communication at first will be by gestures made with a pistol."

"He's probably right."

"He's not right! Logically, perhaps, but not psychologically. Or morally. He sits in his suite with a case of brandy and a box of cigars. The cook, who could be down here helping you, is kept aboard the yacht to fix him his damned gourmet meals. You'd think he didn't care if we're blown out of the sky!"

He remembered his oath of fealty, his official position, and so on and so on. They felt nonsensical, here on the edge of extinction. But habit was strong. He swallowed and said harshly, "Sorry. Please ignore what I said. When you're ready, Freeman Yamamura, we'll test the gorilloids."

Six men and Jeri stood by in the passage with drawn blasters. Torrance hoped fervently they wouldn't have to shoot. He hoped even more that if they did have to, he'd still be alive.

He gestured to the four crewmen at his back. "Okay, boys." He wet his lips. His heart thuttered. Being a captain and a Lodgemaster was very fine until moments like this came, when you must make a return for your special privileges.

He spun the outside control wheel. The airlock motor hummed and opened the doors. He stepped through, into a cage of gorilloids.

Pressure differentials weren't enough to worry about, but after all this time at one-fourth G, to enter a field only ten percent less than Earth's was like a blow. He lurched, almost fell, gasped in an air warm and thick and full of unnamed stenches. Sagging back against the wall, he stared across the floor at the four bipeds. Their brown fleecy bodies loomed unfairly tall, up and up to the coarse faces. Eyes overshadowed by brows glared at him. He clapped a hand on his stun pistol. He didn't want to shoot it, either. No telling what supersonics might do to a nonhuman nervous system; and if these were in truth the crewfolk, the worst thing he could do was inflict serious injury on one of them. But he wasn't used to being small and frail. The knurled handgrip was a comfort.

A male growled deep in his chest, and advanced a step. His pointed head thrust forward, the sphincters in his neck opened and shut like sucking mouths; his jaws gaped to show the white teeth.

Torrance backed toward a corner. "I'll try to attract that one in the lead away from the others," he called softly. "Then get him."

"Aye." A spacehand, a stocky slant-eyed nomad from Altai, uncoiled a lariat. Behind him, the other three spread a net woven for this purpose.

The gorilloid paused. A female hooted. The male seemed to draw resolution from her. He waved the others back with a strangely humanlike gesture and stalked toward Torrance.

The captain drew his stunner, pointed it shakily, resheathed it, and held out both hands. "Friends," he croaked.

His hope that the masquerade might be dropped became suddenly ridiculous. He sprang back toward the air lock. The gorilloid snarled and snatched at him. Torrance wasn't fast enough. The hand ripped his shirt open and left a bloody trail on his breast. He went to hands and knees, stabbed with pain. The Altaian's lasso whirled and snaked forth. Caught around the ankles, the gorilloid crashed. His weight shook the cubicle.

*"Get him! Watch out for his arms! Here—"*

Torrance staggered back to his feet. Beyond the melee, where four men strove to wind a roaring, struggling monster in a net, he saw the remaining three creatures. They were crowded into the opposite corner, howling in basso. The compartment was like the inside of a drum.

"Get him out," choked Torrance. "Before the others charge."

He aimed his stunner again. If intelligent, they'd know this was a weapon. They might attack anyway. . . . Deftly, the man from Altai roped an arm, snubbed his lariat around the gargantuan torso, and made it fast by a slip knot. The net came into position. Helpless in cords of wire-strong fiber, the gorilloid was dragged to the entrance. Another male advanced, step by jerky step. Torrance stood his ground. The animal ululation and human shouting surfed about him, within him. His wound throbbed. He saw with unnatural clarity the muzzle full of teeth that could snap his head off, the little dull eyes turned red with fury, the hands so much like his own but black-skinned, four-fingered, and enormous. . . .

"All clear, Skipper!"

The gorilloid lunged. Torrance scrambled through the air-lock chamber. The giant followed. Torrance braced himself in the corridor and aimed his stun pistol. The gorilloid halted, shivered, looked around in something resembling bewilderment, and retreated. Torrance closed the airlock.

Then he sat down and trembled.

Jeri bent over him. "Are you okay?" she breathed. "Oh! You've been hurt!"

"Nothing much," he mumbled. "Gimme a cigarette."

She took one from her belt pouch and said with a crispness he admired, "I suppose it is just a bruise and a deep scratch. But we'd better check it, anyway, and sterilize. Might be infected."

He nodded but remained where he was until he had finished the cigarette. Farther down the corridor, Yamamura's men got their captive secured to a steel framework. Unharmed but helpless, the brute yelped and tried to bite as the engineer approached with his equipment. Returning him to the cubicle afterward was likely to be almost as tough as getting him out.

Torrance rose. Through the transparent wall, he saw

a female gorilloid viciously pulling something to shreds, and realized he had lost his turban when he was knocked over. He sighed. "Nothing much we can do till Yamamura gives us a verdict," he said. "Come on, let's go rest awhile."

"Sick bay first," said Jeri firmly. She took his arm. They went to the entry hole, through the tube, and into the steady half-weight of the *Hebe G.B.* which van Rijn preferred. Little was said while Jeri got Torrance's shirt off, swabbed the wound with universal disinfectant, which stung like hell, and bandaged it. Afterward he suggested a drink.

They entered the saloon. To their surprise, and to Torrance's displeasure, van Rijn was there. He sat at the inlaid mahogany table, dressed in snuff-stained lace and his usual sarong, a bottle in his right and a Trichinopoly cigar in his left. A litter of papers lay before him.

"Ah, so," he said, glancing up. "What gives?"

"They're testing a gorilloid now." Torrance flung himself into a chair. Since the steward had been drafted for the capture party, Jeri went after drinks. Her voice floated back, defiant:

"Captain Torrance was almost killed in the process. Couldn't you at least come watch, Nick?"

"What use I should watch, like some tourist with haddock eyes?" scoffed the merchant. "I make no skeletons about it, I am too old and fat to help chase large economy-size apes. Nor am I so technical I can twiddle knobs for Yamamura." He took a puff of his cigar and added complacently, "Besides, that is not my job. I am no kind of specialist, I have no fine university degrees, I learned in the school of hard knockers. But what I learned is how to make them do things for me, and then how to make something profitable from their doings."

Torrance breathed out, long and slow. With the tension eased, he was beginning to feel immensely tired. "What're you checking over?" he asked.

"Reports of engineer studies on the Ekser ship," said van Rijn. "I told everybody should take full notes on what they observed. Somewhere in those notes is maybe a clue we can use. If the gorilloids are not the Eksers, I mean. The gorilloids are possible, and I see no way to eliminate them except by Yamamura's checkers."

Torrance rubbed his eyes. "They're not entirely plausible," he said. "Most of the stuff we've found seems meant for big hands. But some of the tools, especially, are so small that—oh, well, I suppose a nonhuman might be as puzzled by an assortment of our own tools. Does it really make sense that the same race would use sledge hammers and etching needles?"

Jeri came back with two stiff Scotch-and-sodas. His gaze followed her. In a tight blouse and half knee-length skirt, she was worth following. She sat down next to him rather than van Rijn, whose jet eyes narrowed.

However, the older man spoke mildly. "I would like if you should list for me, here and now, the other possibilities, with your reasons for thinking of them. I have seen them too, natural, but my own ideas are not all clear yet and maybe something that occurs to you would joggle my head."

Torrance nodded. One might as well talk shop, even though he'd been over this ground a dozen times before with Jeri and Yamamura.

"Well," he said, "the tentacle centaurs appear very likely. You know the ones I mean. They live under red light and about half again Earth's gravity. A dim sun and a low temperature must make it possible for their planet to retain hydrogen, because that's what they breathe, hydrogen and argon. You know how they look: bodies sort of like rhinoceri, torsos with bone-plated heads and fingered tentacles. Like the gorilloids, they're big enough to pilot this ship easily.

"All the rest are oxygen breathers. The ones we call caterpiggles—the long, many-legged, blue-and-silver ones, with the peculiar hands and the particularly intelligent-looking faces—they're from an oddball world. It must be big. They're under three Gs in their cage, which can't be a red herring for this length of time. Body fluid adjustment would go out of kilter, if they're used to much lower weight. Nevertheless, their planet has oxygen and nitrogen rather than hydrogen, under a dozen Earth-atmospheres' pressure. The temperature is rather high, fifty degrees. I imagine their world, though of nearly Jovian mass, is so close to its sun that the hydrogen was boiled off, leaving a clear field for evolution similar to Earth's.

"The elephantoid comes from a planet with only about half our gravity. He's the single big fellow with a trunk ending in fingers. He gets by in air too thin for us, which indicates the gravity in his cubicle isn't faked either."

Torrance took a long drink. "The others live under pretty terrestroid conditions," he resumed. "For that reason, I wish they were more probable. But actually, except for the gorilloids, they seem like long shots. The helmet beasts—"

"What's that?" asked van Rijn.

"Oh, you remember," said Jeri. "Those eight or nine things like humpbacked turtles, not much bigger than your head. They crawl around on clawed feet, waving little tentacles that end in filaments. They blot up food through those, soupy stuff the machines dump into their trough. They haven't anything like effective hands—the tentacles could only do a few very simple things—but we gave them some time because they do seem to have better developed eyes than parasites usually do."

"Parasites don't evolve intelligence," said van Rijn. "They got better ways to make a living, by damn. Better make sure the helmet beasts really are parasites—in their home environments—and got no hands tucked under those shells, before you quite write them off. Who else you got?"

"The tiger apes," said Torrance. "Those striped carnivores built something like bears. They spend most of their time on all fours, but they do stand and walk on their hind legs sometimes, and they do have hands. Clumsy, thumbless ones, with retractable claws, but on all their limbs. Are four hands without thumbs as good as two with? I don't know. I'm too tired to think."

"And that's the lot, ha?" Van Rijn tilted the bottle to his lips. After a prolonged gurgling he set it down, belched, and blew smoke through his majestic nose. "Who's to try next, if the gorilloids flunk?"

"It better be the caterpiggles, in spite of the air pressure," said Jeri. "Then . . . oh . . . the tentacle centaurs, I suppose. Then maybe the—"

"Horse maneuvers!" Van Rijn's fist struck the table. The bottle and glasses jumped. "How long it takes to catch and check each specimen? Hours, *nie?* And in between times, takes many more hours to adjust the apparatus and chase out the hiccups it develops under a new set of conditions. Also, Yamamura will collapse if he can't sleep soon, and who else we got can do this? All the whiles, the forstunken Adderkops get closer. We have not got time for that method! If the gorilloids don't pan out, then only logic will help us. We must deduce from the facts we have who the Eksers are."

"Go ahead." Torrance drained his glass. "I'm going to take a nap."

Van Rijn purpled. "That's right!" he huffed. "Be like everybody elses. Loaf and play, dance and sing, enjoy yourselfs the liver-long day. Because you always got poor old Nicholas van Rijn there, to heap the work and worry on his back. Oh, dear St. Dismas, why can't you at least make some *one* other person in this whole universe do something useful?"

Torrance was awakened by Yamamura. The gorilloids were not the Eksers. They were color blind and incapable of focusing on the ship's instruments; their brains were small, with nearly the whole mass devoted to purely animal functions. He estimated their intelligence as equal to a dog's.

The captain stood on the bridge of the yacht, because it was a familiar place, and tried to accustom himself to being doomed.

Space had never seemed so beautiful as now. He was not well acquainted with the local constellations, but his trained gaze identified Perseus, Auriga, Taurus, not much distorted since they lay in the direction of Earth (and of Ramanujan, where gilt towers rose out of mists to catch the first sunlight, blinding against blue Mount Gandhi). A few individuals could also be picked out: ruby Betelgeuse, amber Spica, the pilot stars by which he had steered through his whole working life. Otherwise the sky was aswarm with small frosty fires, across blackness unclouded and endless. The Milky Way girdled it with cool silver, a nebula glowed faint and green, another galaxy spiraled on the mysterious edge of visibility. He thought less about the planets he had trod, even his own, than about this faring between them which was soon to terminate. For end it would, in a burst of violence too swift to be felt. Better go out thus cleanly when the Adderkops came, than into their dungeons.

He stubbed out his cigarette. Returning, his hand caressed the dear shapes of controls. He knew each switch and knob as well as he knew his own fingers. This ship was his—in a way, himself. Not like that other, whose senseless control board needed a giant and a dwarf, whose emergency switch fell under a mere slap if it wasn't hooked in place, whose—

A light footfall brought him twisting around. Irrationally, so strained was he, his heart flew up within him. When he saw it was Jeri, he eased his muscles, but the pulse continued quick in his blood.

She advanced slowly. The overhead light gleamed on her yellow hair and in the blue of her eyes. But she avoided his glance, and her mouth was not quite steady.

"What brings you here?" he asked. His tone fell even more soft than he had intended.

"Oh . . . the same as you." She stared out the viewscreen. During the time since they captured the alien ship, or it captured them, a red star off the port bow had visibly grown. Now it burned baleful as they passed, a light-year distant. She grimaced and turned her back to it. "Yamamura is readjusting the test apparatus," she said thinly. "No one else knows enough about it to help him, but he has the shakes so bad from exhaustion he can scarcely do the job himself. Old Nick just sits in his suite, smoking and drinking. He's gone through that bottle already, and started another. I couldn't breathe in there any longer; it was too smoky. And he won't say a word. Except to himself, in Malay or something. I couldn't stand it."

"We may as well wait," said Torrance. "We've done everything we can, till time to check a caterpiggle. We'll have to do that spacesuited, in their own cage, and hope they don't attack us."

She slumped. "Why bother?" she said. "I know the situation as well as you. Even if the caterpiggles are the Eksers, under those conditions we'll need a couple of days to prove it. I doubt if we have that much time left. If we start toward Valhalla two days from now, I'll bet we're detected and run down before we get there. Certainly, if the caterpiggles are only animals too, we'll never get time to test a third species. Why bother?"

"We've nothing else to do," said Torrance.

"Yes, we do. Not this ugly, futile squirming about, like cornered rats. Why can't we accept that we're going to die, and use the time to . . . to be human again?"

Startled, he looked back from the sky to her. "What do you mean?"

Her lashes fluttered downward. "I suppose that would depend on what we each prefer. Maybe you'll want to, well, get your thoughts in order or something."

"How about you?" he asked through his heartbeat.

"I'm not a thinker." She smiled forlornly. "I'm afraid I'm just a shallow sort of person. I'd like to enjoy life while I have it." She half turned from him. "But I can't find anyone I'd like to enjoy it with."

He, or his hands, grabbed her bare shoulders and spun her around to face him. She felt silken under his palms. "Are you sure you can't?" he said roughly. She closed her eyes and stood with face tilted upward, lips half parted. He kissed her. After a second she responded.

After a minute, Nicholas van Rijn appeared in the doorway.

He stood an instant, pipe in hand, gun belted to his waist, before he flung the churchwarden shattering to the deck. "So!" he bellowed.

"Oh!" wailed Jeri.

She disengaged herself. A tide of rage mounted in Torrance. He knotted his fists and started toward van Rijn.

"So!" repeated the merchant. The bulkheads seemed to quiver with his voice. "By louse-bitten damn, this is a fine thing for me to come on. Satan's tail in a mousetrap! I sit hour by hour sweating my brain to the bone for the sake of your worthless life, and all whiles you, you illegitimate spawn of a snake with dandruff and a cheese mite, here you are making up to my own secretary hired with my own hard-earned money! Gargoyles and *Götterdämmerung!* Down on your knees and beg my pardon, or I mash you up and sell you for dogfood!"

Torrance stopped, a few centimeters from van Rijn. He was slightly taller than the merchant, if less bulky, and at least thirty years younger. "Get out," he said in a strangled voice.

Van Rijn turned puce and gobbled at him.

"Get out," repeated Torrance. "I'm still the captain of this ship. I'll do what I damned well please, without interference from any loud-mouthed parasite. Get off the bridge, or I'll toss you out on your fat bottom!"

The color faded in van Rijn's cheeks. He stood motionless for whole seconds. "Well, by damn," he whispered at last. "By damn and death, cubical. He has got the nerve to talk back."

His left fist came about in a roundhouse swing. Torrance blocked it, though the force nearly threw him off his feet. His own left smacked the merchant's stomach, sank a short way into fat, encountered the muscles, and rebounded bruised. Then van Rijn's right fist clopped. The cosmos exploded around Torrance. He flew up in the air, went over backward, and lay where he fell.

When awareness returned, van Rijn was cradling his head and offering brandy which a tearful Jeri had fetched. "Here, boy. Go slow there. A little nip of this, ha? That goes good. There, now, you only lost one tooth and we get that fixed at Freya. You can even put it on expense account. There, that makes you feel more happy, *nie?* Now, girl, Jarry, Jelly, whatever your name is, give me that stimpill. Down the hatchworks, boy. And then, upsy-rosy, onto your feet. You should not miss the fun."

One-handed, van Rijn heaved Torrance erect. The captain leaned awhile on the merchant, until the stimpill removed aches and dizziness. Then, huskily through swollen lips, he asked, "What's going on? What d' you mean?"

"Why, I know who the Eksers are. I came to get you, and we fetch them from their cage." Van Rijn nudged Torrance with a great splay thumb and whispered almost as softly as a hurricane, "Don't tell anyone or I have too many fights, but I like a brass-bound nerve like you got. When we get home, I think you transfer off this yacht to command of a trading squadron. How you like that, ha? But come, we still got a damn plenty of work to do."

Torrance followed him in a daze through the small ship and the tube, into the alien, down a corridor and a ramp to the zoological hold. Van Rijn gestured at the spacemen posted on guard lest the Eksers make a sally. They drew their guns and joined him, their weary slouch jerking to alertness when he stopped before an air lock.

"Those?" sputtered Torrance. "But—I thought—"

"You thought what they hoped you would think," said van Rijn grandly. "The scheme was good. Might have worked, not counting the Adderkops, except that Nicholas van Rijn was here. Now, then. We go in and carry them all out, making a good show of our weapons. I hope we need not get too tough with them. I expect not, when we explain by drawings how we understand their secret. Then they should take us to Valhalla, as we can show by those pretty astronautical diagrams Captain Torrance has already prepared. They will cooperate under threats, as prisoners, at first. But on the voyage, we can use the standard means to establish alimentary communications . . . no, terror and taxes, I mean rudimentary . . . anyhows, we get the idea across that all humans are not Adderkops and we want to be friends and sell them things. Hokay? We go!"

He marched through the air lock, scooped up a helmet beast, and bore it kicking out of its cage.

Torrance didn't have time for anything en route except his work. First the entry hole in the prize must be sealed, while supplies and equipment were carried over from the *Hebe G.B.* Then the yacht must be cast loose under her own hyperdrive; in the few hours before her converter quite burned out, she might draw an Adderkop in chase. Then the journey commenced, and though the Eksers laid a course as directed, they must be constantly watched lest they try some suicidal stunt. Every spare moment must be devoted to the urgent business of achieving a simple common language with them. Torrance must also supervise his crew, calm their fears, and maintain a detector-watch for enemy vessels. If any had been detected, the humans would have gone off hyperdrive and hoped they could lie low. None were, but the strain was considerable.

Occasionally he slept.

Thus he got no chance to talk to van Rijn at length. He assumed the merchant had had a lucky hunch, and let it go at that.

Until Valhalla was a tiny yellow disc, outshining every other star; a League patrol ship closed on them; and, explanation being made, it gave them escort as they moved at sublight speed toward Freya.

The patrol captain intimated he'd like to come aboard. Torrance stalled him. "When we're in orbit, Freeman Agilik, I'll be delighted. But right now, things are pretty disorganized. You can understand that, I'm sure."

He switched off the alien telecom he had now learned to operate. "I'd better go below and clean up," he said. "Haven't had a bath since we abandoned the yacht. Carry on, Freeman Lafarge." He hesitated. "And—uh—Freeman Jukh-Barklakh."

Jukh grunted something. The gorilloid was too busy to talk, squatting where a pilot seat should have been, his big hands slapping control plates as he edged the ship into a hyperbolic path. Barklakh, the helmet beast on his

shoulders, who had no vocal cords of his own, waved a
tentacle before he dipped it into the protective shaft to
turn a delicate adjustment key. The other tentacle remained buried on its side of the gorilloid's massive neck,
drawing nourishment from the bloodstream, receiving
sensory impulses, and emitting the motor-nerve commands of a skilled space pilot.

At first the arrangement had looked vampirish to Torrance. But though the ancestors of the helmet beasts
might once have been parasites on the ancestors of the
gorilloids, they were no longer. They were symbionts.
They supplied the effective eyes and intellect, while the
big animals supplied strength and hands. Neither species
was good for much by itself; in combination, they were
something rather special. Once he got used to the idea,
Torrance found the sight of a helmet beast using its claws
to climb up a gorilloid no more unpleasant than a man
in a historical stereopic mounting a horse. And once the
helmet beasts were used to the idea that these humans
were not enemies, they showed a positive affection for
them.

*Doubtless they're thinking what lovely new specimens
we can sell them for their zoo,* reflected Torrance. He
slapped Barklakh on the shell, patted Jukh's fur, and
left the bridge.

A sponge bath of sorts and fresh garments took the
edge off his weariness. He thought he'd better warn van
Rijn, and knocked at the cabin which the merchant had
curtained off as his own.

"Come in," boomed the bass voice. Torrance entered
a cubicle blue with smoke. Van Rijn sat on an empty
brandy case, one hand holding a cigar, the other holding
Jeri, who was snuggled on his lap.

"Well, sit down, sit down," he roared cordially. "You
find a bottle somewhere under those dirty clothes in the
corner."

"I stopped by to tell you, sir, we'll have to receive
the captain of our escort when we're in orbit around
Freya, which'll be soon. Professional courtesy, you know.

He's naturally anxious to meet the Eks—uh—the Togru-Kon-Tanakh."

"Hokay, pipe him aboard, lad." Van Rijn scowled. "Only make him bring his own bottle, and not take too long. I want to land, me; I'm sick of space. I think I'll run barefoot over the soft cool acres and acres of Freya, by damn!"

"Maybe you'd like to change clothes?" hinted Torrance.

"Ooh!" squeaked Jeri, and ran off to the cabin she sometimes occupied. Van Rijn leaned back against the wall, hitched up his sarong and crossed his shaggy legs as he said: "If that captain comes to meet the Eksers, let him meet the Eksers. I stay comfortable like I am. And I will not entertain him with how I figured out who they were. That I keep exclusive, for sale to what news syndicate bids highest. Understand?"

His eyes grew unsettlingly sharp. Torrance gulped. "Yes, sir."

"Good. Now do sit down, boy. Help me put my story in order. I have not your fine education, I was a poor lonely hard-working old man from I was twelve, so I would need some help making my words as elegant as my logic."

"Logic?" echoed Torrance, puzzled. He tilted the flask, chiefly because the tobacco haze in here made his eyes smart. "I thought you guessed—"

"What? You know me so little as that? No, no, by damn. Nicholas van Rijn never guesses. I *knew*." He reached for the bottle, took a hefty swig, and added magnanimously, "That is, after Yamamura found the gorilloids alone could not be the peoples we wanted. Then I sat down and uncluttered my brains and thought it over.

"See, it was simple eliminations. The elephantoid was out right away. Only one of him. Maybe, in emergency, one could pilot this ship through space—but not land it, and pick up wild animals, and care for them, and all else. Also, if somethings go wrong, he is helpless."

Torrance nodded. "I did consider it from the spaceman's angle," he said. "I was inclined to rule out the elephantoid on that ground. But I admit I didn't see the animal-collecting aspect made it altogether impossible that this could be a one-being expedition."

"He was pretty too big anyhow," said van Rijn. "As for the tiger apes, like you, I never took them serious. Maybe their ancestors was smaller and more biped, but this species is reverting to quadruped again. Animals do not specialize in being everything. Not brains and size and carnivore teeth and cat claws, all to once.

"The caterpiggles looked hokay till I remembered that time you accidental turned on the bestonkered emergency acceleration switch. Unless hooked in place, what such a switch would not be except in special cases, it fell rather easy. So easy that its own weight would make it drop open under three Earth gravities. Or at least there would always be serious danger of this. Also, that shelf you bumped into—they wouldn't build shelves so light on high-gravity planets."

He puffed his cigar back to furnace heat. "Well, might be the tentacle centaurs," he continued. "Which was bad for us, because hydrogen and oxygen explode. I checked hard through the reports on the ship, hoping I could find something that would eliminate them. And by damn, I did. For this I will give St. Dismas an altar cloth, not too expensive. You see, the Eksers is kind enough to use copper oxide rectifiers, exposed to the air. Copper oxide and hydrogen, at a not very high temperature such as would soon develop from strong electricking, they make water and pure copper. Poof, no more rectifier. Therefore ergo, this shop was not designed for hydrogen breathers." He grinned. "You has had so much high scientific education you forgot your freshlyman chemistry."

Torrance snapped his fingers and swore at himself.

"By eliminating, we had the helmet beasts," said van Rijn. "Only they could not possible be the builders. True, they could handle certain tools and controls, like that buried key, but never all of it. And they are too slow and small. How could they ever stayed alive long enough to invent spaceships? Also, animals that little don't get room for real brains. And neither armored animals nor parasites ever get much. Nor do they get good eyes. And yet the helmet beasts seemed to have very good eyes, as near as we could tell. They looked like human eyes, anyhows.

"I remembered there was both big and little cubbyholes in these cabins. Maybe bunks for two kinds of sleeper? And I thought, is the human brain a turtle just because it is armored in bone? A parasite just because it lives off blood from other places? Well, maybe some people I could name but won't, like Juan Harleman of the Venusian Tea & Coffee Growers, Inc., has parasite turtles for brains. But not me. So there I was. Q.," said van Rijn smugly, "E.D."

Hoarse from talking, he picked up the bottle. Torrance sat a few minutes more, but as the other seemed disinclined to conversation, he got up to go.

Jeri met him in the doorway. In a slit and topless blue gown which fitted like a coat of lacquer, she was a fourth-order stunblast. Torrance stopped in his tracks. Her gaze slid slowly across him, as if reluctant to depart.

"Mutant sea-otter coats," murmured van Rijn dreamily. "Martian firegems. An apartment in the Stellar Towers."

She scampered to him and ran her fingers through his hair. "Are you comfortable, Nicky, darling?" she purred. "Can't I do something for you?"

Van Rijn winked at Torrance. "Your technique, that time on the bridge—I watched and it was lousy," he said to the captain. "Also, you are not old and fat and lonesome; you have a happy family for yourself."

"Uh—yes," said Torrance. "I do." He let the curtain drop and returned to the bridge.

NOT LONG AGO, I HAD THE PLEASURE of sharing a banquet table with the distinguished scientific thinker Harrison Brown, and of telling him how shamelessly I had ransacked his work.

In particular, some two decades before he had published a prescient book, *The Challenge of Man's Future*. Along with much else, this work made certain points that today are beginning to jab us harder and harder—points about unrestrained industrial growth brought up short by shortages as well as by the limits of what the biosphere can stand. Technological civilization can, we hope, find technological solutions to the problems it creates for itself. But suppose it collapses. Will there be any physical possibility of rebuilding it?

Thinking about this at the time, I considered a mitigating factor that had been emphasized by L. Sprague de Camp and others. Worldwide catastrophe would probably not produce a worldwide, permanent loss of knowledge. There are simply too many printed books lying around. (And it's worth noting that when societies in the past went under, much or all of their art and literature might forever have vanished, but seldom any

9

235

appreciable amount of their technology.) Eventually someone would use that information to rebuild—though, as Dr. Brown explained, the result might have to be a civilization based on low energy and lean resources.

And its people wouldn't think like us today. In fact, the chances are that several new cultures would arise, alien to each other. Could they achieve understanding? With our many advantages, we who now live on Earth haven't done any too well at that.

# THE SKY PEOPLE

‹‹‹‹‹‹‹‹‹‹‹‹‹‹‹‹‹‹‹‹‹‹‹‹‹‹‹‹‹‹‹‹‹‹‹

THE ROVER FLEET GOT THERE JUST BEFORE sunrise. From its height, five thousand feet, the land was bluish gray, smoked with mists. Irrigation canals caught the first light as if they were full of mercury. Westward the ocean gleamed, its far edge dissolved into purple and a few stars.

Loklann sunna Holber leaned over the gallery rail of his flagship and pointed a telescope at the city. It sprang to view as a huddle of walls, flat roofs, and square watchtowers. The cathedral spires were tinted rose by a hidden sun. No barrage balloons were aloft. It must be true what rumor said, that the Perio had abandoned its outlying provinces to their fate. So the portable wealth of Meyco would have flowed into S' Antón, for safekeeping—which meant that the place was well worth a raid. Loklann grinned.

Robra sunna Stam, the *Buffalo*'s mate, spoke. "Best we come down to about two thousand," he suggested. "To make sure the men aren't blown sideways, to the wrong side of the town walls."

"Aye." The skipper nodded his helmeted head. "Two thousand, so be it."

Their voices seemed oddly loud up here, where only the wind and a creak of rigging had broken silence. The sky around the rovers was dusky immensity, tinged red gold in the east. Dew lay on the gallery deck. But

237

when the long wooden horns blew signals, it was somehow not an interruption, nor was the distant shouting of
orders from other vessels, thud of crew feet, clatter of
windlasses and hand-operated compressor pumps. To a
Sky Man, those sounds belonged in the upper air.

Five great craft spiraled smoothly downward. The
first sunrays flashed off gilt figureheads, bold on sharp
gondola prows, and rioted along the extravagant designs
painted on gas bags. Sails and rudders were unbelievably white across the last western darkness.

"Hullo, there," said Loklann. He had been studying
the harbor through his telescope. "Something new. What
could it be?"

He offered the tube to Robra, who held it to his remaining eye. Within the glass circle lay a stone dock
and warehouses, centuries old, from the days of the
Perio's greatness. Less than a fourth of their capacity was
used now. The normal clutter of wretched little fishing
craft, a single coasting schooner . . . and yes, by Oktai
the Stormbringer, a monster thing, bigger than a whale,
seven masts that were impossibly tall!

"I don't know." The mate lowered the telescope. "A
foreigner? But where from? Nowhere in this continent—"

"I never saw any arrangement like that," said Loklann.
"Square sails on the topmasts, fore-and-aft below." He
stroked his short beard. It burned like spun copper in
the morning light; he was one of the fair-haired blue-
eyed men, rare even among the Sky People and un-
heard of elsewhere. "Of course," he said, "we're no experts on water craft. We only see them in passing." A
not unamiable contempt rode his words: sailors made
good slaves, at least, but naturally the only fit vehicle
for a fighting man was a rover abroad and a horse at
home.

"Probably a trader," he decided. "We'll capture it if
possible."

He turned his attention to more urgent problems.
He had no map of S' Antón, had never even seen it before. This was the farthest south any Sky People had
yet gone plundering, and almost as far as any had ever

visited; in bygone days aircraft were still too primitive
and the Perio too strong. Thus Loklann must scan the
city from far above, through drifting white vapors, and
make his plan on the spot. Nor could it be very complicated, for he had only signal flags and a barrel-
chested hollerer with a megaphone to pass orders to the
other vessels.

"That big plaza in front of the temple," he murmured.
"Our contingent will land there. Let the *Stormcloud*
men tackle that big building east of it . . . see . . . it
looks like a chief's dwelling. Over there, along the north
wall, typical barracks and parade ground—*Coyote* can
deal with the soldiers. Let the *Witch of Heaven* men
land on the docks, seize the seaward gun emplacements
and that strange vessel, then join the attack on the
garrison. *Fire Elk*'s crew should land inside the east
city gate and send a detachment to the south gate, to
bottle in the civilian population. Having occupied the
plaza, I'll send reinforcements wherever they're needed.
All clear?"

He snapped down his goggles. Some of the big men
crowding about him wore chain armor, but he preferred
a cuirass of hardened leather, Mong style; it was nearly
as strong and a lot lighter. He was armed with a pistol,
but had more faith in his battle ax. An archer could shoot
almost as fast as a gun, as accurately—and firearms were
getting fabulously expensive to operate as sulfur sources
dwindled.

He felt a tightness which was like being a little boy
again, opening presents on Midwinter Morning. Oktai
knew what treasures he would find, of gold, cloth, tools,
slaves, of battle and high deeds and eternal fame. Possibly death. Someday he was sure to die in combat; he
had sacrificed so much to his josses, they wouldn't
grudge him war-death and a chance to be reborn as a
Sky Man.

"Let's go!" he said.

He sprang up on a gallery rail and over. For a moment
the world pinwheeled; now the city was on top and
now again his *Buffalo* streaked past. Then he pulled the

ripcord and his harness slammed him to steadiness. Around him, air bloomed with scarlet parachutes. He gauged the wind and tugged a line, guiding himself down.

## II

Don Miwel Carabán, calde of S' Antón d' Inio, arranged a lavish feast for his Maurai guests. It was not only that this was a historic occasion, which might even mark a turning point in the long decline. (Don Miwel, being that rare combination, a practical man who could read, knew that the withdrawal of Perio troops to Brasil twenty years ago was not a "temporary adjustment." They would never come back. The outer provinces were on their own.) But the strangers must be convinced that they had found a nation rich, strong, and basically civilized, that it was worthwhile visiting the Meycan coasts to trade, ultimately to make alliance against the northern savages.

The banquet lasted till nearly midnight. Though some of the old irrigation canals had choked up and never been repaired, so that cactus and rattlesnake housed in abandoned pueblos, Meyco Province was still fertile. The slant-eyed Mong horsemen from Tekkas had killed off innumerable peons when they raided five years back; wooden pitchforks and obsidian hoes were small use against saber and arrow. It would be another decade before population had returned to normal and the periodic famines resumed. Thus Don Miwel offered many courses, beef, spiced ham, olives, fruits, wines, nuts, coffee, which last the Sea People were unfamiliar with and didn't much care for, et cetera. Entertainment followed—music, jugglers, a fencing exhibition by some of the young nobles.

At this point the surgeon of the *Dolphin,* who was rather drunk, offered to show an Island dance. Muscular beneath tattoos, his brown form went through a series of contortions which pursed the lips of the dignified

Dons. Miwel himself remarked, "It reminds me somewhat of our peons' fertility rites," with a strained courtesy that suggested to Captain Ruori Rangi Lohannaso
that peons had an altogether different and not very nice
culture.

The surgeon threw back his queue and grinned. "Now
let's bring the ship's wahines ashore to give them a real
hula," he said in Maurai-Ingliss.

"No," answered Ruori. "I fear we may have shocked
them already. The proverb goes, 'When in the Solmon
Islands, darken your skin.'"

"I don't think they know how to have any fun," complained the doctor.

"We don't yet know what the taboos are," warned
Ruori. "Let us be as grave, then, as these spike-bearded
men, and not laugh or make love until we are back on
shipboard among our wahines."

"But it's stupid! Shark-toothed Nan eat me if I'm
going to—"

"Your ancestors are ashamed," said Ruori. It was about
as sharp a rebuke as you could give a man whom you
didn't intend to fight. He softened his tone to take out
the worst sting, but the doctor had to shut up. Which
he did, mumbling an apology and retiring with his
blushes to a dark corner beneath faded murals.

Ruori turned back to his host. "I beg your pardon,
S'ñor," he said, using the local tongue. "My men's command of Spañol is even less than my own."

"Of course." Don Miwel's lean black-clad form made
a stiff little bow. It brought his sword up, ludicrously,
like a tail. Ruori heard a smothered snort of laughter
from among his officers. And yet, thought the captain,
were long trousers and ruffled shirt any worse than
sarong, sandals, and clan tattoos? Different customs, no
more. You had to sail the Maurai Federation, from
Awaii to his own N'Zealann and west to Mlaya, before
you appreciated how big this planet was and how much
of it a mystery.

"You speak our language most excellently, S'ñor," said
Doñita Tresa Carabán. She smiled. "Perhaps better than

we, since you studied texts centuries old before embarking, and the Spañol has changed greatly since."

Ruori smiled back. Don Miwel's daughter was worth it. The rich black dress caressed a figure as good as any in the world; and, while the Sea People paid less attention to a woman's face, he saw that hers was proud and well formed, her father's eagle beak softened to a curve, luminous eyes and hair the color of midnight oceans. It was too bad these Meycans—the nobles, at least—thought a girl should be reserved solely for the husband they eventually picked for her. He would have liked her to swap her pearls and silver for a lei and go out in a ship's canoe, just the two of them, to watch the sunrise and make love.

However—

"In such company," he murmured, "I am stimulated to learn the modern language as fast as possible."

She refrained from coquetting with her fan, a local habit the Sea People found alternately hilarious and irritating. But her lashes fluttered. They were very long, and her eyes, he saw, were gold-flecked green. "You are learning cab'llero manners just as fast, S'ñor," she said.

"Do not call our language 'modern,' I pray you," interrupted a scholarly-looking man in a long robe. Ruori recognized Bispo Don Carlos Ermosillo, a high priest of that Esu Carito who seemed cognate with the Maurai Lesu Haristi. "Not modern, but corrupt. I too have studied ancient books, printed before the War of Judgment. Our ancestors spoke the true Spañol. Our version of it is as distorted as our present-day society." He sighed. "But what can one expect, when even among the well born, not one in ten can write his own name?"

"There was more literacy in the high days of the Perio," said Don Miwel. "You should have visited us a hundred years ago, S'ñor Captain, and seen what our race was capable of."

"Yet what was the Perio itself but a successor state?" asked the Bispo bitterly. "It unified a large area, gave law and order for a while, but what did it create that was new? Its course was the same sorry tale as a thousand kingdoms before, and therefore the same judgment has fallen on it."

Doñita Tresa crossed herself. Even Ruori, who held a degree in engineering as well as navigation, was shocked. "Not atomics?" he exclaimed.

"What? Oh. The old weapons, which destroyed the old world. No, of course not." Don Carlos shook his head. "But in our more limited way, we have been as stupid and sinful as the legendary forefathers, and the results have been parallel. You may call it human greed or el Dío's punishment as you will; I think the two mean much the same thing."

Ruori looked closely at the priest. "I should like to speak with your further, S'ñor," he said, hoping it was the right title. "Men who know history, rather than myth, are rare these days."

"By all means," said Don Carlos. "I should be honored."

Doñita Tresa shifted on light, impatient feet. "It is customary to dance," she said.

Her father laughed. "Ah, yes. The young ladies have been getting quite impatient, I am sure. Time enough to resume formal discussions tomorrow, S'ñor Captain. Now let the music begin."

He signalled. The orchestra struck up. Some instruments were quite like those of the Maurai, others wholly unfamiliar. The scale itself was different. . . . They had something like it in Stralia, but—a hand fell on Ruori's arm. He looked down at Tresa. "Since you do not ask me to dance," she said, "may I be so immodest as to ask you?"

"What does 'immodest' mean?" he inquired.

She blushed and tried to explain, without success. Ruori decided it was another local concept which the Sea People lacked. By that time the Meycan girls and their cavaliers were out on the ballroom floor. He studied them for a moment. "The motions are unknown to me," he said, "but I think I could soon learn."

She slipped into his arms. It was a pleasant contact,

even though nothing would come of it. "You do very well," she said after a minute. "Are all your folk so graceful?"

Only later did he realize that was a compliment for which he should have thanked her; being an Islander, he took it at face value as a question and replied, "Most of us spend a great deal of time on the water. A sense of balance and rhythm must be developed or one is likely to fall into the sea."

She wrinkled her nose. "Oh, stop," she laughed. "You're as solemn as S' Osé in the cathedral."

Ruori grinned back. He was a tall young man, brown as all his race but with the gray eyes which many bore in memory of Ingliss ancestors. Being a N'Zealanner, he was not tattooed as lavishly as some Federation men. On the other hand, he had woven a whalebone filigree into his queue, his sarong was the finest batik, and he had added thereto a fringed shirt. His knife, without which a Maurai felt obscenely helpless, was in contrast: old, shabby until you saw the blade, a tool.

"I must see this god, S' Osé," he said. "Will you show me? Or no, I would not have eyes for a mere statue."

"How long will you stay?" she asked.

"As long as we can. We are supposed to explore the whole Meycan coast. Hitherto the only Maurai contact with the Merikan continent has been one voyage from Awaii to Calforni. They found desert and a few savages. We have heard from Okkaidan traders that there are forests still farther north, where yellow and white men strive against each other. But what lies south of Calforni was unknown to us until this expedition was sent out. Perhaps you can tell us what to expect in Su-Merika."

"Little enough by now," she sighed, "even in Brasil."

"Ah, but lovely roses bloom in Meyco."

Her humor returned. "And flattering words in N'Zealann," she chuckled.

"Far from it. We are notoriously straightforward. Except, of course, when yarning about voyages we have made."

"What yarns will you tell about this one?"

"Not many, lest all the young men of the Federation come crowding here. But I will take you aboard my ship, Doñita, and show you to the compass. Thereafter it will always point toward S' Antón d' Inio. You will be, so to speak, my compass rose."

Somewhat to his surprise, she understood, and laughed. She led him across the floor, supple between his hands.

Thereafter, as the night wore on, they danced together as much as decency allowed, or a bit more, and various foolishness which concerned no one else passed between them. Toward sunrise the orchestra was dismissed and the guests, hiding yawns behind well-bred hands, began to take their departure.

"How dreary to stand and receive farewells," whispered Tresa. "Let them think I went to bed already." She took Ruori's hand and slipped behind a column and thence out onto a balcony. An aged serving woman, stationed to act as duenna for couples that wandered thither, had wrapped up in her mantle against the cold and fallen asleep. Otherwise the two were alone among jasmines. Mists floated around the palace and blurred the city; far off rang the *"Todos buen"* of pikemen tramping the outer walls. Westward the balcony faced darkness, where the last stars glittered. The seven tall topmasts of the Maurai *Dolphin* caught the earliest sun and glowed.

Tresa shivered and stood close to Ruori. They did not speak for a while.

"Remember us," she said at last, very low. "When you are back with your own happier people, do not forget us here."

"How could I?" he answered, no longer in jest.

"You have so much more than we," she said wistfully. "You have told me how your ships can sail unbelievably fast, almost into the wind. How your fishers always fill their nets, how your whale ranchers keep herds that darken the water, how you even farm the ocean for food and fiber and . . ." She fingered the shimmering material of his shirt. "You told me this was made by

craft out of fishbones. You told me that every family has
its own spacious house and every member of it, almost,
his own boat . . . that even small children on the lone-
liest island can read, and have printed books . . . that
you have none of the sicknesses which destroy us
. . . that no one hungers and all are free—oh, do not
forget us, you on whom el Dío has smiled!"

She stopped, then, embarrassed. He could see how
her head lifted and nostrils dilated, as if resenting him.
After all, he thought, she came from a breed which for
centuries had given, not received, charity.

Therefore he chose his words with care. "It has been
less our virtue than our good fortune, Doñita. We suffered less than most in the War of Judgment, and our
being chiefly Islanders prevented our population from
outrunning the sea's rich ability to feed us. So we—
no, we did not retain any lost ancestral arts. There are
none. But we did re-create an ancient attitude, a way
of thinking, which has made the difference—science."

She crossed herself. "The atom!" she breathed, drawing from him.

"No, no, Doñita," he protested. "So many nations we
have discovered lately believe science was the cause of
the old world's ruin. Or else they think it was a collection of cut-and-dried formulas for making tall buildings
or talking at a distance. But neither is true. The scientific method is only a means of learning. It is a . . . a
perpetual starting afresh. And that is why you people
here in Meyco can help us as much as we can help
you, why we have sought you out and will come knocking hopefully at your doors again in the future."

She frowned, though something began to glow
within her. "I do not understand," she said.

He cast about for an example. At last he pointed to a
series of small holes in the balcony rail. "What used to
be here?" he asked.

"Why . . . I do not know. It has always been like
that."

"I think I can tell you. I have seen similar things
elsewhere. It was a wrought-iron grille. But it was pulled

out a long time ago and made into weapons or tools. No?"

"Quite likely," she admitted. "Iron and copper have grown very scarce. We have to send caravans across the whole land, to Támico ruins, in great peril from bandits and barbarians, to fetch our metal. Time was when there were iron rails within a kilometer of this place. Don Carlos has told me."

He nodded. "Just so. The ancients exhausted the world. They mined the ores, burned the oil and coal, eroded the land, until nothing was left. I exaggerate, of course. There are still deposits. But not enough. The old civilization used up the capital, so to speak. Now sufficient forest and soil have come back that the world could try to reconstruct machine culture—except that there aren't enough minerals and fuels. For centuries men have been forced to tear up the antique artifacts, if they were to have any metal at all. By and large, the knowledge of the ancients hasn't been lost; it has simply become unusable, because we are so much poorer than they."

He leaned forward, earnestly. "But knowledge and discovery do not depend on wealth," he said. "Perhaps because we did not have much metal to cannibalize in the Islands, we turned elsewhere. The scientific method is just as applicable to wind and sun and living matter as it was to oil, iron, or uranium. By studying genetics we learned how to create seaweeds, plankton, fish that would serve **our** purposes. Scientific forest management gives us adequate timber, organic-synthesis bases, some fuel. The sun pours down energy which we know how to concentrate and use. Wood, ceramics, even stone can replace metal for most purposes. The wind, through such principles as the airfoil or the Venturi law or the Hilsch tube, supplies force, heat, refrigeration; the tides can be harnessed. Even in its present early stage, paramathematical psychology helps control population, as well as—no, I am talking like an engineer now, falling into my own language. I apologize.

"What I wanted to say was that if we can only have

the help of other people, such as yourselves, on a
worldwide scale, we can match our ancestors, or surpass
them . . . not in their ways, which were often short-
sighted and wasteful, but in achievements uniquely
ours. . . ."

His voice trailed off. She wasn't listening. She stared
over his head, into the air, and horror stood on her face.

Then trumpets howled on battlements, and the cathedral bells crashed to life.

"What the nine devils!" Ruori turned on his heel and
looked up. The zenith had become quite blue. Lazily
over S' Antón floated five orca shapes. The new sun
glared off a jagged heraldry painted along their flanks.
He estimated dizzily that each of them must be three
hundred feet long.

Blood-colored things petaled out below them and
drifted down upon the city.

"The Sky People!" said a small broken croak behind
him. "Sant'sima Marí, pray for us now!"

### III

Loklann hit flagstones, rolled over, and bounced to
his feet. Beside him a carved horseman presided over
fountain waters. For an instant he admired the stone,
almost alive; they had nothing like that in Canyon,
Zona, Corado, any of the mountain kingdoms. And the
temple facing this plaza was white skywardness.

The square had been busy, farmers and handicrafters
setting up their booths for a market day. Most of them
scattered in noisy panic. But one big man roared,
snatched a stone hammer, and dashed in his rags to
meet Loklann. He was covering the flight of a young
woman, probably his wife, who held a baby in her arms.
Through the shapeless sack dress Loklann saw that her
figure wasn't bad. She would fetch a price when the
Mong slave dealer next visited Canyon. So could her
husband, but there wasn't time now, still encumbered
with a chute. Loklann whipped out his pistol and fired.

The man fell to his knees, gaped at the blood seeping between fingers clutched to his belly, and collapsed. Loklann flung off his harness. His boots thudded after the woman. She shrieked when fingers closed on her arm and tried to wriggle free, but the brat hampered her. Loklann shoved her toward the temple. Robra was already on its steps.

"Post a guard!" yelled the skipper. "We may as well keep prisoners in here, till we're ready to plunder it."

An old man in priest's robes tottered to the door. He held up one of the cross-shaped Meycan josses, as if to bar the way. Robra brained him with an ax blow, kicked the body off the stairs, and urged the woman inside.

It sleeted armed men. Loklann winded his oxhorn bugle, rallying them. A counterattack could be expected any minute. . . . Yes, now.

A troop of Meycan cavalry clanged into view. They were young, proud-looking men in baggy pants, leather breastplate and plumed helmet, blowing cloak, fire-hardened wooden lances but steel sabres—very much like the yellow nomads of Tekkas, whom they had fought for centuries. But so had the Sky People. Loklann pounded to the head of his line, where his standard bearer had raised the Lightning Flag. Half the *Buffalo's* crew fitted together sections of pike tipped with edged ceramic, grounded the butts, and waited. The charge crested upon them. Their pikes slanted down. Some horses spitted themselves, others reared back screaming. The pikemen jabbed at their riders. The second paratroop line stepped in, ax and sword and hamstringing knife. For a few minutes murder boiled. The Meycans broke. They did not flee, but they retreated in confusion. And then the Canyon bows began to snap.

Presently only dead and hurt cluttered the square. Loklann moved briskly among the latter. Those who weren't too badly wounded were hustled into the temple. Might as well collect all possible slaves and cull them later.

From afar he heard a dull boom. "Cannon," said Robra, joining him. "At the army barracks."

"Well, let the artillery have its fun, till our boys get in among 'em," said Loklann sardonically.

"Sure, sure." Robra looked nervous. "I wish they'd let us hear from them, though. Just standing around here isn't good."

"It won't be long," predicted Loklann.

Nor was it. A runner with a broken arm staggered to him. "*Stormcloud*," he gasped. "The big building you sent us against . . . full of swordsmen. . . . They repulsed us at the door—"

"Huh! I thought it was only the king's house," said Loklann. He laughed. "Well, maybe the king was giving a party. Come on, then, I'll go see for myself. Robra, take over here." His finger swept out thirty men to accompany him. They jogged down streets empty and silent except for their bootfalls and weapon-jingle. The housefolk must be huddled terrified behind those blank walls. So much the easier to corral them later, when the fighting was done and the looting began.

A roar broke loose. Loklann led a dash around a last corner. Opposite him he saw the palace, an old building, red-tiled roof and mellow walls and many glass windows. The *Stormcloud* men were fighting at the main door. Their dead and wounded from the last attack lay thick.

Loklann took in the situation at a glance. "It wouldn't occur to those lardheads to send a detachment through some side entrance, would it?" he groaned. "Jonak, take fifteen of our boys and batter in a lesser door and hit the rear of that line. The rest of you help me keep it busy meanwhile."

He raised his red-spattered ax. "A Canyon!" he yelled. "A Canyon!" His followers bellowed behind him and they ran to battle.

The last charge had reeled away bloody and breathless. Half a dozen Meycans stood in the wide doorway. They were nobles: grim men with goatees and waxed mustaches, in formal black, red cloaks wrapped as shields on their left arms and long slim swords in their right hands. Behind them stood others, ready to take the place of the fallen.

"A Canyon!" shouted Loklann as he rushed.

*"Quel Dío wela!"* cried a tall grizzled Don. A gold chain of office hung around his neck. His blade snaked forth.

Loklann flung up his ax and parried. The Don was fast, riposting with a lunge that ended on the raider's breast. But hardened six-ply leather turned the point. Loklann's men crowded on either side, reckless of thrusts, and hewed. He struck the enemy sword; it spun from the owner's grasp. *"Ah, no, Don Miwel!"* cried a young person beside the calde. The older man snarled, threw out his hands, and somehow clamped them on Loklann's ax. He yanked it away with a troll's strength. Loklann stared into eyes that said death. Don Miwel raised the ax. Loklann drew his pistol and fired point blank.

As Don Miwel toppled, Loklann caught him, pulled off the gold chain, and threw it around his own neck. Straightening, he met a savage thrust. It glanced off his helmet. He got his ax back, planted his feet firmly, and smote.

The defending line buckled.

Clamor lifted behind Loklann. He turned and saw weapons gleam beyond his own men's shoulders. With a curse he realized—there had been more people in the palace than these holding the main door. The rest had sallied out the rear and were now on his back!

A point pierced his thigh. He felt no more than a sting, but rage flapped black before his eyes. "Be reborn as the swine you are!" he roared. Half unaware, he thundered loose, cleared a space for himself, lurched aside and oversaw the battle.

The newcomers were mostly palace guards, judging from their gaily striped uniforms, pikes, and machetes. But they had allies, a dozen men such as Loklann had never seen or heard of. Those had the brown skin and black hair of Injuns, but their faces were more like a white man's; intricate blue designs covered their bodies, which were clad only in wraparounds and flower wreaths. They wielded knives and clubs with wicked skill.

Loklann tore his trouser leg open to look at his
wound. It wasn't much. More serious was the beating
his men were taking. He saw Mork sunna Brenn rush,
sword uplifted, at one of the dark strangers, a big man
who had added a rich-looking blouse to his skirt. Mork
had killed four men at home for certain, in lawful fights,
and nobody knew how many abroad. The dark man
waited, a knife between his teeth, hands hanging loose.
As the blade came down, the dark man simply wasn't
there. Grinning around his knife, he chopped at the
sword wrist with the edge of a hand. Loklann dis-
tinctly heard bones crack. Mork yelled. The foreigner
hit him in the Adam's apple. Mork went to his knees,
spat blood, caved in, and was still. Another Sky Man
charged, ax aloft. The stranger again evaded the weapon,
caught the moving body on his hip, and helped it along.
The Sky Man hit the pavement with his head and moved
no more.

Now Loklann saw that the newcomers were a ring
around others who did not fight. Women. By Oktai
and man-eating Ulagu, these bastards were leading out
all the women in the palace! And the fighting against
them had broken up; surly raiders stood back nursing
their wounds.

Loklann ran forward. "A Canyon! A Canyon!" he
shouted.

"Ruori Rangi Lohannaso," said the big stranger politely. He rapped a string of orders. His party began to
move away.

"Hit them, you scum!" bawled Loklann. His men rallied and straggled after. Rearguard pikes prodded them
back. Loklann led a rush to the front of the hollow
square.

The big man saw him coming. Gray eyes focused on
the calde's chain and became full winter. "So you killed
Don Miwel," said Ruori in Spañol. Loklann understood
him, having learned the tongue from prisoners and
concubines during many raids further north. "You lousy
son of a skua."

Loklann's pistol rose. Ruori's hand blurred. Suddenly

the knife stood in the Sky Man's right biceps. He dropped his gun. "I'll want that back!" shouted Ruori. Then, to his followers: "Come, to the ship."

Loklann stared at blood rivering down his arm. He heard a clatter as the refugees broke through the weary Canyon line. Jonak's party appeared in the main door —which was now empty, its surviving defenders having left with Ruori.

A man approached Loklann, who still regarded his arm. "Shall we go after 'em, Skipper?" he said, almost timidly. "Jonak can lead us after 'em."

"No," said Loklann.

"But they must be escorting a hundred women. A lot of young women too."

Loklann shook himself, like a dog coming out of a deep cold stream. "No. I want to find the medic and get this wound stitched. Then we'll have a lot else to do. We can settle with those outlanders later, if the chance comes. Man, we've a city to sack!"


## IV

There were dead men scattered on the wharves, some burned. They looked oddly small beneath the warehouses, like rag dolls tossed away by a weeping child. Cannon fumes lingered to bite nostrils.

Atel Hamid Seraio, the mate, who had been left aboard the *Dolphin* with the enlisted crew, led a band to meet Ruori. His salute was in the Island manner, so casual that even at this moment several of the Meycans looked shocked. "We were about to come for you, Captain," he said.

Ruori looked toward that forest which was the *Dolphin*'s rig. "What happened here?" he asked.

"A band of those devils landed near the battery. They took the emplacements while we were still wondering what it was all about. Part of them went off toward that racket in the north quarter, I believe where the army lives. But the rest of the gang attacked us. Well, with our gunwale ten feet above the dock, and us trained to repel pirates, they didn't have much luck. I gave them a dose of flame."

Ruori winced from the blackened corpses. Doubtless they had deserved it, but he didn't like the idea of pumping flaming blubber oil across live men.

"Too bad they didn't try from the seaward side," added Atel with a sigh. "We've got such a lovely harpoon catapult. I used one like it years ago off Hinja, when a Sinese buccaneer came too close. His junk sounded like a whale."

"Men aren't whales!" snapped Ruori.

"All right, Captain, all right, all right." Atel backed away from his violence, a little frightened. "No ill-speaking meant."

Ruori recollected himself and folded his hands. "I spoke in needless anger," he said formally. "I laugh at myself."

"It's nothing, Captain. As I was saying, we beat them off and they finally withdrew. I imagine they'll bring back reinforcements. What shall we do?"

"That's what I don't know," said Ruori in a bleak tone. He turned to the Meycans, who stood with stricken, uncomprehending faces. "Your pardon is prayed, Dons and Doñitas," he said in Spañol. "He was only relating to me what had happened."

"Don't apologize!" Tresa Carabán spoke, stepping out ahead of the men. Some of them looked a bit offended, but they were too tired and stunned to reprove her forwardness, and to Ruori it was only natural that a woman act as freely as a man. "You saved our lives, Captain. More than our lives."

He wondered what was worse than death, then nodded. Slavery, of course—ropes and whips and a lifetime's unfree toil in a strange land. His eyes dwelt upon her, the long hair disheveled past smooth shoulders, gown ripped, weariness and a streak of tears across her face. He wondered if she knew her father was dead. She held herself straight and regarded him with an odd defiance.

"We are uncertain what to do," he said awkwardly. "We are only fifty men. Can we help your city?"

A young nobleman, swaying on his feet, replied: "No. The city is done. You can take these ladies to safety, that is all."

Tresa protested: "You are not surrendering already, S'ñor Dónoju!"

"No, Doñita," the young man breathed. "But I hope I can be shriven before returning to fight, for I am a dead man."

"Come aboard," said Ruori curtly.

He led the way up the gangplank. Liliu, one of the ship's five wahines, ran to meet him. She threw arms about his neck and cried, "I feared you were slain!"

"Not yet." Ruori disengaged her as gently as possible. He noticed Tresa standing stiff, glaring at them both. Puzzlement came—did these curious Meycans expect a crew to embark on a voyage of months without taking a few girls along? Then he decided that the wahines' clothing, being much like his men's, was against local mores. To Nan with their silly prejudices. But it hurt that Tresa drew away from him.

The other Meycans stared about them. Not all had toured the ship when she first arrived. They looked in bewilderment at lines and spars, down fathoms of deck to the harpoon catapult, capstans, bowsprit, and back at the sailors. The Maurai grinned encouragingly. Thus far most of them looked on this as a lark. Men who skindove after sharks, for fun, or who sailed outrigger canoes alone across a thousand ocean miles to pay a visit, were not put out by a fight.

But they had not talked with grave Don Miwel and merry Don Wan and gentle Bispo Ermosillo, and then seen those people dead on a dance floor, thought Ruori in bitterness.

The Meycan women huddled together, ladies and servants, to weep among each other. The palace guards formed a solid rank around them. The nobles, and Tresa, followed Ruori up on the poop deck.

"Now," he said, "let us talk. Who are these bandits?"

"The Sky People," whispered Tresa.

"I can see that." Ruori cocked an eye on the aircraft patrolling overhead. They had the sinister beauty of as many barracuda. Here and there columns of smoke reached toward them. "But who are they? Where from?"

"They are Nor-Merikans," she answered in a dry little voice, as if afraid to give it color. "From the wild highlands around the Corado River, the Grand Canyon it has cut for itself—mountaineers. There is a story that they were driven from the eastern plains by Mong invaders, a long time ago; but as they grew strong in the hills and deserts, they defeated some Mong tribes and became friendly with others. For a hundred years they have harried our northern borders. This is the first time they have ventured so far south. We never expected them—I suppose their spies learned most of our soldiers are along the Río Gran, chasing a rebel force. They sailed southwesterly, above our land—" She shivered.

The young Dónoju spat. "They are heathen dogs! They know nothing but to rob and burn and kill!" He sagged. "What have we done that they are loosed on us?"

Ruori rubbed his chin thoughtfully. "They can't be quite such savages," he murmured. "Those blimps are better than anything my own Federation has tried to make. The fabric . . . some tricky synthetic? It must be, or it wouldn't contain hydrogen any length of time. Surely they don't use helium! But for hydrogen production on that scale, you need industry. A good empirical chemistry, at least. They might even electrolyze it . . . good Lesu!"

He realized he had been talking to himself in his home language. "I beg your pardon," he said. "I was wondering what we might do. This ship carries no flying vessels."

Again he looked upward. Atel handed him his binoculars. He focused on the nearest blimp. The huge gas bag and the gondola beneath—itself as big as many a

Maurai ship—formed an aerodynamically clean unit. The gondola seemed to be light, woven cane about a wooden frame, but strong. Three-fourths of the way up from its keel a sort of gallery ran clear around, on which the crew might walk and work. At intervals along the rail stood muscle-powered machines. Some must be for hauling, but others suggested catapults. Evidently the blimps of various chiefs fought each other occasionally, in the northern kingdoms. That might be worth knowing. The Federation's political psychologists were skilled at the divide-and-rule game. But for now . . .

The motive power was extraordinarily interesting. Near the gondola bows two lateral spars reached out for some fifty feet, one above the other. They supported two pivoted frames on either side, to which square sails were bent. A similar pair of spars pierced the after hull: eight sails in all. Shark-fin control surfaces were braced to the gas bag. A couple of small retractable windwheels, vaned and pivoted, jutted beneath the gondola, evidently serving the purpose of a false keel. Sails and rudders were trimmed by lines running through block and tackle to windlasses on the gallery. By altering their set, it should be possible to steer at least several points to windward. And, yes, the air moves in different directions at different levels. A blimp could descend by pumping out cells in its gas bag, compressing the hydrogen into storage tanks; it could rise by reinflating or by dropping ballast (though the latter trick would be reserved for home stretches, when leakage had depleted the gas supply). Between sails, rudders, and its ability to find a reasonably favoring wind, such a blimp could go roving across several thousand miles, with a payload of several tons. Oh, a lovely craft!

Ruori lowered his glasses. "Hasn't the Perio built any air vessels, to fight back?" he asked.

"No," mumbled one of the Meycans. "All we ever had was balloons. We don't know how to make a fabric which will hold the lifting-gas long enough, or how to control the flight. . . ." His voice trailed off.

"And being a nonscientific culture, you never thought

of doing systematic research to learn those tricks," said Ruori.

Tresa, who had been staring at her city, whirled about upon him. "It's easy for you!" she screamed. "You haven't stood off Mong in the north and Raucanians in the south for century after century. You haven't had to spend twenty years and ten thousand lives making canals and aqueducts, so a few less people would starve. You aren't burdened with a peon majority who can only work, who cannot look after themselves because they have never been taught how because their existence is too much of a burden for our land to afford it. It's easy for you to float about with your shirtless doxies and poke fun at us! What would you have done, S'ñor Almighty Captain?"

"Be still," reproved young Dónoju. "He saved our lives."

"So far!" she said, through teeth and tears. One small dancing shoe stamped the deck.

For a bemused moment, irrelevantly, Ruori wondered what a doxie was. It sounded uncomplimentary. Could she mean the wahines? But was there a more honorable way for a woman to earn a good dowry than by hazarding her life, side by side with the men of her people, on a mission of discovery and civilization? What did Tresa expect to tell her grandchildren about on rainy nights?

Then he wondered further why she should disturb him. He had noticed it before, in some of the Meycans, an almost terrifying intensity between man and wife, as if a spouse were somehow more than a respected friend and partner. But what other relationship was possible? A psychological specialist might know; Ruori was lost.

He shook an angry head, to clear it, and said aloud: "This is no time for inurbanity." He had to use a Spañol word with not quite the same connotation. "We must decide. Are you certain we have no hope of repelling the pirates?"

"No unless S' Antón himself passes a miracle," said Doñoju in a dead voice.

Then, snapping erect: "There is only a single thing you can do for us, S'ñor. If you will leave now, with the women—there are high-born ladies among them, who must not be sold into captivity and disgrace. Bear them south to Port Wanawato, where the calde will look after their welfare."

"I do not like to run off," said Ruori, looking at the men fallen on the wharf.

"S'ñor, these are *ladies!* In el Dío's name, have mercy on them!"

Ruori studied the taut, bearded faces. He did owe them a great deal of hospitality, and he could see no other way he might ever repay it. "If you wish," he said slowly. "What of yourselves?"

The young noble bowed as if to a king. "Our thanks and prayers will go with you, my lord Captain. We men, of course, will now return to battle." He stood up and barked in a parade-ground voice: "Atten-tion! Form ranks!"

A few swift kisses passed on the main deck, and then the men of Meyco had crossed the gangplank and tramped into their city.

Ruori beat a fist on the taffrail. "If we had some way," he mumbled. "If I could do something." Almost hopefully: "Do you think the bandits might attack us?"

"Only if you remain here," said Tresa. Her eyes were chips of green ice. "Would to Marí you had not pledged yourself to sail!"

"If they come after us at sea—"

"I do not think they will. You carry a hundred women and a few trade goods. The Sky People will have their pick of ten thousand women, as many men, and our city's treasures. Why should they take the trouble to pursue you?"

"Aye . . . aye. . . ."

"Go," she said. "You dare not linger."

Her coldness was like a blow. "What do you mean?" he asked. "Do you think the Maurai are cowards?"

She hesitated. Then, in reluctant honesty: "No."

"Well, why do you scoff at me?"

"Oh, go away!" She knelt by the rail, bowed head in arms, and surrendered to herself.

Ruori left her and gave his orders. Men scrambled into the rigging. Furled canvas broke loose and cracked in a young wind. Beyond the jetty, the ocean glittered blue, with small whitecaps; gulls skimmed across heaven. Ruori saw only the glimpses he had had before, as he led the retreat from the palace.

*A weaponless man, his head split open. A girl, hardly twelve years old, who screamed as two raiders carried her into an alley. An aged man fleeing in terror, zigzagging, while four archers took · potshots at him and howled laughter when he fell transfixed and dragged himself along on his hands. A woman sitting dumb in the street, her dress torn, next to a baby whose brains had been dashed out. A little statue in a niche, a holy image, a faded bunch of violets at its feet, beheaded by a casual war-hammer. A house that burned, and shrieks from within.*

Suddenly the aircraft overhead were not beautiful. To reach up and pull them out of the sky!

Ruori stopped dead. The crew surged around him. He heard a short-haul chantey, deep voices vigorous from always having been free and well fed, but it echoed in a far corner of his brain.

"Casting off," sang the mate.

"Not yet! Not yet! Wait!"

Ruori ran toward the poop, up the ladder and past the steersman to Doñita Tresa. She had risen again, to stand with bent head past which the hair swept to hide her countenance.

"Tresa," panted Ruori. "Tresa, I've an idea. I think— there may be a chance—perhaps we can fight back after all."

She raised her eyes. Her fingers closed on his arm till he felt the nails draw blood.

Words tumbled from him. "It will depend . . . on luring them . . . to us. At least a couple of their vessels . . . must follow us . . . to sea. I think then—I'm not sure of the details, but it may be . . . we can fight . . . even drive them off—"

Still she stared at him. He felt a hesitation. "Of course," he said, "we may lose the fight. And we do have the women aboard."

"If you lose," she asked, so low he could scarcely hear it, "will we die or be captured?"

"I think we will die."

"That is well." She nodded. "Yes. Fight, then."

"There is one thing I am unsure of. How to make them pursue us." He paused. "If someone were to let himself . . . be captured by them—and told them we were carrying off a great treasure—would they believe that?"

"They might well." Life had come back to her tones, even eagerness. "Let us say, the calde's hoard. None ever existed, but the robbers would believe my father's cellars were stuffed with gold."

"Then someone must go to them." Ruori turned his back to her, twisted his fingers together and slogged toward a conclusion he did not want to reach. "But it could not be just anyone. They would club a man in among the other slaves, would they not? I mean, would they listen to him at all?"

"Probably not. Very few of them know Spañol. By the time a man who babbled of treasure was understood, they might be halfway home." Tresa scowled. "What shall we do?"

Ruori saw the answer, but could not get it past his throat.

"I am sorry," he mumbled. "My idea was not so good after all. Let us be gone."

The girl forced her way between him and the rail to stand in front of him, touching as if they danced again. Her voice was altogether steady. "You know a way."

"I do not."

"I have come to know you well, in one night. You are a poor liar. Tell me."

He looked away. Somehow, he got out: "A woman—

not any woman, but a very beautiful one—would she not soon be taken to their chief?"

Tresa stood aside. The color drained from her cheeks. "Yes," she said at last. "I think so."

"But then again," said Ruori wretchedly, "she might be killed. They do much wanton killing, those men. I cannot let anyone who was given into my protection risk death."

"You heathen fool," she said through tight lips. "Do you think the chance of being killed matters to me?"

"What else could happen?" he asked, surprised. And then: "Oh, yes, of course, the woman would be a slave if we lost the battle afterward. Though I should imagine, if she is beautiful, she would not be badly treated."

"And is that all you—" Tresa stopped. He had never known it was possible for a smile to show pure hurt. "Of course. I should have realized. Your people have your own ways of thinking."

"What do you mean?" he fumbled.

A moment more she stood with clenched fists. Then, half to herself: "They killed my father; yes, I saw him dead in the doorway. They would leave my city a ruin peopled by corpses."

Her head lifted. "I will go," she said.

"You?" He grabbed her shoulders. "No, surely not you! One of the others—"

"Should I send anybody else? I am the calde's daughter."

She pulled herself free of him and hurried across the deck, down the ladder toward the gangway. Her gaze was turned from the ship. A few words drifted back. "Afterward, if there is an afterward, there is always the convent."

He did not understand. He stood on the poop, staring after her and abominating himself until she was lost to sight. Then he said, "Cast off," and the ship stood out to sea.

# V

The Meycans fought doggedly, street by street and house by house, but in a couple of hours their surviving soldiers had been driven into the northeast corner of S' Antón. They themselves hardly knew that, but a Sky chief had a view from above; a rover was now tethered to the cathedral, with a rope ladder for men to go up and down, and the companion vessel, skeleton crewed, brought their news to it.

"Good enough," said Loklann. "We'll keep them boxed in with a quarter of our force. I don't think they'll sally. Meanwhile the rest of us can get things organized. Let's not give these creatures too much time to hide themselves and their silver. In the afternoon, when we're rested, we can land parachuters behind the city troops, drive them out into our lines and destroy them."

He ordered the *Buffalo* grounded, that he might load the most precious loot at once. The men, by and large, were too rough—good lads, but apt to damage a robe or a cup or a jeweled cross in their haste; and sometimes those Meycan things were too beautiful even to give away, let alone sell.

The flagship descended as far as possible. It still hung at a thousand feet, for hand pumps and aluminum-alloy tanks did not allow much hydrogen compression. In colder, denser air it would have been suspended even higher. But ropes snaked from it to a quickly assembled ground crew. At home there were ratcheted capstans outside every lodge, enabling as few as four women to bring down a rover. One hated the emergency procedure of bleeding gas, for the Keepers could barely meet demand, in spite of a new sunpower unit added to their hydroelectric station, and charged accordingly. (Or so the Keepers said, but perhaps they were merely taking advantage of being inviolable, beyond any kings, to jack up prices. Some chiefs, including Loklann, had begun to experiment with hydrogen production for themselves, but it was a slow thing to puzzle out an art that even the Keepers only half understood.)

Here, strong men replaced machinery. The *Buffalo* was soon pegged down in the cathedral plaza, which it almost filled. Loklann inspected each rope himself. His wounded leg ached, but not too badly to walk on. More annoying was his right arm, which hurt worse from stitches than from the original cut. The medic had warned him to go easy with it. That meant fighting left-handed, for the story should never be told that Loklann sunna Holber stayed out of combat. However, he would only be half himself.

He touched the knife which had spiked him. At least he'd gotten a fine steel blade for his pains. And . . . hadn't the owner said they would meet again, to settle who kept it? There were omens in such words. It could be a pleasure to reincarnate that Ruori.

"Skipper. Skipper, sir."

Loklann glanced about. Yuw Red-Ax and Aalan sunna Rickar, men of his lodge, had hailed him. They grasped the arms of a young woman in black velvet and silver. The beweaponed crowd, moiling about, was focusing on her; raw whoops lifted over the babble.

"What is it?" said Loklann brusquely. He had much to do.

"This wench, sir. A looker, isn't she? We found her down near the waterfront."

"Well, shove her into the temple with the rest till—oh." Loklann rocked back on his heels, narrowing his eyes to meet a steady green glare. She was certainly a looker.

"She kept hollering the same words over and over: '*Shef, rey, ombro gran!*' I finally wondered if it didn't mean 'chief,' " said Yuw, "and then when she yelled 'khan' I was pretty sure she wanted to see you. So we didn't use her ourselves," he finished virtuously.

"*Aba tu Spañol?*" said the girl.

Loklann grinned. "Yes," he replied in the same language, his words heavily accented but sufficient. "Well enough to know you are calling me 'thou.' " Her pleasantly formed mouth drew into a thin line. "Which means you think I am your inferior—or your god, or your beloved."

She flushed, threw back her head (sunlight ran along crow's-wing hair) and answered: "You might tell these oafs to release me."

Loklann said the order in Angliz. Yuw and Aalan let go. The marks of their fingers were bruised into her arms. Loklann stroked his beard. "Did you want to see me?" he asked.

"If you are the leader, yes," she said. "I am the calde's daughter, Doñita Tresa Carabán." Briefly, her voice wavered. "That is my father's chain of office you are wearing. I came back on behalf of his people, to ask for terms."

"What?" Loklann blinked. Someone in the warrior crowd laughed.

It must not be in her to beg mercy, he thought; her tone remained brittle. "Considering your sure losses if you fight to a finish, and the chance of provoking a counterattack on your homeland, will you not accept a money ransom and a safe-conduct, releasing your captives and ceasing your destruction?"

"By Oktai," murmured Loklann. "Only a woman could imagine we—" He stopped. "Did you say you came back?"

She nodded. "On the people's behalf. I know I have no legal authority to make terms, but in practice—"

"Forget that!" he rapped. "Where did you come back from?"

She faltered. "That has nothing to do with—"

There were too many eyes around. Loklann bawled orders to start systematic plundering. He turned to the girl. "Come aboard the airship," he said. "I want to discuss this further."

Her eyes closed, for just a moment, and her lips moved. Then she looked at him—he thought of a cougar he had once trapped—and she said in a flat voice: "Yes. I do have more arguments."

"Any woman does," he laughed, "but you better than most."

"Not that!" she flared. "I meant—no. Marí, pray for me." As he pushed a way through his men, she followed him.

They went past furled sails, to a ladder let down from the gallery. A hatch stood open to the lower hull, showing storage space and leather fetters for slaves. A few guards were posted on the gallery deck. They leaned on their weapons, sweating from beneath helmets, swapping jokes; when Loklann led the girl by, they yelled good-humored envy.

He opened a door. "Have you ever seen one of our vessels?" he asked. The upper gondola contained a long room, bare except for bunk frames on which sleeping bags were laid. Beyond, a series of partitions defined cabinets, a sort of galley, and at last, in the very bow, a room for maps, tables, navigation instruments, speaking tubes. Its walls slanted so far outward that the glazed windows would give a spacious view when the ship was aloft. On a shelf, beneath racked weapons, sat a small idol, tusked and four-armed. A pallet was rolled on the floor.

"The bridge," said Loklann. "Also the captain's cabin." He gestured at one of four wicker chairs, lashed into place. "Be seated, Doñita. Would you like something to drink?"

She sat down but did not reply. Her fists were clenched on her lap. Loklann poured himself a slug of whiskey and tossed off half at a gulp. "Ahhh! Later we will get some of your own wine for you. It is a shame you have no art of distilling here."

Desperate eyes lifted to him, where he stood over her. "S'ñor," she said, "I beg of you, in Carito's name— well, in your mother's, then—spare my people."

"My mother would laugh herself ill to hear that," he said. Leaning forward: "See here, let us not spill words. You were escaping, but you came back. Where were you escaping to?"

"I—does that matter?"

Good, he thought, she was starting to crack. He hammered: "It does. I know you were at the palace this dawn. I know you fled with the dark foreigners. I know their ship departed an hour ago. You must have been on it, but left again. True?"

"Yes." She began to tremble.

He sipped molten fire and asked reasonably: "Now, tell me, Doñita, what you have to bargain with. You cannot have expected we would give up the best part of our booty and a great many valuable slaves for a mere safe-conduct. All the Sky kingdoms would disown us. Come now, you must have more to offer, if you hope to buy us off."

"No . . . not really—"

His hand exploded against her cheek. Her head jerked from the blow. She huddled back, touching the red mark, as he growled: "I have no time for games. Tell me! Tell me this instant what thought drove you back here from safety, or down in the hold you go. You'd fetch a good price when the traders next visit Canyon. Many homes are waiting for you: a woods runner's cabin in Orgon, a Mong khan's yurt in Tekkas, a brothel as far east as Chai Ka-Go. Tell me now, truly, what you know, and you will be spared that much."

She looked downward and said raggedly: "The foreign ship is loaded with the calde's gold. My father had long wanted to remove his personal treasure to a safer place than this, but dared not risk a wagon train across country. There are still many outlaws between here and Fortlez d' S' Ernán; that much loot would tempt the military escort itself to turn bandit. Captain Lohannaso agreed to carry the gold by sea to Port Wanawato, which is near Fortlez. He could be trusted because his government is anxious for trade with us; he came here officially. The treasure had already been loaded. Of course, when your raid came, the ship also took those women who had been at the palace. But can you not spare them? You'll find more loot in the foreign ship than your whole fleet can lift."

"By Oktai!" whispered Loklann.

He turned from her, paced, finally stopped and stared out the window. He could almost hear the gears turn in his head. It made sense. The palace had been disappointing. Oh, yes, a lot of damask and silverware and whatnot, but nothing like the cathedral. Either the calde was less rich than powerful, or he concealed his hoard. Loklann had planned to torture a few servants and find out which. Now he realized there was a third possibility.

Better interrogate some prisoners anyway, to make sure—no, no time. Given a favoring wind, that ship could outrun any rover without working up a sweat. It might already be too late to overhaul. But if not—h'm. Assault would be no cinch. That lean, pitching hull was a small target for paratroops, and with rigging in the way . . . Wait. Bold men could always find a road. How about grappling to the upper works? If the strain tore the rigging loose, so much the better: a weighted rope would then give a clear slideway to the deck. If the hooks held, though, a storming party could nevertheless go along the lines, into the topmasts. Doubtless the sailors were agile too, but had they ever reefed a rover sail in a Merikan thunderstorm, a mile above the earth?

He could improvise as the battle developed. At the very least, it would be fun to try. And at most, he might be reborn a world conqueror, for such an exploit in this life.

He laughed aloud, joyously. "We'll do it!"

Tresa rose. "You will spare the city?" she whispered hoarsely.

"I never promised any such thing," said Loklann. "Of course, the ship's cargo will crowd out most of the stuff and people we might take otherwise. Unless, hm, unless we decide to sail the ship to Calforni, loaded, and meet it there with more rovers. Yes, why not?"

"You oathbreaker," she said, with a hellful of scorn.

"I only promised not to sell you," said Loklann. His gaze went up and down her. "And I won't."

He took a stride forward and gathered her to him. She fought, cursing; once she managed to draw Ruori's knife from his belt, but his cuirass stopped the blade.

Finally he rose. She wept at his feet, her breast marked red by her father's chain. He said more quietly, "No, I will not sell you, Tresa. I will keep you."

# VI

"Blimp ho-o-o-!"

The lookout's cry hung lonesome for a minute between wind and broad waters. Down under the mainmast, it seethed with crewmen running to their posts.

Ruori squinted eastward. The land was a streak under cumulus clouds, mountainous and blue-shadowed. It took him a while to find the enemy, in all that sky. At last the sun struck them. He lifted his binoculars. Two painted killer whales lazed his way, slanting down from a mile altitude.

He sighed. "Only two," he said.

"That may be more than plenty for us," said Atel Hamid. Sweat studded his forehead.

Ruori gave his mate a sharp look. "You're not afraid of them, are you? I daresay that's been one of their biggest assets, superstition."

"Oh, no, Captain. I know the principle of buoyancy as well as you do. But those people are tough. And they're not trying to storm us from a dock this time; they're in their element."

"So are we." Ruori clapped the other man's back. "Take over. Tanaroa knows what's going to happen, but use your own judgment if I'm spitted."

"I wish you'd let me go," protested Atel. "I don't like being safe here. It's what can happen aloft that worries me."

"You won't be too safe for your liking." Ruori forced a grin. "And somebody has to steer this tub home to hand in those lovely reports to the Geoethnic Research Endeavor."

He swung down the ladder to the main deck and hurried to the mainmast shrouds. His crew yelled around him, weapons gleamed. The two big box kites quivered taut canvas, lashed to a bollard and waiting. Ruori wished there had been time to make more.

Even as it was, though, he had delayed longer than seemed wise, first heading far out to sea and then tacking slowly back, to make the enemy search for him while he prepared. (Or planned, for that matter. When he dismissed Tresa, his ideas had been little more than a conviction that he could fight.) Assuming they were lured after him at all, he had risked their losing patience and going back to the land. For an hour, now, he had dawdled under mainsail, genoa, and a couple of flying jibs, hoping the Sky People were lubbers enough not to find that suspiciously little canvas for this good weather.

But here they were, and here was an end to worry and remorse on a certain girl's behalf. Such emotions were rare in an Islander; and to find himself focusing them thus on a single person, out of earth's millions, had been horrible. Ruori swarmed up the ratlines, as if he fled something.

The blimps were still high, passing overhead on an upper-level breeze. Down here was almost a straight south wind. The aircraft, unable to steer really close-hauled, would descend when they were sea-level upwind of him. Regardless, estimated a cold part of Ruori, the *Dolphin* could avoid their clumsy rush.

But the *Dolphin* wasn't going to.

The rigging was now knotted with armed sailors. Ruori pulled himself onto the mainmast crosstrees and sat down, casually swinging his legs. The ship heeled over in a flaw and he hung above greenish-blue, white-streaked immensity. He balanced, scarcely noticing, and asked Hiti: "Are you set?"

"Aye." The big harpooner, his body a writhe of tattoos and muscles, nodded a shaven head. Lashed to the fid where he squatted was the ship's catapult, cocked and loaded with one of the huge irons that could kill a sperm whale at a blow. A couple more lay alongside in their rack. Hiti's two mates and four deckhands poised behind him, holding the smaller harpoons—mere six-foot shafts—that were launched from a boat by hand. The lines of all trailed down the mast to the bows.

"Aye, let 'em come now." Hiti grinned over his whole round face. "Nan eat the world, but this'll be something to make a dance about when we come home!"

"If we do," said Ruori. He touched the boat ax thrust into his loincloth. Like a curtain, the blinding day seemed to veil a picture from home, where combers broke white under the moon, longfires flared on a beach and dancers were merry, and palm trees cast shadows for couples who stole away. He wondered how a Meycan calde's daughter might like it . . . if her throat had not been cut.

"There's a sadness on you, Captain," said Hiti.

"Men are going to die," said Ruori.

"What of it?" Small kindly eyes studied him. "They'll die willing, if they must, for the sake of the song that'll be made. You've another trouble than death."

"Let me be!"

The harpooner looked hurt, but withdrew into silence. Wind streamed and the ocean glittered.

The aircraft steered close. They would approach one on each side. Ruori unslung the megaphone at his shoulder. Atel Hamid held the *Dolphin* steady on a broad reach.

Now Ruori could see a grinning god at the prow of the starboard airship. It would pass just above the topmasts, a little to windward. . . . Arrows went impulsively toward it from the yardarms, without effect, but no one was excited enough to waste a rifle cartridge. Hiti swiveled his catapult. "Wait," said Ruori. "We'd better see what they do."

Helmeted heads appeared over the blimp's gallery rail. A man stepped up—another, another, at intervals; they whirled triple-clawed iron grapnels and let go. Rutor saw one strike the foremast, rebound, hit a jib. . . . The line to the blimp tautened and sang but did not break; it was of leather. . . . The jib ripped, canvas thundered, struck a sailor in the belly and knocked him from his yard. . . . The man recovered to straighten out

and hit the water in a clean dive. Lesu grant he lived.
. . . The grapnel bumped along, caught the gaff of the
fore-and-aft mainsail, wood groaned. . . . The ship
trembled as line after line snapped tight.

She leaned far over, dragged by leverage. Her sails
banged. No danger of capsizing—yet—but a mast could
be pulled loose. And now, over the gallery rail and seizing a rope between hands and knees, the pirates came.
Whooping like boys, they slid down to the grapnels
and clutched after any rigging that came to hand.

One of them sprang monkeylike onto the mainmast
gaff, below the crosstrees. A harpooner's mate cursed,
hurled his weapon, and skewered the invader. "Belay
that!" roared Hiti. "We need those irons!"

Ruori scanned the situation. The leeward blimp was
still maneuvering in around its mate, which was being
blown to port. He put the megaphone to his mouth
and a solar-battery amplifier cried for him: "Hear this!
Hear this! Burn that second enemy now, before he
grapples! Cut the lines to the first one and repel all
boarders!"

"Shall I fire?" called Hiti. "I'll never have a better
target."

"Aye."

The harpooner triggered his catapult. It unwound
with a thunder noise. Barbed steel smote the engaged
gondola low in a side, tore through, and ended on the
far side of interior planking.

"Wind 'er up!" bawled Hiti. His own gorilla hands
were already on a crank lever. Somehow two men found
space to help him.

Ruori slipped down the futtock shrouds and jumped
to the gaff. Another pirate had landed there and a third
was just arriving, two more aslide behind him. The man
on the spar balanced barefooted, as good as any sailor,
and drew a sword. Ruori dropped as the blade whistled,
caught a mainsail grommet one-handed, and hung there,
striking with his boat ax at the grapnel line. The pirate
crouched and stabbed at him. Ruori thought of Tresa,
smashed his hatchet into the man's face, and flipped him

off, down to the deck. He cut again. The leather was tough, but his blade was keen. The line parted and whipped away. The gaff swung free, almost yanking Ruori's fingers loose. The second Sky Man toppled, hit a cabin below and spattered. The men on the line slid to its end. One of them could not stop; the sea took him. The other was smashed against the masthead as he pendulumed.

Ruori pulled himself back astride the gaff and sat there awhile, heaving air into lungs that burned. The fight ramped around him, on shrouds and spars and down on the decks. The second blimp edged closer.

Astern, raised by the speed of a ship moving into the wind, a box kite lifted. Atel sang a command and the helmsman put the rudder over. Even with the drag on her, the *Dolphin* responded well; a profound science of fluid mechanics had gone into her design. Being soaked in whale oil, the kite clung to the gas bag for a time—long enough for "messengers" of burning paper to whirl up its string. It burst into flame.

The blimp sheered off, the kite fell away, its small gunpowder load exploded harmlessly. Atel swore and gave further orders. The *Dolphin* tacked. The second kite, already aloft and afire, hit target. It detonated.

Hydrogen gushed out. Sudden flames wreathed the blimp. They seemed pale in the sun-dazzle. Smoke began to rise, as the plastic between gas cells disintegrated. The aircraft descended like a slow meteorite to the water.

Its companion vessel had no reasonable choice but to cast loose unsevered grapnels, abandoning the still outnumbered boarding party. The captain could not know that the *Dolphin* had only possessed two kites. A few vengeful catapult bolts spat from it. Then it was free, rapidly falling astern. The Maurai ship rocked toward an even keel.

The enemy might retreat or he might plan some fresh attack. Ruori did not intend that it should be either. He megaphoned: "Put about! Face that scum-gut!" and led a rush down the shrouds to a deck where combat still went on.

For Hiti's gang had put three primary harpoons and half a dozen lesser ones into the gondola.

Their lines trailed in tightening catenaries from the blimp to the capstan in the bows. No fear now of undue strain. The *Dolphin,* like any Maurai craft, was meant to live off the sea as she traveled. She had dragged right whales alongside; a blimp was nothing in comparison. What counted was speed, before the pirates realized what was happening and found ways to cut loose.

*"Tohiha, hioha, itoki, itoki!"* The old canoe chant rang forth as men tramped about the capstan. Ruori hit the deck, saw a Canyon man fighting a sailor, sword against club, and brained the fellow from behind as he would any other vermin. (Then he wondered, dimly shocked, what made him think thus about a human being.) The battle was rapidly concluded; the Sky Men faced hopeless odds. But half a dozen Federation people were badly hurt. Ruori had the few surviving pirates tossed into a lazaret, his own casualties taken below to anesthetics and antibiotics and cooing Doñitas. Then, quickly, he prepared his crew for the next phase.

The blimp had been drawn almost to the bowsprit. It was canted over so far that its catapults were useless. Pirates lined the gallery deck, howled and shook their weapons. They outnumbered the *Dolphin* crew by a factor of three or four. Ruori recognized one among them—the tall yellow-haired man who had fought him outside the palace; it was a somehow eerie feeling.

"Shall we burn them?" asked Atel.

Ruori grimaced. "I suppose we have to," he said. "Try not to ignite the vessel itself. You know we want it."

A walking beam moved up and down, driven by husky Islanders. Flame spurted from a ceramic nozzle. The smoke and stench and screams that followed, and the things to be seen when Ruori ordered cease fire, made the hardest veteran of corsair patrol look a bit ill.

The Maurai were an unsentimental folk, but they did not like to inflict pain.

"Hose," rasped Ruori. The streams of water that followed were like some kind of blessing. Wicker that had begun to burn hissed into charred quiescence.

The ship's grapnels were flung. A couple of cabin boys darted past grown men to be first along the lines. They met no resistance on the gallery. The uninjured majority of pirates stood in a numb fashion, their armament at their feet, the fight kicked out of them. Jacob's ladders followed the boys; the *Dolphin* crew swarmed aboard the blimp and started collecting prisoners.

A few Sky Men lurched from behind a door, weapons aloft. Ruori saw the tall fair man among them. The man drew Ruori's dagger, left-handed, and ran toward him. His right arm seemed nearly useless. "A Canyon, a Canyon!" he called, the ghost of a war cry.

Ruori sidestepped the charge and put out a foot. The blond man tripped. As he fell, the hammer of Ruori's ax clopped down, catching him on the neck. He crashed, tried to rise, shuddered, and lay twitching.

"I want my knife back." Ruori squatted, undid the robber's tooled leather belt, and began to hogtie him.

Dazed blue eyes looked up with a sort of pleading. "Are you not going to kill me?" mumbled the other in Spañol.

"Haristi, no," said Ruori, surprised. "Why should I?"

He sprang erect. The last resistance had ended; the blimp was his. He opened the forward door, thinking the equivalent of a ship's bridge must lie beyond it.

Then for a while he did not move at all, nor did he hear anything but the wind and his own blood.

It was Tresa who finally came to him. Her hands were held out before her, like a blind person's, and her eyes looked through him. "You are here," she said, flat and empty voiced.

"Doñita," stammered Ruori. He caught her hands. "Doñita, had I known you were aboard, I would never have . . . have risked—"

"Why did you not burn and sink us, like that other

vessel?" she asked. "Why must this return to the city?"

She wrenched free of him and stumbled out onto the deck. It was steeply tilted, and bucked beneath her. She fell, picked herself up, walked with barefoot care to the rail and stared out across the ocean. Her hair and torn dress fluttered in the wind.

# VII

There was a great deal of technique to handling an airship. Ruori could feel that the thirty men he had put aboard this craft were sailing it as awkwardly as possible. An experienced Sky Man would know what sort of thermals and downdrafts to expect, just from a glance at land or water below; he could estimate the level at which a desired breeze was blowing, and rise or fall smoothly; he could even beat to windward, though that would be a slow process much plagued by drift.

Nevertheless, an hour's study showed the basic principles. Ruori went back to the bridge and gave orders in the speaking tube. Presently the land came nearer. A glance below showed the *Dolphin*, with a cargo of war captives, following on shortened sail. He and his fellow aeronauts would have to take a lot of banter about their celestial snail's pace. Ruori did not smile at the thought or plan his replies, as he would have done yesterday. Tresa sat so still behind him.

"Do you know the name of this craft, Doñita?" he asked, to break the silence.

"He called it *Buffalo*," she said, remote and uninterested.

"What's that?"

"A sort of wild cattle."

"I gather, then, he talked to you while cruising in search of me. Did he say anything else of interest?"

"He spoke of his people. He boasted of the things they have which we don't . . . engines, powers, alloys . . . as if that made them any less a pack of filthy savages."

At least she was showing some spirit. He had been

afraid she had started willing her heart to stop; but he remembered he had seen no evidence of that common Maurai practice here in Meyco.

"Did he abuse you badly?" he asked, not looking at her.

"You would not consider it abuse," she said violently. "Now leave me alone, for mercy's sake!" He heard her go from him, through the door to the after sections.

Well, he thought, after all, her father was killed. That would grieve anyone, anywhere in the world, but her perhaps more than him. For a Meycan child was raised solely by its parents; it did not spend half its time eating or sleeping or playing with any casual relative, like most Island young. So the immediate kin would have more psychological significance here. At least, this was the only explanation Ruori could think of for the sudden darkness within Tresa.

The city hove into view. He saw the remaining enemy vessels gleam above. Three against one . . . yes, today would become a legend among the Sea People, if he succeeded. Ruori knew he should have felt the same reckless pleasure as a man did surfbathing, or shark fighting, or sailing in a typhoon, any breakneck sport where success meant glory and girls. He could hear his men chant, beat war-drum rhythms out with hands and stamping feet. But his own heart was Antarctic.

The nearest hostile craft approached. Ruori tried to meet it in a professional way. He had attired his prize crew in captured Sky outfits. A superficial glance would take them for legitimate Canyonites, depleted after a hard fight but the captured Maurai ship at their heels.

As the northerners steered close in the leisurely airship fashion, Ruori picked up his speaking tube. "Steady as she goes. Fire when we pass abeam."

"Aye, aye," said Hiti.

A minute later the captain heard the harpoon catapult rumble. Through a port he saw the missile strike the enemy gondola amidships. "Pay out line," he said. "We want to hold her for the kite, but not get burned ourselves."

"Aye, I've played swordfish before now." Laughter bubbled in Hiti's tones.

The foe sheered, frantic. A few bolts leaped from its catapults; one struck home, but a single punctured gas cell made slight difference. "Put about!" cried Ruori. No sense in presenting his beam to a broadside. Both craft began to drift downwind, sails flapping. "Hard a-lee!" The *Buffalo* became a drogue, holding its victim to a crawl. And here came the kite prepared on the way back. This time it included fish hooks. It caught and held fairly on the Canyonite bag. "Cast off!" yelled Ruori. Fire whirled along the kite string. In minutes it had enveloped the enemy. A few parachutes were blown out to sea.

"Two to go," said Ruori, without any of his men's shouted triumph.

The invaders were no fools. Their remaining blimps turned back over the city, not wishing to expose themselves to more flame from the water. One descended, dropped hawsers, and was rapidly hauled to the plaza. Through his binoculars, Ruori saw armed men swarm aboard it. The other, doubtless with a mere patrol crew, maneuvered toward the approaching *Buffalo*.

"I think that fellow wants to engage us," warned Hiti. "Meanwhile number two down yonder will take on a couple of hundred soldiers, then lay alongside us and board."

"I know," said Ruori. "Let's oblige them."

He steered as if to close with the sparsely manned patroller. It did not avoid him, as he had feared it might; but then, there was a compulsive bravery in the Sky culture. Instead, it maneuvered to grapple as quickly as possible. That would give its companion a chance to load warriors and rise. It came very near.

Now to throw a scare in them, Ruori decided. "Fire arrows," he said. Out on deck, hardwood pistons were shoved into little cylinders, igniting tinder at the bottom; thus oil-soaked shafts were kindled. As the enemy came in range, red comets began to streak from the *Buffalo* archers.

Had his scheme not worked, Ruori would have turned off. He didn't want to sacrifice more men in hand-to-hand fighting; instead, he would have tried seriously to burn the hostile airship from afar, though his strategy needed it. But the morale effect of the previous disaster was very much present. As blazing arrows thunked into their gondola, a battle tactic so two-edged that no northern crew was even equipped for it, the Canyonites panicked and went over the side. Perhaps, as they parachuted down, a few noticed that no shafts had been aimed at their gas bag.

"Grab fast!" sang Ruori. "Douse any fires!"

Grapnels thumbed home. The blimps rocked to a relative halt. Men leaped to the adjacent gallery; bucketsful of water splashed.

"Stand by," said Ruori. "Half our boys on the prize. Break out the lifelines and make them fast."

He put down the tube. A door squeaked behind him. He turned, as Tresa reentered the bridge. She was still pale, but she had combed her hair, and her head was high.

"Another!" she said with a note near joy. "Only one of them left!"

"But it will be full of their men." Ruori scowled. "I wish now I had not accepted your refusal to go aboard the *Dolphin*. I wasn't thinking clearly. This is too hazardous."

"Do you think I care for that?" she said. "I am a Carabán."

"But I care," he said.

The haughtiness dropped from her; she touched his hand, fleetingly, and color rose in her cheeks. "Forgive me. You have done so much for us. There is no way we can ever thank you."

"Yes, there is," said Ruori.

"Name it."

"Do not stop your heart just because it has been wounded."

She looked at him with a kind of sunrise in her eyes. His boatswain appeared at the outer door. "All set,

Captain. We're holding steady at a thousand feet, a man standing by every valve these two crates have got."

"Each has been assigned a particular escape line?"

"Aye." The boatswain departed.

"You'll need one too. Come." Ruori took Tresa by the hand and led her onto the gallery. They saw sky around them, a breeze touched their faces and the deck underfoot moved like a live thing. He indicated many light cords from the *Dolphin*'s store, bowlined to the rail. "We aren't going to risk parachuting with untrained men," he said. "But you've no experience in skinning down one of these. I'll make you a harness which will hold you safely. Ease yourself down hand over hand. When you reach the ground, cut loose." His knife slashed some pieces of rope and he knotted them together with a seaman's skill. When he fitted the harness on her, she grew tense under his fingers.

"But I am your friend," he murmured.

She eased. She even smiled, shakenly. He gave her his knife and went back inboard.

And now the last pirate vessel stood up from the earth. It moved near; Ruori's two craft made no attempt to flee. He saw sunlight flash on edged metal. He knew they had witnessed the end of their companion craft and would not be daunted by the same technique. Rather, they would close in, even while their ship burned about them. If nothing else, they could kindle him in turn and then parachute to safety. He did not send arrows.

When only a few fathoms separated him from the enemy, he cried: "Let go the valves!"

Gas whoofed from both bags. The linked blimps dropped.

"Fire!" shouted Ruori. Hiti aimed his catapult and sent a harpoon with anchor cable through the bottom of the attacker. "Burn and abandon!"

Men on deck touched off oil which other men splashed from jars. Flames sprang high.

With the weight of two nearly deflated vessels dragging it from below, the Canyon ship began to fall. At five hundred feet the tossed lifelines draped across flat

rooftops and trailed in the streets. Ruori went over the
side. He scorched his palms going down.

He was not much too quick. The harpooned blimp
released compressed hydrogen and rose to a thousand
feet with its burden, seeking sky room. Presumably no
one had yet seen that the burden was on fire. In no
case would they find it easy to shake or cut loose from
one of Hiti's irons.

Ruori stared upward. Fanned by the wind, the blaze
was smokeless, a small fierce sun. He had not counted
on his fire taking the enemy by total surprise. He had
assumed they would parachute to earth, where the Meycans could attack. Almost, he wanted to warn them.

Then flame reached the remaining hydrogen in the
collapsed gas bags. He heard a sort of giant gasp. The
topmost vessel became a flying pyre. The wind bore it
out over the city walls. A few antlike figures managed
to spring free. The parachute of one was burning.

"Sant'sima Marí," whispered a voice, and Tresa crept
into Ruori's arms and hid her face.


# VIII

After dark, candles were lit throughout the palace.
They could not blank the ugliness of stripped walls
and smoke-blackened ceilings. The guardsmen who
lined the throne room were tattered and weary. Nor
did S' Antón itself rejoice, yet. There were too many
dead.

Ruori sat throned on the calde's dais, Tresa at his
right and Páwolo Dónoju on his left. Until a new set of
officials could be chosen, these must take authority. The
Don sat rigid, not allowing his bandaged head to droop;
but now and then his lids grew too heavy to hold up.
Tresa watched enormous-eyed from beneath the hood
of a cloak wrapping her. Ruori sprawled at ease, a little
more happy now that the fighting was over.

It had been a grim business, even after the heart-
ened city troops had sallied and driven the surviving

enemy before them. Too many Sky Men fought till
they were killed. The hundreds of prisoners, mostly
from the first Maurai success, would prove a dangerous
booty; no one was sure what to do with them.

"But at least their host is done for," said Dónoju.

Ruori shook his head. "No, S'ñor. I am sorry, but you
have no end in sight. Up north are thousands of such
aircraft, and a strong hungry people. They will come
again."

"We will meet them, Captain. The next time we shall
be prepared. A larger garrison, barrage balloons, fire
kites, cannons that shoot upward, perhaps a flying navy
of our own . . . we can learn what to do."

Tresa stirred. Her tone bore life again, though a life
which hated. "In the end, we will carry the war to them.
Not one will remain in all the Corado highlands."

"No," said Ruori. "That must not be."

Her head jerked about; she stared at him from the
shadow of her hood. Finally she said, "True, we are
bidden to love our enemies, but you cannot mean the
Sky People. They are not human!"

Ruori spoke to a page. "Send for the chief prisoner."

"To hear our judgment on him?" asked Dónoju. "That
should be done formally, in public."

"Only to talk with us," said Ruori.

"I do not understand you," said Tresa. Her words
faltered, unable to carry the intended scorn. "After everything you have done, suddenly there is no manhood
in you."

He wondered why it should hurt for her to say that.
He would not have cared if she had been anyone else.

Loklann entered between two guards. His hands were
tied behind him and dried blood was on his face, but
he walked like a conqueror under the pikes. When he
reached the dais, he stood, legs braced apart, and grinned
at Tresa.

"Well," he said, "so you find these others less satis-
factory and want me back."

She jumped to her feet and screamed: "Kill him!"

"No!" cried Ruori.

The guardsmen hesitated, machetes half drawn. Ruori stood up and caught the girl's wrists. She struggled, spitting like a cat. "Don't kill him, then," she agreed at last, so thickly it was hard to understand. "Not now. Make it slow. Strangle him, burn him alive, toss him on your spears—"

Ruori held fast till she stood quietly.

When he let go, she sat down and wept.

Páwolo Dónoju said in a voice like steel: "I believe I understand. A fit punishment must certainly be devised."

Loklann spat on the floor. "Of course," he said. "When you have a man bound, you can play any number of dirty little games with him."

"Be still," said Ruori. "You are not helping your own cause. Or mine."

He sat down, crossed his legs, laced fingers around a knee, and gazed before him, into the darkness at the hall's end. "I know you have suffered from this man's work," he said carefully. "You can expect to suffer more from his kinfolk in the future. They are a young race, heedless as children, even as your ancestors and mine were once young. Do you think the Perio was established without hurt and harm? Or, if I remember your history rightly, that the Spañol people were welcomed here by the Inios? That the Ingliss did not come to N'Zealann with slaughter, and that the Maurai were not formerly cannibals? In an age of heroes, the hero must have an opponent.

"Your real weapon against the Sky People is not an army, sent to lose itself in unmapped mountains. . . . Your priests, merchants, artists, craftsmen, manners, fashions, learning—there is the means to bring them to you on their knees, if you will use it."

Loklann started. "You devil," he whispered. "Do you actually think to convert us to . . . a woman's faith and a city's cage?" He shook back his tawny mane and roared till the walls rung. "No!"

"It will take a century or two," said Ruori.

Don Páwolo smiled in his young scanty beard. "A refined revenge, S'ñor Captain," he admitted.

"Too refined!" Tresa lifted her face from her hands,
gulped after air, held up claw-crooked fingers and
brought them down as if into Loklann's eyes. "Even if it
could be done," she snarled, "even if they did have
souls, what do we want with them, or their children or
grandchildren . . . they who murdered our babies today? Before almighty Dío—I am the last Carabán and
I will have my following to speak for me in Meyco—
there will never be anything for them but extermina-
tion. We can do it, I swear. Many Tekkans would help,
for plunder. I shall yet live to see your home burning,
you swine, and your sons hunted with dogs."

She turned frantically toward Ruori. "How else can
our land be safe? We are ringed in by enemies. We
have no choice but to destroy them, or they will destroy
us. And we are the last Merikan civilization."

She sat back and shuddered. Ruori reached over to
take her hand. It felt cold. For an instant, unconsciously,
she returned the pressure, then jerked away.

He sighed in his weariness.

"I must disagree," he said. "I am sorry. I realize how
you feel."

"You do not," she said through clamped jaws. "You
cannot."

"But after all," he said, forcing dryness, "I am not just
a man with human desires. I represent my government.
I must return to tell them what is here, and I can predict their response.

"They will help you stand off attack. That is not an aid
you can refuse, is it? The men who will be responsible
for Meyco are not going to decline our offer of alliance merely to preserve a precarious independence of
action, whatever a few extremists may argue for. And
our terms will be most reasonable. We will want little
more from you than a policy working toward conciliation
and close relations with the Sky People, as soon as they
have tired of battering themselves against our united
defense."

"What?" said Loklann. Otherwise the chamber was very still. Eyes gleamed white from the shadows of helmets, toward Ruori.

"We will begin with you," said the Maurai. "At the proper time, you and your fellows will be escorted home. Your ransom will be that your nation allow a diplomatic and trade mission to enter."

"No," said Tresa, as if speech hurt her throat. "Not him. Send back the others if you must, but not him—to boast of what he did today."

Loklann grinned again, looking straight at her. "I will," he said.

Anger flicked in Ruori, but he held his mouth shut.

"I do not understand," hesitated Don Páwolo. "Why do you favor these animals?"

"Because they are more civilized than you," said Ruori.

"What?" The noble sprang to his feet, snatching for his sword. Stiffly, he sat down again. His tone froze over. "Explain yourself, S'ñor."

Ruori could not see Tresa's face, in the private night of her hood, but he felt her drawing farther from him than a star. "They have developed aircraft," he said, slumping back in his chair, worn out and with no sense of victory; *O great creating Tanaroa, grant me sleep this night!*

"But—"

"That was done from the ground up," explained Ruori, "not as a mere copy of ancient techniques. Beginning as refugees, the Sky People created an agriculture which can send warriors by the thousands from what was desert, yet plainly does not require peon hordes. On interrogation I have learned that they have sunpower and hydroelectric power, a synthetic chemistry of sorts, a well-developed navigation with the mathematics which that implies, gunpowder, metallurgics, aerodynamics. . . . Yes, I daresay it's a lopsided culture, a thin layer of learning above a largely illiterate mass. But even the mass must respect technology, or it would never have been supported to get as far as it has.

"In short," he sighed, wondering if he could make

her comprehend, "the Sky People are a scientific race—
the only one besides ourselves which we Maurai have
yet discovered. And that makes them too precious to
lose.

"You have better manners here, more humane laws,
higher art, broader vision, every traditional virtue. But
you are not scientific. You use rote knowledge handed
down from the ancients. Because there is no more fossil
fuel, you depend on muscle power; inevitably, then,
you have a peon class, and always will. Because the iron
and copper mines are exhausted, you tear down old
ruins. In your land I have seen no research on wind
power, sun power, the energy reserves of the living cell
—not to mention the theoretical possibility of hydrogen
fusion without a uranium primer. You irrigate the desert
at a thousand times the effort it would take to farm the
sea, yet have never even tried to improve your fishing
techniques. You have not exploited the aluminum
which is still abundant in ordinary clays, not sought to
make it into strong alloys; no, your farmers use tools
of wood and volcanic glass.

"Oh, you are neither ignorant nor superstitious. What
you lack is merely the means of gaining new knowledge.
You are a fine people; the world is the sweeter for you;
I love you as much as I loathe this devil before us. But
ultimately, my friends, if left to yourselves, you will slide
gracefully back to the Stone Age."

A measure of strength returned. He raised his voice
till it filled the hall. "The way of the Sky People is the
rough way outward, to the stars. In that respect—and it
overrides all others—they are more akin to us Maurai
than you are. We cannot let our kin die."

He sat then, in silence, under Loklann's smirk and
Dónoju's stare. A guardsman shifted on his feet, with a
faint squeak of leather harness.

Tresa said at last, very low in the shadows: "That is
your final word, S'ñor?"

"Yes," said Ruori. He turned to her. As she leaned
forward, the hood fell back a little, so that candlelight

touched her. And the sight of green eyes and parted lips gave him back his victory.

He smiled. "I do not expect you will understand at once. May I discuss it with you again, often? When you have seen the Islands, as I hope you will—"

"You *foreigner!*" she screamed.

Her hand cracked on his cheek. She rose and ran down the dais steps and out of the hall.